My Lousy Life

Stories

Enhanced Edition

Author's Books
(As of June 20, 2020)[*]

Non-fiction

The Nature of Love and Relationships 2011, **2016**
Doubts and Decisions for Living:
   Volume I: The Foundation of Human Thoughts **2014**
   Volume II: The Sanctity of Human Spirit **2014**
   Volume III: The Structure of Human Life **2014**
Relationship Facts, Trends, and Choices **2016**
The Mysteries of Life, Love, and Happiness **2016**
Marriage and Divorce Hardships **2016**
Gender Qualities, Quirks, and Quarrels **2016**
Relationship Needs, Framework, and Models **2016**
Being Better Beings **2020**

Fiction

Persian Moons 2007, **2016**
Midnight Gate-opener 2011, **2016**
My Lousy Life Stories **2014**
Persian Suns **2021** (Planned)

[*] 12 older books are Enhanced Editions and printed in 2020. They were resubmitted to the Library and Archives Canada Cataloguing as well. If a book's 'print date' on the copyright page is older, the newest version is available at Amazon and bookstores.

My Lousy Life

Stories

An Abstract Novel

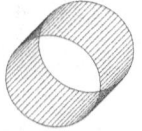

Tom Omidi, Ph.D.

Omidi, Tom, 1945-, author
My Lousy Life Stories: an abstract novel /Tom Omidi.

ISBN 978-1-988351-09-4 (paperback)

I. Title.

Old edition at
Library and Archives Canada Cataloguing in Publication
PS8629.M53M9 2014 C813'.6 C2014-903381-8

Cover page design: From a painting by Tom Omidi

Published by Eros Books,
Vancouver, British Columbia
Canada

erosbooks2020@gmail.com

Enhanced and Printed in 2020

I did my best everywhere,
Hoping to find that whatever!
Now I believe it is not anywhere,
Even if you looked for it forever.

Table of Contents

Prologue *1*

The Beginning
CONFUSION

The Middle
REFLECTION

The End
RESIGNATION

Epilogue *395*

Prologue

The upcoming fifteen related essays and short stories depict the crucial stages of the protagonist's life in an abstract style. Starting as a young boy with an ambitious mission in the first story—*The Big Plan*—various emotional episodes carry him and the readers toward the last story—*The Final Plan*—when he is old, lost, and disheartened. Like most of us, he faces the biggest contrast with his initial dreams when future had appeared quite promising.

The story is about a loner's unsettling fate and mind during his breakaways from city to city, while he staggers in the journey of life itself, grapples with dire dilemmas, satiates his curiosities, gets old, encounters complex people and situations, fights with his friends and family, and strives to make sense of it all.

The protagonist, who appears under different pseudonyms in most stories, represents either my personal experiences (over sixty percent) or plays my role as a secondary character in some stories. He recounts a mass of real encounters and perplexing thoughts that have propelled the course of my lousy life, but also made it bearable and even interesting on some days. Our daily encounters best illustrate the peculiarities of our habits, cultures, mentalities, resilience, and coping mechanisms. If we muse over them long enough, they show the intricacy of human nature, ego, and spirit that function in a clever, humorous, and mysterious manner. Accordingly, we discover an enigmatic, deeper reality that authors strive to capture in their tales. For example, the rather bizarre story of *Trumpet Man* reveals the lively atmosphere and culture in downtown Vancouver in line with a fine perspective of the convoluted humanity. Conversely, the poignancy of random events and our fates often make us wonder about some kind of magic or power always directing our lives and plans.

All stories are based on actual events, although some aspects or endings of a few stories have been slightly altered to offer a more dramatic outcome, but only because they could have easily been the cases in those circumstances. Yet, I have tried to remain fully faithful to the gist of the stories and characters' quirks in the way they had intrigued me to write about them in the first place. At the same time, using many pseudonyms for the main character in this book reflects the mixed personalities that everybody holds and demonstrates erratically a lifetime in line with his/her bizarre urges and thoughts.

These fifteen essays and stories were written randomly during the last fifteen years, but they cover three distinct stages of the protagonist's life nicely. The first phase—the beginning—covers youths' narrow vision of life while they struggle with daunting dilemmas and **confusion** in hopes of building their characters and plans. Their mental unrest erupts in the form of their exaggerated attitude and silliness. The second phase—the middle—contains our serious experiences and involvement with life as we strive to survive financially and emotionally, while we wonder regularly also about the purpose of all that hard work. We face middle-age crisis and do a great deal of soul-searching and **reflection**. The third phase—the end—arrives as we feel old and defeated, realize life's vanity, and eventually reach the point of **resignation**.

Depicting humans' mental transition through the three life phases has been one of my intentions for creating this abstract novel. The innocent daftness of characters in the first few stories, during their youthful life explorations and confusions, contrasts the sombre humour of the protagonist's resignation in the last few stories while he compares his earlier dreams with the gloomy outcome of his struggles. Meanwhile, the stories in the middle reflect our slow, painful growth as we gain some wisdom through our encounters and contemplations. During this dreary transformation, our daily experiences affect our psyches and souls very deeply, while we all follow a narrowly structured, meaningless path of life. All along, we feel obliged to define the meaning of life, thus keep paining ourselves for our inability to do so. Ironically, our actions in all three life phases remain quite meaningless and comical in fact, anyway.

It is bizarre that humans have not yet been able to develop a sensible life philosophy, based on all their growing wisdom and historical lessons, to live together in a relative peace instead of hurting and humiliating one another forever. Even weirder, we do not seem capable of benefiting personally from our maturity even in the latter stages of our lives. Instead, we merely stick to our crippling mentalities and lifestyles until the very end.

The effect of the pervasive social mayhem is that life often feels lousy to most of us, but also quite funny if we get the gist of it. The stories in this and my other novels have meant to show this humorous drama in the new era. They also reflect my joys and pains during adolescence with my peculiar parents, during middle age with my nagging bosses, lovers, and wife, and during old age with my beloved children and conscience, while I have tried sincerely, but uselessly, all along to keep a civil relationship with everybody, including the nasty devil inside me. What a pity!

The mixed use of first person voice or a narrator (with mixed pseudonyms for the novel's mystery protagonist) fitted each story's particular structure best when written independently many years ago. They have been kept intact to create this abstract novel. This variety actually offers an additional layer of mystery and challenge to follow a particular character's interests and thoughts throughout the book. Accidentally, the stories' level of sophistication, intonation, and complexity also seems to build up progressively in line with the protagonist's maturity during his three life phases. This merely literary observation is bizarre in one respect, but logical if we consider the likely effects of rising personal dilemmas and self-realization as people age and learn more about society and themselves. Thus, reading the stories chronologically shows both personal growth and the peculiarities of life's three phases more vividly. However, reading them out of order or skipping some stories of less interest to you would not ruin their intended effects as an abstract novel too much.

As my main field of interest and study, 'relationships' has emerged as a recurring theme in almost all the stories in this book as well. Social welfare and individuals' health are in big jeopardy, while people strive to balance their sexual urges, independence, and emotional needs. Companionship is a basic human need, especially in our stressful and harsh societies. However, sexual deprivation and relationship complexities are getting more out of hand and burdensome for every generation. Accordingly, we feel lonelier every day as our need for compassion accelerates.

I do not believe in writing or reading stories for fun alone or merely making indirect hints about social issues. It is crucial now to address the fast deterioration of our social structure and values clearly in any manner we can. We must find and fight the roots of social problems. We must admit the urgent need to change our mentalities and lifestyles in order to relate more effectively. Maybe we can learn to spread more compassion and sincerity, instead of promoting more arrogance and greed every day.

By the way, although many incidents in this abstract novel may sound silly or bizarre, their realness actually makes them most appropriate to recount and wonder about human nature. They are true stories. Also, as long as I keep living and pondering my existences, adding a few points now and then to my writings, especially to the last story in this novel, '*The Final Plan*,' seems inevitable when timely new thoughts erupt. *Then, when I die, the dust will settle and maybe even the universe will stand still!*

Tom Omidi, Ph.D.
Vancouver, 2014

The Beginning

CONFUSION

The Big Plan

The 'big plan' began rolling officially with a hectic and heroic 25-day journey from Tehran to Los Angeles on planes, trains, automobiles, and the U.S. Steamship—the biggest and fastest passenger ship at the time according to the overzealous travel agent. He was ecstatic about finally finding a fool from this part of the world eager to send his cranky son to the other side with so much hassle, including a wearing voyage on a vessel.

"My first sale of a seat on this magnificent ship," he informed Father in particular with triumph, as if dispatching a spaceship to Mars. Yet I was too depressed and dismayed those days to fall for this kind of nonsense about a ship.

"But your *magnificent* ship will still take five days to reach New York from Southampton! Right?" I asked with a tense grin, trying hard to be as patient and cooperative as possible. "Going to Southampton would be another big hassle." Both he and Father stared at me blankly, as if just realizing I was in the room, too.

"May I fly straight to Los Angles or to New York at least?" I asked boldly, still trying hard to keep my idiotic grin as a show of my continued cooperation.

This time, the cagey agent and Father peeped at each other in disbelief, quite unhappy about my childish intrusion with such an expensive request, not to mention my total disregard for all the fun and adventure they were planning for me. Then they resumed their keen collaboration on the cheapest travel itinerary for me, as if nobody had asked any question! Drained and desolate, I just leaned back in my chair, admitting at last that certainly no part of this whole shenanigan was for adventure or fun as Father had stressed, but merely for penny-pinching.

The three-week, tedious journey was merely Father's cheap scheme for shipping me to America for higher education and returning to Iran to become a cabinet minister—a feat the poor man had himself pursued all along in vain. Instead, he always claimed—with a heartbreaking sigh—that not having a graduate degree from a prominent U.S. university, or at least Oxford, had been the only obstacle for his final promotion to a cabinet post. He just ploughed on as a testy deputy-minister, year after year, despite his friendship with the long-lasting prime minister.

Father's Big Plan for me was absurd, anyway. In fact, I had told him a hundred times already that I was not really up to taking on all the hassles involved for an iffy political career in a flimsy monarchy. Yet, he seemed to have gone deaf. He only smirked, as if watching a moron not appreciating the wisdom of his free advice today, at this point, yet keeping faith in my ability to catch up with him soon when the Big Plan began to come to fruition. It was only a matter of time for me to grow up a bit. My cynicism about the Shah's future irritated Father the most, though, which nicely soothed my tension a bit at least.

"Do you wanna help this country or not?" Father had asked me one time with frustration while glaring at my blank face. "Do you wanna let the communists take over our country and grab everything we have, too, including this house?"

"Of course not...," I had replied politely, trying to be a bit more cooperative before he hit the roof or had a heart attack.

"Then you must go to America to get the right education and come back soon," he stressed in a soft, charismatic tone of voice that often left me paralysed and convinced. Let us give him that!

Then again, I believed my life was perfect already without becoming just another greedy official like many of Father's snotty friends! I had a good job, a bright prospect, and a pretty girlfriend, Haydeh. In fact, we had finally vowed to marry soon —a blissful triumph I had cherished after pleading and promising to behave myself from now on, and her generosity to forgive my past childish infidelities. Then again, that was all a few months before Father's brainwashing me gradually about the proper path to a ministerial position as the ultimate purpose of life. In the end, in fact, I was so carried away I had decided to shoot for the Prime Minister's job, after all. Too bad we had a king already with a bunch of heirs, quite cosy with America, too. The monarch's humiliating loyalty, for such a haughty royalty, felt embarrassing, indeed, way beyond my patience and pride. So, I had to get over my crude political dispositions in a hurry as well, on top of all the necessary technical education in the U.S. of A. I wondered if it also entailed CIA, or whoever, giving me a *big* lecture!

Anyhow, I set out to break my promise to proud Haydeh and renounce our love very calmly and rationally just like Humphrey Bogart in *Casablanca*. My meticulous reasoning for abandoning her, after our eventful romance for two years, sounded bizarre even to my own ears. Not merely inventing such lame excuses, but the way I offered them so briskly with no shame, revealed a new depth of my shallowness. I was now quite puzzled about my character even myself, especially when I recalled my pitiful pleas to her only a few months earlier to forgive my infidelity and promising to love her forever. Worst of all, after spending so much logic and energy, she did not buy any of my bullshit.

She was more stubborn and annoying than I had anticipated. My pitiful presentation was simply going nowhere, despite all the fine justifications I had diligently prepared and practised in the last few days for my great speech today. I felt like an idiot all along, sorry for my honourable intention to justify our break-up like a gentleman. My tone of voice had probably been ineloquent and maybe even girlish when she challenged me and I tried to hide my frustration with more excuses. Learning that I lacked the slightest trace of Father's power of persuasion was embarrassing as well. She only rolled her eyes with a smirk and overruled my strong reasoning, one after another, with a lousy argument of her own like saying, "Okay, what else have you got?"

"I'll come back in three or four years eventually, if you want to wait and see what happens."

"Are you kidding me? Those horny American girls will eat you alive—with your skin, balls, and everything."

"Just imagine I'm going to war and dying, if it helps," I said as my final offer, now totally exhausted.

"Don't talk to me like a child," she yelled.

"I feel really terrible," I said helplessly, tears flooding my eyes from despair, which she apparently attributed to the jam I was stuck in because I just did not have the balls to stand up to my father and tell him to go to hell.

Magically, the mere notion of my clear entrapment causing me so much grief from the big loss of leaving her calmed her and she swiftly looked convinced. "Go, go... Just leave me alone, you selfish bastard," she shrieked.

The way weeping alone seemed to solve one's problem most naturally so fast was enlightening—a big lesson I learned about women that day! *They respect and trust the legitimacy of certain tactics best, apparently, regardless of the gender using it!* Had I known this huge secret sooner, I would have wept right at the beginning and gotten the matter over with fast instead of wasting an hour and all that sound logic. Yet my subsequent attempts to use this trick on other women have never worked, unfortunately. Maybe women have learned about some jerks like me abusing their delicate, corny strategies!

A bunch of tricky questions haunted me later, though, like what would I have done had Haydeh cried and begged me to stay? Why had not she wept herself, instead of only arguing with me so much? Had she grown her own doubts about me—to ever mature and become a real man, despite my pathetic promises just a few months earlier? Had she realized my frailty around Father? Was she upset merely for losing her chance of dumping me first, right after finalizing her own lame excuses in a few days or so? The idea of her possible doubts about us hurt my pride despite my own disloyalty. As a result, my conscience and pride wrestled for a week on top of many other painful dilemmas that Father's big plan had caused me already.

Fortunately, things got a little clearer during the send-off party, as Haydeh moaned furtively in a corner with vengeful stares. Both my pride and sense of guilt were restored quickly as her few tears seemed genuine. All along, Father's victorious grin all night was annoying, though, as if he had discovered America himself. He mingled among his flashy friends with glee, gloated like Christopher Columbus, and snubbed the fuming, vengeful Haydeh with his sneering smirk. You could imagine he would burst out of his skin any second now from all that pride, for being such an insightful, persuasive father.

"I'm glad you finally understood my advice about your future in politics," he told me after having informed everybody else in the party about his wisdom and my marvellous prospects upon returning from the U.S., all thanks to him, of course.

Sad and embarrassed already from Father's charade, Haydeh shamed me even more with her own last minute advice:

"Get off the devil's donkey, forget your stupid fantasy, let's get on with our own fancy," she murmured to me softly after such a long time, with her cute, subtle grin trying to lure me back again in the last minute perhaps.

Then again, it was too late to abort that masterfully laid plan. Too late now for any amount of charm or even tears, including my poor mother's, to abandon the big plan! She looked even more miserable than Haydeh. She had witnessed the making of the big plan with mixed feelings all along, cried her heart out, and savoured the last few days with her spoiled son. She just kept making the best Persian foods she knew I loved with basmati rice and saffron, constantly hinting and fretting about my life without this kind of luxury for many years.

"Do you wanna take five kilos of basmati rice to cook there?" she asked me with a sigh.

"No, thanks. I believe they have rice in Los Angeles, too."

"But not this kind of Persian Basmati!" she replied with pity.

"Don't worry, I'll survive," I said with confidence. Yet, she stared at me with serious scepticism, as if not sure I would really survive without basmati rice. In fact, she seemed worried even more about my sanity the way I seemed so casual about the kind of rice available in L.A., if at all! She looked extremely sad and concerned, but also helpless. Dealing with a nutty husband and a naughty son had soured her spirits and senses over the years.

She had started my luggage two weeks prior to my departure. Soon two big suitcases and a huge carryon were filled with all kinds of stuff she believed I needed no matter how much I swore to god that I did not, including pistachio, dried vegetables and fruits, delicacies, and a large assortment of winter clothing and boots. I kept telling her that winters are nowhere nearly as cold in California as they are in Tehran, but she insisted that it was better to be safe than sorry. "You never know," she said. Every time I turned my head or left my room for a second, she sneaked back in and hid a few more things underneath the presently approved pile, as though I would not double-check and take them out again. At the end, my luggage weighed over forty kilos at the airport, even though the winter clothing was restricted to four wool sweaters and a long heavy overcoat like Dr. Zhivago's. All along, my poor mom's narrow, sad eyes were buried behind her heavy tears anytime I had looked at her. So, how could I refuse hauling most of the things she wanted me to take with me?

Naturally, Father insisted that maybe I could kindly wear the overcoat when checking in at the airport to save the cost of five kilos of extra baggage. However, I put my foot down and refused to do so, on account of dying of heat on top of looking ridiculous entering the airport like that in May.

Anyway, past all those treachery, turmoil, and tear-sheds, the lengthy, messy mission of getting to Los Angeles, as frugally as possible, began one early morning in May 1969. I hit the rocky road with an admission letter from the University of Southern California, my backbreaking luggage, a journey itinerary, a load of tickets, all my personal savings turned into $1,250 traveller's cheques, and Father's moronic promise that I could find work in Los Angeles immediately—hinting not to expect any money once I got there. He always had better use for his money, even though, in this case especially, only his ego and rivalry with his friends was behind this preposterous project that felt pointless and undoable from the beginning even financially.

"Bah…! Any young man can find a good job in a jiffy in the great land of opportunities," the bigheaded Father had repeated every time I had complained about the difficulty of finding a job and working to pay for the steep tuition and living expenses while going to school, too. His idiotic cool and apathy was odd and frustrating. Still odder, his confidence and persistence had finally calmed my nerves and I set out to get a job, find time and energy to go to school, and learn something, too—at least enough to reform the economy of my chaotic country immediately upon my triumphant return to Iran in a few years! Going by Father's diligent descriptions of my forthcoming role and responsibilities, I had to save the Shah from the rising unrest all over the country!

I imagined myself already back from the U.S. and being the Prime Minister with Father always sitting in my office—maybe even behind my desk—to advise me, or expecting me to go visit him every night (in case he couldn't come to the office himself), so that he could outline my duties and decisions for the next day. I was merely his last hope to be someone at least through me!

"Come back soon and make me proud, my smart son," Father whispered in my ears at the airport before I left.

I nodded sceptically.

The Iran Air flight had long stops in Athens, Rome, and Paris, before the plane finally landed at London's Heathrow after eight hours for going such a relatively short distance. It seemed to need a major tune-up at every stop and we had to change planes in Paris, after all. Surviving this ordeal was a miracle all by itself considering the coughing sound of the engines.

My close friend, Jafar, who had started his own education in London a year earlier, was waiting for me. Holding his English girlfriend like a shield, he looked tense with a passive smile and made weird gestures. First, I thought he was showing off that pretty girl by clinging to her so tightly.

"Let's only shake hands," he whispered to me in Persian at last with stress from a safe distance.

Exhausted and disoriented, finally I gathered that Persian's sappy greeting was not cool in the Western culture. Jafar would have been immensely embarrassed before his girlfriend and the entire English public if we had hugged and kissed on the cheeks. So, I froze like a Popsicle, timid and confused, as we shook hands formally like two jackasses.

Jafar's coyness in that episode feels funnier nowadays when TV clippings show the U.S. Presidents and European leaders hugging and kissing the beardy sheikhs and other Middle Eastern officials so eagerly. George W. Bush's, in particular, looked quite cosy and educational. All the hypocrisy spreading fast around the world nowadays, for money and politics, makes any sane person dizzy. Jafar is probably surprised the most these days about oil diplomacy alone making everybody so affectionate; changing even world cultures now in just a few decades. Maybe Jafar had already predicted and abhorred this masquerade with his mystical foresight! He was often a smart boy, after all! Nowadays, I only shake hands even with my cousins and close friends, too.

Jafar drove me to a hotel and left me lonely and homesick quickly. With daylight still out there, I lingered in the middle of the room, bemused like an abandoned orphan. Equally rude, I was too tired and sad to thank him for his help and waiting for my late arrival, too. Only a few weeks later when my brain began working somewhat normal again, I realized my insolence and felt bad, although I still blamed Jafar's bizarre behaviour for my clumsiness. Actually, these odd formalities between two intimate friends, such as thanking him, had suddenly felt necessary only because he had changed.

First thing the next day, I found a cheaper accommodation. Then I wandered around the city on the subway, wondering about my dwindling identity in London—out of Tehran actually. According to the journey itinerary, I had to wait five days in London before going to Southampton. So, all I could do was to eat fish and chips every day, do some drab sightseeing with stress, and practise solitude. I spent one whole day at the zoo whispering curses about the hassles of being a human to animals that were already burdened by pesky insects. It was hard not to envy their simplicity and irresponsibility, although their blank stares felt purposeful and sardonic, as if mocking my stupidity. All day, I missed Haydeh badly, especially when the lioness glared at me and then yawned.

I did not find Jafar until my last day in London despite my earnest attempts. I went to his flat tensely to say goodbye and complain about his hiding. He blamed his final exams uselessly with no conviction. This time, we did not even shake hands and I left with dire despair. Now, I was sure he had really changed—so fast! He was no longer the Jafar I had known and felt so natural around before his departure to England. He did not even offer to take me and my big luggage to the train station at least, if not all the way to Southampton! Asshole! I worried only about myself, of course; about the necessity or inevitability of becoming aloof myself very soon. I was feeling weird already! I had imagined leaving Iran would cause pain and confusion, but not this much so soon. Learning all this new stuff felt tough and tacky. I took a taxi, the subway and trains, hauling my heavy luggage in streets, panting and perspiring like a dog, to get to Southampton. I feared getting lost somewhere or missing a train or the U.S. Steamship, thus the entire travel itinerary falling apart.

So, boarding the ship in the final minutes felt like winning a major triathlon. I gasped a sigh of relief despite the grimness of the tiny cabin I had to share with a tough-looking, impatient guy. Soon, however, the rhythmic, loud sound of several heavy chains banging the shipboard shattered my tentative peace, especially at night when the racket impeded my sleep. I complained to a ship steward about the matter. He listened impatiently with surprise, glared, and then left coolly, murmuring mostly to himself some words like, "What do you expect for the price you've paid? You think we can move the anchor and chains for your convenience, Mr. Big Shot."

I felt damned in that damp cabin for five nights, as if trapped in one of those medieval dungeons with hundreds of chains and cylinders clashing around me non-stop. The scene of Father's keen collaboration with the travel agent on the 'most economical arrangement' singed my brain and I cursed them both. Nothing else I could do other than jumping into the ocean! I wished I had the guts to return to Iran and move out of my parents' house right away, too. My cellmate was hardly around to at least chat and whine together instead of trying to sleep. His absence, even for sleep, remained an unsolved mystery all by itself. Most likely, he preferred to sleep in the lounge or on the deck.

A thrilling moment raised my hopes a little at dinnertime, though, when I looked for my pre-assigned seat in the dining hall. While faxing my profile, the jolly travel agent had stressed proudly *again* that the ship's crew—or some experts—arranged the seating according to passengers' profiles. I had not given any thought to the outcome of such scrutiny until I saw the only empty chair at Table 21 next to a gorgeous blonde, assuming quickly to be mine—the chair, I mean. Although my inane brain promised that soon she would be mine, too. *The crew's wisdom to join us must surely mean something*, all the logic in my head whispered boastfully. She would hopefully be as intelligent to not disappoint the crew or waste their expertise. So I moved fast with revived confidence, hoping that my late arrival had not pained a

Scandinavian heart too much. *I felt guilty and sad about the high chance of my delay causing her so much grief in anticipation,* while I had dozed off in the lounge with a headache, unaware of the fate's funny plan for me. *Maybe she would take my late big entrance as a sign of class, though!*

I greeted everyone around the table fast to focus on the blonde girl with my big grin and murmuring a heartfelt 'Sorry' to her before taking my seat politely. In return, she showed no hesitance to express her disappointment even quicker with a smug smirk. Not even my well-groomed mustache had apparently impressed her the way it made me feel proud. She said her name was Marie coldly after I introduced myself to everybody and asked hers. Instead, she used the occasion to announce giddily that she *must* visit the first class section of the ship right after dinner. It sounded like she had been waiting for my arrival to warn us when all were accounted for at the table. Then, she whispered to me, for good measure and my special interest, that she *must* go dance with her friends on that side instead of joining us in the lounge. A blonde so blunt felt bizarre! I only grinned at her as a show of support. Was she lying only out of courtesy? Would she hide in her cabin five nights just to avoid us? Nah! Had I looked a bit more stylish or assertive, I reckoned, she might have taken me with her for a glimpse of the better world *on the other side* at least.

The next day, nausea and vomiting aggravated my agony when the ship hit a rough storm and the banging of the chains got fiercer. The Atlantic Ocean looked mad at something or the ship, too, for its own reasons. Most passengers staggered and stared at one another awkwardly like zombies. Not even the comfy sofas in the lounge offered any relief, though at least my ears rested awhile when I slumbered around there.

As though I did not have enough worries and grief, soon the idea of sneaking into the first class somehow, at least out of spite for Marie, but also to check out her charm in that cheery crowd, tickled me. My cynical mind and curiosity began driving me nuts like a plague and I felt obliged to penetrate and watch that society for a few minutes. Real life should be on the other side then, judging by Marie's tension during her short presence at Table 21. Her gloom for half an hour merely for a measly meal saddened me, too, anytime I looked at her. The burden dulling her beautiful eyes, for being among us, was surely heartbreaking and so unfair. Yet, I could see how hard she was trying not to break our hearts entirely, either! The poor girl had a hard time balancing her pity and pride. Anyhow, we chatted enough for etiquette only, before she vanished quickly after finishing her meal somewhat hastily and excusing herself with a cold courtesy goodbye to all of us losers at the table.

My small consolation was that Marie snubbed everybody around the table more than she humiliated me. At least she did not ignore me completely the way she dismissed others casually! "Now I'm going to escape this hellhole," she usually whispered *only to me* just as she rose to leave. Her rising motherly patience with me was soothing, especially coming from such a young, pretty girl! Yet she seemed to really enjoy torturing me as well with her timely sarcasms and random putdowns! In return, I cursed the travel agent—*now* for faxing my profile.

For five nights, bingo or dancing to a measly record player amused the rest of us after Marie left. We pretended everything was fine, although Marie's words kept rolling in my nosy head. I imagined those people dancing the real dance, unaware of our existence, or fully assured about the safety of our presence. My half-assed attempts to find the gate to the high society failed, too, and I never saw the lucky boys who danced with snotty Marie. I stopped looking soon, anyway, thanks to my low stamina for exploration—unlike any bold, adventurous son that could make Captain Columbus or Father proud. Of course, one problem was that sneaky Marie always rushed away right in the middle of my feast, when I was totally absorbed in all the food I took from the buffet as if making up for my sleep deprivations. So, although the option of following her to discover the gate to the other side had felt like a rather worthy trade-off, I always remained loyal to the food. I guess I was not devoted enough to this cause, after all.

At least the young man from Pasadena amused me with his friendly attitude and conversations. Glen Wymore was enchanted by Marie's charm, too, while enjoying my pitiful efforts to soften her. Yet, he also seemed jealous about me sitting next to her and chatting and chuckling with her occasionally. He was probably wondering why his profile had placed him next to an old couple instead of Marie! He realized our dismal fortune with her, yet kept grilling me about her, as if still gauging his chance, anyway, or merely for laughing some more at my expense. He consoled me with devious joy and offered silly suggestions with a chuckle anytime I recounted her words. He confessed to his flying phobia and taking this very ship and several trains every few years to travel to Europe for sightseeing and visiting relatives. I was dying to know, or ask him, why he liked to travel so much with all these hassles and efforts. At the end, I kept my mouth shut when I imagined he would probably give me only an idiotic response, anyway, such as, "Because I like it." Then, his surprise and thoughts about my idiocy would be humiliating as well when I ask him, "So why do I hate it already in my first trip?"

Instead, I asked Glen once, "Do you think those first classers know about us in the way we're so carefully hidden from them?"

"Probably not," he replied with gloom, as if swiftly disturbed by the idea of being a rather nobody on this ship, too.

"Unless Marie tells some of them at least about our petty life in their neighbourhood," I said.

"Nah, I rather believe Marie won't tell on us just to hide her own secret," Glen said with another chuckle.

"You think so?"

"I guess…"

"On the other hand, maybe they know and are in fact trying to tell us something through her."

"Like what?" Glen asked.

"Like, 'What idiot let you lowlifes share this luxury vessel with us?'" I said wittily to tease Glen. "Doesn't her presence at our table and non-stop bragging feel odd to you, like a clever plot?"

"It looks fishy alright! She never stops blabbering about the other side, especially the big music band, as if they were paying her and dying to make sure we realize our pettiness," he replied.

"Oh, gosh, where does she get all that vulgar energy?" I said with a sigh and Glen burst into laughter again.

"I bet nobody at our table would've found out about the first class, either, if it weren't for Marie's tenacity to educate us," Glen replied with a tense chuckle.

"Yeah, our grazing pasture is huge enough already, isn't it?" I said. "Without Marie's big mouth, I would've kept imagining that this was the whole passengers' area."

"Then just imagine how large the better side of the ship must be," Glen replied.

"My travel agent had bragged about it enough, thank you!"

In New York, Glen helped me with the customs formalities and securing my luggage in a big locker at the Grand Central Station before continuing his journey. He gave me his address and phone number and explained that Pasadena was only a twenty-minute drive away from downtown L.A. Despite his tempting invitation to stay with him a few days before settling down, I refused to go along with him to L.A. I just had to follow Father's instructions and stay in New York for a week with Mr. Ganji's family—another snotty friend of Father—to learn about life in America, as Father had put it. But, I imagined, it was mainly to save money on hotel and food before my school started in fall.

I was thrilled to be in America, at least for Father's sake and on his behalf. His love and admiration for this country was both amazing and amusing considering that he had never traveled to the U.S. himself. He had, however, read many books and grilled people who had been there. He also watched a lot of American shows and movies on the U.S. TV channel that broadcasted in Tehran for the Americans living in Iran. After traveling all over Europe, somehow America, especially New York, remained a holy place for Father, beyond all the splendours and cultures that even Paris could offer.

I strolled in Manhattan proudly with a miraculous, mysterious lightness, like walking on clouds. I believed it all related to the thrill of pacing such sacred grounds, exactly like the way Father had anticipated in his description of life in the New World. But, unfortunately, I lost both my interest and lightness rather quickly. My high expectations gradually died down, since the streets seemed dull like in any other city despite all those noises and skyscrapers. My anticipation for attaining a huge milestone and a swift enlightenment was fast punctured. The sense of lightness evaporated soon, too. Then, I figured it had been all due to the effect of the ship's rigorous, rhythmic bobbing for five days. Soon, instead of my feet, only my head felt dizzy when checking all those outrageous prices or looking up at the skyscrapers.

I peered at the seascape stretched widely beyond the glass wall of Mr. Ganji's large, impressive office. The U.S. Steamship anchored like a sleeping giant at the harbour. It indeed looked quite big. Its proud stillness, like a small toy in the bathtub, felt soothing after so much bobbing and throbbing. It needed a rest, too, after hitting and defeating all those wild surfs for four days. I missed it somehow, despite my gloomy memories, wondering whether I would ever dare to board another ship. Still I pointed it to Mr. Ganji and bragged about my fabulous adventure, anyway. I mentioned Marie to him, too—only vaguely just to complete a fanciful picture of my splendid experience on the ship—all for Father's benefit, of course. His gloating habit had infected me as well apparently. But, in that moment, I sounded more like the travel agent in Tehran. I bet he wished he had a generous father, too, like me, to send him to America on a boat so big!

The next day, I tried to use the subway to go around in New York like I had experienced and enjoyed it in London—oh, what a big mistake. I learned my lesson after getting lost a couple of times and paying a hefty cab fare to return to Manhattan. So, the rest of the week, I restricted my adventures to window shopping and walking to museums and the Central Park around downtown. Despite my confusion and boredom, I tried to act like an eager, genuine tourist for a whole week—such a daunting endeavour.

Then I was on the train to Chicago. Changing trains entailed three hours of waiting—enough time to take a glimpse of Lake Michigan. Back at the station, I went to a coffee shop for a snack and sat at the counter next to an elegant woman. She opened up to me quickly, probably because I looked like a lost child needing some quick motherly attention.

"Where're you heading?"

"Los Angeles," I replied with pride like I were L.A.'s mayor.

"Uh-oh!"

"What?!"

"I'm myself running away from L.A."

"You are? Why?"

"Haven't you heard?"

"What about?"

"The big one…"

"The big one…?" I asked with deep shame for my ignorance. Everybody probably knew about the 'big one' except for stupid me—just fresh off the boat.

"Yeah… The earthquake…!"

"No, I didn't know. Was there an earthquake?"

"No, but it's coming soon…"

"Really?"

"Yeah, it'll cause a major chaos," she said with horror.

"Are you sure?"

"Of course."

"You're serious?"

"Of course…"

Abandoning a big city just for a possible earthquake sounded absurd. Was everybody warned about this looming disaster, or the secret was shared only with privileged pretty people like her? Unless, of course, she was either a psychic or a psycho!

"When is it coming?" I asked like an imbecile.

"Well, nobody knows exactly, but it'll happen sooner or later. Believe me... I'm not gonna wait for it to kill me."

"Sooner or later...?" I mumbled, not sure what it meant, due to my poor English perhaps.

"Yes, one of these days," she replied.

"Oh, my God...," I said with panic.

"Forget L.A., I say. I'm going to New York myself."

"I just came all the way from New York," I said with gloom.

She was simply too cute and elegant to doubt her judgment. Otherwise, I would have not gotten anxious so quickly. In fact, she was perhaps a godsend to save me from the hassle of going all this distance to an empty city with no jobs. The university would surely close down soon, too, if it had not already. The Big One clearly put a big dent in Father's big plan for me! It was hard to believe he had missed this major bottleneck. Yet I did not want to go all the way to L.A. just to realize my stupidity, either. I surely did not want to be the only one arriving in L.A. with my big luggage and all, while everybody else was scrambling to get out! How could I push through the crowd rushing in the opposite direction? Why were they actually still selling train tickets to this doomed city, anyway?

Despite causing me a big dilemma, I appreciated her warning and concern for a stranger just in time. I thanked her a few times, dying to kiss her gorgeous hands, too.

"When's your train leaving?" she asked to break my pensive shock and despair.

"In about an hour," I murmured timidly.

"You'd better decide quickly. The New York train is leaving in forty-five minutes."

"I don't know what to do. I'm confused."

"Then listen to me. Go change your ticket and come to New York with me."

"Really?"

"Really… I'll help you settle there and go to another school. You can go to school anywhere."

Never mind the earthquake, merely her promise to help me had wrecked my resolve already. Suddenly I needed her *help*! Now I wanted to go to New York for her more than I feared of dying in Los Angeles, or anywhere else. I wondered only briefly about her intentions and quickly assured my cynical brain that she really wanted me—finally a positive sign about my groovy mustache. Especially after Marie's torturous coldness on the ship, so much warmth from such a gorgeous woman was ripping my heart. She was even prettier than Marie! "But who's she, you moron?" my nosy brain kept butting in. "Who cares, stupid!? Leave me alone!" my boisterous heart yelled back at it with a threat to stop sending blood to it any second. She was too pretty to fuss over her identity or intentions—that is how we men think and react in emergency, in case anybody had any doubts still.

I was falling for her fast and feeling powerless to say no to her. Making a radical decision quickly was unwise, too, but not following her felt stupid and excruciating. As I opened my mouth to say, "Okay," the image of Father, shaking the journey itinerary before my face with anger, popped up in front of my eyes and I froze. How could I disobey him, especially after following his instructions to the letter up to that moment? It would be an utter mutiny. He would probably not buy my excuse about the Big One, either! What if I lost my heart to this mysterious woman instead of going to university to become the prime minister of Iran, so that Father could brag to his friends? He would never ever forgive me and I would never forgive myself for spoiling everything for him. I needed more time to think, but her stern, enticing eyes made it difficult to even concentrate!

One of Father's teachings was to *eventually* marry an Iranian girl, because mixed marriages always lead to disaster. Of course, *'eventually'* meant, *'If you really have to, and only after you are at least in your thirties.'* He had a reservation about marriage, anyway—a big one! To prove his point, he often said that the big secret for the existing Prime Minister's success and longevity had been his lifetime bachelorhood! The liberal family lifestyle was the only Father's cynicism about America, and that was a big deal considering his undivided devotion to this country.

"Oh, what a mess," I uttered with a sigh.

"Just listen to my advice…, will you?"

The way she sounded like Father was odd, pushing her advice like the eleventh Commandment instead of a friendly suggestion only. Choosing between two eminent experts with clashing plans for me was tough now. I liked and trusted them both equally in that instant, although I had just met her. A big war continued for about two minutes in my head between these two pushy advisors before Father finally prevailed with a very narrow margin.

"I must go to L.A. at least for a while," I murmured with shame, totally mortified about Father's pitiful power over me, considering this stranger's beauty and my dire desire to go with her anywhere she wanted. Resisting pretty women's charms, not to mention dropping my darling Haydeh, just to humour Father, was an absolute proof of my rising insanity all by itself.

"That's too bad. I wouldn't do that if I were you," she replied tensely with a smirk. Then she got up to leave.

"Maybe we can meet later sometime?" I asked anxiously. "Maybe I go to New York in a few weeks or so."

"I have no address or number in New York to give you."

I gazed at her sadly, feeling guilty and lonely. The thought of not seeing her again felt just too catastrophic, but also odd and unacceptable. I had no address or telephone number to give her, either. Besides, she was already quite disappointed with me and walked away too fast for my overheated brain to react creatively. I just stared at her disappear in the crowd before realizing that I could have given her the address of the English language school to contact me. Still better, I could have given her the telephone number of Glen Wymore, my Pasadena friend.

I smacked my forehead hard to punish that slow brain, rushed out, and looked for her everywhere, but she had simply vanished the way a fairy would after giving you an advice or a gift. Those times, I really admired older women, so unlike my exact opposite preference nowadays—like all wise old man, I suppose. In that moment, especially, the beauty of this goddess, who looked about fifteen years older than I was, had mesmerized me. How could I be both stupid and selfish? How could I be so rude after all her kindness and efforts to save my life? I could never forgive myself for everything I had done to her—my gorgeous saviour—on top of breaking her heart in our very first meeting. No wonder she had left me with such an attitude—rolling her eyes and all! It seemed she really wanted me *today*, not later.

Running around the station frantically, suddenly I did not give a damn about my education or Father's diligent plan for me anymore. Thank God, I had at least realized my big mistake soon, while there was still a chance to find her and apologize. I missed her miserably already, as if we had been lovers for two decades. I was now willing to sacrifice everything for her and forget my patriotic obligations, too. I could not care less about the Shah's problems, either. *I will follow that woman to the edge of the earth if only I find her,* I promised the devil and ran faster.

For ten minutes, I rushed around the station frantically with a lump clogging my throat and tears blurring my eyes. I ran along the windows of the train bound for New York and checked inside a few wagons, too. All I wanted now was only the warm cuddle of this elegant woman whom I had forgotten to even ask her name. No sign of her was anywhere like she had been only a dream. I would have exchanged my ticket and gone to New York if I knew she was on the train. But what if she had decided to stay around to find a more cooperative lover to take with her to New York. With a jolt of jealousy, I wondered whether not enough eligible men lived in New York, or she had really liked me!

I plummeted onto a bench in pain and stared at her train for three minutes, until it hauled out of the station. I had decided to run along the moving train and yell to her jubilantly that I would be on the next train to New York if she were looking for me, too, from the train's open widow—the way it usually happens in movies. But no such luck. She had just disappeared.

Miserable and guilt-ridden, I collected my luggage from the lockers and boarded the train to L.A., still cursing my slow brain and the big plan all along. I mused in a haze with gloom about the pretty angel who had shattered my life in a moment and then abandoned me so casually, with no hope of ever seeing her again. She could have been my greatest lover and advisor, but I had lost my opportunity out of sheer gutlessness. I believed God would never bless me this way again, even if He ever forgave my gross, ancient sins!

Then I was struck with a shocking and humiliating revelation, as if God did not wish to wait even another day for punishing me: Had I become so lonely and desperate already to fall in love with a stranger so fast after abandoning Haydeh with such arrogance only a few weeks earlier? Did I suddenly love this new woman more than what I had felt for Haydeh after our long romance to the extent that I was now willing to go back to New York just in hopes of building a relationship with a woman whose name I did not even know? What had happened to me in a matter of weeks? Why did not I feel the same dire urge to return to Tehran then, where I already knew Haydeh lived and would be thrilled to see me back only for her? Did this mean that something was terribly wrong with me both emotionally and mentally? Yes, it was quite likely…! But was I at least smart enough to use this information, like a tiny awakening this minute perhaps, when another woman mesmerizes me in the future? *I doubted it already!*

Sitting and sleeping on the economy seat of the train, with so many weird characters looking around for someone to chat with, was exhausting. It looked bizarre how most passengers moved around restlessly, as if playing musical chairs to remedy their boredom, or maybe just to elude some weirdoes bugging them.

At the same time, being one of the few sitting so politely in my seat made me an attractive bugging target for those wacky wanderers. Some passengers' stories sounded outright appalling or just too personal even if I had the patience and mood to hear their gibberish. An ugly, middle-aged guy whispered to me after only three minutes of sitting next me abruptly that he must have sex with a different woman every day. The way he said, 'I must,' almost threw me off my seat. It surely implied a clear 'or else' subtext, but I did not have the guts to challenge him about the consequence of not achieving his sacred goal on a particular day. Or else what? I wanted to know. Besides, what was he expecting me to do with this vital piece of information, from someone I had just met, right in the middle of my exhausting, horrific journey? His way of forcing a dialogue after imposing his acquaintance upon me so zealously had felt silly already. But doing it merely to tell me about his daily triumphs, adventurous personality, vulgar sexual habit…, I was lost! I still could not figure out his intention or message after ten hours! Meanwhile, my jealous, nosy brain posed a few dozen corny questions of its own, anyway: "Was he telling the truth? How could he do it? How was he going to do it on this train? What was his secret? Why could not I find even one woman for myself then? …" For such rubbish, this boring brain of mine was quite fast and active suddenly, when it kept missing its urgent tasks, like reminding me of contact information I could give to the woman in Chicago. What a useless brain! Really…! What kind of a brain would fret about a stranger and how he would fill his daily quota on this busy train?!

I congratulated the guy for his audacity and stamina, anyway, and hoped he would now go bug somebody else with his exciting news. I was also thrilled for not being a woman with that ugly Casanova on the train! People's energy and enthusiasm to talk nonsense with strangers was just amazing, I tell you. Maybe they were hoping to cheer up a polite, miserable looking guy like me with their lies and gibberish. I liked to put out a sign that said, "Don't worry about me. My melancholy is incurable!" Weirdly enough, though, everybody's first question during this journey had always been, "Where're you from?", as if they had conspired to remind me that was a lost foreigner. The only exception had been the women in Chicago, who had asked the exact opposite question. It showed a lot about her character already, I thought. *Where one is going is always more important than where one comes from!* Anyhow, I listened to people politely and explained my origin, plus bits and pieces of my story, too, when a few of them insisted on grilling me. Some of them were quite pesky and looked like the FBI agents, anyway.

Besides the lack of sleep and shower, fatigue, and my painful experiences on this trip so far, the slow approach of the train to L.A. in the last fifty kilometres or so was the added torture. If I did not have all those heavy suitcases, I could have walked the rest of the way and gotten to L.A. faster. I wondered whether it had anything to do with the fear of the Big One. At last, a train attendant told me the reason was that the train was ahead of the schedule. I started to believe I must learn a whole set of new logic in the New World. Many intriguing phenomena during this long journey had already signalled the peculiarity of the environment I had come to to educate myself: The slow train that was ahead of the schedule, the commotion surrounding a *possible* Big One, the matchmaking scheme on the steamship causing me such comical humiliation, the guy devoting his life to conquering at least one new pussy a day, my dear friend in London mysteriously losing all his compassion within one year, and on and on. *Welcome to the Wonderland,* I whispered to myself as I prepared my brain for many more weird 'phenomena' during the next three years of living in America.

All these silly thoughts and enigmas were torturous enough. Then I got even more anxious whenever I imagined I could have been in New York already, strolling in Manhattan, hand in hand with that pretty woman. Instead, I was stuck on this slow train with so many bored, nosy, horny passengers. Apparently, I still could not shake that mysterious woman off my head. Resuming my previous analyses and efforts to apply that pathetic incident only as an educational reminder, or a basic awakening, about my idiocy amused me somewhat to mitigate my growing sense of loneliness on this ridiculous journey! *How and when a young person matures, if ever?*

Finally, on the fifth day of traveling from New York through Chicago, the turtle train arrived at the Union Station in L.A.—*on schedule..., not a minute sooner, thank god!* With wobbly legs on the unmoving ground again, I secured my luggage in two lockers and took the bus to the English language school, ELS, where I met Alan Dewitt, the young, friendly, student advisor. We hit it off quickly for no logical reason to think of right away. He helped me settle in a cheap hotel near the school after I took a placement test and registered at a relatively high level for the next session. Still Mr. Dewitt encouraged me to show up every day, get to know other students, and practise speaking English in the lobby. This rather big shot also found time in his busy schedule to chat with me informally at least once daily in a crowded school that looked like a serious academy.

I feel embarrassed now to recall or recount everything about the rest of that summer, particularly Mr. Dewitt's influence on me, but it is necessary to mention at least the gist of this odd friendship that started the demise of Father's big plan in a big way. Only later, I realized that letting Alan manipulate me was my worst sin among all the silly things I did that summer.

Soon I learned that Alan was friendlier with some students whom he assembled as a team of extravagant thrill-seekers. Yet, he used only me for contacting the elite gang and whispering the after-school plans into their ears carefully. This way, he meant to observe some general boundaries and to preclude the impression of favouring some students above others. So, my role became quite sensitive and important quickly as Alan's *sole* messenger— *Dewill*'s privileged prophet perhaps.

Besides exploiting me as his free personal butler, Alan also encouraged my dull sense of humour by laughing at my silliest remarks, especially before the gang. Being portrayed as a fun and funny person was an entirely new image for an uptight boy like me—a new phenomenon in itself! Still, I did not mind gauging my chance of developing a smoother personality now that I seemed to be stuck with Alan. In spite of his scheme to drive me for his needs, while also laughing at my wacky wit (and maybe gullibility), I enjoyed my sudden popularity and authority among the students.

Soon we forgot our main mission in L.A.—to study. Instead, we focused on partying and drinking most evenings. We danced to the fresh music of Santana and screamed along with the Blood, Sweat and Tears' tune: *What goes up, must come down.* Yet I was mostly *up* with my new friends and hardly went *down* to the apartment that my roommate, Sid, and I shared. My social life soon accelerated like a spinning wheel. Sid was happy, too, to enjoy the quiet suite and gorge on the food we shared, like milk, cereal, and bread. Anytime I happened to go home for a quick change of cloth or something, he insisted on going shopping since we were running out of essential groceries. "Can't you see I'm in a rush?" I barked at him in return.

Alan had several influential friends (or bosses!) in L.A. who craved the opportunity of meeting so many beautiful young girls from all over the world in our gang, including some of our pretty teachers. They kept inviting us to their luxurious mansions. We partied at various houses many nights, gathered at Malibu beach, or went to fancy discotheques to practise our mischief. Once we went to Mr. X's mansion—a famous actor I do not wish to name merely to avoid being sued for libel. In the absence of spicier plans, we explored Hollywood Boulevard and Sunset Strip, which were popular and full of tourists those days. The thrill of mingling amongst hippies with their weird scents and marijuana smoke satiating the air and shops was endless. Hare Krishna's singing and dancing in those bright, colourful streets with their exotic attires, shaved heads, and tambourines also added to the ambiance. Then, of course, we occasionally sneaked into topless bars for a peek as well, all under Alan's crooked influence.

Intriguing phenomena in America, including girls' liberalism, seemed endless and often amusing and educational, exactly as I had predicted on the train from Chicago. Even Persian girls, who played shy and pure in Iran, showed off their real talents in L.A. immediately, albeit not around Iranian boys. Apparently, any other nationality could *help* them better with their passion for perversion without judging their hypocrisy or leaking their juicy secrets to their ultra conservative parents. I was especially pissed off when a particularly beautiful Persian girl at the school rejected me outright even though I promised I would never tell on her to anybody if she just let me *help* her catch up with the American culture immediately. Instead, she chose an ugly, short Thai guy. Her foolishness was maddening. Yet, the boy's smirk and idiotic bragging was even more irritating and insulting to my country's flag. The only thing I could do was to prevent the odd couple from joining our elite club. Meanwhile, I remained content with my mediocre luck around the South American girls who were almost as pretty and horny.

No doubt, my language education that summer was a major fiasco and waste of money. The fact that we, this big bunch of misguided students, could at least sit straight in the classroom or language laboratory all day and pretend to be alive was a huge accomplishment though—something to say about our resilience, at least, I presume! How could our deadbeat brains grasp any grammar or vocabulary? More astonishing, we all passed all the tests with flying colours. I received a certificate of outstanding achievement, too.

All along, Alan performed his day job as 'Student Advisor' perfectly the whole summer! Absolutely! I wondered what the school principal was thinking. Nobody could imagine he was unaware of what was going on. My guess was that someone out there had told him not to worry about this particular educational aspect of that school. Alan was perhaps only someone else's puppet or pimp himself and not too guilty. Then, what was I? I worried a bit sometimes about being a puppet's butler or a pimp's jester without even getting paid in proper kind, such as cash, for my vital services.

Mostly I wondered what specific qualifications in my school application or appearance had convinced Alan to pick me for such a prestigious, honorary job. Handing in my resignation felt foolish, too, especially since I was now addicted to these parties myself. I was now taking my responsibilities very seriously. So at the end, I learned to stop fussing about anything just to keep my evenings exciting around Alan. *That is exactly what you are here for in America, right?* my nosy brain often asked me whenever it tried to be clever or cute again. I merely ignored it, though, as I had lost my trust in it long time ago. I have already mentioned some of my reasoning in the earlier pages about my random doubts about my mental and emotional stability. Still its sneaky attempts to spoil my spirit were infuriating, anyway. I wished I could deport it to another city or a remote island for the summer.

Sometimes, I recalled the woman at the Chicago train station, in a different context now, and giggled about my silly speedy infatuation, sense of guilt for ignoring her advice, devastation for losing her, and running around the station like a lunatic. I also laughed, even harder, whenever I recalled my initial high regard for Alan's authority when I had just arrived in L.A. Then, I laughed the hardest when I imagined Father's face, bragging to his snotty friends about my continuing triumph in America, while also looking for a job tirelessly—all according to my well-crafted letters. He would have had a heart attack if somebody sent him a few pictures of our nightly rituals.

Then, one day in June, Françoise Guinn showed up at the school. She was petit, pretty, and sexy in her tight stylish attire that highlighted her enticing dance manoeuvres. Alan recruited her swiftly and I reacted even quicker to lure her by abusing my sham popularity in the elite club, as a fair reward for my services,

I reckoned. Her arrival made things even more interesting right away, while L.A. proved so much fun and friendly, after all. And no sign of the Big One, despite the thumping of a few dozen drunken feet shaking the grounds as we danced the nights away. Then we went to a coffee shop for breakfast before going to the school—if you want to call it 'school.' We hardly remembered where and when we slept, but there were usually some beds to accommodate a few bushed bodies at a time.

For six weeks, my romance with Françoise flourished, while Alan kept looking for excuses to throw more parties. Once, when he had run out of any remotely sensible idea, he had suggested a surprise belated birthday party for me. It was a memorable event by the way the gang expressed their embellished affection with presents and a huge birthday card full of funny comments about my bushy mustache and commendable leadership—all Alan's idea again, I reckoned. Among the idiotic presents was a sexy red bra from Alan. Such a bizarre gift! Yet I danced with it hanging from my neck for a bit before collapsing in the bed, exhausted and drunk.

Starting in early August, Alan, who dreamed of becoming a movie star and director someday, chased Françoise and me around constantly. He made a frame with his forefingers and thumbs to view our movements through it like making a romance movie. We bore his hollow humour and annoying attention, but he had become a constant nuisance. Françoise rather enjoyed the flirtation despite her occasional comments about Alan's sanity. Soon, he lost interest in his role as the gang leader and entertainer for his rich friends, too, and at the end it appeared my lucrative job was being phased out as well. He was also losing track of his job at the school. Françoise had simply mesmerized him, and finally one day they confessed to being in love and wanting me out of their way. Alan had known what he had wanted all along and what her sizes were. I had already given the red silk, stylish bra—Alan's brilliant gift—to Françoise the morning after my birthday party. It fitted her perfectly.

The sudden emptiness Françoise left me with was unfair but not unfamiliar to me. Something about my crude personality had goaded a couple of my previous girlfriends to dump me without notice or pity. They just ran after more assertive and adventurous boys eventually. Luckily, all that experience helped me shrug off Françoise's tyranny somewhat easily and to wish the hot lovers eternal happiness together. I had to get ready for hard work at university and maybe some real work to pay my bills. Besides, maybe Alan deserved a pretty woman in his life as a handsome, decent man himself. Let us forgive his simple, weird personality. I also owed him a lot for letting me hang around the school every day, despite my refusal to register in more than one three-week session. Alan proved to be at least a sincere and conscientious person, too, since he always said, 'You're right, Tootoo,' when I asked him, 'What is the point of registering for another session?' Of course, he had needed me around him all along as well. By the way, Tootoo was my new nickname, as I will explain later.

That my affection for Françoise need not be taken to the next level was a big relief for me in fact. The thought of living in Paris with Françoise and learning French felt rather tough and bizarre! She had already softened me enough to follow her anywhere if she simply asked me to. By then I knew what a useless, pitifully impressionable boy I had become around pretty girls. Luckily, most girls have dumped me fast enough before I was trapped! All my life, I have often wondered if my pathetic sentimentality and repeated failures have been a curse that Haydeh had spelled on me after I had dumped her in Tehran so rudely, if not ruthlessly.

Anyway, Alan's betrayal shook me back into reality a bit, thank goodness. I rejoiced despite the hurt feelings and hurried to find another girlfriend—this time merely for settling down. Now I needed a stable and possibly rich girlfriend—while thinking sneakily about Sachiko Hiroi all along. She was fussy about boys and sexual adventures, which had stopped us practical boys from exploring her. But now, her cute face, nice body, subtle humour, shy sexuality, brand new Toyota Corolla, and lots of money, made her a perfect candidate for me to exploit quickly. Therefore, I expressed my rising affection and insisted on the purity of my intention, which was a hard sale considering the wickedness of Kitty Yamato, Sachiko's roommate. Apparently, Kitty had taken on the mission of consoling her all along after Sachiko's break-up with her boyfriend in Tokyo. The rumours had it that Sachiko had brought her for continuous support and been even paying for Kitty's tuition at the school. Accordingly, I found my resolve to rescue Sachiko from Kitty an urgent mission in itself as a divine duty perhaps, and maybe even redeeming myself in God's eyes.

I went to ELS every day to see Sachiko and plan something together if Kitty would let us. Competing with her for Sachiko's time and affection was an added pain, though—a disheartening affair, in fact, after all my triumphs throughout the summer. Of course, Sachiko savoured all the attention and kept both of us on short leashes skilfully, despite kitty's seeming hold over her and my manly arrogance and eagerness to rescue her.

Kitty kept brainwashing Sachiko against me, anyway. Yet, I always believed my perseverance and groovy mustache would convince Sachiko eventually, despite Kitty's higher aptitude in wickedness and appetite for war. Sachiko's importance for me to reform my lifestyle fuelled my resolve rampantly—something that Kitty had not anticipated. She reminded me of Kamikazes, especially when she wore her cap and hauled her short chubby body around in swift decisive paces. She looked even fiercer when she rushed to inform Sachiko of my latest atrocity, such as looking at or talking to a pretty girl.

At last, Sachiko made the right decision after watching me sweat long enough. It ended three months of my recklessness and then loneliness after Françoise. Access to a car, the luxury I could not afford for the near future, was the added benefit. If I ran out of my last few hundred dollars, she might insist on lending me a few bucks, too, I imagined with delight. What else did I need, except a good-paying job soon, of course, if Sachiko would not push me to forget about any job other than being her bodyguard!

Obviously, all the hoopla in L.A. had prevented me from looking for a job—Father's main priority for me upon arrival. In fact, defying his instructions had felt gratifying and necessary to find my hidden talents in the new world—never mind the big plan, for now at least. Instead, I was planning to use the phrase, "I told you so," in one of my letters to Father along with my regular nagging about the impossibility of finding a job, which then dented all other parts of his big plan, too!

By the way, a war of nerves had been percolating behind the scene between Father and me the whole summer. That is, while I refused to move a finger for making money, I just kept stressing my failure to find a job in my letters to Father. In return, despite all my elaborate hints, he just refused to offer any financial aid, as if he knew I was lying. So eventually, I realized I was on my own regardless of my decision to stay in the U.S. or return to Iran empty-handed. Sadly, however, I was both too proud to accept defeat and stupid enough to stay loyal to him. For a mysterious reason or pure gutlessness, I abhorred disappointing him in me, despite his persistence to ignore the financial requirements of the Big Plan—his Big Plan, I should reiterate!

Casually, I had enquired about job opportunities a couple of times when I had met employed or job-hunting students. Their inputs and exhausted souls gave me enough clues to stay put and keep believing in the difficulty of getting the kind of work I was willing to do, certainly not as a busboy or parking valet. Of course, a few months later I was forced to do exactly those very jobs to pay for the stiff tuition and food.

In early September, Françoise returned to Paris. Her departure depressed Alan and the state of our nightly affairs even more. We all began going our own ways and worrying about our immediate concerns, like money, job, and education.

Alan showed me Françoise's postcards and expected me to be as much depressed, perhaps even shed some tears with him, for our loss of Françoise. Now he suddenly wanted me to share our memories of her together for hours, which felt like still another

bizarre phenomenon in the new world. Alan was a phenomenon
all by himself already, I should say! But he sounded particularly
weird when he insisted on sharing and expressing our gloom
about Françoise's reckless departure after all the love we had
given her, albeit alternately, during the summer. He did not seem
to remember or care that she had broken my heart so that they
could parade their silly romance in front of my sad face every
day. Or the fact that he had been the one luring Françoise and
breaking our affair. Now, in his mind, she was just a love idol in a
common domain for both of us to cherish with anguish, and that
the situation was bringing us even closer together. By this time,
we were the closest buddies we had ever had in our lives, or at
least this is what he imagined and expressed a few times. One
night, he took me to the newly released movie, *Romeo and Juliet*,
and cried his heart out throughout the movie and afterward in his
apartment. I was going nuts, but still felt obliged to stay with him
after he begged me a lot.

He looked pathetic, but also surprised, and rather angry, by
my continued lack of enough enthusiasm to mourn Françoise's
absence, although I tried hard to appear quite miserable and to
sympathize with him as much as I could act before sounding or
looking silly. I worried that soon I would be a much better actor
than he would ever be. I was proud of myself for not confessing
that I had already gotten over Françoise and he was on his own
for missing her. I did not want to be his deputy anymore, anyway,
especially since he hardly arranged any parties. The amount of
bizarre phenomena and bemusing logic in the New World just
seemed endless! I was also extremely happy that so many more
pathetic people than me lived in this world!

Later in September, Alan could no longer bear the separation
from Françoise. He was tired of my lukewarm cooperation and
my stubborn reluctance to grasp the depth of his misery, and
maybe sob a little, too. He quit his job and went to Paris. I felt
happy for him, and for being rid of him, until two months later
when a common friend mentioned his rising misery. She said

Alan had lost all his money and dignity in the streets of Paris and cheap hotels after Françoise had kicked him out. He had stayed around, though, hoping to find a way back to her cruel heart eventually. But we never heard any news about either of them. Knowing Alan's wild passion, maybe he jumped into the Seine and drowned himself. Did any of you see a desolate American in his early thirties, very handsome, blonde, with blue eyes, a real Romeo, in Paris in the fall of '69 or later, pretending to be a movie director or star?

After Kitty's catastrophic defeat and sudden return to Tokyo, the task of consoling Sachiko was all mine now, not only for the loss of her previous boyfriend, but also kitty's spiteful departure. Both Françoise's and Kitty's departures had been taking so much of my time and energy, while Alan's departure and disappearance had brought me a sense of peace and relief despite missing him. Anyway, I moved in with Sachiko right away—out of my tiny lodging to her luxury suite. I think I did a good job of reviving her deflated self-image, which finally led to her finding true love in Jesus—although she still made love to me regularly, rather tensely though, as if she felt guilty about something.

I could not have imagined such a drastic, dramatic change in Sachiko's mentality in a million years. In fact, I was surprised immensely when she confessed that she had been thinking about Jesus for sometime behind my back and loved him a lot. She was so serious and excited about Jesus and looked forward to the formal ritual of joining him, being baptized and all. She asked me *so politely* eventually if it would be all right to stop our sex—to avoid a taboo or cheating on Jesus, I presumed. I said fine gladly. I knew nothing about Christianity rules nor wanted to challenge her. Maybe she had the same dilemmas! It felt easier for me to grant her wish and suffer the sudden sexual drought than trying to mislead her again or compete with Jesus. I was happy for her despite my erratic and confusing gloom. Losing my sweetheart to another man seemed to have become the story of my life! But then no reason to be testy about the matter, either, especially this time.

She tried to convert me, too, of course, as though hoping I could or would push such an odd thing into my head merely for resuming our sexual relationship immediately. Unfortunately, I had never been a believer. She gave up on me altogether at last and returned to Tokyo after two marvellous years of shacking up together in L.A. In fact, she also seemed relieved to be rid of me at last, after maybe figuring out that I was vastly immature and unreliable, especially compared to Jesus. She was probably tired of all regular boys, especially her last two lousy boyfriends. Jesus was a much better option than a husband could ever be, for sure, I kept telling her! Yet, when she seemed to agree with me, too, I wondered if it showed only her naiveté or a divine wisdom that even I could not fathom! She was anxious to return to Tokyo to tell her parents the good news, anyway. Maybe even hoping to convert them, too?

Anyhow, this outcome seemed to be the best scenario for our separation without hurt feelings. Sometimes, during those years of cohabiting with her, and enjoying the well-deserved reputation of Japanese women for pampering their men, I had suffered of conscience attacks about the high chance of misleading Sachiko emotionally. My sole consolation was that I had stopped Kitty's relentless abuse of her soft heart at least. I have never had a woman in my life as empathetic and mature, despite her huge, appealing simplicity. Sometimes, nowadays, I imagine she might have become my wife and saved my life if we had lived together a few more years without Jesus butting in and cluttering a young girl's head. Anyhow, the fact that my lousy lifestyle and attitude drove Sachiko to Jesus at my expense should be worth something to some divine authorities, I imagine! I hope at least Lord Jesus appreciates my sacrifice! *Perhaps I deserve some credit for my good deeds, after all, or an absolution for my sins and sacrilege at least. I'm trying hard here, people… Please work with me…*

My attempts to find a trace of my fascinating friend, Mr. Alan Dewitt, in the following years failed. I wished to satiate my dire curiosity at least about the outcome of such a scorching passion goading him to give up everything he had in L.A. to go after a moody lover. All along, however, I was glad I was not the man homeless in Paris craving Françoise. 'Better him than me,' I often thought. Then I met Françoise by accident in Rodeo Drive in Beverly Hills in the summer of 1972. She had returned to L.A. for a short visit, she said, and knew nothing about Alan, either. I could not say whether she was telling me the truth or not, though. I did not care to grill her. She did not show even a bit of remorse for ruining poor Alan's life and possibly causing his death, which she might known about already as well. I did not even ask her what happened to their love affair and all that fiery passion. I merely watched her saunter away, although I was a bachelor again at the time and loved to spend at least one night with her. She looked fantastic.

Anyway, neither the Big Plan nor the Big One materialized. No *Big* deal! Instead, all the events around me have been petite and pitiful since my departure from Tehran in 1969. Surely, I disappointed Father in all respects, including a moronic marriage, which led to divorce after plenty of headaches. I failed to make him proud. I have not felt proud of myself yet, either, despite my rather long life and some illusive success that most people envy. Actually, I often feel guilty for so many catastrophes caused by my simple disobedience of Father's orders and deviating from the path of life he had so diligently chosen for me. Maybe if I had returned to Iran and reformed the economic condition of that country, the level of unrest in Iran had not risen so high and led to the Islamic Revolution. I feel guilty for betraying my country and the Shah and causing so much agony and chaos in Iran and around the world single-handedly. I was destined to save the world but failed! A few times, when drunk and sentimental, I wished the BIG ONE had killed me to at least not witness the outcome of my disregard for the BIG PLAN! I hope that people forgive my recklessness while I salute my late father's wisdom, including his warning about the devilish temptations in America.

Clearly, America itself is responsible for the world's growing hostility toward Iran's current international stand. How do you expect things improve in the world when America lures most of the brilliant youths of developing countries—especially me—and reduces the chance of their return to become cabinet or prime ministers?! Of course, Alan ~~Dewitt~~ Dewill deserves a lot of credit for making me flop so fast as well. Yet, ultimately, I know that all my failures, as evident in this and future stories are my own fault due to my impressionable personality stirring many bad decisions all my life. Meanwhile, I feel I have been lucky every day, as though an angel watching over me part time, for example for not returning to New York with the women I met in the train station in Chicago, for not returning to Iran, for not going to Paris with Françoise, and on and on as the future stories would reveal.

*****

Today is October 5, 2013. I am sitting in my study in despair, reflecting on those haunting experiences of yesteryears, feeling lonely, though enjoying my peace, despite the rain hitting the windows fiercely and obstructing the view of the city and the ocean—just another gloomy fall afternoon in Vancouver.

Room

'Room' sounded like a nasty little word in the English dictionary as I walked in pain with my roomy, Sid. He was leading me to the nearby clinic, while carrying four heavy bags of groceries for five blocks, too. Staggering pensively and hoping not to faint, I pressed the leaking veins in my bloody forehead with a roll of toilet papers Sid had just bought at Safeway. When he had come out of the supermarket ten minutes earlier, I was sitting on the bench in awe and agony. After an initial shock, he burst into laughter as I managed to mumble the course of events. Luckily, he recalled a nearby clinic and insisted on taking me there since the gash appeared too deep to clot on its own. We were almost at the clinic when Sid stopped abruptly and put the grocery bags down.

"What happened?" I asked. "Are you tired?"

"No... But how much do you think it's gonna cost you?" Sid asked with a sudden panic for suggesting the clinic.

"I don't know...," I said with some concern myself.

"You'd better ask for a quote first when we go in," he said.

"And then what?"

"If it's too much, we'll ask them for direction to the nearest public clinic or hospital."

"I'll be dead by the time we get to the hospital. But I'm so glad to have a frugal and concerned roomy like you."

"I hope you always remember this," Sid replied with pride as he picked up the groceries and we resumed toward the clinic.

"At least we have five more rolls of toilette papers."

"Yeah, just keep pressing the gash."

When we reached the clinic, I asked Sid, "Go ask the cost."

"Are you crazy? They must see you before giving us a quote."

A pretty nurse rinsed the wound and a young doctor did the stitching. "Eight of them," he emphasized with impatience, as if planning to charge me extra. He was probably testy for my lie, too, about that big cut.

"What *really* happened to you?" the nurse asked me sternly when the doctor left. Clearly, the gibberish I had told the doctor had tickled her intelligence a little, too. Her angelic name was engraved on a blue tag garnishing her white uniform right at the summit of her Everesty breast—Carla. It resonated romantically in my head… Carla… Carla... And I felt breathless and dizzy imagining myself conquering the Everest. Losing all that blood was probably helping my hallucination, too. If only I could kiss that sacred crest… Feeling so horny suddenly under my present condition, with the big headache and all, was bizarre. Normally, not even sexier girls made me so restless so fast! I gasped and chuckled, wondering about the possible side effect of my head injury—a concussion perhaps.

"It's a long story…, Carla," I replied with a sigh, despite the thrill of pronouncing her name aloud and praying to God to give me Carla.

"I'll listen if you wanna tell me," she said a bit more tenderly this time, giving me hope about good God's plan to make up for the bad time He had bestowed upon me in front of Safeway an hour earlier.

I was not really in the mood too much to recount the long, humiliating story. But her alluring scent and warm breath near my face, while bandaging the wound diligently, obliged me to be less selfish. I pulled my head back stealthily so that she had to move closer and closer and lean more. Her knees touched mine, her slim gorgeous hands caressed my skin and hair, and her large black eyes mesmerized me as she gazed down at my forehead. I pondered the striking contrast between her slender, pretty fingers and her round, extra large buttocks. They obstructed my view of the room and Sid who watched us from a corner—assuming he was still standing there, of course. Yet, every one of her body parts had its charm. She was quite a delicious, full package, not to mention her blissful empathy, as if tending lonely souls like me, especially foreign students, were her sole mission on earth. She seemed to sense my urgent need for her love today, considering my sad face and all the blood she had cleaned from my forehead. She resembled my mother, too, whom I had not seen for so long and missed a lot. The image of my mom's agony and tears the last few days before my departure, while filling my suitcases with all kinds of junk so seriously, rolled in my head and I chuckled.

"What?" Carla asked. "Is the story funny?"

"Maybe a little…"

"So, are you gonna tell me or not?"

"Only if you go for coffee with me," I said like a spoiled brat, like those good old times when I coaxed my mom for a toy I wanted so badly.

"Umm… Okay… My break is in twenty minutes if you wanna wait."

Suddenly the reason for all my pains that morning near the end of summer 1969 became obvious. The opportunity of dating Carla, after all my prayers, felt like another sign of God's random boons, maybe as omens or peace offerings—to quit my regular sacrilege. Oh, how I craved a nightlong of worshipping Him atop those sacred mountains!

Sid hauled the grocery bags again without whining as we rushed to the coffee shop to wait for Carla. Strong enough to even climb the Everest now, still I kept nagging about needing some food quickly before fainting, anyway, just in case Sid felt I looked happy and rejuvenated. Such a smart, considerate guy Sid was, he seemed to agree I was still not ready to carry any bags despite my free hands, although I did not like his suspicious stare for a minute.

Carla arrived on time and I began my story.

"I came from Tehran a few months ago to go to university here. We hear a lot about crimes and poverty in America. So my father had warned me about suspicious strangers, mostly blacks. He'd scared me so much I'd almost decided against coming to America altogether. 'It's not wise to go then,' I'd insisted. But he persisted, 'No, you must go. How many times should I tell you that it is your patriotic duty…? Just be very careful.'

"I'm sure you realize his worry about my delicate physique," I told Carla, trying to be funny, "although not even the risk of my getting killed could stop his big plan for my travel to the U.S."

Carla checked my flimsy figure slyly and smiled playfully. I might be blown away if she exhaled hard near me by accident.

"Sid and I study English at this language school," I continued. "Three weeks ago, we went to Safeway at Western Avenue. As we left the store, Sid realized he had forgotten to buy onions. A bench in front of the store lured me, so I waited for him outside.

"I settled in the middle of the bench, put five large bags of groceries on my left and right, laid my arms across the top of the bench, and stretched my legs out in front of me, very much like King Solomon at his fancy throne ready for a foot massage or something more thrilling perhaps. Soon, a big young black man, ferocious-looking and strong, approached the bench. The sight of him coming fast toward me scared the hell out of me already. After an abrupt break next to me, he stood speechless and kept staring at me, as if I should read his mind. His stern gaze and a subtle nod made me wonder if handing over one's wallet was so automatic nowadays that his asking would be silly. Anyway, I figured the best thing to do was to stay cool and hold my ground. With the daylight and people walking by, I could always scream if he insisted, although I had only four dollars in my wallet. So I just glared back at him, while my dad's words of wisdom rolled in my head and forced me to be brave.

"After a long mutual gazing, at last he troubled himself to say something that blew my mind after all that suspense and trauma.

'You got any room for me?' he asked with tension.

'No,' I said firmly with irritation, like a fixed reaction I had memorized in Iran several months earlier.

"Just imagine, Carla: me leaning back casually on the bench, staring seriously at the guy's baffled eyes, though almost wetting my pants, and he standing before me in shock, dying to know the meaning of my arrogance, but also his options. I was—"

"First, tell her what you were thinking," Sid interrupted me.

"Yeah, in my foreign mind, I'd imagined he was a homeless man looking for a place to sleep for a night or two. Or maybe his request for a 'room' was only an excuse for getting a few bucks at least, as a best second option he could offer me today."

"So, you thought the guy was asking for a place to stay over night?" Carla asked with a giggle.

"Yeah," I replied, recalling my thoughts in that moment about the guy. *What a nerve! He'd scared the hell out of me already, standing tall above my face, and asking me for a room or money, too! My father's wisdom and advice had come handy again, I'd kept thinking with pride all along. How direct and pushy these people could be, really? What kind of a modern city is this?*

"But the guy looked even more pissed off and puzzled than I was," I continued. "He was frozen for fifteen seconds, frowning at the grocery bags resting comfortably on the bench, then glaring at my serious face with my arms still stretched across the back of the bench and my legs spread-out before me. After measuring me long enough so uselessly, he walked away at last with absolute disgust and I breathed a sigh of relief. Still, he turned and glared at me every few steps before disappearing behind a corner."

Carla burst into laughter and I enjoyed her cute stare before continuing, "Sid got equally astonished when he returned with the onions and I told him the story. We discussed the risks and eeriness of living in L.A. and worried about going to school in this rough neighbourhood and city for a few years. 'This tramp actually looked like a pervert and murderer,' I swore to Sid."

"Oh boy…! Aren't we clever?!" Carla blurted with a chuckle.

"Are you mocking me?" I asked teasingly.

"Of course not. Whatever for?"

"He'd startled and scared me, coming so fast and standing above me closer than you were when bandaging my head."

"Okay, what happened next?" Carla asked with laughter.

"The following Friday night, we went to a pizza place with a bunch of classmates and teachers," I continued. "I like these pizza places that show classic movies, usually Charlie Chaplin."

"Me too…," Carla said.

Thank God, we have so much in common, this lovely chubby Carla and I, I mused; *although walking together we'd look like Laurel and Hardy.*

"Anyway, I offered more pizza to one of our young, beautiful teachers and she said, 'No, thanks, I don't have room.'

'What do you mean?' I asked her with surprise.

'I mean, I'm full. I have no more *space* in my stomach.'

"This odd meaning of the word 'room' instantly pricked my mind about the incident last Sunday with the black guy."

"Boy, oh boy…!" Carla murmured with a grin.

"I felt guilty for all the wicked things I'd assumed about him. I still remembered his rage and disbelief, and then the scene of his exhausted legs hauling his big body away sluggishly, but still turning every few steps to glare at me like a warning—probably memorizing my face. Now suddenly his confusion after my loud, 'No,' to his polite request felt hilarious, too. But thinking that he could've smashed my skull with one punch, just for a simple misunderstanding, also made me tremble. Luckily, he'd just left, dumbfounded about the wild animal he'd faced so unexpectedly in the middle of L.A. Maybe he'd imagined I was a martial art master or an insane, suicidal killer. Anyhow, I thanked God for surviving the dire dangers of language barrier."

"You were really lucky," Sid said and Carla nodded.

"This English language sometimes sounds freaky with many weird meanings for the same word," I said, "especially when a giant, black guy stands over your head with a grimace. In Persian, the word 'room' is never used for 'space'."

"You must learn English fast before getting killed," Carla said with a chuckle.

"Do you like to be my private tutor?"

"Maybe… We'll see…"

"I've been studying English in Iran, too, but there is still *room* for big mistakes. Here we go again—yet another meaning for this damn word," I said. "Why don't you invent more words to stop all these mix-ups, at least for foreigners' sake?"

"We enjoy confusing and torturing you guys any way we can…," Carla said with another giggle.

"It's not funny, Carla. I could've died! Is this what *you* want?"

"So the guy found you today and gave it to you, finally?"

"Right; except for two major twists."

"What twists?"

"First of all, I found him. Second, he probably smacked me for a different reason than my rudeness three weeks ago."

"Oh…?" Carla said with a smirk.

"After fussing enough about my mistake and luck, I told Sid we must find him to make things right for my innocent rudeness. I wanted to thank him for his patience and generosity."

Sid interjected, "I told him to forget about everything and stay away from this guy."

"I would've told you the same thing myself," Carla added.

"But I felt awful for treating him like shit; excuse my poor language. I owed him my life anyway. Besides, I worried about facing him in the neighbourhood by accident someday. What if he attacked me now that he'd gotten over his initial shock from my idiotic arrogance?" I asked.

"You really have a wild imagination," Carla said.

"He had to do something about his shattered self-image, didn't he?" I said. "Besides, I felt I had to at least apologize."

"Are you always this polite and caring?" Carla asked wittily.

"Of course... I'm the kindest person on the planet."

"How'd you find him?" she asked.

"I figured the best way to find him would be to go to Safeway on Sunday mornings around the time the incident had happened. For two weeks, he was no show. But today, I left Sid in the checkout line and got out. The black guy was smoking a cigarette on the bench. I imagined it must be him, although I did not quite remember his face. So I went close and asked him very politely, 'Do you have room for me?'

"The guy moved to his left but ignored me after a suspicious glimpse. He was in deep thoughts, probably counting his debts. I couldn't say if he'd recognized me, but I decided to straighten out the three-week-old misunderstanding as quickly as possible.

'I'm from Iran,' I said as a friendly gesture and a hint about my English language deficiency. He turned briefly and gazed at me with amazing disgust, which I couldn't say whether related to my ethnicity or his three-week-old grudge. This guy is a master of disgust, I tell you. He could be an actor for his horrific gesture of disgust alone.

'My name is Tootoo,' I added nicely. He still did not react, as if I were talking to the bench. Embarrassed, suddenly it dawned on me that perhaps he was intimidated, again, if he still assumed I was a sick lunatic, a martial art master, or a psychotic murderer.

'Excuse me... do you remember me?' I asked him.

"He stared at me for five seconds and frowned deeper before looking away again impatiently, possibly recognizing me only then. Maybe he was too mad at me or too dumb to understand my efforts to explain the three-week-old mix-up. Then I realized that perhaps he imagined I was mocking him again, and maybe even crazy enough to ask him any second to vacate the bench. Especially my last comment, 'Do you remember me,' could've implied I'm still the same crazy guy who made you flee last time. Should he leave again or start a fight this time if I kept bugging him? So, I said hastily before he lost his patience or ran away.

'I'm sorry about my behaviour three weeks ago.'

"He peeped at me with anger again for six seconds, while I smiled coolly in hopes of softening him. Yet , he kept grimacing, which made me wonder if he was taking my friendly grin as a smirk or maybe even considering my apology sarcastic. He just turned his face away again. Ten seconds later, I felt he may think my behaviour three weeks before had been deliberate, based on perfect knowledge of what I was doing and saying. So I added fast, 'You see, I thought you were asking me for a place to sleep. Maybe you thought I did not want you to sit on the bench just because you were black or something. I don't mind you sitting on the bench with me.' The guy just kept gazing at me pensively and smoking his cigarette. I wasn't still sure if he quite understood—"

"Why did you tell him all these stuff?" Carla interrupted me.

"How else could I say I was sorry?" I replied with surprise. "I wanted him to know that this whole matter had been only a funny misunderstanding."

"Were you even sure he was the same guy?" Carla asked.

"I think so... I'm ninety percent sure..."

Carla and Sid started laughing as if facing a crazy, cute alien.

"So what happened finally?" Carla asked after they stopped their silly laughter.

"I told him, 'Maybe you imagined I was rude or brave like a martial art master, did you? Actually, I took some karate lessons but I sucked. Was this whole thing funny or what?'"

"Oh, boy, you really talk too much, don't you?" Carla said.

"I guess so... because that's exactly when he lost it, I believe. Maybe he assumed I was either crazy or still mocking him. He dropped his cigarette butt on the pavement in front of him and smothered it with his right sneaker slowly. Then he turned swiftly and smacked my forehead with a fast fling of his right hand as he leaped out of the bench and fled. The fierce impact flapped my head back and his huge sharp ring ripped my forehead. Thank God, at least my neck didn't break."

"And still you don't know why he hit you?" Carla asked with another cute chuckle.

"No. Why did he ignore or misunderstand my apology?"

Sid and Carla giggled again.

"Apology...?" Sid asked. "He'd been angry with himself for three weeks for not killing you and then you show up today to poke his old wound with all that new nonsense."

"What nonsense, idiot?" I said to Sid before turning my face to Carla. "But I learned a couple of good lessons today, Carla."

"What lessons, Tootoo?" Carla asked.

"First, my father had been right, after all, about all these senseless violence in Los Angeles. Second, being humble and admitting to one's mistake never pays off nowadays."

"It's a funny story, alright!" Carla said, laughing with Sid.

"I have many other real stories like this about my stupidities in L.A. if you wish to laugh at me some more," I told Carla, proud of finding a line quickly to lure her for a date perhaps.

"Is it because you're a troublemaker?"

"Maybe only around pretty girls..."

"Is that a fact!?" Carla said teasingly.

"I keep getting mixed up with weird people and situations since I started my journey for America. You can't believe some people's words and actions around me last few months. Even the English Language School I've gone to has been a fiasco..."

"Maybe it's your face or grimace," Sid said and they giggled.

"So maybe things gonna get even crazier around me in L.A.?"

"It will. But don't worry, you'll get used to all the lunacy in America soon enough. Or it'll just make you crazier," Carla said before bursting into laughter with Sid again.

My effort to grin and humour their silly waves of laughter and teasing felt so idiotic and unnatural against my grimacing habit.

"I'll go to Safeway every Sunday until I find him," I said.

"Why? To kick his ass this time?" Sid yelled with stress.

"Just to find out why he hit me."

"Sid told you why... And I agree with him... Don't you still get it?" Carla asked.

"I do, but I'd like to explain everything to him slower this time, from the very beginning, including my father's advice about guns and crimes in America and all."

"Your explaining has only confused him more and given you a big wound to heal." Carla said.

"Then either something is wrong with my explanations or you people get confused so quickly?"

"Never mind that. Just forget him," Carla said, sounding tired or stressed.

"Okay... But how...?" I asked anyway, now totally confused about people's mentality to leave matters unresolved so casually. *By the way, bigger proofs of my uptightness about unresolved matters appear in future stories, especially the next one.*

"Because I cannot keep repairing your face," Carla snapped. "You'll probably have a big scar after we take out the stitches."

"Well, that's even worse..."

"Why?" Carla asked.

"Because with this dent in my forehead, I'll remember him and get upset every time I look into a mirror," I said. "I'm really surprised how you guys prefer to forget things so easily..."

"Don't count on me to go with you, anyway, although I'm sure he'll never show up around there again. You can have the bench all to yourself every Sunday," Sid said.

"Maybe I've actually forced him escape this neighbourhood altogether to avoid more troubles?" I said wittily.

"Didn't you just say you've learned your lessons about life in L.A. and about the risks of apologizing to people?" Carla asked.

"But this one is especially hard to forget," I said like an idiot again. I was apparently incapable of learning any lesson, not even from my own firsthand, painful experiences. Carla was right. *How could I still hope to explain the matter to a moron who had no sense of humour, never mind a brain?*

"No wonder your father has been concerned about you!" Carla said with a giggle and a bit of reservation in her eyes about dating a foreigner with doubtful mental stability.

"You mean I'm crazy, and my father knew it too?"

"At least you're rather handsome," Carla said playfully after a long pause and staring at my sad eyes.

"Not without that mustache," Sid said quickly.

"What about his mustache?" Carla asked with surprise.

"Ask him to shave it if he dares," Sid replied with a giggle. "He's not even brave to shave his mustache for a few days, but keeps talking nonsense about teaching that black guy a lesson."

"He's just jealous, Carla...," I said with angst, "Shut up, Sid."

Sid's urge to compete with me often erupted unexpectedly and he got nasty and jealous despite his rather good mannerism and friendliness on most occasions. He suddenly turned into a spiteful devil as though making up for his normal timidity around people, especially girls.

"If you want to be brave, just shave your mustache," Sid said.

"Don't mind this joker, Carla. Sometimes he loses his brain."

"I usually don't like mustache on most men, but it looks good on you!" Carla said.

"Thanks, Carla... So, can we go out for pizza and movies?"

"Maybe..."

"'Maybe' is good! Maybe I conquer and kiss the Everest..."

"What?" Carla asked.

"I'll explain later... I hope. When you come to my room..."

"Room?"

"Room!"

*****

It may be hard for people to believe this true story and appreciate the variety of hassles foreign students must endure, especially when we arrive with little knowledge of the English language and so many meanings for even a simple word like 'Room.'

Roomies

The exhilarating summer of 1969, with all its commotion and bizarre episodes, was winding down quickly and nothing felt fun or funny anymore. The fall's approach was closing a confusing chapter of our youthful, but not useful, lives, while I wrestled with the idea of returning to Iran or finding a job to stay in the U.S. We all seemed anxious suddenly, as though wakened from a curious dream or regaining our senses at last after three months of abusing our gaudy freedom in a boisterous, foreign land under the influence of a weird advisor now better known as Alan *Dewill*. I had mixed feelings, too, about leaving the language school and my exotic friends to start at university. Big nostalgia in line with my memories of the long summer—fooling around the lobby or in the downtown streets near the school and partying most evenings—still haunted me. All that fun and friendships were too precious to let go. Some students had come to L.A. only for the summer, which almost eliminated the prospect of seeing them again. The rest of us looked forward to, or worried about, the new challenges ahead at universities and colleges.

With all the extra time on my hands suddenly, I tried to keep myself busy with a different kind of wasteful, silly stuff, now. I abhor to recollect or recount this new line of childish adventures —yet I do it, anyway, for perpetuating the perturbing moments of my adolescence. For instance, the following true story mostly reflects the sad state of affairs around me at the time, when we few remaining friends needed some type of madness to replace our reckless idiocy throughout the summer. At the same time, the main practical joke in the story is amusing all by itself for setting an unprecedented record in the history of the United States and perhaps the entire world. Most of all, we all need lots of humour nowadays, in the 21st century, to withstand the world's absolute, growing misery as humans get crazier and lonelier every day.

At the beginning of the summer, Sid and I had rented a tiny apartment close to the school in order to save money and savour our memories of Iran together. We were both homesick, although I got absorbed in Alan Dewi*ll*'s elite club soon. Such a misguided student advisor of ELS, Alan taught me well to relax a little, yet my nostalgia grew five folds whenever I went home and faced Sid's chronic nagging about our gloomy prospects in the U.S.; mostly since his remarks made perfect sense to me and matched my own sentiments about the Big Plan and the U.S. readily. Sid was his nickname, of course, the same way I had chosen Tootoo to make life easier for everybody, including myself. Most of us with difficult names had been rather forced to choose nicknames.

By the way, choosing nicknames sounding rather close to our real names, in hopes of keeping our identities and dignities a bit, too, had been hard and humiliating. I felt awkward responding politely to a different name, as if I had always been that dude. Although I had chosen my silly nickname myself, I had done so in a moment of distress under duress during my first visit with Mr. Alan Dewi*ll* when he had proposed abruptly that I needed an easier name urgently and I had felt timid and obliged to comply. Still, anytime I heard my nickname, I looked behind me, thought twice, and doubted my identity before getting ready to respond with scepticism. The mere fact that all this hassle and mental burden was merely for accommodating others felt outlandish in itself. This charade felt like another outrageous inconvenience of living in a foreign land, which worked in favour of my idea of returning to Iran, where I could reclaim my name and pride! I had reckoned with joy and humour that 'hating my nickname' could have actually been a good excuse to give Father promptly upon his demand for my justification to abandon his Big Plan!

Sid's uptightness surpassed even mine. He studied hard all evenings to get the best value for the tuition he paid to ELS and hopefully avoid more English courses at university. We mocked each other's wasteful lifestyle—me merely partying and he solely studying—but we got along just fine since I was hardly at home, anyway. He enjoyed the seclusion to concentrate on studying and consuming more foods that we shared their costs. His incentive for staying home alone to study intensively most evenings took so many calories at my expense!

Although Sid's dormitory at the University of Utah opened near the middle of September, he had told me not to count on him for sharing the September rent. He seemed unconcerned about my warnings and intention to find another roommate or a cheaper apartment. I teased him about his plan for a place to stay before traveling to Salt Lake City. Yet, he always only grinned slyly without offering a straight answer, as if his ingenious plan might be jinxed. I sensed he was planning to stick around a few extra days without paying a share of the rent, even if I got a new roommate or a smaller apartment.

Usually, I would just let the matter go—merely out of laziness or more pressing concerns. Yet, the problem was that I could not forget or resolve logically a secret that had jumped out of Sid's mouth one night when we both had been drunk. *As you probably recall from the previous story, I hate leaving matters unresolved!* He had confessed that, based on his family teachings, one should build his life and fortune around people's gullibility. He believed most people were naïve and it was fine to take advantage of this loophole readily for personal benefit. *Was he pulling my leg?* I wondered. So I tricked him a few times, even when he was sober, to restate his position. And he had always reiterated his belief with pride. In fact, he had bragged about it, looking quite serious and fully committed to his stinking ideology, even if it were not a pronounced traditional conviction.

Besides his arrogance, admitting to such an outrageous crime as a principle was boggling my mind. Of course, I wondered about the accuracy of Sid's assertion as a traditional teaching. A few times, I considered confirming the matter with proper Jewish authorities, but I felt I would never receive a reliable answer, for obvious reasons, of course. *What if I told them I was interested in becoming a Jew? Would they reveal this one secret at least if I indeed converted to Judaism?* I wondered. *That's why I want to convert, anyway—to learn and practice this principle perfectly,* I'd insist. *Would they tell me all their traditional principles right away or only after years of training and proving my sincerity?*

Naturally, most people in all religions ignore their conscience when they get a chance to exploit others, but nobody goes around admitting it or advertising it as a traditional conviction. So why would a smart guy like Sid make a fool of himself and me? Was not this a sign of his own gullibility in fact? Had he felt obliged to reciprocate after I had revealed the big secret about my mustache to him? Had he tried to outdo me with an even bigger secret of his own? It was all just so damn confusing!—although I knew he always tried to compete with me about everything to prove being smarter than I was. Or maybe he was merely fooling me, hoping to make me suffer from my normal uptightness and cynicism that he mocked me about so often—now by making me think and do exactly what I had been doing: Wondering and suffering about his words and intention! Despite these possibilities, I still could not let the matter go, which was indeed a perfect proof for his solid view of my impressionable personality and uptightness.

Anyway, the idea of letting Sid stick around a week or ten days without paying rent was driving me nuts. It reminded me of many instances my friends had betrayed me and I had shrugged it off coolly at the time. But that was all before Sid's confession provoking me. At least this once, I had to prove to Sid and myself that I could be assertive, too. Too bad for Sid, but he had started it. Of course, this sudden obsession for assertiveness was in itself just another proof of my rooted uptightness while criticizing Sid's, plus my chronic urge to never leave matters unresolved.

An Iranian guy, Bob Zarkesh, lived close to us. He had been taking English classes at a public school since his arrival in L.A. a year earlier only for extending his student visa. He was carefree and bold, always kidding around with people—even strangers—and laughing. Most evenings, he worked as a parking valet at a famous restaurant in Hollywood where celebrities often came for dining. Of course, some of them, like Bob Hope, usually waited in their cars for their takeout orders, which meant no tip for Bob Zarkesh. This was one of many colourful stories Bob repeated to amuse people. He was particularly proud of his encounters with Sammy Davis Jr., whom he had supposedly lifted and carried to his limousine a few times for humour. Then Sammy would tip him a five-dollar bill, apparently enjoying Bob's silliness and boldness. Bob repeated these types of stories frequently and bragged about his chummy relationships with celebrities.

In all, Bob was a free-spirited guy who was fun to spend a couple of hours with sometimes. He was just a complete contrast to Sid and me and thus we enjoyed his silliness. He was not an intellectual by any sense, nor did he waste time on serious people or talks. He would rather go to bars and fool around with patrons despite his terrible command of English and awkward accent. He had become popular for his generosity and funny stories, though. Even if he were not telling the truth always, he had the greatest imagination to create all those amusing stories.

I liked Bob's wit, but he appeared reckless to me, especially after I somewhat regained my sense of responsibility and normal uptightness. How could he ignore his education, unlike all Iranian youth coming to America with great ambitions—some even with a Big Plan of their own perhaps? How could he focus only on making money and spending it in bars and on women? What a waste! Besides my puzzlement about Bob's seeming empty head, I wondered about his father's thoughts and plans for him!

Therefore, when Bob invited me to stay with him after Sid's presumed departure, I was not too thrilled with the idea. Besides, his apartment was a dump. I nauseated anytime I visited him. Still having this option as a last resort, I gave my notice to the building manager without telling Sid. I intended to surprise him in the last minute by just packing my luggage and leaving. I was dying to watch his reaction after realizing that a fool like me had played him all along. I also had the option of shacking up with Tania—a plain, short, semi-hunchbacked girl from a wealthy Brazilian family—who had lost her heart to me. Especially, after Françoise dumped me to love Alan, Tania sent messages through mutual friends at the school that she wanted me. The matter had become too annoying, as she no longer hid her intention to lure me with her extravagant lifestyle and an offer to live with her free of charge. *Tania after Françoise?!* That was just such a crazy idea! Without a girlfriend, job, or money, even the mere chance of flirting with a few attractive girls still felt more honourable than selling myself to Tania.

I wondered whether Tania would take me as a roomy without romance. But what if she agreed, but then attacked me in the middle of the night? Anyhow, I just knew that between Tania's unflattering love and Bob's unlovely flat I would find a place for my slumber, although both options sucked. I felt sad for having to pick one of these two painful remedies just for teaching Sid a lesson. But a man must do what his silly ego tells him so, even if it only proves his own foolishness on top of lots of hassle.

At last, I chose to stay with Bob for a month while looking for another place. Moving in with Tania was just too risky for both my manhood and reputation. I still hid my decision from Sid who believed more every day that I would stay put and he was safe. Meanwhile, Bob and I enjoyed Sid's devious questions regarding my plans and my innocent playacting, casually murmuring, "Nothing yet." Watching Sid's glittering eyes and the party going on in his brain was hilarious. Especially Bob was having a ball testing Sid stealthily and laughing whenever he got a chance.

Bob had always teased Sid without a shred of nastiness. He merely craved for subjects rendering a chance to keep his tempo high. Poor Sid had shown a lot of patience in humouring Bob. But now Bob was haunted by the possibility of missing the expression on Sid's face when he learned about my plot and his homelessness on September 1. He was losing his patience and insisted on hitting Sid with the news one of these nights in his presence. But I believed it was still too early to warn Sid. The gist of the plan lied in breaking the news to Sid abruptly at the very last minute, actually by just letting him witness my packing and leaving. That would be a real Kodak moment.

I promised Bob to ensure his presence for breaking the news to Sid on August 31st, maybe while Bob helped me pack and leave. But Bob was restless. He argued he might be away on that particular day or something. For a man thriving on gossiping and storytelling, losing the chance of witnessing the main scene with Sid would be a real catastrophe. He was suffocating for keeping the secret this long already. Our stealthy whispers, quarrels, and giggling—Bob dying to tell, and I struggling to keep his big mouth shut—was getting out of hand and making Sid suspicious.

Finally, in the evening of August 29th, Bob just shouted out the secret and then had a ball watching both Sid's and my startle. I wanted to strangle that moron, yet my fury only helped Bob laugh more heartily and gather more funny material for sharing with people later. Of course, I enjoyed Sid's sudden panic, too—though not as much as it would have been had we waited until the last minute.

"Is this true?" Sid asked me with terror ripping his heart.

"Yep," I replied.

"You're moving out without telling me?"

"Well, you've given your notice to leave, anyway. What's it to you what I'll decide to do?"

"But we're roommates," Sid said.

"Not as of September 1," I replied.

"Have you found a new place?"

"No, I'll stay with Bob for a while."

"Hmm… What should I do then?"

"Go to a motel or something."

"Oh, no. That's too expensive. Can I stay with you too, Bob?"

"No. My apartment is small for three people," Bob replied. "Besides, my landlady wouldn't allow it, anyway."

"There's not enough *room* for you," I added cleverly with a giggle, enjoying every chance to use this nasty little word, *which might have actually caused my extra assertiveness urges recently as well, if you recall the story!*

"Oh, please, I won't take any space or *room*; just a place to sleep. I'll stay out all day and sleep on the couch," Sid implored.

"No. That's out of the question," Bob replied.

"Please, Bob. Please," Sid begged.

"Bob's apartment is full of ghosts," I said. "That old building with that witch landlady. Do you remember Bob's stories?"

"They're all nonsense. Bob is fooling us," Sid replied.

"No, they're true. Bob, tell him," I said.

"People say she's killed two young tenants and buried their bodies in the basement," Bob said. "Their spirits come out every night to haunt the residents. Ghostly voices and foggy shadows roam around regularly."

"And still you haven't moved out, ha?" Sid asked.

"Because I like fooling with them and they enjoy teasing me. Tootoo is safe, too, since he believes in ghosts, unlike you. They will haunt and hurt you out of spite," Bob said in a solemn tone.

"Yeah, yeah… Can I stay with you for ten days, anyway?" Sid said with a nervous smile.

"No, it's impossible…"

"How about only a week then?" Sid kept bargaining.

"No. The ghosts will get angry with me, too," Bob said.

The ghosts' story was not a new gimmick. We had discussed them on several occasions when Sid and I had visited Bob and strange noises had erupted late at night. Bob's building was old and wrecked, with a few suites that an ugly landlady rented out at cheap prices. The sight of her chubby body wrapped in a tiny, thin, wrinkled negligee, walking in the dim corridors with her Doberman almost matching her weight, was horrific all by itself. Some tenants had sworn to Bob that two foreign girls renting a suite there had suddenly disappeared. The building was dark and spooky at night, particularly in the narrow, smelly corridors. However, for the carefree, adventurous Bob, the low rent was a big incentive to avoid bearing a roommate. Sid, in particular, had lost his nerve on several occasions when noises had echoed and Bob had exaggerated with his ghost stories.

Yet, Sid's fear of a costly motel far exceeded his fear of ghastly ghosts. Bob and I tried hard to dissuade him, but Sid was too desperate and persistent.

"Okay, okay" Bob said at last, getting exhausted arguing with Sid. "But I won't be responsible for whatever happens to you."

"Yeah, okay. I'll take care of the ghosts myself, don't worry," Sid replied with a teasing tone and a triumphant smirk to me.

"Hey, Sid, you're so brave again all of a sudden?" I said.

"You two clowns better stop fooling around, you know?" Sid said, leaning back leisurely on the couch now that he had secured a place to stay free.

Sid's revived arrogance and his last remark added fuel to our already bungled outlook of his exploiting attitude. He looked too satisfied with the outcome of his begging, which had fooled even Bob finally, too. I was certain that at the end of one week of free accommodation, Sid would simply stay on for the few extra days he needed before travelling to Utah. His silly smirk pierced my brain, as though whispering in my ear, 'Hey, Tootoo, was this just another good proof of people's gullibility or what?' Bob and I glanced at each other and nodded about the need for a plot to kid Sid some more, in a more serious way this time. We figured that if we were going to let him stay free and bear his arrogance all along as well, we should at least get our money's worth in laughter and teasing Sid a bit.

"Remember, we told you so," Bob said.

The first three nights, we chewed over the neighbours' creepy tales about the landlady and her Doberman chopping off the heads of those two poor girls. They believed she had punished the girls for spreading rumours about her making the dog leak her fat ugly private parts every night and then some. That was just another creepy story in itself that tenants had been collaborating on and disseminating fast beyond the building's confines now to the whole neighbourhood. Accordingly, the taunted landlady and her dog had turned meaner in return every day.

The building's atmosphere was spooky enough to break Sid's nerve already, let alone the elaborate, lengthy tales Bob delivered in a sombre tone so masterfully with patience. Night after night, we witnessed Sid's nervous grins to cover his terrified eyes and gasping. We invented weirder stories every night and exploited the occasional sharp noises from outside or in the walls. Rats and cats rummaged the garbage bins in the silence of the night, too, as though eagerly supporting our cause. Still, the outcome seemed inadequate for the free rent Sid was enjoying with a big smirk on his face at least during the daylight. Bob and I agreed it was time for a direct ghost attack to scare Sid, yet we did not know how.

On the fourth day, I suggested to Bob to use his tape recorder, which had a remote control with a long cord, to play haunting messages in the middle of the night as a start. We practised ghostly girl voices before recording a bunch of wacky phrases. We planted the tape recorder logistically and hid the long remote control's cord carefully under the mattresses and beds. The sound level and dampening effects were tested and perfected.

At least I, and possibly even Bob, realized how silly, wasteful, and totally pointless our infantile efforts were, other than possibly making us, including Sid, laugh a little to forget our gloomy prospects in a foreign land. That was all! Sadly, I must repeat I was bored to my bones with no job or school. I just had nothing better to do those days after Alan Dewi*ll* had left for Paris to join Françoise and I felt horribly lonely and useless again, while also worrying about my future as a broke foreign student. I felt out of place in L.A. even more now, while my daily routines grew more painful in line with my sad cohabitation with Bob and my hurtful indecision about returning to Iran. Living in a meagre condition with a perturbed state of mind was at best frustrating. So, teasing Sid seemed like a brilliant distraction or tonic to beat my worries about future on top of my nostalgia of losing my eccentric friends after our endless fun throughout the summer.

That fateful night, Bob and I initially brainwashed Sid with our senseless, horrific stories of ghosts and goblins again. We had learned to keep our faces straight while expressing sorrow for the murdered girls, cursing the cruelty of human nature, analyzing ghosts' knack for revenge, and showing a lot of personal fear and vulnerability. In particular, a clown like Bob showing so much grief for the girls had impressed Sid a lot. By now, the poor guy, that snotty Sid, seemed quite susceptible to any kind of silly claim about supernatural interfering with our daily affairs.

At last, we turned off the light to sleep. The three of us slept in the same bedroom in that tiny apartment, Bob and I on two single beds, and Sid on a mattress on the floor. We always had to watch, and remember even in our sleepy minds, not to walk all over Sid and smash his silly head in the middle of night when going to the washroom or getting a glass of water.

We believed Sid would be struggling with ghosts' images in the darkness of the bedroom before falling asleep. So Bob waited fifteen minutes before pressing the remote control button.

"Hey... Sid...," a ghostly voice whispered softly from the far corner of the room closest to Sid's ears, where the tape recorder was hidden behind the dresser.

"Cut it off, guys," Sid said sluggishly.

We did not reply, pretending to be asleep. After a while, Bob released the second part.

"Hey, Sid... Get up... Come to me, Sid... Help me..."

"I said stop, I'm warning you," Sid shrieked. "It's not funny."

"What? What's the matter, Sid?" I asked irately as if wakened by Sid's noise.

"You know what! Stop whispering my name," Sid said.

"Who's whispering, stupid? Just shut up and let us sleep. Will you?" Bob yelled. He then released the next segment when Sid was quiet for two minutes.

"Hey, Sid … Come to me. Please save me, Sid," the ghost whispered so softly and convincingly.

Sid jumped out of his mattress, turned on the light, and kept gazing at Bob and me with terror covering his pale face.

"What's wrong with you tonight?" I yelled at him. "Why are you acting crazy?"

"You want me kick you out of here, asshole?" Bob shouted. "Why are you making so much noise and turning on the light?"

"The voice, the voice. Stop whispering my name like ghosts."

"What're you talking about? What voice?"

"The voice… The voice calling me…"

"It's only your imagination from the stories. Turn off the light and go back to sleep."

"Swear on your parents' lives you're not whispering my name."

"I swear I'm not whispering. Will you let us sleep," I said.

"How about you, Bob?"

"Are you crazy? I'm not even opening my mouth," Bob cried.

"You don't hear any voice or whispers?" Sid asked.

"No, idiot," Bob replied and I shook my head.

"Not now… before, I mean. When the light was off?" Sid asked with stutter, suddenly appearing rather convinced about the possible presence of ghosts, while questioning his sanity, too.

Bob and I shook our heads.

"You're imagining it. Just go to bed and forget about it. Don't think about those two girls and ghosts," I said.

"What kind of a college student are you?" Bob said giddily, which was funny in itself, sounding like his jealousy or insecurity around college students. "You're not too smart, are you?"

Reluctantly, Sid turned off the light and returned to his puny mattress. Bob and I had assumed Sid would have by now figured out the trick we were playing on him, especially since he knew about Bob's new tape recorder with a remote control. But, for a guy so full of himself about his intelligence, Sid appeared too carried away by the ghost stories to use even a single brain cell. Silence ruled for three minutes before Bob released the recorded whispers again.

"Hey, Sid... I'm your friend, I promise... Come to me... Nowww... Nowww..."

"You hear this? You hear this? It's coming from that wall," Sid screamed after jumping out of the mattress again and turning on the light. He was shaking, sweating, and screaming in the middle of the room. We leaped out of our beds, too, as Sid danced like a rooster on a hot plate. Then he ran erratically, from one corner of the room to the other, hitting the walls and floor, rising, sprinting again, and yelling. We tried to catch and calm him, but he fled to the living room. We were startled, too, ready to confess before he collapsed from a heart attack. Yet he eluded us as though we were in cahoots with the ghosts.

Bob had not had a chance to stop the tape recorder after Sid's swift panic attack and turning on the light. It kept whispering its ghostly messages from the bedroom while we chased Sid. He was running a marathon around the apartment, holding his ears, banging his head with his fist, and sometimes hitting the floor and up again like a beheaded chicken. It seemed like he might faint any second and die right in front of our eyes. Yet, as much as we worried about him, the amazing success of the theatrics we had caused inadvertently was funny, too. Bob and I had never imagined such a drastic outcome and felt horrible. We meant to stop this silliness and save Sid's nerves if not his life, but we could not catch him or stop laughing. We also worried about the landlady or neighbours rushing over to check out the cause of the racket and shrieks in the middle of the night.

"It was us... We made the voices...," we shouted amidst Sid's screams, while the ghosts' whispers still echoed from the bedroom and haunted Sid as well.

"No, no. It isn't you. I can still hear them... They are in the bedroom. Don't you hear them?"

The terror in our eyes from Sid's condition and the whole commotion had unnerved Sid even more. So, the more we tried to catch and calm him down, the more he fought with us. At last, Bob grabbed and shook him, and swear that we had made the whispers on the tape recorder. Still Sid was too overwhelmed to think. His mind seemed totally out of commission, as he shook himself loose again and kept sprinting around the apartment. He charged toward the apartment door to flee, but halted swiftly in his tracks, as though recalling the landlady's Doberman and the hallway's spookiness. He turned back, banged the door shut, and resumed running around the apartment.

Bob grabbed and held him tight and thrust him harder toward the bedroom, while Sid kept screaming and struggling to flee, thinking that Bob was going to deliver him to the ghosts in the bedroom. I ran and started pushing Sid into the bedroom, too, and then pulled out the tape recorder from behind the dresser. It was still whispering its beckoning words, but now louder without the dampening effects. All the main haunting words were now going to waste since the few early words had already broken Sid. The cord and remote control also surfaced from underneath the sheets and Bob's pillow. The sight and sound of the tape recorder shocked Sid and he calmed down gradually, though he was still pale and shaking. I brought him a glass of water and held his hand until he regained his composure after ten minutes. He probably had a mini heart attack that night.

"Didn't you often claim Jews are so brave?!" Bob murmured.

"That was a stupid thing we did, I'm sorry," I said.

"Who's responsible for this?" Sid mumbled at last when he could breath properly again.

"Tootoo planned the whole thing," Bob said quickly.

"He's lying. You know that he's the mastermind," I said.

"You're both crazy," Sid said and walked toward the fridge to take his revenge on our food even though it was near two A.M.

"He's right about our silliness," I whispered to Bob. "He might've fainted and died right before our eyes. Enough playing jokes on him."

"Tell it to yourself!" Bob said with a chuckle.

"I'm telling it to both of us."

"I didn't know he's such a gutless, gullible boy. Who could imagine he's such a chicken, not to mention his slow brain?" Bob replied, still giggling and enjoying the success of our plan beyond our wildest dreams. "What kind of a college student is he?"

I burst into laughter from Bob's ironic comments in such a horrific situation, especially repeating the 'college student' point. A numbskull like Bob accusing Sid of having a 'slow brain' was really both funny and insulting.

"But don't forget that this gullible boy even fooled you to let him stay here free of charge," I said in a mocking tone.

The next day, I shared the ghost story with our few leftover friends at ELS and teased Sid while everybody laughed. Besides the event's humiliation in itself, Sid hated me for publicizing his gullibility and gutlessness everywhere so casually. His gloom touched me at last and I abhorred my crude behaviour. *How and when I had became so callous?* I mused in despair. I was really changing for the worse, just as I had anticipated a few months earlier when witnessing Jafar's dwindling personality in London!

"I thought we were good friends after all this time, being roomies and all," Sid whispered to me with resignation. "But no… you're only a jerk, now siding with Bob to mock me."

"Yeah?"

"You bully only gentle people," Sid insisted.

"Gentle…!? You? That's fresh…" I replied. "You forget how you sometimes get jealous and compete with me in front of girls yourself."

"Like when?"

"Like the time we were in the coffee shop with that nurse, Carla, and you started mocking me and my mustache."

Sid giggled with satisfaction. "That was your fault too, flirting so much with every girl you see all the time."

"Exactly my point... You're just too jealous."

"You've become Bob's puppet, anyway."

"Then you're wrong. I'm nobody's puppet," I replied.

"Then prove it."

"How?"

"Play a trick on Bob if you dare."

My pride was pricked before his classmates, especially a few gorgeous girls, and I abhorred Sid's accusation of gutlessness and only bullying timid guys. I had to prove Sid wrong and make up for my wrong toward him. Most importantly, I felt I must show off my guts and ingenuity to those snobbish girls.

"Okay. That's a deal. I'll think of a perfect plot," I said loudly.

"Hurry up then. If you can do anything to him, it must be soon before I leave L.A."

"Okay, but it's gonna cost you," I replied.

"Why?"

"Because I still have to live with Bob long after you're gone. I must get something from you for all my troubles and annoying Bob, too."

"I'll give you one dollar."

"Don't be so generous! Do you want to bankrupt your dad or give him a heart attack?" I said while laughing along with our classmates. "You must pay me $100 if you want me play a good trick on Bob."

"See, everybody...! He's afraid of Bob like a chicken. I don't have $100."

"Okay, buy me a big cake," I said.

"Tell me about your trick first. If I like it, I'll decide."

"Do you have to consult your father about it, too?" I asked.

"We'll see... I'll buy you a cake, anyway, don't worry."

"Not any cake. A big cake from the French bakery."

"Only if your trick is huge and worth it."

Getting a tasty cake out of Sid could be a major triumph all by itself—still another phenomenon, in fact, during that summer to write in the history books! But the idea of playing a terrific trick on Bob suddenly felt even more intriguing, at least for getting even with him for warning Sid prematurely regarding my plan to vacate the apartment. Yes, a real nasty trick could demonstrate my ingenuity to him and everybody else at last. Let me stress *again* that this story is entirely true and those days I was simply desperate to distract myself somehow to curb my melancholy and missing my friends who were leaving L.A. one after another, except for Tania who showed no sign of returning to Brazil or stopping her gimmicks to seduce me!

Later that afternoon, I remembered Bob's plan to take his driver's test the next morning and that was enough for me to cook up a crazy scheme. Sid loved it too.

Since Bob did not have a car, he had begged his ultra-busy cousin, Jimmy Ferdousy, to come all the way from San Fernando Valley early next morning and let Bob use his car for the driving test after passing the written part. Bob had also planned to beat the system on the written test instead of preparing for it. His poor English and laziness to study the driver's guide had goaded him to come up with his elaborate, ingenious plan during the last seven months. The practice in 1969 was to return the marked tests to applicants, in order to review their mistakes and learn the material more thoroughly. Bob had checked out the tests that his friends and classmates had brought back with them during the last seven months. He had figured out that only five sets of tests were available and given to applicants randomly. All he had to do was to memorize the correct answers for the five sets of tests.

Yet even this task had felt too horrendous for Bob, although only around 36 multiple-choice questions were on each set. He had copied all the right answers in his English-Persian dictionary that he was allowed to take with him to the examination. He had numbered the test sets from one to five. Set one started on page 101 of the dictionary, set two on page 201, and so on and so forth. The correct answer to question one of set one was faintly penciled with a Persian letter on page 101, the answer for the second question on page 102, and so on. If an examiner checked the dictionary, he could not detect any abnormality in it and would not suspect the possibility of cheating. Bob's plan was foolproof and he was ecstatic and proud about beating the system and getting his driver license the next day. All along, he had used his international driver's license issued in Iran, but time had long come for him to have a California driver's license, especially for his job of parking cars.

All these efforts revealed Bob's personality, especially his laziness and eagerness to beat the system on top of his limited knowledge of the English language. The amount of energy and time to collect the tests, draw his conclusions, and prepare his dictionary had been much more than the amount of time any normal person would spend on reading the driver's guide and preparing for the test in a usual manner. Then again, bob was not really what you may call a normal person!

For altering the answers in Bob's dictionary, I needed around thirty minutes alone with it. He usually returned home with the dictionary around six p.m. Unlike his routine, that particular night, he was not planning to go out in preparation for an early rise the next day. Therefore, we somehow had to convince him to leave the apartment without raising his suspicion. After mulling over several options, Sid and I finally agreed on a plot that sounded rather believable.

Bob arrived on time and we had our super before I initiated the well-rehearsed plot. I started teasing Sid about buying us a cake in return for refuge against Bob's tricks and for not paying rent, either. Bob liked the idea, too, and joined me in pushing Sid. Masterfully, Sid refused for forty minutes, according to the plan, before finally giving in. Bob was, of course, still shocked and looked suspicious when Sid agreed! Sid then insisted that he was afraid to go out alone in the dark, especially in the corridors of the house. At last, Bob went with him.

I found Bob's dictionary and altered all the marks in it, so that now all the answers were wrong. It was a big chore under time pressure. But I also had to fight my conscience about screwing Bob's elaborate, seven-month planning, not to mention the total waste of Jimmy's time, lost wages, and the hassle of driving from San Fernando Valley only for Bob's driving test. Bob's job of hiding the pencil marks in the pages of the dictionary also proved more professional than I had anticipated. Anyway, I erased and replaced about two hundred pencil marks in a similar number of pages with a different letter of the Persian alphabet. I imitated his handwriting and made sure no eraser mark or residue was left behind to raise Bob's slightest suspicion. Besides, clever Sid had insisted and received my guarantee that if the plot failed for any reason, I had to refund the full price of the cake he was buying. He was a shrewd ass and hard to bargain with, I tell you.

Everything progressed smoothly. Sid and I giggled all night behind Bob's back and sometimes in his presence. Sid had last minute jitters about partaking in this callous scheme, however small his role was. What if Bob kicked him out, despite Sid's denial of any knowledge of my plan? We believed Bob would figure out the plot soon. Even if he did not, the secret should be revealed somehow; otherwise how would the whole thing be funny? Everybody must learn about it to make this plot worth our efforts and also prove my guts to fool Bob. The humour, and not Bob's failing the driver's test per se, was the main point.

Sid's severe agitation and fear of Bob's retaliation were clear and funny. But he also had to control his jitters, as he would have to absorb the cost of the cake if he himself ruined our plot, so he pushed me and hoped I would confess to Bob in the last minute. His mind and nerves were all over the place, while he was dying to tell on me just to get some credit from Bob. I hated his endless duplicity and cowardice, and yet had to humour him to keep his mouth shut and relax. My struggle throughout the evening felt like my previous squabbles with Bob to keep the secret about my plot against Sid. Anyhow, we ate the tasty French cake and went to bed earlier than usual before Sid's nerves or duplicity could spoil everything.

The next day, Sid and I told the story to our friends at ELS and giggled the whole day, while we feared our encounter with Bob later in the afternoon, too. He would surely suspect some kind of sabotage. He would definitely double-check the marks in his dictionary with the original test sheets that he kept in a safe place, too, as soon as he got home. So he would discover our plot, or at least suspect Sid and me. Still, I asked Sid to be extra careful with his words and attitude, instead of trying to get funny or somehow raise Bob's suspicions.

Bob was not home when we arrived around four p.m., but his dictionary and other papers were on the desk. Sid and I waited nervously. Around six o'clock, our hearts thumped as the sound of the key in the lock echoed. But, he stepped inside solemnly with a heartbreaking look of desperation and resignation instead of rage or suspicion. The sudden absence of his normal clowning and laughing felt so weird and depressing, too, but also funny.

"What's wrong, Bob?" Sid asked hastily with a mocking tone and grin, quite slyly—so unlike a gentle person he often claimed to be.

"Wow... That was real gentle, Sid!" I said gladly, happy for the chance to give him a live proof of his slyness, especially after my earlier warning to him to stop being funny or provocative.

"I screwed up the whole test and everything else today," Bob replied with an unprecedented gloom, as if he had been sentenced to death.

"What happened?" I asked softly with my crafty compassion, hoping to stop Sid from saying or doing something stupid fast.

"I failed," Bob replied with terror on his face. "That's what happened."

"Why?" I asked.

"I guess they've changed the tests," Bob replied impatiently.

His response and the fact that he had not still checked the marks in his dictionary with the original test sheets said a lot about Bob's character, especially his laziness and naivety. That would have been the first thing that Sid or I would have done, if we had been in Bob's place. But Bob, he had just come home earlier, dropped his books on the desk, and gone out to a bar or something, instead of checking anything.

"That's strange. So how many mistakes did you have?" Sid asked, winking to me privately as we giggled callously. He just could not stop himself as I had suspected.

"All my answers were wrong. Everything was wrong. I got zero and then ridiculed, too," Bob replied, almost ready to bang his head against the wall from anguish. Sid and I burst into loud laughter, which made Bob both nervous and amused. He simply did not understand how the matter could be so funny in the way we blasted with laughter repeatedly. There was some humour in it, he said, but our outbursts were extravagant and childish. His comment and reaction—for a person who thrived on fooling around with people and laughing senselessly at silliest things all the time—was extra amusing and it made us laugh even harder.

"Why were you ridiculed?" Sid asked with a sly smirk, rather disappointed that Bob had not yet put two and two together to figure out we had been behind this charade.

"Well, the ugly examiner stared at me like I was a complete ass and she peeped at Jimmy standing beside me as if he were an idiot, too, to be even around me. Jimmy was offended even more than I was, so he kept peeping at me with contempt, too. Then she spoke with a smirk: 'I've been working here for over twenty years and I've never seen such a score. How could you manage not to get even one answer correct, not even by accident? What's the matter with you, huh?'" Bob repeated her words with anguish and humiliation still covering his face. "She then tossed another driving guide at me and ordered me to study it good or get a tutor. I can't understand what went wrong?"

"Because you're lazy," I said, hoping he would get my drift.

Bob still did not get my hint about his laziness to check the original tests with his dictionary to discover what had exactly gone wrong. Sid and I laughed our hearts out again and Bob imagined that only the story amused us, and not his laziness in addition to the tremendous success of our plot. He just cursed us and left. He simply could not imagine the possibility of his naughty roomies being crazy enough to conspire against him on such an important matter so heroically.

Bob's grave desperation showed in his contemplative face the next few days. He believed his scheme to defeat the system had failed and his chance of passing the driver's written test was slim, considering his poor English. Besides, Jimmy had told him that he would not come back again. In addition, without a license, his lucrative parking job was in jeopardy. Sid and I enjoyed his rising agony, which felt like an extra layer of icing on the French cake Sid had bought and we had finished already.

I felt guilty for not only having destroyed Bob's plan for cheating on the test, but also abolishing his hope of ever passing it. I was also ecstatic that my simple practical joke had created such an unprecedented record in the whole history of the United States and perhaps the entire world. Most likely, no one had ever been dumb enough to get a 'zero' on the driving test and nobody would be able to break this record ever. I had left my mark on history, albeit the public might never discover and appreciate my nifty initiative and the immense amount of laughter generated by it. Even today, I believe that those officials should have framed and kept Bob's historical score for posterity and recorded it in the Guinness Book as well! I want some credit, too, for all this. My ingenuity had been cute, although perhaps weird like Picasso's paintings that only certain smart people would really appreciate. Sid, on the other hand, was hardly worried or happy about Bob's anguish, but dying to reveal our secret and then blaming me for everything. He was itching to start a conflict between Bob and me before leaving L.A. in a few days. He wanted to get so much more mileage out of the price of the cake he had bought for us.

The situation was quite amusing for a few days, especially watching Bob's incredible torment, yet commendable optimism, in search of an alternative means of beating the system. He was determined to invent a new scheme, but got only more frustrated when no easy solution came to his mind. Sometimes, Sid and I offered silly ideas and made more fun of him.

"Pay someone who resembles you to take the written test for you, then switch places for the driving test and taking the license picture. The examiners are different, so they won't notice the switch," I suggested teasingly once.

Bob's sudden shock and delight, while contemplating my suggestion seriously, indicated that I might have accidentally stumbled upon a brilliant idea.

"Wow, this might actually work," Bob said with great joy in his eyes after so long.

Had I known he would like my idea so much, I could have tried to exchange it for cash or something. Still, both Sid and I had personal motives for revealing our mischief, especially now that he could actually start looking for an impostor to do what I had suggested. Me and my big mouth! On the other hand, at least I, and maybe Sid too, remained apprehensive about triggering Bob's rage. Therefore, we fooled around with him about his failed test long enough, *very cautiously*, time after time, until Bob smelled a rat, finally… At last! By then, Sid and I were exhausted from all our hard work just to raise Bob's dull curiosity a tad. Sid and I exhaled a sigh of relief and congratulated each other for our stamina to finish phase one for now. We hoped to get a chance to clear our conscience soon, too, while testing Bob's intelligence and character along the way. We preferred to confess eventually somehow in phase two, instead of letting him suffer for God knew how much longer—if not forever.

Thanks to our regular push when he was around to goad his marginally activated curiosity, Bob indulged us with confusion, while Sid and I strived to bring him into picture little by little. His growing confusion was too funny to end soon, while finding the exact points to keep his interest were hilarious and amusing for a few more days, too, until, at last… Eventually, the severity of our hints hit his brain and he realized the conspiracy, while Sid and I accused each other of being the mastermind behind the plot. He accepted Sid's version of the story, rationalizing I did not mind doing one up on him just to show-off my nerve and creativity, at least parallel to what Bob had become famous for among our mutual friends. By this time, Sid and I were really exhausted and needed a long vacation to recuperate, yet deep down felt we had given Bob too many direct clues despite our efforts to be stingy, otherwise we would be still at it.

Despite his fury about two amateur clowns causing him so much hassle, disgrace, and grief, Bob was relieved that at least his scheme for the driver's written test was still intact as soon as he copied the right answers back into the dictionary—perhaps in inerasable ink this time—and safeguarded it with his life until passing the test. He regained his good humour soon and joined us in recounting the event and laughing. In particular, he enjoyed explaining the examiner's growing grimace when every single answer had been wrong, one after another, and then pulling a deriver's guide out of the shelf and shoving it onto Bob's face, patting him on the shoulder, and whispering her sarcastic remarks to him and Jimmy.

"Just imagine the same woman examiner correcting my test again the next time I go there," Bob said. "I bet she'd go crazy to see me get all the answers right this time after getting zero only a week earlier. She'd probably be quite proud of herself to make me study so hard."

"Go find her and tell her you got 100%, even if she is not the one correcting your test," I suggested jokingly, but again Bob liked this idea a lot, too. He seemed dying to take his revenge on that ugly examiner at whatever cost! *I should really stop giving away my ideas so freely left and right!*

"Yeah, I'll certainly do it to teach that bitch a lesson," Bob said with a blast of laughter.

"But, tell me, Bob, honestly…" I kept teasing him, "How did it really feel watching her growing grimace and then saying zero instead of hundred percent?"

"I couldn't imagine you're such an asshole," Bob replied.

"I swear, Sid started the whole thing," I said, knowing that my claim had some truth behind it.

"I'll get you for this, jerk. Mark my words…," Bob reiterated, although he was not still sure how to take his revenge.

"Why don't you shave his mustache?" stupid Sid suggested.

"Yeah, that's a great idea. I'll shave your mustache one of these nights in your sleep."

"No. No, Bob. Not my mustache, please."

My mustache had always played an important role for my ego and popularity. It had been my secret weapon for masking my narrow, sullen upper lip. Without a mustache, my plain long face, not to mention the enormity of my nose, would come to life. It was amazing how a bushy mustache could hide or subdue all those flaws. Most of our friends at ELS had learned about this secret through Sid's big mouth and teased me about it now and then. They had begged me to shave it just to satisfy their curiosity —but mostly for their fun, I was sure. Those jerks had abused my sensitivity about it throughout the summer and mocked me whenever an occasion had risen. With his sneaky proposal, Sid had now taken his revenge on me, sucked up to Bob, and could brag to students at ELS, too.

The irony was that if Sid and I had not shared our secrets with each other at the beginning of the summer when we were drunk one evening, none of the events in this true story had taken place and everybody would have lived in peace all along.

"Ask for something else," I begged Bob again.

"No, your mustache. I will cut it one of these nights. Now you cannot get a good night sleep, either, fearing the moment of my revenge, when I arrive in the middle of night with the scissors. Oh, how much I enjoy this plan! Thanks for suggesting it, Sid. You're forgiven, but must help me cut his mustache, too."

"Okay. I'll help you," Sid replied, chuckling at my expense with unprecedented fearlessness about my wrath. He probably thought he would be leaving in a few days, anyway, far away from my reach and possible wrath.

"Be ready to hold his hands tight if he wakes up," Bob said.

"I'll take care of you, traitor, you bastard," I told Sid. "Bob, that's a silly plan. If you try to do it in my sleep, the scissors may pierce my face or eye if I get startled. Don't do it."

"Then let me cut it right now," Bob replied.

"Are you crazy? I'm gonna look silly at school without my mustache. I'm just in the middle of finding a new girlfriend," I said, pondering my efforts to soften Sachiko those days.

"No, your mustache," Bob insisted.

"Do something else," I implored. "Sid'll give you one dollar!"

"No. I'll cut your damn mustache. Now or in your sleep, one of these nights. Your choice…" Bob said while chuckling.

"Yeah, Tootoo, let him shave it now if you're afraid of the scissors getting into your eye," the bastard Sid said with a wicked grin, full of satisfaction for causing my anguish and final defeat.

I could slit his throat at that moment for putting this idea into Bob's crazy head in the first place and now making his cheap shots and giving me advice, too, so fearless of me so suddenly. Sneaky sly! Always pretending to be timid and gentle, too! I was glad I had overcome my sense of pity for Sid at some moments when I had felt he might be a simpleton, after all!

I knew when Bob put his mind into doing something, he would never give up. He would definitely cut my mustache one night and I might as well let him do it when I was awake at least. Losing the symbol of my pride and charisma would be a disaster, but I had no other choice. Everybody would tease my ugly face at ELS, but it was better than getting the scissors in my eye in the middle of the night or delaying Bob's inevitable revenge. I could go shack up with Tania, to save my mustache, pride, and all the rest of it, but that option felt even riskier than losing my eye. At the end, I decided that the sooner I let Bob do it, the sooner my mustache would grow back, hopefully in time for starting at the university at least. Deep down, I felt I deserved a punishment for my naughtiness with both Sid and Bob, anyway.

They enjoyed shaving my beautiful mustache slowly and laughing at me every step of the way and the following days until getting used to my plain face. It is funny and weird that mustache can make so much effect on one's looks. Even creepier is how the word mustache is made of the two words 'must' and 'ache.' I did ache without it for almost a month until it grew long enough to trim it properly.

At ELS, the next day, I was ridiculed, as expected, while Sid bragged about his vital role in getting my mustache shaved. He was having the last laugh after all the tricks we had played on each other throughout the summer. *Bastard!* I wished I were a Muslim woman to hide my big nose and mouth behind one of those so practical face veils for a while. The most humiliating part of it was Tania's sudden loss of love and joining the crowd at ELS to mock my lousy looks. Once, I overheard her telling her friends, "I'm so glad he never kissed me, or I'd be throwing up right about now. How could I have been in love with such an ugly face? Now I know that God loves me."

Of course, I knew that ugly Tania was exaggerating only out of spite. Poor girl! I should have given her a kiss at least. *It would have not killed you, you stingy boy!*

By the way, another weird phenomenon during this period worth mentioning here is that I had been going to ELS and fooling around the lobby with the students even after Alan *Dewill* had left for Paris and I was not a student, either. The principal and teachers knew about my daily visits and staying there for hours. The principal seemed to despise the liberty I had given myself. Still, he probably did not dare confronting me or prohibiting my presence. I bet he had felt I had too many dirty secrets about that school's after-hour extracurricular activities during the time I had been Alan's communication runner. Actually, it seemed I had established myself a special right at ELS to come and go as I wished for as long as I desired—apparently for everything I had done for the school during the summer of 1969 free!

And, for me, ELS had still felt like a good refuge all along, until Sachiko finally took me on as her new boyfriend. In fact, I felt that the more other students made fun of my looks without a mustache, the more Sachiko showed pity and love towards me. It appeared, in the end, that shaving my mustache had been another mysterious omen stirring Sachiko's decision to take me on as her boyfriend.

By the way, she remained one of those lucky people who never used a nickname, but more importantly called only my real name cutely. How could I not love her true nature and identity? In contrast, I believe using a nickname, combined with the shock of being in an idiotic new world, especially around Alan Dewi*ll*, changed my personality for the worse within a few months of my arrival in the U.S. I believe the events during that short period of my life provoked the dormant devil inside me, so it has erupted and made me do outrageous things from time to time beyond my deeper convictions and good nature! The point is that the bad things I happen to do in the future stories are not my fault or a reflection of who I really am! That is another reason for using pseudonyms and a passive voice in some of those stories as well.

*****

Just another 'by the way,' Bob Zarkesh got his driver's licence by cheating on the written test and setting another record in the U.S. history for getting 100% mark. He drove all over the city without knowing a single thing about traffic rules in California. That is cause for concern about driving safety in California with people like Bob around! How useful are traffic rules then, anyway?

Change of Heart

To boost Holly's mood, her mom is planning a party at home for her twentieth birthday with family and friends, minus Curt, she hopes. Holly is hesitant herself to call and invite him, especially since he has not called her for nearly two weeks again, bastard! The family has seen him before, including the few times they had invited him to dinner. He has not come around, however, or been invited to their house for over one year now. They tolerate him for Holly's sake only, while everybody remains sceptical about the future of their murky relationship. They avoid interfering, though, considering Holly's melancholy and reckless obsession with Curt—a sad situation the whole world admits and abhors adamantly.

Only God knows how many times Curt has broken Holly's heart during the last four years, while she has been struggling to salvage their hectic courtship. She simply cannot renounce her passion for him. Despite his aloofness and possible cheating, her attempts to abandon him have always failed, unable to say no to him whenever he calls and uses his charm and lies to coax her. Curt Beasmarth is a jerk, Holly Klint admits overtly, especially when pondering the gist of their dubious dates—spending a few hours together occasionally, dining and lovemaking, then Curt returning her home casually without sharing any romance or even committing to the next date. She must just wait and hope he would call soon, wondering all along about his affairs and fun with other girls, or whether he is truly busy. He is an enigmatic monster by all accounts. But, God, he is also cute and caring sometimes, thus a tough challenge for Holly, especially when she reminisces about their initial splendid times together.

Holly is not a dumb or desolate creature, either. Tall and sexy like a fashion model, plenty of men chase her all the time. Yet, she cannot engage in a serious relationship with an eligible man as if pinned by Curt's spell. A few times, she courted other men, but failed to bring herself to kiss them goodnight or accept their invitation for a second date. After any one of those experimental or retaliatory dates—to incite Curt's jealously perhaps—she just flees to her room and cries herself to sleep. She has tried different gimmicks to hurt Curt or play hardball when he calls and asks for a date, to no avail. He always accepts her rejection or flirtation with other men coolly without showing any sign of softening. In fact, after any one of her mutinous games, Holly finds herself in a weaker position, since Curt stops calling her on the assumption that she is finally getting on with her life. She must call him and apologize for her behaviour or wait much longer than usual for Curt to call her casually on peculiar pretences leading to another date again.

For Curt, Holly is a godsend convenience to depend on for his sudden need for sex or a pretty partner for an important social function. He often feels guilty, however, and tells her to find a tamer man for herself, especially when she seeks higher attention and commitment. Actually, Curt is a softhearted, caring person by nature, if things around him were not always so hectic. One problem is that several women imagine outfoxing him and their rivals eventually. Therefore, while they fight to steal him from one another, he does not have the heart to reject any of those sad sexy faces and fragile souls hovering around him like butterflies.

In his naïve mind, he is doing these delicate creatures a favour by not holding on to them selfishly. Let them be free and share him leisurely as they wish. They all need his nectar of love. And when they finally perish, a fresh flock of butterflies normally pop up to put his fire off. The butterflies come and go regularly except for Holly, who deserves a Nobel Prize for patience and optimism in the way she ignores Curt's repeated clues to forget about him and a permanent relationship together.

At least he tries to be honest with her, and women in general, about his erratic lifestyle. Most are offended and leave him with anger and insults eventually. The way they suddenly become rude and hostile toward him is truly educational. It feels weird how most women reveal their true personality when they fail to tame him. All their profuse passion quickly turns into rowdy rage and spite in a matter of minutes. Nobody wants friendship only, yet they all claim to be compassionate and caring! So how can he trust any of them? Still, some women, especially Holly, discount his naive sense of honesty and cynicism. He would be charmed and outfoxed soon enough, this hopeful group presumes sneakily, no matter what he says and how clever he thinks he is. *He'll be tamed, all mine and immune against other women's temptations forever,* they all imagine sincerely with confidence, especially Holly.

Against her better judgment, at last Holly decides to invite Curt. He accepts when she refutes his excuses about the weirdness of visiting her parents again after so long. Besides, he feels obliged to respond to Holly's wishes periodically, particularly on this momentous occasion of her twentieth birthday.

At least, she'll no longer be a teenager after the party, Curt ponders wittily and chuckles. *It is a nice, round number, too, to remember for a year when she asks to test his degree of devotion!*

The party indeed cheers up Holly, friends and family showing their love with genial words and gifts. Especially, Curt's presence and present delight her immensely. A heart-shaped diamond pendent, not a particularly expensive gift, to her appears as a sign of his tacit deep affection. On the other hand, his flirtations with women throughout the party crush her hopes—for the thousandth time—regarding Curt's change of heart. Of course, she mostly condemns other women for spoiling him, anyway, although that night, in particular, only his exceeding charm could be blamed for the ladies' zeal. As a busy hostess, Holly cannot stick around him all night like usual, either, to shoo those sneaky women away —that large flock of pesky admirers, old and young—all those bees and butterflies.

"Some of the young people here are coming to our ranch for a picnic tomorrow. Why don't you come too?" Suzy Hollinger, a young, attractive guest, proposes to Curt.

"I'll check with Holly," Curt replies.

"I suppose... I hope I'll see you soon, anyway... tomorrow hopefully," she says and saunters away as Holly approaches them with tension.

"She just invited me to her picnic tomorrow. Are you going?"

"Yeah, sure... You like to go?"

"Maybe... Where's the ranch?"

"It's in Riverside. We'll leave around ten-thirty. You can come with us if you like."

"We...? Who else is going with you?"

"Only Hammond and our cousin Rudy."

"Hammond is now quite grown up."

"Yeah... My mom feeds him well and he's a great athlete."

"Yeah...? You love him a lot, don't you?"

"Of course. He's my man... and quite mature for his age, too, unlike most men," Holly says tensely, hoping desperately to stir some jealousy in Curt.

"Of course he is! I wish I had a brother."

"But he's more than a brother to me. He understands me and we share a lot of secrets."

"Maybe that's why he doesn't like me?"

"Why do you say that?"

"That's the impression I got tonight. Maybe you've told him bad things about me?" Curt asks jokingly.

"I never say anything bad about you to anybody."

"But your family can see through you."

"Well, I can't hide my feelings."

"Can you guys pick me up on your way tomorrow then?"

Around one p.m., they arrive at the ranch. Curt, Hammond, and Rudy scuffle noisily to get out of the car and race one another to the washroom. The beer they have consumed is about to burst their bladders, while Holly had been driving soberly and scorning their clowning and noise.

A large group of guests mingle around the big campground designated for barbeque and the games organized for later in the afternoon. The villa stands farther out in the background where another group enjoys the swimming pool in front of it. Many stagger back and forth between the villa and the picnic area, but most people focus on the food and drinks laid out delectably on four long tables. The heavy smoke from three gigantic barbeques gushes toward the villa in massive waves.

Curt reappears from inside the villa at last and approaches Holly, who is standing near the pool and watching the main crowd in the picnic area. They exchange blank grins and start strolling together toward the crowd.

"Why, do you think, the picnic area is set out so far away from the villa?" Curt asks Holly just to make conversation.

She only shrugs without troubling herself with a guess or a few words.

"Don't you even wanna guess?" Curt asks irately.

Holly only shakes her head.

"Maybe because all that smoke would've covered the whole house even if all the doors and windows were shut tight, not to mention blinding the guests around the pool," he murmurs to Holly casually, while his gaze chases Suzy whom he has just spotted in the crowd. Holly only nods.

Rather intimidated by each other's growing defensive attitude, they hardly find topics to discuss. Curt attributes the shallowness of their communication and affair to their age and educational differences. An added pain for Curt has been Holly's tenuous shyness, which he believes is a clear symptom of her suppressed volcanic tension and anger within her. Conversely, her occasional blasts of frustration and aggression might be the effects of her deep shyness and low self-esteem. Either way, the outcome is a lousy communication between them. He should make small talks to instigate some chitchat without hitting a nerve. Then again, this situation has posed a big obstacle, in Curt's opinion, to build any kind of effective relationship. Often their dialogue sounds pure silly if someone listens to them.

Holly stays close to Curt all afternoon to minimize his flirtations with other girls. At last, she is relieved of her strenuous mission by Hammond around four p.m.

"Rudy and I are going for a walk around the river," he tells Curt. "You wanna go?"

"Okay," Curt replies, hoping to sneak back after a short walk and get lost in the crowd away from Holly's eyes. All afternoon, he has been dying to find Suzy in private. They have flirted from a distance after she had warmly greeted him upon arrival. But Holly's persistent protection has ruined his mood. So, a decoy to get away from Holly sounds like a great opportunity. He also suspects that Hammond's invitation has been prompted by Holly herself, merely in hopes of getting him out of this place to cut his chance of flirting with Suzy—a new threatening competition. Anyhow, Curt decides to oblige Hammond, while figuring out how to deal with Suzy later. Things always get tricky and tough when Holly is around. *She is quite a cunning shrew in her own right,* Curt ponders as he kisses her cheek before walking away.

"Let's grab a couple of six-packs to drink later," Rudy says as he hurries toward the bar.

"How can you guys drink so much beer?" Curt exclaims.

The trio departs westbound toward the river, just beyond a narrow line of trees visible from the picnic area. Close to the woods, the roar of the river reverberates and soon they must shout to hear one another around the rapids. The atmosphere is soothing, particularly when Curt stares into the hypnotic river rush to enjoy the amusing wooziness, like riding a speedy roller coaster. These occasional opportunities to get absorbed into the refreshing moods of Nature have always stirred his erratic sense of divinity. He would have certainly fallen into a deep trance if not for the boys' non-stop silliness around him and his mind still so engaged with the desire of seducing Suzy in the ranch. She is probably wondering about him, too, and why he has not found her in a quiet corner to snatch a kiss at least, Curt muses with melancholy.

They hike uphill on the riverbank counter to the currents. Soon, they reach a small inlet with a shallow flow, shaded by trees and bushes. Its serenity contrasts the rough rolling waters only ten meters away. The ambience and clear, cold water entice Hammond and Rudy promptly to undress fully and jump in with noise. Their daylong beer consumption manifests in their juvenile zest and energy. Curt grabs a beer from the pack immersed in a safe corner of the inlet and settles on a rock. He has done his best to humour those clowns and play along with their foolish games, but cannot do it anymore. He likes to be on friendly terms at least with Hammond, to prove he is not a selfish jerk set to hurt Holly —not intentionally, anyway. Oh, gosh, how can he make people believe him? For half an hour, he ponders his indefinable affairs and purposeless life, while watching the cousins' silliness and wrestling in the water, swimming, drinking beers, and throwing the cans filled with water at him. He simply ignores them, while feeling sick and ready to smash their heads. He begins to scheme a plan, an excuse, to sneak away and go back to the ranch to kiss Suzy behind Holly's back. He envies them in a way, for their simplicity and careless life. Then, he thinks he does not desire to be like them, despite his own purposeless and painful existence.

"Come on in, you sissy," Rudy yells with a mocking snigger.

Curt only flings his hand to them and murmurs with a smirk, *No, thanks, idiot.*

"Aren't you hot? Just take off your clothes and jump in," Rudy insists while Hammond grins and beckons Curt with repeat hand motions as well.

"No, I'm fine here," Curt yells back, shaking his head and murmuring to himself, *You clowns play with each other; morons.*

"I just can't imagine what Holly likes about this sissy?" Rudy shouts.

"Don't mind him, Curt. He's drunk," Hammond yells, while slapping Rudy's head.

"You know what she likes about me, you asshole? You want me to show you?" Curt shrieks, hoping to start a scene to find an excuse to abandon these kids.

"You're drunk too, man," Hammond shouts and splashes some water toward Curt.

"She loves me because I'm more of a man than ten of you put together."

"Yeah? You think so, idiot?" Rudy yells back.

"Yeah, I'm sure, asshole," Curt barks, while savouring the brewing excuse this deliberate skirmish gives him to go away.

"No, I think she's lost her mind. Why don't you leave her alone?" Rudy shouts.

"Stop it, you two," Hammond yells and punches the water.

"Why are you defending him? He's screwing your sister real bad and you just sit there and tell me to shut up. Why don't you go throw him in the river?"

"Rudy, this ain't your business," Hammond screams, staring at Curt intently, trying to control his anger.

For a moment, Curt feels the hidden rage behind Hammond's appeasing voice, but decides to keep his calm and prevent the situation from getting out of hand. *You never know what that lout is capable of!*

"I'd better go back," Curt shouts and starts to leave, happy that his plan has worked perfectly.

"No. Wait," Hammond says as he leaps out of the lagoon and grabs a couple of beers. "We came here together and must return together. Rudy's drunk, and we still have things to do."

"What things? It's gonna get dark soon; we better move on," Curt says, trying to at least keep Hammond somewhat on his side, while confirming his earlier hunch about Hammond's likely mission to keep him away from the ranch.

"Why don't we walk up the trail and see how the river turns behind the mountains before going back... Deal?"

"Okay. But let's get moving then," Curt says, again trying to find a way to Hammond's heart.

Hammond beckons Rudy out of the water. They put on their pants and sneakers and follow Curt who is already lurching up the trail. They leave their shirts and beers to collect on the way back after their brief expedition. In ten minutes, the riverbank reaches the foot of a hill where the river turns sharply behind a huge protruding rock. They stand silent and gauge their options. The smooth boulders sneak out of the torrents like a path and they look inviting, but crossing the rough river to the opposite bank seems dangerous, even to their drunken heads. Hammond steps on the first rock and skids into the river. He pulls his wet leg out of the water, shakes it a few times, and stands on the bank with a smile.

"They're slippery, especially with our sneakers," he says.

"Let's go back," Curt says.

"Or we could climb this hill and see how the river turns," Rudy suggests.

"Nah, I don't have proper shoes for climbing a hill now," Curt replies.

"Come on, man. Let's go up a little. This is easy, you sissy," Rudy says.

"You don't need climbing shoes for this, Curt. Let's go," Hammond says with a teasing tone and a smirk.

The idea of two college freshmen contradicting him non-stop and now forcing him to hike the damn hill annoys Curt. Why are they so eager to see how the river turns, like National Geographic explorers or something? How dare they boss him around? He is nine years older, has a master's degree, and a job that these kids can only dream about. Even worse, how dare this ass, Hammond, insult his dear sister's beloved, the one she cherishes helplessly? What is this moron thinking? However, for the same reasons, he should prove himself even more. If they can climb this hill with their sneakers, so can he, Curt decides despite his surging urge to go find Suzy without Holly spotting him.

By the time he calms his ego and stops to catch his breath, the rascal cousins have gained fifty meters over him. He decides to stick to them. *Not because I am afraid of walking alone in the woods for an hour, but rather because I am responsible for these juveniles, especially since they are drunk. You are right…!* his conscience nags. He follows the 'stupid cousins' up the hill with hesitation and angst. They climb up to the left in order to see the turn of the river and discover its course behind the hills. The cousins are just racing each other, while Curt trails behind them with a longer distance to catch up every minute. They stop now and then and mock Curt's struggle. Curt notices the morons' mumbling and laughing while flinging their arms to him. He considers returning now that these drunk kids are out of control and he does not even have enough breath to yell at them to wait. He motions them to descend but they beckon him to ascend. Somehow, he finds it improper or unsafe to return by himself. He could sit right there and wait for their return, but that would prove their superiority over him for sure. Not a charming option! So, he curses the cousins and pushes upward.

The river finally reappears behind the hill, rushing even more ferociously at a sharp angle between two narrowing lines of mountains. It is a breathtaking view and even Curt thinks their exploration had been a worthwhile effort. But the crazy cousins are still climbing and he simply following them. Hiking another ten minutes, the hill starts to turn into a full-fledged steep rocky mountain. The softer grounds of the initial passage have long vanished as they press on a heavy layer of fine gravel covering the streaks of greyish rocks. The river recedes below them as they climb another twenty minutes. It looks narrower and longer while the mountain becomes wider and steeper. Panting and thirsty, Curt finally catches up with the stupid cousins. Maybe they have finally decided to descend; thank goodness.

Curt stands next to them to gulp some air and rest his wrecked legs. When his body recovers partly and his tongue rolls to curse those morons, he notices them perplexed by the huge protruding cliff above their heads this time. It extends to the left and right with no manageable way around it. Besides the small path just below them, only a steep, rocky wall surrounds the cliff as far as they can see.

"Okay, that's it. Let's go back," Curt blurts with disgust.

"See if you can, Curt," Hammond says in a mocking tone.

Curt takes a small step and skids on the loose gravel as though walking on ball bearings. He grabs Hammond's shirt to regain his balance. The sight of the long steep rocky mountain below, covered with a thick layer of loose gravel, alarms him.

"Oh, shit," Curt shrieks.

"Yeah, shit. How come we didn't notice this?" Rudy asks.

"It's all your fault, assholes," Curt blurts.

"Oh, shut up," Rudy snarls.

"Everybody shut up," Hammond shouts. "We must climb this cliff and find a better way to go down."

Curt stares at the cliff, surveys its angles and smooth surface, trembles from the horror, and laughs hysterically. Climbing this huge rock is merely unconceivable. *Are these kids crazy or only joking?* He then looks down to reassess the downhill option closer. Their footsteps are etched on a path where the gravel is partly shifted during their uphill climb. How could their ascent on such dry, slippery gravel have been so manageable? Apparently, the combination of the gravel's friction on the rocks and the tip of their sneakers pressing on the solid surface of the mountain had somehow made the climbing relatively easy. For going down, however, the pressure point and the rather flat position of their feet and body weight promptly release a load of gravel and they slide. A few times Hammond ventures a step while holding to the end of Rudy's belt. But every time he skids and Rudy pulls the belt to prevent his plunge to the bottom of the mountain, which is at least a kilometre deep. Such a bizarre situation, where a rocky mountain is so treacherously covered by slippery gravel, is a new experience even for the cousins who seem at ease with these types of adventures. In particular, Curt is learning firsthand that climbing a mountain is easier than descending it without proper gears. It is a good lesson to remember for the future, but too late for their situation today.

Climbing the massive hanging cliff above them and finding a way down from another route, despite its apparent impracticality, seems to be their only option. Hammond and Rudy discuss the ways of mounting the cliff while Curt sits down cautiously in despair. Rudy makes a foothold for Hammond with his joined hands to boost him up the rock. After a few trials, Hammond at last sticks his sweaty chest to the rock and scrambles smoothly toward a tiny crack four meters away. Slowly he crawls until his fingers reach the crack and hold on to the rock tight. Then, he presses his feet and hands over the rock to pull his body up a few inches at a time. Under Curt's astonished eyes, Hammond thrusts up with diligence until he is halfway on the cliff with a solid grip on a rugged corner. He is now ready to help Rudy or Curt with the strap made of his and Rudy's belts, but it is still short. He cannot bend any lower either without losing his grip. Rudy offers a boost to Curt to climb up and crawl on the rock toward the strap. Once he reaches Hammond, his belt can be attached to the strap, to make it long enough for Rudy to get a start on the big rock. But Curt refuses after gauging the distance he must crawl even if he succeeds to stick to the rock in the first place. The risk of losing his control and plunging all the way down to the river is simply horrendous.

"Come on man, you can do it… It's easy, you sissy," Rudy insists.

"Just leave me alone, asshole."

"You give me a boost then," Rudy asks.

"No, I can't," Curt replies passively, struggling nervously with the panic rising inside him.

"Why not?"

"Because I may slip and go down."

"Don't worry, I'll be careful."

"No, I can't do it."

"Come on man, don't be a baby," Rudy yells rudely.

"But then how am I going to get out of here?" Curt asks with desperation.

"Give me your belt and I'll attach it to the strap up there."

"It still won't be long enough."

"What other option do we have, man? We'll try to figure out something for you up there, I promise. Yeah, I know… I'll join the three belts to my pants and throw it down to you."

Rudy's offer sounds like the only viable option. He gives his belt to Rudy and puts his hands together to give him a boost. Like Hammond, Rudy sticks his naked chest to the rock after a few tries and begins inching forward toward the crack in the rock and the strap. *These crazy cousins crawl like lizards,* Curt ponders as Rudy reaches the strap and clambers toward Hammond. Curt can hear them laughing, perhaps mocking him again. Shortly after, they shout from the middle of the rock and release the long strap for Curt to grab. With three belts and Rudy's pants tied together, Curt can barely reach it. Even so, he would still have difficulty pulling himself up. The lizard cousins could possibly pull him up if the strap were longer to tie around his chest or something. But surely, he cannot haul himself up or even be sure about holding on to the strap tightly enough when they pull him. What if he loses his grip of the strap and goes all the way down to the river? Besides, Rudy's pants might rip or the belts could break, which means the end of him. *Maybe I am a sissy after all.* The cousins giggle even harder while teasing his indecision and fear, and he curses them in return.

"Listen, Curt, we'd better go all the way to the top of the cliff then, to find a long stick or something," Hammond suggests with a teasing tone. Curt only curses them repeatedly. They sound lax and clownish when he is losing his mind by the thought of being stranded.

"Don't leave me here, you assholes."

"We must go find something to pull you up, Curt. Just sit tight."

"Guys… You bastards…"

"Take care, Curt," Hammond chuckles and Rudy blasts into laughter. "Don't worry, man. We'll come back for you. For sure! Just wait there."

"Yeah… Just sit tight," Rudy shouts and they giggle again.

"Go find a helicopter or the rangers to rescue me, you sons of the bitches. Hurry up, it'll be dark soon. Hurry up, please."

Curt hears the lizard cousins move away and soon a horrific silence besieges the valley except for the faint hiss of the river gushing at the bottom of the mountain. It is not visible anymore for the darkness filling the valley rapidly. The lines of shadows on the opposite mountains climb higher and turn greyer, hinting the speedy end of the day. He screams unconsciously for help, hoping his voice would echo and reach somebody, Holly maybe, who is probably worried sick about him at that very instant. If only she knew what jam he is in! But his voice vanishes quickly without any echo, which feels creepy when all those mountains are surrounding him. Still he keeps shouting louder to break the horrifying silence and the shattering sense of loneliness in such an awful position. Not even the tall mountains care to echo back to give him even a tiny hope! Then he stops howling in hopes of hearing the crazy cousins returning for him. He listens to the quiet vacuum, which immediately crushes his chest, as if pulling his pounding heart out of his mouth. Ten more minutes pass without any sound or sign from the cousins.

The space on the tiny ledge below the big cliff is too tight. Switching between the sitting and standing positions is also tricky due to the cliff's big, curvy protrusion and inadequate surface to manoeuvre his feet or hands around it. He can move his feet only a few inches cautiously, because a small mistake might result in sliding to his death. He yells, 'Hammond... Rudy,' a few times, hoping beyond all hopes they would come to his rescue with a long stick or rope. But nobody answers. "Where would they find a rope, stupid?" he yells at himself mostly to distract his crushing fear. *My life is over!*

The daylight dies along with his hopes for rescue. A cold breeze blows through the valley and he shivers of a combination of cold and terror. He cringes and clutches the collar of his shirt as he shifts his butt on the ledge a little and then stretches his numbing legs on the loose gravel carefully. He frets about his ability to get up again and stand on his feet in such a tiny space, especially if his legs and butt go numb from sitting on the hard rock too long. A flock of small birds fly by just before his eyes and he wishes he had wings, too, to fly away with them to safety. They are probably returning to their nests to rest for the night, and he is trapped here with no chance of getting back to his elegant apartment anytime soon, if ever.

The birds fly by him a few rounds as if gloating or teasing him before going home. Would he ever lie in his warm, comfy bed again? Would he ever embrace any of those pretty girls who cuddle him all night after they make passionate love? He would give anything to have his normal life back. It is all Hammond's fault that he is in such a mess; Rudy was drunk, anyway. He curses both of them loudly, nonetheless, and hopes they hear him and curse him back, which would surely sound like music to him instead of insulting. He utters the coarsest swears he had seldom used only as a teenager when gotten into fierce arguments with bullies. Now they all sound appropriate for the occasion. Those bastards deserve the darkest damnation, yet the sound of them cursing him in return would be a blessing.

He is surprised how all these filthy profanities feel so good and liberating under the present circumstance. So he goes up one notch every time, until he cannot think of anything dirtier to add. Only now, he truly appreciates the healing power and psychology behind profanities that people use as their ultimate refuge to curb their frustration and despair. The challenge to make up filthier curses keeps his mind busy awhile and he laughs with tension again. Then he keenly resumes swearing and hoping the cousins would hear him and yell back at him.

Yet only the sound of a smooth wind wheezes through the valley. The situation is getting more desperate every minute as Curt screams and bitches unconsciously. He considers letting himself go, maybe sliding on the gravel and mountain rocks bit by bit, and hoping for the best. He firms his right foot to slide a few inches down, but he skids promptly, barely able to restrain the rest of his body. Sliding is a silly proposition, he realizes. If he let himself go, his descent would accelerate. He would certainly lose control, plummet to his death, and disappear in the river. With darkness approaching fast, especially, he is unable to see the path downhill, anyway, even if he believed having a remote chance of surviving a long slide on the gravel.

How it could have been rather easy coming up so far, yet so mysteriously impossible to go down even a meter, he wonders again anxiously. Apparently, the toes' pressure, bent knees, and arched back had created the balance needed to climb, which is an impossible posture to imitate for descending. Maybe he could try descending by replicating the exact motions of climbing: facing the mountain and pressing the gravels with his toes. Then again, he realizes that only ascending produces the proper pressure needed on one foot to release the other one safely in a timely manner. Imitating that exact pressure points for descending would be too cumbersome and dangerous, if possible at all.

With horror now completely crippling his normal wisdom and courage, Curt cringes and curses the crazy cousins again. *They will not come back for me.* Maybe they are still looking for a long stick or rope, or maybe even more formidable obstacles have stopped them on their way up. Perhaps they are trapped in a horrible situation themselves. Before long, darkness surrounds Curt and his mind and body start freezing of despair, while the chilly wind blows rampantly, too. It seems as if the nippy wind had been hiding behind the sun and then hurried to whip him as soon as it had set.

"They won't return... The lizard cousins won't come back to get me," Curt mumbles. Suddenly a crazy thought crushes his nerves: Maybe this whole episode had been a premeditated plot by the cousins to punish him for his bad treatment of Holly all these years. Even if it had not been premeditated, this situation still gives them a grand opportunity to avenge her. She would be free at last, forever. Curt recalls Hammond's and Rudy's rage and rude insults at the river inlet earlier this afternoon. They had seemed quite pissed off with him and could not hide their hatred. That was why they kept asking him to go for swimming in the inlet. They would have definitely pushed him into the rapids if he had joined them in the inlet. Thus, they had to invent a new plan. Yes, yes, it all makes sense now. Hammond is taking revenge for Curt's handling of Holly. He is trying to set Holly free, finally, and also restore his family's honour after all the humiliation that a snob jackass like him has caused them. *I never meant to harm or humiliate anybody, but I have, haven't I? Life's bizarre events and circumstances cause sinful outcomes that we are blamed and punished for! How ironic!*

The added terror about Hammond's revenge makes Curt shiver even harder, while the chilly wind blows faster and howls louder, too. He is doomed and the taunting reality begins to sink in with all its bitterness: he is on his own because they would never return. His tongue and throat are dry and he can no longer even curse or cry for help. He is thirsty and hungry and his body is getting number every minute. What if he loses his senses and collapses down the mountain with the next wind? That, in fact, might be a fine solution to relieve him from his misery. A sudden death feels preferable to all these physical and emotional tortures. He can no longer calm his nerves or squeeze his muscles to stop quivering within four square feet of space. If he could see a little better, he would at least try to stand up for a while. But the fear of losing his balance stops him to move even an inch outside the tiny area his body is occupying.

Oh, God, please help me... I know I have not been a good person, but I promise to become one as soon as I put my foot on flat grounds again. I promise not to ever come close to another mountain again. I promise to go to a church or something and confess to all my sins, especially the nasty things I have done to Holly. Oh, Holly, please help me... please forgive me...please, Your Hollyness...

He feels the depth of horror even in his tiniest bones, past his thumping heart and trembling brain cells, beyond both the literal and imaginable meanings of HORROR. Not enough Rs and Os in the word, going by the way he is trembling this minute! How terribly petrified the young girl in Stephen King's novel must have felt when she got lost in the woods. How did she cope with such horrendous terror for several days when he cannot imagine surviving even another minute? She had imagined talking with Tom Gordon all along to mitigate her loneliness and horror. *For how many days? What was her name? She must've really loved baseball...Did she cry? Most likely she did...* He decides to read the novel again to verify all these crucial facts if he survives this ordeal. Anyway, he is about to cry even if she did not. However, hallucination comes to his rescue.

In the daunting darkness, white-winged angels hover around him and play soothing music with their little harps and horns. Suddenly he feels happy and oblivious of any danger. He rises freely, ready to reach out and hug them. A tiny angel floats right above him, and as he turns his head and looks up, two shining red dots appear at a near distance. Startled, he still manages to hold his composure and hang on instead of howling for help. Sniffing and purring, the pair of the shimmering lights moves closer to him on the huge jutting rock. As the parallel shining red dots stop only three meters from him, Curt's exhausted mind perceives the approach of an animal, probably a ferocious one. Shaking from the shocking discovery, he senses the animal losing its control or pouncing toward him. His jerky retreat throws him out of balance and he slides ten meters before hitting a sharp object and halting. He witnesses the animal fly by him to the bottom of the mountain before he faints.

One hour later, he comes to from the sound of a helicopter hovering near the mountain. The left side of his head aches, and as he touches it, he feels a burning bump and a gooey substance. He shivers and screams frantically with angst as he recalls his doomed situation, the animal, and his fall. He wonders where he might be and what had stopped him from plummeting all the way to the bottom of the valley. The fact that he is still alive gives him a tentative sense of security and satisfaction, though, despite the ambiguity of his location. The wind blows gentler as if the cold and hot airs have finally mixed and now merely danced together smoothly like placid lovers. He wishes the silky wind could glide him gently across the valley and guide him safely into Holly's arms. Poor Holly; she is surely devastated by his disappearance. No longer does he desire to kiss Suzy. He hears the helicopter overhead again and looks up. It approaches slowly and radiates the light from its projectors on the mountain. He shouts hoarsely with his dry throat, which is a futile effort against the roar of the helicopter. His eyes trail the reflection from the projectors on the mountain desperately, hoping it would come his way.

The projectors' beams dance in all directions except his. It concentrates on the tiny spot he had been trapped on for five hours before sliding to his new location. If he were still up there, the crew would have detected him. Obviously, they are looking for him. Alas, the light cannot reach him on the new ledge where he lies flat in shock, hesitant to move even a finger lest he falls again perhaps a longer distance this time. He is not even sure he can move, as if paralyzed after the fall. He does not know where he is, but can distinguish the silhouette of limbs and leaves of a tree obstructing much of his view of the helicopter. At least the fact that they are looking for him is encouraging.

The helicopter hovers for another minute before moving away slowly, now focusing on the nearby mountains. In ten minutes, it disappears and the haunting silence returns. Recalling the view of the mountain slope just below him while he had lingered next to the big cliff, Curt realizes at last that he must have slid to the small ridge near a tree. He had considered slithering to this point, but the distance had appeared too long and risky. Besides, he had wondered about the purpose of reaching the new ledge, even if he had succeeded to do so. Is he better off now that he has reached it by sheer accident? *Well, at least it seems to offer a larger area for him to rest.* Exactly for the same reason, though, he had remained hidden from the lights of the copter. If he had known where he was sooner, he might have found the guts to stand up and fling his arms, and possibly fallen within the range of the helicopter's beams. Instead, lying flat on the mountain motionless cowardly, fearful of falling to his complete demise this time, had eliminated his chance of rescue. Oh, what a bizarre bad luck, he groans. *What a sissy I am, after all. Or maybe I am actually paralyzed?*

The darkness is too daunting and the thought of the animal causing his fall to this ledge aggravates his agony. Maybe wild animals are around and would come by soon for a late supper. What a delicious dish he would become! What kind of an animal was it? Perhaps a wolf or a wildcat? Nah, they cannot be around here. Perhaps a raccoon or a coyote? Nah, they don't dwell at this altitude. Could they? Maybe it was only a squirrel or a chipmunk, or an owl or vulture perhaps? *Oh, damn Holly, it's all your fault… But I'll forgive you if I survive this ordeal. And I promise to love you forever. Please do something. You don't know how cruelly your silly brother and cousin have abandoned me here, perhaps having fun right now down there on the ranch, claiming they don't know how I got lost. Or maybe they claim I left with another girl or something. They're lying. They're only taking their revenge and you will never find out the truth if I die here tonight.*

Curt rests on the ledge, which now feels like a luxury bed compared to the tiny spot he had occupied next to the large cliff up there. At least this is a safer place to fall asleep, if he could. It seems to be the only option left for him at this time, despite all the conceivable hazards. Nobody would probably look for him in the dark, he cannot see even a few inches ahead of him, his body feels paralyzed, and his brain is starting to freeze, too. *I'll never lie in my cosy bed again,* he sighs and then laughs hysterically about the irony—about the chance to lie again in his bed and lie to girls. No more! He would never lie to anybody in that bed any more, especially Holly, because he is going to die tonight. *Die for all your lies, bastard!*

He closes his eyes, but Holly's image and memories of their long, adventurous relationship amuse him. First, he recalls her timid face this afternoon after he agreed to go for a walk around the river with the crazy cousins. She looked pale and worried for no obvious reason. Maybe she knew about Hammond's plan to avenge her, or maybe at least she suspected that Hammond might somehow harm him. Maybe she had planned or at least agreed with this stiff punishment for him. She seemed nervous and maybe even trying once to tell him not to go. Then she had stopped saying anything and only looked at him with stress and passion as if she would never see him again. Could she have been part of this plot? *Nah.* He dismisses this possibility, because the only person who might have instigated a search must have been Holly. Nobody else in the party knew or remembered him and if the crazy cousins meant to harm him, then the only individual who could have alerted others to dispatch a helicopter must have been Holly. Well, Suzy Hollinger might have been the only other person initiating a search, except that Hammond and Rudy would have most likely convinced her that he had left without saying goodbye. He knows Holly would never betray him despite his relentless disregard of her passion and devotion. Now Holly's ceaseless loyalty, a trait he had normally attributed to her low self-esteem, means a world to Curt. He had always thought that any other girl in Holly's position—any girl with some pride— would have left him long time ago. But not hopeful Holly. She has remained loyal hoping that someday Curt would realize what a gem she was. Now, tonight, alone, abandoned in the absolute darkness of the universe, Curt finally seems to have reached the same conclusion. Alas, his life is about to expire with no hope of seeing Holly again and proving his sudden awakening. He is now dying for a chance to tell her how wrong he had been and how sorry he is, although deep down he has always believed in his innocence and good intention to set Holly free. Yet, none of those thoughts and excuses matters now, anyway. The reminiscing continues as Curt recalls the beginning of his affair with Holly five years earlier.

In 1975, Curt was a graduate student at UCLA. After spending the summer in Washington D.C. with his parents, he was looking for a place to rent near the school. He was the first one to call Lucien Stratton, a studious freshman, who had placed an ad in the student union for a quiet roommate. The spacious suite enticed Curt and he convinced Lucien to choose him despite their age, education, and lifestyle differences. He also kept his promise to respect Lucien's condition for peace and privacy to concentrate on university demands. Seldom did he bring his girlfriends to the apartment, and even then, he strived to minimize their activities in the living room and to contain their lively erotic noises in the bedroom.

After four months, however, the situation reversed as Lucien realized university life need not be too restrictive and serious. The change was quite drastic for a rather uptight geek, thanks to his new friends' influence. They came by frequently and urged him to throw parties. With his good looks and new Corvette, Lucien became popular and reckless quickly. Curt did not mind the new atmosphere and indeed encouraged Lucien's new lifestyle. The situation in fact rekindled his own memories of a similar reckless lifestyle and partying just a few years earlier before he had started university. To study these days, he often went to library if Lucien had a party going on or something, but stayed around sometimes to tease Lucien's juvenile friends, too, especially pretty girls.

Curt met Holly in Lucien's crowded birthday party during the Christmas break. Luther, Lucien's younger brother, a popular football player in high school, had invited her. She was fifteen years old and even more naive and reserved than her age. Tall and slender, however, she was gorgeous enough to entice Curt's imagination quickly. He teased Luther often in the party and later about the intensity of sex with a girl like her. Luther only laughed and nodded agreeably. Nonetheless, Curt flirted with Holly whenever he got a chance, which was never enough in his dirty mind. Holly's relationship with Luther appeared odd to him, anyway, as Luther chased other girls under her nose. She came by occasionally to visit Luther, who was now practically living with Lucien. Since the apartment was large, and while nobody intruded Curt's privacy, neither Lucien nor Curt minded Luther's increasing visits and long stays, sometimes one or two weeks at a time. Actually, it helped Curt's desire to see Holly more.

Four months later, at last Curt grilled Luther, "What's the deal between you and Holly?"

"Nothing, we're friends," Luther replied.

"Isn't she your girlfriend?"

"Not really, you know."

"No… I do not understand. Are you together or not?"

"Sometimes… But she ain't my type," Luther said, his eyes betraying his attempt to appear cool about it.

"Why isn't she your type?"

"She's too emotional, uptight, and still a virgin. I don't wanna mess up her mind. Or become her slave if we get too close."

"But she's gorgeous. How you've resisted her all this time?"

"I wanna enjoy my life; not arguing with her or explaining myself to anybody."

"So you don't mind if she dates somebody else?"

"Nah…"

"Are you sure?"

"Yeah I'm sure… Why? Now you're interested too?"

"Maybe… Do you mind?"

"No, but it's crazy. You and her…?" Luther said and burst into laughter.

"What's wrong with that?"

"You're old. She's not gonna be interested in a guy your age."

"Just shut up, silly boy."

"But don't tell me I didn't warn you."

"I'll try to remember your advice, professor."

"Go stay in line then. So many guys are ahead of you already trying to tame her."

The next time Holly came by the suite, and Curt happened to be conveniently around and aroused, he showered her with his charm and invited her to dinner. For the showy, young girl, this unexpected attention from an older, handsome guy was precious, to restore some of her lost confidence around Luther for so long. She seemed to have been waiting for a special occasion to parade her suppressed charm to the entire world. The candlelight dinner at the lavish Japanese restaurant in Century Plaza, while Curt showed off his extravagance and mannerism, created the right atmosphere—too romantic for Holly to suspect his trap. They dated for two months without any close encounter of the sexual kind. She was determined to keep both him and her virginity, which soon turned into a major dilemma for both of them. Her psyche could not bear another loss after her historical fights with Luther and other horny boys who still ridiculed her offhanded manner. She also wished to teach those snotty boys, especially Luther, a lesson. But giving in to Curt's demands felt too risky at the same time. In all, her inner conflict, mostly goaded by her family's catholic values, spoiled their relationship and moods more every week.

While Holly sought a refuge and a means of becoming more popular in social circles, Curt set out to make the most of her frustration. The challenge of conquering a reserved, sentimental creature was too exciting to pass over. He was quite determined to explore and exploit her needs and state of mind for an ultimate, divine purpose; especially that he had never had the privilege of befriending a virgin despite his sexually enriching adolescence. That was just too humiliating for a person of his stance. All the girls in his life so far had been initially conquered by other boys. They had all been sluts or in love with somebody else already, neither case offering a flattering position for an egocentric person like Curt. Overall, the novelty of Holly's situation only increased his attraction to her sexy face and physique. He had to experience a virgin for once at least in his life—a challenge getting more and more unreachable nowadays, with hardly any presentable girl close to his age and taste available for such crafty experiment.

So Holly had turned into a holy mission desperately needing a resolution, most likely through a miracle. Yet, as a fundamental aspect of his character noted before already in earlier stories, Curt simply could not leave this matter unresolved, either. Despite her moodiness and resistance to his sexual advances, Curt stayed around hoping to wear her down and eventually give her the real taste of lust. Like the devil, he was driven by bizarre fantasies and feelings beyond his control and against his primary conviction to ignore difficult or underage girls. He believed Holly would come around on her own as long as he respected her desire and never forced himself upon her. Luther's words about 'not wishing to mess her up' always rang in Curt's ears, especially since she was a minor. However, the devil inside him just would not quit. It wanted her at whatever price. On some occasions, when drunk, he considered even the option of marrying her if that must be the last resort for conquering her. She was simply too sexy to set free and he was just *unable to leave this challenge unresolved.*

Then the nightmare that both Holly and the conscientious side of Curt had adamantly dreaded for nearly one year occurred one

evening when they got drunk. Their casual foreplay led to unruly
erotic adventures and soon Holly was not a virgin. Suddenly her
drunkenness evaporated, as though she had been submerged into
an icy pool and revived by a pot of hot black coffee, all in two
seconds. She began screaming in bewilderment and desperation
for the taboo brought upon her.

"I must call my mom to come and get me; I must tell her right
away," she shrieked, rushing toward the phone. Curt charged
after her and grabbed the receiver off her trembling hands with
difficulty. Crying hysterically, she scuffled with Curt fiercely like
a cornered cougar.

"Come on, honey, it's nothing. You'll be all right. It's not the
end of the world, believe me," he pleaded calmly and desperately
after regaining his composure somewhat.

Her sudden insanity and rage had startled and confused him,
but he was also getting frustrated for his inability to restrain her,
as if fighting a two-ton bull. Considering his drunkenness and
anger, his scuffle to control the situation looked futile and funny
at the same time. Breathless from all the wrestling, he also felt
remorse for luring her and worried about the consequence of the
racket she had started, especially if his neighbours ran over to
check out the cause of the commotion. If her family found out, he
could be in big trouble.

"No, no, it's not all right… You stupid… Take me home,"
Holly screamed, dressed quickly in anger, and left the apartment.

Curt was still in shock from such an unexpected turn of
events, especially her sudden sobriety, agility, and strength. He
was starting to believe that perhaps it was really a catastrophe and
he deserved a severe punishment for it. Or maybe she had been a
lunatic all along and he had not realized it until now. Nonetheless,
there was no time to speculate. He must find a way to calm her
before the neighbours and the police got involved. He dressed up
quickly, too, and followed her to the parking lot. He caught up
with her near his car and helped her to get in. He gave her a few
napkins to wipe off her tears, held her hands and caressed her

hair, but she only cringed, cursed him and cried louder. Then she yelled for more tissues to dry her tears. Curt continued kissing her awkwardly and passing on more tissues to her, although she kept punching and shoving him away.

"Let's go. Let's go," she screamed.

"Where to…? Let's wait awhile and talk before we go."

"No. Take me home now. Actually, go to a hospital. Go…"

"Why? Why are you so childish, Holly? Please believe me, it's nothing. It is not the end of the world, my darling."

"No. I don't believe you. Go to the hospital, hurry up."

Her hysteria felt too bizarre despite Curt's historical exposures to wild women. Especially, he had often witnessed his own bitchy mother's outrageous outbursts around people, especially his dad. Yet none of those experiences compared with the scene Holly had created tonight. Drawing on his psychology courses at UCLA, he finally rationalized that many years of suppression and strict conditioning environment of her family, combined with the effect of alcohol tonight, had erupted such vile perception of a taboo for her and Curt's responsibility for it. He should not have given alcohol to a minor, for one thing. For this mistake alone, he could be in a big mess. Justifying the cause of her explosion helped him a little to behave even more sympathetically toward her. He should calm her down at all cost to prevent any major embarrassment, not to mention some kind of a legal punishment, too. Deep down, however, he wished to slap her a few times back to her senses. Alas, he had to control his urge and nerves to quiet her diplomatically. *Too bad!*

He started the car to leave before alarming the neighbours, and to show his intention to oblige her. Driving slowly, he could not avoid the nearby hospital. Damn luck! Having a hospital right in your path and neighbourhood was bizarre. It felt as though the devil had cunningly anticipated this fateful night when Curt had searched for and rented this particular apartment many months ago. The sign, lights, and the commotion reignited Holly's fury to a new high.

"There, there. Just go to the emergency entrance," she yelled while grabbing and stirring the steering wheel toward the curb.

Curt held the wheel tight, stopped the car at a short distance from the hospital, and turned off the engine. He approached her cautiously and hugged her tenderly, all along repeating soothing words and promises. She tried a few times to escape and rush toward the hospital, but Curt succeeded to hold her back and close the car's door.

"Come on, honey. They cannot do anything for you. Why do you want to embarrass both of us in front of people?" Curt begged. "You know how much I care for you. You know that?"

"You shouldn't have done that."

"I know. I'm sorry. But now we can't help it anymore."

"But I must see a doctor. Maybe he can fix it."

"You'll be okay, I promise."

"I must tell my mom now."

"Not a good idea either."

"Why? Why?"

"If you tell her, she won't let you see me anymore. Is that what you want? Now we can be together even more and start a fun relationship. I'll take care of you, I promise."

"You're not gonna leave me?"

"No. Why would I leave you? We're now closer than ever."

"You promise?"

"I promise. Here, wipe your tears," he said, passing a few more tissues to her. "Let's go eat hamburgers and relax. Okay?"

"We should marry then…"

"Don't worry about this stuff tonight, okay?"

She did not answer, but her relative calm gave Curt enough courage to start the car and drive toward the Burger King a few blocks away. He watched her sullen face in total silence while eating her sandwich timidly. Avoiding Curt's eyes, she gazed at her trembling hands and nibbled on her sandwich with anger and desperation.

"You feel better?"

She shook her head subtly, giving Curt only fifty-one percent assurance that her gesture was a positive inclination. He gasped a sigh of relief now that the possibility of an embarrassing chaos was almost over.

"I'll take you home to rest, but don't talk to anybody tonight."

"I must tell my mom. She can take me to a doctor to fix it."

"If you tell her, she won't let us meet again. How many times should I repeat this?"

She stayed quiet for two minutes without even peeping at Curt. Her rage seemed to be resurfacing fast, however, and she seemed determined to tell her mom. Curt spent another twenty minutes begging and reasoning with her until she looked rather calm eventually.

"Just don't worry about your mom. It's none of her business," Curt cried. "You're almost a sixteen-year-old lady. You agree?"

Deafening silence…

"Go home and rest…, my lady… I'll call you tomorrow night and we'll go to a fancy restaurant like a loving couple. Do you like that?"

More silence…

Back in his apartment, Curt felt mildly relieved that Holly had somewhat calmed down by the time they had arrived at her house. At least tonight, she would not make a scene at home. He had waited in the street and noticed that only Holly's bedroom light had come on and turned off shortly after, which probably indicated that the rest of the family had been sleep—thank God! He had decided to go home, pack a few personal items quickly, and go hide in a friend's place for a while, in case of suspicious activity in her house. Fortunately, it seemed he was safe in his apartment at least tonight.

Yet the image of Holly's outburst revolted him. He sensed his attraction toward her diminishing rapidly. He had never imagined any girl would be so naive or worry so much about such a simple matter. In fact, his experience with girls so far had indicated that this matter was the least of their worries, merely for the sake of becoming a slut as soon as possible. Holly was just an amazing contrast to all the evidences out there about girls' hot sexuality. He laughs hysterically when he recalls Holly's comment about asking her mom to take her to a doctor to fix her vagina and his explanation that such an action would surely make her mom stop her from seeing him again. *Why…? Why would she do that?* she had asked. *Because she doesn't want me to break it again!* he had replied, which had apparently sounded like a legitimate reason to Holly, too, at last! Only at this point, she had finally surrendered after weighing the risk of not being allowed to see Curt, on top of losing her chance, again, to become a full-fledged slut, which was starting to feel like a very tempting option.

The scars of that one long episode felt too deep. He had never begged for anything ever in his life, and then tonight he had to beg a juvenile for two hours for something that was as much her fault as his. All that begging, especially for such a silly matter, had singed his self-image and totally ruined his feelings for her. His promises to stay with her, take care of her, and go out to a restaurant the following evening, disturbed him already. A weird sense of bitterness was creeping up within him rapidly, especially about the possibility of having inadvertently implied to marry her as well. *Had he really given her that impression? Was he now on the hook?* He could not comprehend the revulsion invading every cell in his body; his change of heart was incredibly fast and deep and out of his control, but, most of all, bizarre.

They went out the next evening as Curt had promised. The first thing he asked her was whether she had talked to anybody about the mishap and her response assured him it was safe to sleep in his own apartment for at least another night or two. He took her out every night for two weeks and treated her like a princess to make sure he was safe to go home and sleep another night. After two weeks, he was quite exhausted, thus gradually reduced their number of dates until such time he barely made any efforts to see her. He invented all kinds of excuses, in particular about being busy at school and work. Yet, they continued to see each other for four years torturously. While Holly's love for Curt turned into an obsession, Curt felt obliged to continue this affair out of guilt and his hasty promise to her in that frightful night. Despite his many personality flaws, he strived to maintain his integrity; a sense of responsibility to keep his words at all cost. He had tried occasionally to convince Holly that he could never be an ideal man for her, but she dismissed such negative ideas, although she suspected his affairs with other girls. Out of pity and desperation for both of them, Curt had strived occasionally to insult her or even slapped her once in hopes of revolting her mind about him. Yet, she had remained faithfully in love with Curt, which in turn obliged him to abide by his initial promise to stick around her. Of course, he was also puzzled by his erratic sexual urge toward her, as it often felt contrary to his deep revulsion and enduring desire to minimize his show of affection and eagerness. She moved out of her parent's house to be more independent and see Curt regularly without her parents' scrutiny. After one year of tolerating Curt's apathy even more harshly, she returned to her parent's house in despair. Her parents discovered her rebellion against family values and engaging in a sexual relationship with Curt, for which they mostly blamed him. Yet, they kept some form of tactful relationship with both Holly and Curt, hoping that perhaps they would at least marry soon to end this taboo.

The morning light awakens Curt with no control of his muscles, as if glued to the rock by the frosty fog and the thick moisture engulfing the mountain. He raises his head with difficulty to look for his hands, which seem to be missing or numb. One of them is stuck under his body and the other is stretched out on the rock and frozen in the direction he had waved at the helicopter. He recalls his ordeal last night and the copter's useless hovering in his vicinity for a while before disappearing. He had apparently fainted of cold and trauma soon after. At least he is still alive and alert, though his body parts feel paralyzed. He focuses on them one by one, hoping to shake them out of coma, but none reacts. His back is a bit responsive, which feels like a good sign about his spine cord and not being paralyzed from the fall. He keeps flexing his back muscles and senses some tingling and movement of his butt. Gradually the numbness gives way. As he moves the middle of his body, the other parts slowly come to life, too, and eventually he rises like a zombie escaping its grave.

Curt stretches for a minute and then sits on the ledge to survey his surroundings. Above him, a line of dark-greyish rock appears where the gravel had been partly expunged last night during his slide from below the big cliff to the top of this ledge. The horrific sight of the canyon below reveals his immense luck last night—that this tiny rock had halted his fatal plummet. It feels like sitting on a cloud in midair. The scary view below his feet also reminds him of the futility of thinking about descending the mountain. What should he do then?

His voice turns hoarser as the sun rises higher above him and its rays bombard his encumbered body. In addition to the thirst, all that screaming and cursing yesterday have burnt his vocal cords. Not even a whisper escapes his mouth, never mind yelling for help. He pushes himself to sing a verse of a song with his rasping voice to test his sense of humour under the circumstance and boost his spirits. At least he has survived an entire torturous night alone. That is a big achievement deserving celebration. He thinks any kind of sound might help his morale and break this monotonous silence. But the sound of his scratchy voice makes him burst into anxiety laughter. He senses his sanity fading, the unrelenting sun not helping, either. He recalls his pitiful promises last night, to love Holly and tell her so if he were ever rescued. Then the idea of the crazy cousins abandoning him on purpose to avenge Holly startles him all over again. If that were the case, nobody would come for him. But how about the helicopter last night? Maybe that was only a sheer coincidence and they were looking for somebody or something else—maybe the animal that had attacked him and caused his fall. If they were looking for him, why are not they coming back today?

Around eleven o'clock, still no sign of a search party or a helicopter, the heat intensifying every minute, again he begins hallucinating. He sees himself lurching in the Arabian Desert with no water or food, completely hopeless. His present situation is actually bleaker, since in a desert at least he could move in one direction in hopes of finding water. A mirage would provide some tentative hope and a target to stagger toward until he dies of thirst and fatigue. But now, he cannot even take any initiative, to move in one direction for water, shade, and survival. He is stuck in one spot; condemned to sit under the scorching sun and be barbequed for the vultures. He imagines them flying overhead already, getting ready for a fiesta soon as he loses consciousness. He imagines a couple of them landing near him, approaching him with caution, and beginning to peck at his still body. Then they peck harder to dig out his guts. He shoos them away with anger. The sight of the tiny river way down below and the sound of its dampened roar resemble the rush of a small burbling creek. He attempts to reach out for it, just for a few drops of water. He keeps failing and cursing and soon the intensity of this bracing imagination only heightens his thirst and frustration. He wishes a strong mirage could hypnotize him to forget where he is. It would help him fall off this horrible mountain and end his tortures.

At two o'clock, still no sign of the crazy cousins, the heat and thirst getting unbearable, he is now certain they had deliberately lured him to this spot and then abandoned him to die in a most torturous and humiliating manner. They will come back, those two crazy cousins, maybe in a month or two, to laugh at his skeleton spread on this ledge with his jaw wide open and two arms stretched on his sides. What a hilarious scene that would be for them! They would probably take a few snapshots to laugh at him in private now and then. Then they would probably kick his skeleton and scatter the rotting bones all over the mountain. What a genius plan! They would never tell anybody about his skeleton, either, and his parents would not even get a chance to bury him and visit his grave. If only he survives this ordeal somehow, he knows how severely to punish those two devils—and maybe Holly, too, if she had been involved in this scheme as well. First, however, he must find a way out of this conundrum, because he is on his own with zero plan of action.

Looking up to the big rock to climb it like those two lizard cousins, he wonders how he can do it today alone if he could not do it yesterday with Rudy's help and the long strap? He would not be able to return to this ledge, either, since only sheer luck last night had precluded his further sliding beyond the ridge. It may not happen again even if he finds the guts to slither on the side of the mountain. The idea of getting stuck in such a small spot up there again after failing to conquer the cliff sounds too risky.

Looking down the mountain repeatedly to find a sensible path to descend also generates no solution. He has uselessly assessed this option a hundred times now, but still cannot help thinking that perhaps there is a way ready for exploration. Nobody would believe him that descending a mountain has been impossible when they had climbed it so intuitively. "How is that possible?" they would ask with a smirk. The irony is that he would not dare to bring them up here to prove his claim. So they would call him a liar and a chicken for the rest of his life. The lizard cousins would probably deny his story, too, and perhaps even add some lies of their own about how he had chickened out descending the trail despite their offer to help him and protect him. Those big liars; sons of the bitches. Hallucination appears to be the only remedy keeping him busy and alive, he realizes with his last grains of sanity. Then he considers occupying himself somehow to stop those maddening imaginations about death and revenge driving him nuts even before the sun fries him. But how?

Singing a song or screaming seems like a good distraction, but his voice is completely shut and nothing comes out. He grabs a fistful of gravel and curses them in his mind madly with fiery eyes and trembling lips: *It's all your fault that I can't go down.*

Where did you bastards come from? How did you cover the whole surface of the mountain so shrewdly to trap anybody who dares to climb it? What is the purpose of protecting this rocky mountain beneath your beady bodies, like hiding a wolf in a sheepskin? Curt examines the gravels closer and marvels at the colourful variety in his palm. He then begins picking one gravel from his palm at a time and tossing it down the valley. Counting the gravels after pitching each into the valley feels like a good exercise both physically and mentally. That is probably what Tom Gordon would have done if he stood in his sneakers up here. *Oh, God, what a humiliating, torturous punishment!*

When the boys did not return yesterday at dusk, Holly got too anxious and asked a couple of friends to go with her to look for them. By the time they got to the river, it was dark. They yelled for the boys, although their voices were mostly muffled by the roaring gush of the river. They finally gave up after one hour and returned. Around ten p.m., when it was completely dark outside and Holly sat in a corner and wept, the host, Mr. Hollinger, called the sheriff's office and eventually a search and rescue helicopter was dispatched to the area near midnight. Another group had also searched around the river for a couple of hours already, despite the darkness. They had returned empty-handed and left soon, acknowledging that nothing more could be done until morning. The sheriff and the search party suspected the boys had probably gotten drunk and were fooling around in a bar or with some friends they might have met in the party. Holly disbelieved this theory, but had no way of proving her premonition about the boys being in danger rather than having a good time somewhere without telling her. *Although those three boys had been trying to bond all day and maybe now had gone to party behind her back,* Holly suddenly entertains with angst but tiny hope.

In the morning, another search party sifted the riverbanks for clues. This time they found a couple of shirts on a tree branch near the river, several empty beer cans, half-full bags of potato chips, and a six-pack submerged in shallow waters, all around a tiny river inlet. Many signs indicated that the boys had been swimming in the inlet, perhaps close to the rapids at some point. The conclusion was not pleasant, all evidences indicating that the boys might have been swept away by the torrents when they had swam near the river or crossed it. They might have lost control when trying to help one another if one of them had been in some danger. The search party also probed within a large radius around the inlet extensively and called the boys with a bullhorn before deciding to focus on the riverbanks downhill where they could possibly find their bodies if deposited by the currents. They knew from experience that even if a body were ever found in these situations, it would be usually down the river far away from where they got drowned. Holly had fainted after hearing the news and the Hollingers had called Holly's parents. Along with Rudy's parents, they had arrived and waited in Hollingers' ranch for more news by the search party. The sheriff, his deputies, and a few volunteers had worked tirelessly all afternoon and gave up again when it was dark, with a promise to continue their search the next day.

Curt has tossed and counted six thousand gravels and kept record of it by using a sharp narrow stone to write the score on the dry soil after every hundred throws. At least this futile exercise has diverted his mind from falling into hallucination and helped him partially forget the heat and his thirst. He revolts at the idea of preserving his urine somehow in case he must drink it as the last resort. The thought has occurred to him based on his recollection of some characters in novels doing it in similar situations. Not having a container for hoarding it feels like a blessing, though. He pisses all over the malicious mountain with rage and regret. His stomach is growling too. The leaves of a few small plants seem tempting to help both his thirst and hunger, but they can kill or sicken him. He chops and chews a leaf and it tastes awful, yet he does not care and eats a few more of them with disgust. A leafy tree stands about eight feet away from him in a sharp angle with the mountain, but he cannot reach it without risking a big fall.

As the sun sets and the cool breeze races through the valley again, he braces himself for another long, scary night at the side of the mountain. No helicopter or person has come around all day and his hopes for anybody ever coming for his rescue is almost gone. He is beginning to believe that his only option is to slide down the mountain for a one in a million chance to survive the fall and drink a few gulps of water from that riveting river before the rapids carry him away. Even that few moments of life with cold water in his mouth would be worth the risk of going for the long slide. He should consider this crazy option more seriously tomorrow, but it is definitely not viable now with total darkness only half an hour away.

He had stopped counting gravels long ago when he had reached exactly ten thousand. It is a good record for the day and a round number to remember in case he continues the next day. His ground palette would be useless at dark and very soon erased when he moves around and lies down for a snooze. He imagines Holly's face, now full of fear and tears, perhaps assuming he is dead already. How could he have been such a jerk around her? Instead of loving her and boosting her self-image, he had belittled her before their friends and her family for so long. Remembering some of the lousy incidents that he wishes had never occurred nauseates him. This sudden enlightenment may also be the effect of the heat and eating those leafs, too. He gags and tries to throw up, but only some sticky green liquid hangs out of his mouth and he spits repeatedly to dislodge it. He lies on his back, stares at the stars nonchalantly, and thinks about Holly again.

To dramatize his indifference about her love, he had tried on several occasions to convince her to have sex with his previous roommate, Lucien, possibly in his presence. He was profoundly confused about his unruly feelings and attitude. The way he had known himself, he had a hard time figuring out the cruelty he felt toward her, his actions not a true characteristic of him at all. Who was that devil inside him? He could not believe being a wicked person or capable of behaving like one. Everybody in his family always thought of him as a real gentleman. Oh, how awfully wrong everybody had been about him! Yet, he had strived often to study and justify his malice toward her. Sometimes, he thought his mind was messed up by that one incident in that fateful night when Holly had insisted on going to a hospital and telling on him to her parents. All that immensely humiliating begging, for two hours, for calming her, had definitely ruined his image of her, not to mention her erratic outbursts, as well as her overall naivety even for a young girl her age. Other times, he felt his heinous actions were noble indeed for the ultimate purpose of getting Holly fed up with him. He truly believed she should be forced to leave him and find a more stable boyfriend and life, especially since he was not planning to marry her, even if he had possibly implied it to Holly at a moment of urgency. Then, of course, he had surely promised her to never leave her, anyway.

Aside from the special incident when she had rebelled so abruptly and threatened to tell on him to her parents, she had also revolted with menace on other occasions. All those explosive rebellions and her recurring hysteria had somehow deepened his aversion, if not hatred, toward her. At the same time, his naive sense of obligation to her—maybe even saving her from her own malice—has been puzzling. The other enigma has been the way her superficial charm and sexy body had made him forgive her temporarily whenever he had needed her somewhat abruptly. For those tentative encounters, apparently his fiery sexual urges had cunningly blocked off the repugnance moulded deep inside his mind and soul about her innate wild nature. It is so interesting how lust has temporarily subdued his disgust about her severe mood swings. How incredibly intricate and enigmatic human psyche is! Once, when she was in his apartment and they were mildly drunk, he had tried to pull down her loose, tube top in front of Lucien and she had resisted while cursing and fighting him. During their scuffle, actually one of her breasts had jumped out without her knowledge. It showed for six minutes while they talked casually and Lucien enjoyed the sight of her gorgeous body. When she eventually noticed the lustful gazes of Curt and Lucien on her naked breast, she screamed, hid it away, and charged out of the apartment after breaking two antique vases.

On another occasion, Curt had let Lucien hide in the bedroom closet with its sliding doors a crack open to watch her incredible display of lust for a girl her age. He had also made special efforts to parade a fabulous sexy show for his past roommate. This live performance had been ten times more exciting for Lucien than watching a porno video, he had told Curt with great appreciation. How could he enjoy displaying such a pungent and private act, revealing his dark side to another person, even if Lucien could be considered a dear old friend? He also remembers the one-time instance he had pissed on her right after having a wonderful sex. He had hated himself for it afterward for a long, long time, though, and again right now, pointlessly. Too late to reverse all that atrocity no matter how remorseful he is at this moment. *I deserve to die here,* he mumbles. *I deserve to drink my own piss to possibly get another chance to beg Holly, maybe for three hours this time, to receive her forgiveness at least, before I die anyway, if she wants me to.*

Similar memories regarding the moments of his wickedness agitate him further beyond his already raging agony of loneliness in total darkness amidst a rugged mountain and the cold wind zapping him rampantly. The memory of his disgusting deeds turns his stomach and he feels sick. *What kind of a man have I been? I should die here tonight for everything I have done to Holly,* Curt contemplates in despair. *My deep senses of disgust, guilt, and obligation have possibly been intensifying one another all these years and confusing me more every day.*

The irony is that Holly had inadvertently brought him to this ranch and mountain to receive his punishment and die alone. On the one hand, it is true that he had been a complete jerk regardless of Holly's behaviour; he realizes it wholeheartedly now. On the other hand, the more he had humiliated Holly, the more she had seemed to loved him. He had wondered frequently about the way human brain works—to accept so much humiliation for love. Actually, Holly's desperate struggles to save their love had probably goaded him subconsciously to mortify her more for at least three reasons: First, to make her dump him—like a Good Samaritan. Second, to test and gauge the level of humiliation she would endure—like a mad scientist. Third, to enjoy the obsession of such a gorgeous creature wasted on him—like a possessed psychopath. The last two reasons might have not been so obvious to him until now, but they somehow must have resided in his psychotic mind all along to make him act like Satan. *The devil will die tonight and Holly will be free at last,* he whispers with tears pouring down his cheeks.

The cold, rage, fear, thirst, desperation, guilt, and nausea make Curt faint again until morning. Weirdly enough, the first thing he ponders briefly upon opening his eyes is human body's magical power to defend itself against physical and psychological hardships automatically, in this case by inducing a nightly coma. He would have died already if his body had not reacted naturally to withstand this torturous situation, although it is numb so nicely again as he is familiar with now. He knows that, in time, his fine, paralyzed body would unfreeze like the morning before. Thirty minutes later, with the hot sun shining directly on him, finally his muscles relax, he flexes them a bit to sit up, and swings his arms to get blood running in them. *So, what should I eat for breakfast?* he thinks and giggles with tension, amazed at his weird sense of humour in his condition this early in the day he would probably die.

Soon after his full consciousness returns, Curt considers the option of sliding down the mountain sometime today despite its danger. What other option does he have? Another day in full sun like yesterday would finally barbeque him and the vultures would attack for sure. Besides, he would go crazy sitting here and doing nothing another day. How long can a man live without any plan or initiative? The only plan he can think of is to resume tossing gravels and counting them like yesterday. What a waste of life, though it is better than being idle! What was the score yesterday? He has to think for a minute to remember, and that is a bad sign. Yeah, it was ten thousand. *Let me see if I can break yesterday's record today.* He finds the sharp narrow stone he had used as a pen, clears the surface of the soil with his palm for writing, and begins tossing the pebbles. One... two... three...

One hour later, nearing three thousand, sweat is covering his face and one drop penetrates past his eyebrow into his eye. The burning also makes him realize the stupidity of expediting his ultimate dehydration through this laborious activity. He stops immediately and lies on the ridge with his two hands wrapping his sweaty hair and face, which he then lowers to his mouth and licks with disgust. He hates the crazy cousins, himself, Holly, and the rest of the world. He waits and hallucinates until four p.m., almost losing his sanity.

He gazes downhill for the last time and decides that waiting and hoping for a rescue are futile. Death would probably be less painful than the torture he has been bearing, and definitely more honourable than the humiliation of sitting here without showing any initiative. The sun is too hot to worry about death, anyway. It is amazing that he can even think after all this time! He imagines again the vultures flying overhead more keenly. They probably know better when their food is ready, and they now seem quite anxious. Curt moves to the side of the ridge, hangs his right leg while pressing the left leg against the corner of the ridge to hold himself in place, closes his eyes, says his last prayer, thinks about Holly for the last time, and gets ready to let himself go. Once he releases his left leg from the tip of the ridge, his agony would be over, very much like standing on a chair with his neck properly planted inside a noose, ready to knock down the chair by his own feet. As soon as he lets go of the left leg, he would not have to think and decide about anything anymore. There would be some horror and pain, but then his misery would end rapidly. And maybe, if he is really lucky, he might even survive. He opens his eyes for a second and peers around with anxiety because he imagines hearing some noise. Everything is quiet and nothing moves around him. He closes his eyes again, holds his breath, and begins releasing the flexed muscles of his left leg. *Goodbye Holly, forever... Sorry, my darling...*

In the big living room of the Hollingers ranch, Holly, her parents and Rudy's parents are occupying the three couches solemnly, or pacing nervously, waiting for the Riverside Sheriff and some news. They know that by the end of the day, when the search party stops working, the Sheriff would come by to give them a report. All day, the families have called everybody who might have an idea about the missing boys and everybody who had been in the barbeque party three days ago. Holly has called Curt's office and they have confirmed that he had not showed up at work or called for two days. She does not know Curt's parents or their telephone number in Washington D.C. But even if she did, she still would not have the heart to call them to report their son's disappearance, possibly in the crushing currents of a river. Some of the mourning guests sip their coffees while Hollingers try to comfort them. Holly and her mom hold hands and weep privately in one corner. Mrs. Hollinger and her daughter, Suzy, sit next to them, ask silly questions or offer them food and refreshments, just to distract their negative premonitions.

Around 3:40 p.m., the Sheriff's patrol car turns into the driveway. He and his deputy greet everybody timidly, while the mourners brace themselves for bad news. Noticing their anxiety, the Sheriff blurts quickly, "I don't have any news. We searched the riverbanks again all day and found nothing new. I'm sorry."

"So what're you gonna do next, Sheriff?" Mr. Hollinger asks.

"Well, we'll resume our search tomorrow down the river and hopefully find more clues. But sometimes it takes a week or maybe a month before a clue is found in an odd spot usually far from these areas. Sometimes we don't find any clue," the Sheriff states solemnly and nods with disappointment all along, while the crowd is amazed of the Sheriff's seemingly cool and candid.

"But you'll find something soon, won't you?" Mr. Klint, Holly's dad, asks with disbelief about the Sheriff's assessment, while monitoring his wife's dismal condition from the corner of his eye.

"Yes. We'll try to find as much as we can. But there's usually no point searching the riverbanks after the third day. If nothing is found in three days, we'd probably find nothing useful around here. I guess I'll call off the search after tomorrow. We'll—"

"That's it? You'll call off the search?" Mrs. Hollinger shrieks.

"We'll send a communiqué to nearby counties and ask them to look out for any clues and we'll continue our routine checks a few times a week. But there's no point sending a full-fledged search party every day to the same area over and over."

Everybody stays quiet, unwilling to challenge the Sheriff at this point. They would push the matter and think about their next move after tomorrow's search.

"Would you like a cup of coffee, Sheriff?" Mrs. Hollinger asks.

"That'd be mighty nice of you, ma'am..."

"Sheriff, why don't we go to my study and drink our coffees there," Mr. Hollinger suggests in hopes of removing the angel of bad news from the agitated guests. Sheriff nods and follows him.

The last grains of strength in Curt's shaky left leg are fading fast and he imagines sliding down the slippery slope any second. His heartbeat is over hundred-twenty.

"Hey... Curt..." a voice echoes over his head. Curt's left foot is relenting, but he manages to flex its muscles quickly and grab the tip of the ridge with both hands. "Where're you, Curt?"

If he is not hallucinating, he has definitely heard somebody's voice. Even if he is hallucinating, he has already changed his mind about skidding to his imminent demise. He merely hangs awkwardly on the side of the ridge, inhales a deep breath, presses his right foot on the side of the ledge, and pulls himself back up on the ridge. He lies quietly for ten seconds to recover from the terror during those two horrific seconds. He then pulls himself together and sits. The sun hits his eyes and prevents him from seeing the big cliff where the voice comes from: "Hey, Curt... Where're you, man?" He thinks he is most likely hallucinating again, yet tries to yell, 'I'm here.' But no sound rolls out of his mouth. With his hand over his eyebrows shading the sun, Curt rises and glances up toward the big rock. He barely distinguishes two silhouettes amidst the sun shimmers. Either they are angels, ready to take him to eternity this time, or the crazy cousins have returned to rescue him. He prays he is not hallucinating the whole thing again. He grabs the sharp stone he had used for writing and throws it toward the voice. It hits the big rock below Hammond's feet just as the cousins are about to give up and go away. They assume he has found a way to rescue himself—unless he is dead flat under the big rock already. No one is standing under it for sure, but as they look further downhill, they detect the shadow of Curt's hand waving to them excitedly.

"There he is. He's down there, Rudy..." Hammond says and flings his arm to Curt.

"Yeah... Apparently he's gathered enough courage to go down twenty feet in two days," Rudy replies.

Curt is relieved for being discovered, but apprehensive about the task of going back up to the cliff. Climbing the mountain feels terribly difficult now with so little energy left in him. Of course, it is also too risky for the crazy cousins to come down the cliff for him. Finally, Hammond's shouting and beckoning convinces Curt to begin ascending. The anticipation of rescue and drinking some water goads him to climb fitfully and fretfully for twenty minutes back up to the cliff.

"Hey, man, how're you?" Hammond shouts mockingly. Curt only shakes his head and waves his fist at him. Hammond laughs again and explains his plan for rescuing him.

A ten-foot tree branch is lowered toward him with the strap made of their three belts secured at a knot near the end of it. They hold the stick tightly as Curt wraps the strap around both his arm and hand. They pull him up the cliff slowly until he is safely stuck to its surface and able to crawl the rest of the way up with the help of the crazy cousins. At the top, a large semi-flat field extends in all directions with a breathtaking view of the valley. Curt takes a deep breath as he stands on the safe ground before bursting into tears from excitement and relief. He then enquires, with hand gestures and whisper, about their delay to rescue him.

"We got lost," Hammond says. "How'd you go down there?"

"I fell when an animal attacked me," Curt murmurs.

"You know...?" Hammond asks.

"What about?" Rudy says.

"Now that I think about it, maybe there's one way for going down that slippery mountain," Hammond says.

"What's that?" Rudy asks.

"If we sit on the clean surface of the mountain after removing the gravel gradually, we could possibly move down a few inches at a time without sliding. Maybe..., I don't know!"

"Yeah, we should've tried it. But it would've taken us five days to clear the gravel on our long path."

"Nah, we could probably do it in two days, I'll say. Gravel is only on half of the mountain. The rest would be easy to descend."

"You wanna bet?" Rudy asks.

"Let's go do it," Hammond says, staring at Curt with a smirk.

"You guys are crazy. How did you get lost," Curt whispers with difficulty.

"We went down toward the woods to find a stick, but the trees seemed to move away from us and soon it got dark. It is a long story we'll tell you later, but after we found a long stick the next day, we were lost somewhere and did not know which direction to take. Long story short, we had to sleep another night under a pile of dead leaves to protect our bare chests from mosquitoes. It is a dense forest down there on that side and it is easy to get lost.

You're lucky, because we got lucky and found our way back out of that creepy forest this afternoon. Then we could not figure out your location from above here. We had to climb down and up a few times until we found your exact spot. We should've marked this spot and our tracks from the beginning. How could have we imagined getting lost ourselves. What a nightmare, man!"

Curt nods and tries to whisper a few more words but cannot. He only nods with apprehension, wondering whether the cousins' story holds water. Had they been camping up here all along, just waiting for Curt to die, or at least get his punishment and maybe learn a lesson?

"What happened to your voice?" Hammond asks.

"Gone," Curt whispers.

"It's all right. We'll find your voice too. Thank God, you're okay. Holly would've killed me if you'd died."

"You think so?!" Curt asks jokingly with pride.

"Oh, yeah... She's nuts about you...Poor girl..."

"We've all been lucky a lot these days for many things," Curt whispers with difficulty.

"Just because of her prayers all along, I bet," Hammond says.

"That's true," Curt whispers, still sobbing quietly.

"Hurry up guys. We better find our way to the ranch before it gets dark again," Rudy yells from a distance as he surveys their surrounding. Sometimes he checks out the grounds, too, like an Indian guide looking for water or animal tracks.

"Water?" Curt murmurs, cupping his hands.

"No. We don't have any water. We drank some this morning from a creek down there near the forest. But we couldn't carry any water with us."

Curt shakes his head with disappointment.

"Don't worry, man, we'll find some water soon. If only we could see that damn river from up here we could at least go down toward it and drink some water," Hammond says while waving to Rudy who is beckoning them impatiently from a distance.

The Riverside Sheriff and Mr. Hollinger return to the living room where the mourners wait gloomily or weep privately. Everybody surveys the Sheriff and Mr. Hollinger with suspicion as if they kept a secret or had a new plan of action for finding the boys. But their timid faces indicate otherwise.

"Another cup of coffee, Sheriff?" Mrs. Hollinger asks.

"No, ma'am, thank you. I'd better go and catch up with some paperwork," the Sheriff replies while noticing Holly's astonished gaze into the dark horizon. She then gets up and walks toward the window and the Sheriff follows her.

"I'll be...You think it's them?" Sheriff exclaims.

Everybody rushes to the window to explore the source of Holly's and the Sheriff's attention. Three tiny blurs move at the far end of the ranch in the dying daylight. With a sudden surge of hopes and commotion, the spectators run outside with curiosity. Holly cannot wait any longer and charges toward the shadows in the dusk and soon her parents and the Sheriff follow her. The Hollingers watch the crowd's affectionate, noisy reunion from a distance and exhale a sigh of relief.

In the backseat of Mr. Klint's car, Curt has wrapped his left arm over Holly's shoulder and holds both her hands with his right hand. Both Holly and Curt feel the deep effect of the experience on Curt by the way he is clinging to her like a baby hiding in his mother's cuddle. He remains quiet the entire time on the road, although his voice has partially returned after drinking hot tea and honey and a couple of shots of cognac. Looking occasionally in the rear mirrors, Holly's parents are amused by Curt's sudden change of heart and showing so much affection to everybody, especially toward Holly. Something seems to have aroused his passion so urgently and profoundly—like Moses or Muhammad returning from their respective mountains. *Where did Jesus go for receiving God's messages?* Holly wonders. *What kind of a Christian am I?* It is pathetic that she does not know these basic facts, she grins amusingly, but promises herself to explore all those details soon. *At least my prayers were answered. He is safe and sound, and maybe he is finally cured and ready to become my... my whatever! I'm happy he got stranded on the mountains,* she thinks with delight as she looks into Curt's eyes with a tender grin, *I'm glad Mother Nature beat the shit out of him for two days and nights.* Then she leans, whispers in Curt's ear, "I love you, Curt...", and kisses his cheek. Curt smiles back and whispers in her ears in return, "I love you, too, forever, my dear Holly..." Curt Beasmarth is surprised about his new mood and change of heart more than anybody else: *Is this feeling permanent?* he wonders. *I really hope so!*

*****

Curt is a classy name I would have loved to have, had I been born in the U.S. However, this fine pseudonym used for this story, would always remind me of some tacky moments in my past. Even recalling that crude Curt and recounting his juvenile malice in any manner is perturbing and humiliating at least! Nonetheless, not tainting my own name or singeing my sorry soul feels like a wiser strategy! My late discovery of some nasty things about Curt's character, both on the mountain then and now in my study writing about him, is also educational and mind-boggling. Then again, I have never claimed to be a perfect character, not until recently at least in my old age! Forgive my youthful flaws and confusion. As future tales will reveal, this bewildered character learns good lessons and matures through life gradually, although his enlightenment has been rather slow for my liking and benefit these days.

REFLECTION

Sting

Prelude

We cannot help revering the ambiance of prominent art galleries in town—if at last we get the guts to go inside one of them. No wonder we stay speechless in awe—*or confusion*—like visiting a museum, church, or big library. Some of these galleries indeed resemble a small museum, with expensive paintings hanging on the walls strategically under sharp spotlights in fancy frames if necessary. Sculptures usually constitute an integral part of the display, too, or get a rotating emphasis in the showroom.

Naturally, the owners and directors of these galleries deserve a lot of credit. How have they done it? How have they selected the artists and brought such a wonderful collection under one roof for us to enjoy? Of course, not many of us get a chance to check out the artworks from close-up. At best, a review of the ones in the window or visible from the crack of the door is enough for us broke art-lovers or cranky art-critics to satisfy our curiosity and cynicism. What are we really going to say when the courteous salesperson takes the trouble of coming out of his or her fancy office just to greet us with a suspicious grin that is supposed to hide his/her deep doubts about our means and intentions? That we are only looking? *This is not a museum...* Or pretend to be a rich art collector? *Who are we trying to kid?* Or make comments about some artistry that hardly anybody grasps nowadays? *We have no such guts.* Maybe one day we take a risk and step inside at last, but surely keep our mouths shut, lest insulting somebody inadvertently or showing our dire ignorance. Timidly, we stare at the innovative (and perhaps idiotic) styles surrounding us with open mouths and minds, maybe even nod with admiration like a moron, then check the outrageous prices, and still keep our faces straight. All these phony efforts clearly consume so much energy, which we surely cannot extend too often.

I am making these cynical observations based on my personal experiences when I was unemployed and had nothing better to do during the day but pace the pavements and browse the galleries gallantly. My bravery was amazing, considering my depleting bank account and doomed employment prospects during those recession years. That was shortly after my arrival in Vancouver in the fall of 1982. I had decided finally to escape my hectic life in busy Los Angeles, including a fanatic lover in an *irresolvable*, frantic affair, and start fresh in a new country and a smaller and quieter city. I did not want to return to Tehran, either. Obviously, I was also depressed about my failure to resolve that bizarre love affair I had been entangled in like an emotional rollercoaster for almost a decade. I merely wanted to take it easy awhile until I had a better feel for Vancouver, which felt like an excellent place to re-examine my life and possibly rebuild my confidence and career.

Actually, my main motivation for visiting those galleries was to decide about becoming an artist myself and making a fortune in case I could not find a decent job soon. Cynically, I wondered how difficult it could be to paint something like the ones in those galleries full of jumbled lines and splashed paints. Maybe I could unlock the mystery in some of the paintings to create similar ones myself, or just draw the lines and smear paint randomly around a large canvas. All I had to do was to think outside the box and start painting like crazy as soon as possible. This option sounded more promising to me than wasting lots of time looking for a real job and getting nowhere, anyway, while unemployment rose. Maybe I could also build a meaningful existence for myself eventually, as has always been my dream. Perhaps I could take the world by surprise as a brilliant artist in a few years, if not months, instead of doing a typical, tedious job. I was in no rush to decide, either, before testing the waters and curbing my confusion about who I was! Maybe I had to move again to another city, after all.

Opening a gallery appeared like another viable option to get rich quickly as well without doing too much work. Not even the big economic recessions seemed to dent the demand for art. With interest rates so low and stock markets so volatile, people were eager to invest in art. So, becoming an artist at least, until I could open an art gallery as well, felt like a great plan!

By the way, I could not dismiss two big questions all along: First, I wondered if my growing cynicism about contemporary art and the galleries promoting them was the side effect of the same vile disease goading my aversion towards office work in recent years! Second, I wondered if this developing mental condition—my dire scepticism about the natures of both modern art and work in general—definitely related to a personal disease or had a profound merit, maybe as a divine omen even. The latter sounded more viable to me, though.

A major dilemma in the art world these days is that the pieces displayed in the higher-end galleries appear so ridiculous or too sophisticated for the public to decipher. Oddly enough, the higher the price of an artwork, the harder it has become to grasp its meaning and aesthetic values. Even our art must be enigmatic and obscure nowadays, like everything else in modern lifestyles! We may have the money, but no mind to realize why a painting resembling a sketch that our four-year-old daughter could have done is priced so outrageously. No longer do we need a serene landscape or a subtle expression in a portrait to get mesmerized. Instead, we should find some mysterious message from some jumbled lines or colours to satiate our artistic imaginations and urges. Even worse, we must be very careful not to say something utterly stupid. We must hide our confusion and keep our honest opinions to ourselves in fear of getting kicked out of the gallery. Or we could let the gallery personnel educate us, if we get honest and brave enough to admit ignorance and ask basic questions, which would still sound sarcastic to gallery personnel. In the end, we could always accept the curator's idiotic interpretation if we are keen to buy a painting, even if we cannot repeat what they have just told us. Instead, we could possibly hire one of those pride curators for our parties, to explain everything to our guests as well, while we would keep nodding and pretending to grasp all the wisdom he or she would be sharing with our guests.

Anyhow, it takes a lot of nerve or money to go inside one of those prominent galleries and indulge their overzealous staff who feel obliged to humour us. They act like art gurus with the sacred mission of enlightening commoners like me. In fact, our mere courage to venture inside the gallery alerts its personnel that we have either guts or money—so now they get anxious to figure out which. The smart ones rapidly detect our type—the poor gutsy browser. They stare at us when we answer a question and quickly figure out who we are! They are trained to invent an excuse and escape rather rudely, hoping that we get the clue and scram. Their swift apathy and departure is irritating even more than their initial peskiness to interrogate and psychoanalyze us as artfully as Freud could do. Some are braver and risk trusting our gullibility and means. As we play rich, they smirk and humour us tentatively, *just in case,* hoping we are also naïve enough to buy into their keen presentation of an artwork that we have paused upon more than a casual glance. They become too friendly and kind to *assist* us decide about that particular piece, which hopefully suits the décor of our mansion and the size of our ballroom. Sometimes, I was tempted to show them the picture of the dump I was living in merely for humour, right before being kicked out of the gallery.

However, as long as we play smug, they think we might be somebody, after all! They offer us a cup of cappuccino and insist on putting our name on their VIP list for invitation to the opening night parties where the artists and the art-loving elites of the city congregate and drink champagne. We apparently qualify to be on the list, we gather. Their invitation supposedly implies that we do, which makes us proud of our knack for posing, though wonder how they figured us out so quickly. Anyway, we hardly comply: "No, thank you," we reply politely, "because I'm often traveling overseas, but will come by to check your new artworks when I'm in town." Once I said exactly the same thing to a gallery goddess myself, which clearly showed my growing courage and conceit during that long autumn in 1982. She smirked at me with pity, nodded desperately, and excused herself to go check on another suspicious guy who had just dared to step inside the gallery so gallantly—probably another lousy, useless browser, like myself. I wondered whether he was also checking those paintings for the same reason I was—to become an artist! Too many of us these days think we can paint even better than all those contemporary artists making millions. The irony is that we might all be quite right, too! All we need is only some nerve and encouragement! At the same time, I feel badly for gallery staff who must deal with so many of us broke, sleazy, browsers as patiently as they do day after day! They have the patience of Noah! In fact, a big war of nerves besieges galleries nowadays: our nerve to go in, gallery owners' nerve to show such trivia as art and ask such high prices, and so many people's nerve calling themselves artists.

Then again, we cannot deny the ingenuity of some artists and the expertise of gallery directors to select sculptures and paintings of various styles. Lots of knowledge and courage is required to put a collection together, on the walls or floor space, to create the right ambience, to invent outrageous prices, and then deal with people of all types, too, especially the gutsy critics like me. We seldom realize the turmoil behind all that seeming tranquility and grandeur in a gallery. We may notice staff moving around in big strides, chatting on the phone energetically, putting art pieces from one corner to another, or in and out of the storage room. We may get cynical and suspect the hoopla as part of the show—to display the energy and activity in the art market. We may ask about the business and they quickly confess how booming it is even if they have not sold one piece the whole month. It is simply amazing, we contemplate, while calculating the 50 or 60 percent commission these galleries charge artists for selling their works. At those prices and commissions, no wonder the art business looks so lucrative and tempting, especially to a bunch of greedy investors around the world, to collect art for speculation in hopes of dumping their hidden treasures with a larger profit on even bigger idiots in the future. You wonder how many more centuries this travesty would continue before suddenly no more fools are around to buy all those fading paintings in millions and trillions of dollars from one another anymore. A new delightful dawn! What an enlightening day it would be, especially the sight of the Devil's dance of jubilation! For now, we have so many rich idiots in this world, thus art prices would climb to the moon.

Running an art gallery is tough, though, let me tell you. I know it mostly from personal contacts and stories that my artist friends have shared with me over the years. Do not let the serene ambiance fool you. It is only a cover for the hectic pace behind the scene, especially in smaller galleries, with little rewards for all that hassle. The bulk of wealth from art is shared among only a bunch of elite galleries, while the rest try to copy their gimmicks uselessly. Sometimes, it is outright heartbreaking to witness the depressing lives of the parties involved: the gallery owner, the curator and director, and the poor artists themselves, of course.

Just to give you a fuller picture, let me share Melinda's story about the times she had been a gallery director. She and I had become good friends after meeting in a party and my confession about my idiotic intention to become an artist. She enjoyed my enthusiasm and optimism and promised to support me, while I agreed to help her settle her old dispute with the gallery owner.

Main Story

In his early thirties, some twenty years ago, Edward Newcomb married Cynthia, an ugly broad with broad shoulders and brazen personality. They opened an art gallery in downtown Vancouver and called it Edward's, although Cynthia and her inheritance money were mostly behind the idea. She planned to display her own paintings on a permanent basis, while saving the outrageous commission other galleries collected, even if she got a chance to show her works. She was a spirited painter, yet her innate rage surged easily in her dark paintings, which scared the hell out of normal art-lovers. Her rigidity annihilated people's constructive criticisms about her murky, monotonous paintings, which at best satisfied only bitter souls like her. And usually those sorts hardly go to a gallery or spend money on art, anyway.

Edward's reaped a modest reputation for itself in Vancouver's art community and built a rather good rapport with local painters and art buyers slowly. Edward's motto to sell more paintings at moderate prices was paying off. Edward learned something about the business, too, but not much about art itself beyond a basic first impression. This appears odd, yet these things happen regularly in the art world. He just was not an artistically gifted person and Cynthia's basic influence had not led him in the right direction, either. He did not quite understand the new styles and techniques and remained sceptical about the artists devoted to modernism, especially after his experience with Cynthia.

Meanwhile, Cynthia's nerves shattered witnessing a decent demand for bright colourful paintings of emerging artists in the gallery, while rarely anybody showed interest in hers. After five years, she gave up on both Edward's and Edward. She eloped with another gloomy artist like herself toward New York one day in pursuit of greener pastures and passionate art-lovers dying for darkness and depression. Edward was left alone with the gallery and the hassles of running it. His few attempts to sell the gallery or find a partner had led nowhere. He had to work much harder to keep the gallery open seven days a week. Eventually, he hired an assistant to help with daily chores and provide artistic input. All tangible galleries had a few personnel and a director. However, at Edward's, like other smaller galleries, the so-called director was responsible for all artistic activities and contacts, as well as many administrative duties, including office maintenance.

With the increasing competition and cost of running a decent gallery in downtown core, Edward's profit margins plummeted every year. Yet he remained optimistic and desperate to keep the gallery. The income was good in some years, but dismal more often now, very much like Cynthia's leftover paintings. Luckily, he had removed her artworks and the gallery looked brighter and livelier. In addition, he decided to concentrate only on 'realism,' since it was the easiest style for him to grasp and judge. Besides, he was getting tired of explaining his idiotic interpretations of modern arts to gallery visitors, especially some cynical jerks like me. Accordingly, he had lost the opportunity of offering modern styles and staying competitive with prominent galleries in town that were setting the trends.

To stay afloat, he found excuses to keep some of the artists' monies after selling their works. He strived to pay the bank loans and expenses before sorting out his debts to the poor artists. The real ones had long gone, forcing Edward to prey on less-known artists—those who were too desperate for displaying their arts to worry too much about Edward's delay or default tactics after a sale, which often was quite remote, anyway.

Edward's unfortunate directors were not immune from his exploitive gimmicks, either. Sometimes, they were not paid fully for a month or so, but hoped Edward would honour his promise to pay them the next day, which prolonged over weeks or months sometimes. Meanwhile, the more their salaries and commissions accumulated, the more they felt trapped and forced to tolerate the situation a bit longer.

Most directors had finally given up and left, and every time Edward had ended up hiring less qualified ones with lesser pay, and usually lesser hassle when he stopped paying them while complaining about their incompetence. Overall, he tried to keep the gallery by abusing some desperate artists and directors. After twenty years, he had become an expert in luring in marginal and desperate directors and underpaying them until they got fed up and left. Yet, coping with his own schemes and many weeks of working alone without an assistant had taken a heavy toll on him, too. The stress of living a lousy life without a companion showed in Edward's tired, anxious, and frail face. His short, tiny body kept depleting as he spent nine or ten hours every day, seven days a week, pacing the gallery and talking with visitors of all natures! Only when a director worked for him, he took Saturdays off.

Two weeks after Melinda, the last director quit with distress, Edward realized the need for a replacement before collapsing of exhaustion. If the gallery closed even for a few days, its frail reputation and income would diminish. The bills were piling up and he was concerned about his health and the gallery's prospect. At last, he called the Vancouver Sun to run his regular infamous ad for a director over the weekend. Two women applied on the phone. After chatting with them briefly, Edward invited them for an interview on Tuesday at 9:30 and 11 a.m.

Marjorie Rufus arrived on time with a pleasant smile and attitude: mid-forties, fit, charming, dressed conservatively, with her hair clustered above her neck with two fancy hairpins. On her way to Edward's office, she surveyed the paintings on the walls and the sculptures in glass displays in the middle and around the gallery. She paused before two paintings more attentively, but overall looked neither thwarted nor thrilled with the collection. With a degree from Alberta Art College, she had been a director at a fine gallery in Calgary before moving to Vancouver recently since her husband was transferred to run a major operation of Chevron in British Columbia. She looked smart and experienced, although rather overqualified for Edward's needs and crooked schemes.

That could be a serious concern, Edward thought, but maybe he could still explore and exploit her somehow.

"So what do you think?" Edward asked her.

"I think $2,000 a month salary is low…" Marjorie replied, sipping her coffee in his office.

"As I said, you get 10% commission on the gallery's share of your sales, too."

"But I can't plan my life on that, can I? What's your annual sales volume, anyway?"

"It changes. Two years ago we sold almost a million dollars."

"But there is no guarantee, right?"

"No, but it depends on your efforts too."

She was sceptical, but failing to find a fitting employment in the last four months, this one offered an opportunity to make some money, while seeking a more suitable employer; Edward seemed weird, anyway. Besides, her commissions might grow if she could revive the business by finding better artists and clients. She had the needed expertise and confidence to do so.

"How about 20%?" she asked.

"What?"

"Would you consider paying 20% commission?"

"No, but I may consider 15% for you… What're you gonna do for me for the fat commission?"

"I'll try to find better artists and sell more paintings."

"You can, eh?"

"What're the director's duties, anyway?"

"The regular stuff… The same duties small galleries expect from their directors. To sell and manage the daily operation. It's only the two of us here. So you must run the business and keep the place tidy, too."

"What do you mean exactly?"

"Art delivery and returns, recording and displaying them, or placing them in the storage room, handling customers, etc."

"Anything else?" Marjorie asked with sarcasm.

"Well, tidiness and cleanliness throughout the day are also important for a good gallery. Cleaners come by twice a week for major cleaning. But dusting and cleaning is required all along."

"Has tidying and cleaning always been the director's job?"

"Yes… Despite the doormat, people bring in mud and leaves with their shoes. Hiring cleaners, every day, requires someone's presence after hours to prevent theft and then perform the security lockup. It'd be inconvenient for me or the director to stick around one or two extra hours for the cleaning people to do their tasks after gallery closes around nine p.m. or so," Edward replied with apprehension, admitting privately that the job description for the gallery director was absurd. Yet what other choice did he have? For a gallery this size, he could not afford, or made sense, to be extravagant and hire another person only for administration or cleaning. Besides, the directors usually sat around and twiddled their thumbs half the time when no customers were in the gallery.

Despite the unsettling nature of the job, Marjorie decided to take it as a steppingstone toward a better opportunity, one without such conflicting nature of duties. *How can this idiot expect any director to be both a sophisticated curator and a coy cleaner?*

Edward liked her and promised to think about giving her 15% commission. He had already decided to do so, considering all the tricks he had learned about calculating and paying as much or little commission as he wanted. Once the poor director was owed a large sum of money, she would dance to his tune and promises. Over the years, he had invented and mastered all kinds of bizarre excuses to pay less commission to past directors, or nothing at all. Sometimes, he blamed certain client's delay of payment. Often he forged the books he kept merely for showing to directors and tax authorities; and he usually postponed paying them for weeks, anyway.

Marjorie seemed timid and desperate enough while bringing a wide range of expertise urgently needed for the business. She was attractive too, though married, sadly for him. Still, he could try to flirt with her at least, Edward imagined giddily; who knows what could happen? He was ready to offer her the job, but decided to call and give her the good news later today or even the next day. He was too clever to show his desperation for a director. He had an obligation to interview the other applicant as well, perhaps for five minutes, before getting rid of her. It was close to eleven o'clock and she should show up any minute now.

Edward returned to his office at the far end of the gallery to do some work while waiting. A convex mirror outside his office helped keeping an eye on things while talking on the phone or doing paperwork. A bell also jingled anytime the door opened.

Around eleven, two couples arrived to survey the artworks. The tourists from Australia seemed like good prospects with the typical profile for buying an expensive art piece. They were in their fifties, well dressed, and seemed to know about art. Tourists have always been the best customers, since they are usually rich and in the buying mood. Edward checked his watch and decided to cut his interview with the other job applicant short on account of being late, if she showed up at all.

The patrons showed interest in a Chinese painter that Edward had recently signed on. He said the artist lived in Hong Kong and both he and his wife were recognized painters in China. As the couples scrutinized over a particular painting, Edward felt elated about the inevitability of the sale, which meant at least two grand in his pocket—his regular 50% commission. Of course, he could also claim to have given the customer a discount to make the sale. According to the contract, he must obtain artists' consent for a discount first. But he often justified his decision by swearing that he had called and nobody answered; he would have lost the sale if he had not acted promptly.

"I'll just pay you the difference out of my pocket, if you don't believe me," Edward usually told the artists and they normally replied, "No, that's fine this time." Desperate artists, especially foreign ones, knew better not to argue with Edward too much if they wished to be represented by Edward's.

The four tourists were collaborating on the purchase, and he was already counting the eggs in the basket, when the doorbell jingled and a gorgeous young woman entered the gallery. They all took an appreciative glimpse at her, though Edward remained mesmerized after checking his watch, which showed 11:23. He forgot about the tourists, the sure sale, and his intention to dismiss this tardy applicant. Instead, he hurried to her with a wide grin.

"Natalie?"

"Yes... hi."

"Come in... Let's go to my office..." Edward muttered with excitement while showing her toward his office. "You want a cup of coffee?"

"Thank you," A sweet grin partially hid her stylish snobbery toward him, the tourists, and the artworks around the gallery.

With a clumsy excitement and idiotic grin, Edward brought her a cup of coffee before rushing out to fetch sugar and cream. He decided to talk to her for a minute before excusing himself to go finish the sale to the tourists.

"Did you have trouble finding the gallery?"

"No... It was straightforward..."

"How about parking? Did you have difficulty finding a spot?"

"No. I parked across the street. A spot opened as I arrived."

"Are you always this lucky?" Edward said, trying to break the ice and get over his tension. His vulnerable emotions had been unhinged the minute he had laid eyes on her. Such a beautiful, elegant woman: average height, wearing a beige dress and stylish shoes, and a color-matching bag, most likely genuine Gucci, with light-brown salon styled hair, and her perfume filling the gallery already. Edward imagined heaven. He recalled his intention to reject her for tardiness, especially if her excuse was not valid. She had not bothered to offer an excuse or at least apologize for being late. Worst, she had not even cared to use any of Edward's direct prompts to justify her tardiness. She could have easily blamed the address, traffic, parking, or anything; just any damn excuse would have been nice and acceptable. Yet she had simply not bothered or cared, and still Edward had not dared to object or cut the interview short. He excused himself to go take care of the customers who seemed annoyed by Edward's abrupt desertion. However, the doorbell jingled and he noticed them leaving. He turned and glimpsed at Natalie with indecision, but did not find the conviction to run after the tourists. He settled back in his chair with a $2,000 sigh. Her first damage already, in five minutes!

Natalie crossed her long, shapely legs and peeped at her cup of coffee with suspicion. Her deep blue eyes then fixated idly on Edward's hypnotized ones. With saliva gathering at the corners of his mouth, he was melting like a marshmallow on the stick near the sizzling bonfire. He had already forgotten Marjorie Rufus, thanks to Natalie Peters. Besides her charm, the mere idea of seeing her every day, chatting with her leisurely for hours, and perhaps touching her occasionally had already inebriated his senses. Even more, the opportunity of bossing such a gorgeous creature around ten hours a day felt like a miraculous blessing. That was the ultimate power and gratification any man dreams about all his life. Yes, he could be the master of such beauty and perhaps more if he played his cards right.

"So tell me about yourself," he said, keenly watching her put the cup back in the saucer after only a sip and pushing it away.

"Like what?" she asked with a teasing smirk.

"What kind of experience do you have with gallery work?"

"Not much, I'm afraid…"

"How much do you know about art?"

"I took an art appreciation course at college."

"So you know something about art."

"Yes, something…"

"Actually, it's not difficult to learn about the gallery work. I did not know anything myself when I started running this place with my ex-wife. She didn't know anything, either, although she was a good painter."

"I'll learn too… What should I do?" Natalie murmured softly with impatience, as if already tired from a full day of exhausting work. Yet, her enthusiasm to learn came across to Edward as a positive attitude and attribute—a definite indication of a tameable employee—never mind her childish show of snobbery.

"Basically charm customers and sell artworks."

"That's easy…"

"Well, the gallery director has other duties, too."

"Such as…?"

"You must help me choose and display artworks, return them to the artists, or organize them in the storage room. You must find new artists to promote sales. Always some artists drop in for presentation and you must get rid of them quickly unless you think they are truly talented. Also…" Edward stopped his tongue just in time before blurting out the cleaning chores. He realized that putting such demands on her would definitely dampen, if not demolish, her interest. Any mention of mundane duties would be an insult to her, a lady with such beauty and poise, not to mention her Gucci bag. To be smart, he must let her start work before bringing up other duties gradually in a week or so, after grasping her moods better. Not paying her salary if she refused his orders would be a good retaliation. But parading Natalie in the gallery would make even mediocre paintings look lively and scarce.

"We can discuss other minor duties later after we decide about your employment. We must work as a team and—"

The telephone shrieked and he answered it.

"Hi Melinda… Yes… Yes… I'll write your cheque soon… next week perhaps… I'll call you. I promise." he said and hung up rather abruptly with anxiety.

As Natalie stared at him with a grimace, Edward felt obliged to explain. He had to cover his anxiety, too, and perhaps even impress Natalie with his openness toward her.

"Melinda was the previous director. I must find some time to calculate her outstanding commission. I am waiting for a few clients to pay for the pieces they have taken or return them. I can't pay her until I figure out all these details, can I?"

Natalie only nodded. "How much is the salary?"

"$2,000 a month, plus 15% commission on the gallery's share of your sales."

"That's not much of a salary…"

"I'm willing to give you $2,500 if you work six days a week. That'd give me a chance to take two days a week off, and you'll be in charge," he said.

Edward figured that the extra $500 a month salary and the higher commission he had already considered paying Marjorie were well justified for having Natalie around. Hopefully her charm would increase sales much beyond the extra money that he may or may not pay her depending on her attitude and his mood. Promising is free, but having Natalie in Edward's even for a month would be priceless.

Natalie only stared at him pensively.

"What do you say?" Edward asked.

"I'll have to think about it."

"What's to think about? Aren't you happy with my offer?"

"First of all, I can work only five days, but not for less than $2,500, minimum."

"Why not six days?"

"Why not? Because I have a life too."

"Oh… well… all right, $2,500. But you must work Saturdays alone then. Okay?"

"Hmm... Okay, I guess."

"You must start at 8:30 to tidy up things and open the gallery at nine. And we're open until six; or nine p.m. some evenings."

"I'm looking for a nine to five job. I can't work so many extra hours for a $2,500 measly salary!"

"That's a tough expectation if you like to work in a gallery."

"That's why I said I'll have to think about it," she said coolly.

He felt her attitude was too annoying already and tried with all his might to keep his cool. He just stared at her for a minute.

"Well… Maybe we could try your schedule for a while and see what happens," he said at last. "I'll come in early myself and open up the gallery. But you must stay until six on Saturdays."

"Well, all right… You really drive a hard bargain!"

"I do?" he asks with wide-open eyes. "Are you kidding me?"

"No, of course not…"

Edward only stared at her with admiration and apprehension.

"What's the pay schedule?" Natalie asked.

"The salary is paid at the end of each month, but it takes a few weeks longer to do the commission calculations."

"Vow…! Now, you must be kidding me!"

"Is that a problem too?"

"Of course… It's too long."

"What do you mean?"

"I mean, I need cash much faster…"

"Much faster? Like what?"

Natalie paused, contemplating, "Well… Like all other places I've worked for…"

"And how is that?"

"Pay the salary and commission together every two weeks."

"Every two weeks…?" Edward shrieked, almost falling off his chair. Quickly he sat back with agitation, gauging his sanity for hiring the smartass goddess sitting before him. He was ready to forget the whole deal. Why hire a rebellious employee the way she was presenting herself? But when he looked up in her eyes, gazing at him blankly, his resolve deflated again. "How do you figure I can pay the commission so fast?"

"Well, I'll keep track of sales and do the calculations every other Saturday. You cut a cheque on Sunday or Monday and give it to me on Tuesday morning."

"But we can never be precise. There're always returns and payment delays and many other irregularities."

"We don't have to be precise. Pay an advance based on sales records and then we'll make any necessary adjustments later."

"It's a lot of extra accounting work and hassle."

"I'll do all that myself. I took accounting at college, too, and done some work for my dad's business."

"You're a really smart girl!" Edward said with sarcasm.

"Thank you…," she said and tugged her bag's strap over her shoulder, ready to go. "Think about it, then, and let me know."

"Okay…" Edward rose and extended his hand to shake hers. The warmth of her touch dissolved the remainder of his already mangled rationality.

"I hope I get the job…," she said with an enticing grin.

"I already said okay… You can have the job…"

"Oh, that's what you meant?" she asked with a fake surprise, enjoying her new record time in impressing another forlorn soul.

"Yes… We'll try your needs and schedule and see if they work for this gallery."

"My offers are always fair."

"But I'm supposedly the person who should be making the offers and you accepting them. You wore me down today."

"If you make your offers fair too, like mine, people will take them more seriously, I promise," Natalie said with a killing smile.

"When can you start? Tomorrow perhaps?"

"No… Tuesday…" She moved toward the door, then turned on her gorgeous white heels and addressed Edward. "How about parking?"

"What about parking?"

"Do employees have a parking spot in this building?"

"No, there's only one for me. You can use the parking facility in the next block."

"I can't walk a block in the rain and cold, even though you'll be paying for the parking."

"You expect me to pay for the parking too?"

"Don't tell me I must pay for it out of my measly salary?" she objected so convincingly poor Edward almost peed in his pants. Luckily, he just kept his mouth shut and drooped in desperation.

"We'll think of something. Maybe I give you my spot in the building and find a cheap parking space for me."

"So where should I park on Tuesday?" Natalie asked.

"Stop in front and I'll come out to give you my card to get in."

"It's a reserved spot, I hope?"

"Yes, it is very safe. I think it's better for you to have it, to feel secure working late in downtown some evenings."

"Oh, don't worry. I won't be working late any evening," she mumbled and turned to leave.

None of the previous directors had made such outrageous demands. However, Natalie was not an ordinary director, Edward rationalized. He hurried to her, next to the entrance, and shook her hand one more time as if some free touching could make up for all his speedy concessions and humiliation. He kept her hand with both his hands firmly and pondered kissing it. But Natalie pulled it and left after giving him a flirty grin at the door, to keep him enchanted for a few days until Tuesday.

Edward watched her cross the street, saunter serenely toward her polished BMW, and drive away. A surging gloom flustered him promptly, especially for giving her his parking spot. He felt ashamed for being such a wuss today all of a sudden. Now he must pay for parking and walk at least two blocks to the gallery. But that particular place charged too much. For a cheaper parking facility, he must go at least five blocks out of the downtown core.

He felt lonely with mixed emotions. On the one hand, it would be a thrill spending seven or more hours a day, four or five days a week, with such a pretty woman. On the other hand, she looked snooty and difficult to boss around. On the third hand, if he were an octopus, he had usually tamed the previous directors to work even longer hours and do harsher chores for even less than the agreed pay, though none of them had been so pretty and snobbish. After divorcing Cynthia, his only source of intimacy with the opposite sex had been his short affairs with two previous directors, both cases ending up in disaster—the directors' abrupt departures, heavier workload, and his deeper self-loathe.

Natalie appeared, however, to be a tough cookie to tame, let alone to sleep with. But he was the boss, after all, surely capable of impressing her somehow and finding a way to her heart, too, one way or another. Clearly, he had been too soft and flexible today, but that would all change next week. He would prepare himself to prove his authority around her. She needed him for job training. That would provide a good opportunity to make her abide by his rules in order to survive and flourish in this tough business. Only he could help her learn about art and the tricks of becoming a successful director. He could even send her to school to expand her art appreciation horizons. He could tell her she had a chance of becoming a partner eventually, *if* she played her cards properly and learned to run a major art gallery! Once he explains all these exciting plans and opportunities to her, on Tuesday, she would certainly be grateful to him and more appreciative of his needs. Then he can mention the mundane duties of the director, too—Tuesday? No. Tuesday would be too soon. Let us give her a few days to settle down first.

Edward was delighted with his decision to hire Natalie— more than delighted... He seemed to have lost his heart and mind after only such a short meeting. He tried to forget his stress about the parking inconvenience, the extra $500 pay, submitting to her unbending personality and unending demands despite her limited knowledge of the job, and losing the opportunity of making a $2,000 profit on an almost sure sale. He succeeded to cool down partially by imagining Edward's turning into a 'Love Gallery' starting Tuesday with Natalie's presence all day, day after day. So many customers would come around and buy paintings just for the mere chance of meeting and chatting with her. She would love him back after realizing what a gentle and generous man he is, how fast he is falling for her, and how much he could help her make a career in the art industry. Maybe she even agrees to marry him, who knows!

Daydreams and nightly dreams about the prospect of seducing Natalie mesmerized Edward for the balance of the week. Luring her felt like a sacred mission in fact—maybe even for her own good! He arrived an hour earlier than usual on Tuesday, cleaned up a little, and made a fresh pot of coffee with an expensive brand today, after a long time, near nine before the goddess's arrival. All this work after walking more than six blocks from the parking lot had already exhausted him. But he considered it a good exercise to start the day. He then paced the gallery and peered through the window for Natalie's arrival. He had to go out quickly before she got testy for waiting in the middle of the road. A few minutes past nine, she stopped her BMW in front of the gallery and flung to Edward. He rushed out clumsily to give her the parking card.

"Hi, Ed," Natalie said from behind the wheel with a pleasant grin. Her precious friendliness, calling him Ed already, warmed his bones and flesh. He smiled from ear to ear and gave her the instructions for getting through the secured entrance and finding the spot to park.

When she arrived ten minutes later, Edward helped her settle at her desk, brought her a cup of coffee, ready to explain her job. She peeped at him and the coffee stealthily, while taking her time to come around and sit behind her desk. At last, she took a sip of her coffee with caution and smiled at him for the fine coffee, probably thinking he was learning quickly. Her beautiful face had brightened his day already. Yet, he got ecstatic after Natalie took another gulp of her coffee and grinned at him again with a sign of softening. His soul was swimming in the clouds for all these fast developments and his initiative to give her a great first impression this morning. He merely sat there in silence with patience and watched her enjoy her coffee in leisure before bothering her with all the job details. *First thing first,* he pondered!

At last, she seemed relaxed and ready to listen to his lecture about the computer set-up for various tasks, including inventory controls, pricelists, artists' websites, etc. After a tour around the gallery floor, she was left alone to lure customers. Each artefact had a tag next to it with the price and related artists' information, including the biography and pictures of their other artworks ready for customers' review. In two hours, Natalie studied the folders for the sixteen artists on display and became comfortable talking with customers about the artists' backgrounds, credentials, and styles. Her diligence impressed Edward even more. Despite her inexperience, she appeared sharper in customer relations than any of the previous gallery directors and Edward himself. Her soft, hypnotic tone of voice, charming face and smile, knowledge of the artists on display, and friendly approach attracted customers quickly; all the more reason for Edward to be ultra proud of his decision to hire her. All the torture she had caused him so far seemed to be fully justified and paying off so quickly. However, more satiating were all the naughty ideas he entertained in his twisted mind about getting close to her. He was just having a ball.

Late in the afternoon, a young, handsome painter arrived with his tiny portfolio. He approached Edward and enquired about the gallery's interest in representing him. Instead of reviewing his portfolio like the usual practice, Edward decided to refer him to Natalie, to test her taste and aptitude in art appraisal as well. And more importantly, to provide a hands-on experience for her in handling pesky artists who dropped in regularly.

"You better talk to the director, Kevin," Edward said, returned his petite portfolio to him, and led the way to Natalie's office. He introduced Kevin to her with a get-rid-of-him wink and left them alone. *Now, let's see how quickly she can dismiss this nuisance.*

It was a good opportunity to teach her this delicate aspect of the job, too, while he was in the gallery himself. Seldom, any of these petty artists had anything worthwhile to offer. Yet, he had followed the policy of checking their portfolios in one minute and telling them, 'Sorry, I don't have a market for these,' and sending them away rather respectfully. Over the last twenty years, he had agreed to take on only four artists who had come by directly.

Edward paced the gallery while monitoring the situation in Natalie's office anxiously. Contrary to his expectation, they kept talking over ten minutes and soon began laughing and flirting. He felt jealous and hurried to her office.

He waited and monitored the scene for a minute before asking with caution, "So how long have you been painting, Kevin?"

"It's been a while!"

He moved forward and leaned over Natalie's shoulder to view the half-dozen silly pictures in Kevin's portfolio, which seemed to have fascinated her. He then stepped back and tried to signal Natalie to get rid of Kevin. However, she was not paying any attention to him, her eyes fixated on one picture or another when not chatting with Kevin. Edward waited two minutes with tension before leaving, embarrassed for being ignored. From the way Natalie behaved, he mused, anybody could assume Edward was only a nosy clerk or something, who had ventured into the director's office without invitation. Maybe she must fire him for intruding. These thoughts aggravated Edward even more.

For half an hour, Edward rambled and raged while Kevin and Natalie chatted and chuckled. At last, Kevin said a fast goodbye to Edward on his way out. He hurried to Natalie to give her some advice and maybe a notice for ignoring him in front of customers.

"Hi, Ed…," she said. And that was enough again to crush his resolve. "I asked Kevin to bring four of his paintings to display for a while."

"You did?" Edward asked softly. "Without consulting me?"

"Didn't you say in front of Kevin that I was in charge of these kinds of decisions?"

"Yes… But—"

"And that's exactly what I did. Why do you complain then?"

"Because I assumed you'd ask for my opinion as well before making a final decision."

"I can't read your mind! Besides, I don't like to be overruled in front of artists."

"His paintings appeared too crude to me. What did you like about them? Besides, we don't even have any space to display this guy's paintings."

"I don't think you're sure what you're doing… I'm either in charge or not… Make up your mind, please…" Natalie said with grimace and an elaborate show of annoyance.

Edward got worried, came forward, and patted her shoulder.

"Oh, I'm sorry. I didn't mean to offend you. Of course you're in charge, but let's do some consulting, too, instead of ignoring me completely before people."

Natalie just ignored him and sat quietly.

Despite his agitation, he reckoned these kinds of emotional exchanges usually brought people closer. Natalie's sensitivity was an opportunity he could capitalize on. She had not recoiled when he had caressed her shoulder, and he had enjoyed both the touching and her soft, sexy cringe. So maybe he was on the right track, after all.

"Well... Then tell me which paintings you want to replace Kevin's paintings with?" Edward asked tenderly to break her silence and possible grudge.

"It's very simple... The ones that haven't sold for over three months," she replied with lethargy. "I believe Johnson's paintings can be put in the storage room for now."

"Are you kidding me? She's our best artist..."

"But when was the last time you sold any of her paintings?"

"Not recently..."

"So...? What's the problem then?"

"You don't understand. She's a famous realist painter."

"I don't understand?" Natalie blurted irately with another big grimace. Edward quickly realized the insensitivity of his remark that had really upset her this time.

"No, I don't mean it that way. Sorry..." He again took the opportunity to caress her shoulder. She did not cringe, and he decided to move his hand a bit higher next time and caress her lustrous hair as a test for touching her face and maybe kissing her soon. Love was in the air. "Come on... Come on. We'll take Johnson's paintings to the storage room when Kevin brings his."

"Are you sure?"

"Yes... I'm sure. If that's what you want!"

"Okay... Thank you..."

"When's Kevin bringing his paintings?"

"Tomorrow..." she replied, strolling toward the washroom.

Edward plummeted onto his chair with despair and watched her gorgeous body saunter toward the gallery's sole washroom next to the office. He imagined her pulling down her panties and sitting on the toilet seat. He contemplated going to the washroom right after her to sit on the sacred spot her soft skin had touched. Maybe a bit of her body heat or dead skins would cling to the seat as well. Even some of her natural odour would be refreshing. All that would be an exhilarating experience for now, especially if he also pumped up his imagination a notch. He gasped a big sigh of relief, happy that at least she was not angry with him after his insensitive remarks all afternoon. *Just look at me, such a pathetic, miserable creature I've become after losing my darling Cynthia to that asshole artist,* Edward ponders with pain and pity. *No wonder I hate all these intruding artists!*

As soon as he heard the sound of the toilette flush, he leaped out of his chair ready to charge to the toilet.

"This washroom isn't clean, you know?" Natalie blurted upon stepping out; Edward froze in his tracks.

"It isn't?"

"No."

"That's another thing I'd meant to talk with you…"

"What…? That I should go to the mall to pee?"

"No…Of course, not. You do it all here," Edward felt irritated by her sarcasm, but amused by her inadvertent sense of humour. She was loosening up already and using common vocabularies liberally, too. "But then…"

"Then what?" she asked.

"Well…" Edward was still hesitant about the timing and risk of mentioning the director's mundane duties, especially after they had already had a few rounds of rows today. He decided against a blunt confrontation, but a hint might be justified.

"Well, together we must keep this place tidy."

"What do you mean?"

"Some cleaning and dusting now and then… Cleaners come on Tuesday and Friday nights only."

"I hope you don't expect me to clean the toilet?"

"There's nobody else to do it... We're the only ones using it."

"So...?"

"All the previous directors did it."

"Not me... I don't know what kind of directors you've been hiring before!"

"Somebody should do these chores..."

"Not me...! I guess now it's your turn after having the poor directors do it all these years."

"But I'm the president and owner, for God's sake."

"Then hire help, Mr. President..."

Edward was flabbergasted, but tried hard to hide his emotions with a grin, which looked outlandishly silly to Natalie, anyway.

"But people bring debris and mud inside the gallery all day long," he said. "We must spot vacuum occasionally if necessary. We can't get a maid here on the spur of the moment only to clean a corner and go away."

"I'd better go now. It's five o'clock and I have lots of things to do," Natalie said with a smirk. "See you in the morning..."

Well, of course, 'she'd better go now...!' after causing him enough damage and humiliation for one day!

Bewildered Edward watched Natalie leave with a flirty grin and gentle goodbye at the door, as if they had not just had a skirmish. He was lost but loved her more every minute. Everything she said made absolute sense. She was a director, after all... How could he expect her to do those dirty, mundane jobs? But she was not an art expert, either, and had already invited a 'nobody' to have a show in this prestigious gallery at the cost of taking down Johnson's paintings. Who the hell was this foreign guy who called himself Kevin and seemed to have been painting only a few months? What were those paintings of his all about, by the way? If Johnson found out her painting were being shipped to the storage room, he would be in trouble. On the other hand, Natalie seemed to have a knack for handling customers and making sales already. *So I must humour her for now,* he reckons. *It'll sure take a bit of patience and trust to bring her around.*

After pondering the situation for a while, Edward closed the gallery, washed the toilet and mopped its floor sparkling clean, emptied the garbage cans—containing mostly Natalie's napkins and food wrappers—into a large bin. He then took the bin to the garbage container in the back of the building and emptied it. Next, he vacuumed the gallery, dusted the frames and artefacts, and cleaned eight display boxes smudged with fingerprints and dirt. Two hours later, he was exhausted, but happy that at least Natalie would not complain about the toilet in the morning. He then walked six blocks to the Parkade, panting and perturbed again, as if deep down he remained sceptical about the bumpy road ahead. Sitting behind the wheel, however, everything made sense to him once more, including all the extra cleaning work and walking he must do from now on just to keep Natalie happy. He found her in complete right to be the way she was, especially now that she had proven to be a good salesperson and let him caress her shoulder.

Kevin brought four of his paintings to the gallery as scheduled and Edward personally removed Johnson's paintings and hauled them to the storage room before hurrying back and hanging Kevin's paintings of skulls and vultures, all with a death theme. Kevin's taste and style reignited the old, painful memories of Cynthia's paintings and her nastiness. He wondered whether Cynthia had a hand in all this, or perhaps they were Cynthia's painting that this guy had somehow found and now wanted to unload under false pretences. Nonetheless, he decided to display them awhile until he could find an excuse to get rid of Kevin and his gloomy paintings.

The rest of the week, Edward kept his mouth shut about the mundane chores. He was careful to avoid any insensitive remarks or advice that might offend her. *Patience, patience, man,* he kept telling his pesky brain. Doing so, however, would defeat the whole purpose of exploiting her vulnerable mood and finding an excuse to caress her shoulder or hair. That was a big dilemma! In fact, Edward's attentiveness gave Natalie more courage every day to run the gallery as she pleased or deemed necessary, while leaving the mundane jobs to Edward. Occasionally, she whined slyly about something, like the smell of garbage cans, apparently caused by the leftover food or drink spills. Edward carried the bins to the washroom and cleaned them thoroughly. He had also noticed the small pad she kept in her pocket and apparently jotted down the particulars of each sale to calculate her commission. Maybe she could not be fooled, after all. But that would be okay as long as she let him touch her shoulder and hair perhaps.

Natalie signed up two other unknown painters, too, one of them specializing on paintings of pillows and blankets meshed up together like unmade beds. Edward was just going nuts, but still convinced himself that it was all part of the learning process for Natalie and he must be more patient with her if he wished to reap the rewards of his generosity later. She worked alone on Saturday to give Edward the day off. When he arrived on Sunday, still more new paintings were piled up in every corner around the walls. The gallery looked untidy and the floor and washroom were dirty. He cleaned up as much as he could and decided to confront Natalie on Tuesday about accepting too many artworks from unknown artists and making the gallery resemble a messy frame shop. For a quick moment, he wondered whether she was deliberately trying to drive him crazy. But what reason could she have for doing all these nasty things to him? More depressing, he wondered why he had been so mysteriously fallen in love with a selfish girl so swiftly, as though she had cast a spell on him.

"Hi, Ed," she said excitedly when she arrived on Tuesday, as if she had missed him after only three days of separation. "Did you have a good weekend?"

Edward's earlier rage was largely pacified again. "Yes, thank you. But we should talk about all these paintings you've brought in. We're running out of space."

"Don't worry, we'll do something about them later... But guess who called me yesterday?"

"I don't know... who?"

"Melinda Fisher."

"Oh...?" Edward frowned.

"She said you'd promised to call her for the money you owe her."

"Yeah... I forgot."

"You owe her $3,440 using your own account of sales during her last month of working for you."

"That much...? I don't think so..." Edward shrieked.

"Yes, I got the sales figures off your ledgers to calculate the commission and then added a grand for the last two weeks salary that she says you haven't paid her yet."

"I'll have to do the calculation myself later..."

"I promised her to have the cheque ready by next Tuesday."

"You shouldn't promise anything on my behalf!"

"Here we go again..." Natalie shrieked with stress.

"But—"

"Am I responsible for administration or not?"

"But financial issues and promises require my approval."

"My job is getting really confusing, I'm telling you."

"Because you avoid consulting me for anything," he said with some rage as softly as he could manage under the circumstance.

"Don't you want to pay the outstanding debts?"

"But I need time to dig out all the records and do everything else," Edward said nervously.

"Here... I have everything written up." Natalie handed him the calculations.

"Just leave it there."

"Let's do all the accounting on Friday afternoon. You issue a cheque to her and one for my two-week salary and commission. I'll get any adjusting figure ready by Saturday, too."

"I may have cash problem for making this much payments next week."

"No… We sold sixteen grand last week alone, thanks to me. We'll have even more money by next Tuesday to pay us."

"Why should I listen to you when you never listen to me?"

"Listen to you!? What do you mean?"

"I mean teamwork and consultation…"

"About what?" she asked with confusion.

"About these Kevin's paintings, for instance. Who's this guy, anyway?"

"Don't you like his paintings?"

"No."

"That's not Melinda's fault too, is it?"

"No, but maybe it is your fault a little."

"My fault…? Are you serious?"

"Well… you know…"

"If you're unhappy with my work, just say so…"

"I didn't say that," Edward said fretfully.

"So, are you gonna write our cheques next week?"

"I will if you get rid of Kevin's paintings and put Johnson's back up."

"Tuesday is fine. I'll call Kevin to come and take them next Tuesday morning. And I'll call Melinda to come by on Tuesday as well to get her cheque. Are you happy now?"

"Hmm…" he said with hesitation, wondering if he could have asked for something romantic as well or instead. "How about helping with other chores?"

"What chores?"

"Helping me in general... including some cleaning… And maybe you could also be nicer to me once in a while…"

"Well, maybe…" Natalie said. "I'll help starting next week too, after you wrote our cheques."

"Okay, that's a deal… You can always trust me."

"I certainly hope so…"

Edward thought he should show his goodwill and prove his nobility now that the opportunity had finally risen. The fact that Natalie had promised to be nicer to him *starting next week* and also help with cleaning—whatever it meant in Natalie's mind compared to his wild imagination—was a major step in the right direction. It was a reasonable price to pay to bring Natalie on board and get closer to her heart.

Edward took care of the mundane duties for the remainder of the week, quite jubilant that help was around the corner. Starting next week a new chapter would start in his affair with Natalie, not to mention the opportunity of restoring a proper boss-employee relationship *at last*. *The way she'd been taking over my soul and pride, very soon I would've been forced to give her the gallery altogether and run away!* he muses with a mix of amusement and amazement. *Now, I'm finally going to reap the rewards of my generosity and patience. Great job, you sly Edward!*

Tuesday morning, Edward wrote the promised cheques with mixed feelings. Melinda arrived at 11 o'clock and collected hers. Natalie got her cheque, too, and suggested taking Melinda for coffee. Edward agreed reluctantly and they left. Instead, they went to the bank and cashed their cheques. Meanwhile, Kevin arrived and collected his paintings as well. Under the baffled eyes of Edward, Natalie's BMW stopped in front of the gallery, Kevin loaded the paintings in the trunk of her car and then settled in the front seat next to Natalie.

"That was easy…" Natalie said as she drove away swiftly.

"I told you Ed is a softy lover boy…" Melinda said with a chuckle from the backseat.

"He was rude about my beautiful paintings, though," Kevin blurted and they all burst into laughter.

Edward remained frozen behind the window, baffled about the whole episode happening before his eyes right across the street, until the BMW screeched away and left him in a deeper haze. He thought maybe Natalie had agreed to help Kevin with the paintings and would return soon. Still no sign of her at noon, he assumed the worst at last. He went inside Natalie's office, sat behind her desk and inhaled some of her lingering perfume. He really missed her. From afar, an envelope next to a sculpture near

Natalie's office drew his attention. He walked over and fetched it. It was unsealed and seemed like a letter that Kevin had left for Natalie just a few minutes earlier. He opened it quickly and found the parking pass and a note from Natalie.

'Dear Ed, I'm sorry to leave you this way. But I didn't have the heart to tell you in your face that I really hate cleaning the toilet or sweeping the floor. I was the director, for God's sake... What were you thinking? Anyway, I quit. Thanks for the training and your affection. Better luck next time.'

Edward sighed with melancholy: *Maybe I was too hard on that poor girl! Maybe I should call her and apologize...!*

*****

As for me, I was glad that my ridiculous paintings were displayed under a fictitious name in a gallery after dreaming about such a miracle at the time, even though it was only for fun and for just two weeks. I was also thrilled to play a naughty role in such a well-orchestrated plot that helped Melinda collect her overdue remunerations from stingy Edward after torturing her for such a long period. The opportunity to know her friend, Natalie, was exhilarating all in itself, although I did not feel so proud about all the atrocities that we, in particular that sneaky gorgeous Natalie, had inflicted upon that poor old man, Edward. She was such an attractive, spoiled goddess she could even make me her slave if so many other realities and beauties of life besides love did not distract me every minute already.

Pondering those good old times and my tenacity to challenge arrogant gallery personnel, I feel both amazed of my drive at the time to fight so much social vanity and ashamed of wasting so much of my and those people's time. Now, I realize I must have lost my mind and spirit those days due to erratic love affairs and unemployment in a new city.

Shoot

Salvador and Maggie Romble hang on tight timidly in the posh Mercedes that Sheila Hamdi, their real estate agent, drives rather recklessly with tension toward their next destination, yet she still strives to amuse her clients as well. She has already shown them four houses this afternoon, in addition to about two dozens in recent weeks. The couple is drained, too, and rather disillusioned about the prospect of finding a decent house according to their taste and budget. Yet Sheila keeps blabbering about the merits of a few houses that the Rombles had found inadequate or pricey. Only one house, in Ranger Street, had somewhat appealed to them mostly due to its partial city view. Alas, the neighbour's tall trees obstructed a good portion of the view. Sheila had suggested to Salvador to sneak into the neighbour's backyard late one night and hammer a few long rusty nails into the trees.

"That'd do the job, I promise. And nobody will find out," She had stressed with a moronic grin and a wink to Salvador. "Both your view and the house value will improve drastically."

"Even suggesting it is a sin, Sheila. Let's get out of here," Salvador had exclaimed and charged toward her car with disgust. *How can a certified agent propose such an outrageous deed? Besides, how does she expect me to sneak into the neighbour's property and hammer a few long rusty nails into his trees in the middle of the night without making a racket and wakening the whole neighbourhood? Where am I gonna find rusty long nails, anyway, or is she expecting me to rust them myself somehow in the first place?*

Now speeding through the streets of North Vancouver, Sheila blurts, "The house I'm showing you next has some view, too, and a potential for much more with some landscaping."

"Landscaping?" Salvador shrieks, wondering with pain about the new scheme she is probably cooking up in her twisted, greedy mind. "How can landscaping improve the view?"

"You'll see... But I still think you should put an offer on the Ranger's house and do what I told you," Sheila says with a tense chuckle.

Sheila's persistence again about maiming the neighbour's trees upsets Salvador all over. He decides to fire her right after viewing this last house today. *How can I work with someone lacking integrity and, even worse, keep assuming so low about my character? I bet she can't even imagine the hassle involved to do this tree-killing job!*

Meanwhile, he imagines himself learning about, and taking the time and hassle of, rusting a large supply of long nails, then planning an attack on the neighbour's backyard, waiting for a moonless dark night, staying up late in hopes of people falling asleep and missing his intrusion with the hammer and a bunch of rusted nails, going around from tree to tree, and hammering as quietly as possible a few of those rusty nails into each tree. Then sneaking back to his own house cautiously, hoping that nobody had noticed him, still shaking from all the terror he has endured for half an hour or so, unable to sleep the whole night, fighting his nosy, guilty conscience, suffering from his mischief, and most of all, hating himself for listening to Sheila's criminal suggestion. Then, assuming he succeeds to go through all these insane, risky steps without a hitch, his real long agony would only begin. He would have to get up every morning for months and check out the neighbour's trees for any sign of succumbing to the poison of the rusted nails. How long would it take before the trees start showing a sign of death? How long should he wait, feel guilty, suffer, fight his conscience, and curse Sheila? Would the poor neighbour detect by himself, or after calling the experts, the cause of all that sudden deaths in his once bounteous backyard? And then, most likely, he discovers that his new, crazy neighbour, this juvenile Mr. Salvador, is responsible for all that havoc, merely because he likes to have a view of the city from his house.

Now, I'm not even going to get into the possibility of my neighbours also retaliating against me or even taking me to court. Oh, stupid Sheila, how could you imagine I'm capable of all this atrocity?

Sheila turns into Jones Avenue and stops in front of a corner lot house. It looks sturdy and clean from outside and the Rombles' hopes rise upon stepping into the foyer. The interior is well planned, too, with spacious rooms and a modern kitchen. The paint and carpets are new and the incomplete basement can be renovated and rented as mortgage helper. The late-afternoon sun shimmers through windows and the cute solarium on the west side of the house. The kitchen and family room are also well lit and have a good ambiance. But the living room and bedrooms are rather dark and damp. The Rombles attribute the gloominess to the time of day as the sun is setting slowly.

"What do you think?" Sheila asks.

"It's not a bad house… But didn't you say it has a view?" Salvador asks.

"Yeah, come here," Sheila replies and rambles to the far end of the living room where the tips of some downtown high-rises show amidst the branches of a dense tree.

Peering through the window, the Rombles stand still in awe, wondering how they had missed the immensity of the tree near the entrance. Its thick branches spread across the house leisurely and block a chunk of the kitchen and dining room windows.

"What is this big tree doing in front of the house?" Salvador asks with frustration.

Maggie also turns toward Sheila with bewilderment, eager to hear her *normally idiotic* explanations, especially after her fervent claim in the car about the 'view.'

"I told you that some landscaping will help. Cut the tree and you'll get more light and view."

Salvador and Maggie shake their heads with despair and rush outside the house to survey the tree. Sheila follows them casually without any hint of remorse. She believes the potential for view is great and her clients should be smart to see it instead of criticizing her and nagging constantly like two spoiled kids.

"Shoot! This tree is really huge!" Salvador shrieks.

"And right near the entrance," Maggie adds with a sigh. "Soon people will have difficulty getting into the house."

"That's another good reason for cutting it," Sheila says keenly with triumph.

"How old is this tree? Do you know?" Salvador asks.

"No... Probably twenty or thirty years," Sheila replies.

"It's over fifty years old, if you ask me..." Salvador says.

"Maybe..." Sheila murmurs irately.

"Why do you keep showing us houses blocked by trees and insist they have views, too?" Salvador asks with agitation.

"You can't help it here in this city. All houses have some trees inside their property or on the neighbours' backyards," Sheila replies with conviction. "But this one is easy to fix. It's your tree and you can do whatever you like with it."

"I don't think so..." Salvador says with distress.

"Are you sure we can hack the tree?" Maggie asks.

"Why not? It's on your property," Sheila replies.

"I don't know about that... Let's go," Salvador says and starts toward the Mercedes, promising himself that this would be the last time he would be riding in her damn car.

"You must decide soon," Sheila says. "I've heard another couple is considering making an offer."

"We'll let you know, Sheila. We should think about this," Salvador growls.

At home, the Rombles discuss the house in Jones Avenue at some length without success. Maggie believes that cutting the tree would make the house ideal for them, considering their budget and extensive house-hunting results. But Salvador abhors buying a house that could be suitable only if an ancient tree is destroyed. He has already expressed his opposition to killing the neighbour's trees in Ranger Street, quite unwilling to change his position and hack an older one now. For this house, of course, he does not have the hassle of sneaking into a neighbour's backyard, rusting any nails, or take the risk of going to jail! Still, killing an old tree is an outrageous and insensitive act regardless of who owns it.

Maggie is frustrated with Salvador's stubbornness and idiotic idealism. She wishes he showed some of this romanticism to her instead of wasting it on trees so passionately. Indeed, he has never been a particularly romantic person and his emerging love of trees feels weird. Anyhow, Salvador's sudden sentimentality can cost them a great house at such a reasonable price. Arguing with him is futile though, so she leaves the room in distress. The phone rings and Salvador answers it.

"Have you decided yet?" Sheila asks on the phone.

"We discussed it and can't buy this one, either."

"But this is a great opportunity. You can't find another house like this again. The owners are really motivated to sell, too."

"Maybe… But I'm against buying a deficient house in hopes of improving it later. I don't feel comfortable with this house the way it stands now."

"Is the tree the only problem?" Sheila asks.

"Yes."

"Is it Sheila?" Maggie interjects upon entering the room. "Let me talk to her." Salvador gives her the receiver and staggers to the kitchen to grab a beer for his nerves.

"Can you take care of the tree, Sheila?" Maggie asks. "And do you think an offer ten grand below the asking price can fly?"

"I think so, about the tree. And about the offer, let's give it a try," Sheila replies.

"Let me talk to Salvador and call you back," Maggie says and hangs up the phone.

"I think we should fire her and get another agent," Salvador says once he returns and finds Maggie deep in thoughts.

"Actually, let's give her a chance to prove herself."

"Give her a chance?"

"What if Sheila can get us a deal and get rid of the tree, too?"

"How?"

"Let Sheila give a low offer for the house. She will also get the tree removed before we move in. Isn't this great?" Maggie says with a triumphant smile as if she has just invented a peace plan for the Middle East. "You won't have to worry about killing an ancient tree or dealing with Sheila anymore."

"It's still because of us that the tree will be cut. It's still the same crime, Maggie."

"But somebody will do it, anyway. The present owner may decide to do it to facilitate the sale. Or the smart new owner will get rid of it to take advantage of the view and increase the value of the property."

"But then I won't be responsible for other owners' stupidity and cruelty."

"How come you're now so passionate for plants and weeds all of a sudden? You've never shown me this much affection?"

"Maggie, stop this nonsense. This isn't the right time…"

"Never is the right time with you!" Maggie says with tension.

"You really like this house?"

"Yes… I think it's a good house."

"But the tree might cause us big hassle."

"Sheila will take care of it."

"That's the problem. She's too arrogant and pushy. She's a novice agent and I don't trust her judgment."

"Come on, honey…" Maggie insists.

"I still think we should fire her and forget about this house."

"Let's make an offer ten grand below the price. If declined, we will walk away. Deal?"

"Okay, okay. Just leave me alone," Salvador shrieks.

The Rombles' offer is accepted for a possession date in forty days. Maggie is ecstatic despite Salvador's cynicism and distress, which is hard to miss while he keeps uttering, "Shoot!" every half an hour or so. She believes he would come around, though, once the tree is gone. Despite the shoddy outcome, Salvador is rather relieved that at least their house hunting is over and no more Sheila to tolerate. *It's outrageous how she makes all that money off naïve people like us and drives that kind of Mercedes—and so recklessly, too, mind you. They should cancel both her driving and real estate licenses.* Regarding the tree, as long as he would not witness the slaughter, he should probably leave the matter alone. Indeed, he now prefers to think of it as being 'taken away,' rather than being killed. *What a hypocrite I am,* he groans again, anyway. *Shoot!*

Sheila calls Maggie the following week to announce that the tree-cutting company requires a city permit to remove such an old tree, for which the owner should apply.

"Can the present owner apply?" Maggie asks.

"They've gone away for a few days. But they probably won't do it anyway."

"Why not?"

"Because they're really pissed off. The husband ignored his wife's objection to sell the house to you under the listed price… She's now blaming him for the screw up."

"Screw up?"

"Two days after accepting your offer, another agent told them that a full-price offer had been in the making while I was pushing yours relentlessly."

"Really?"

"Yes. You should thank me for sneaking your offer through quickly."

"I thank you, but don't count on Salvador doing it, too."

"I can imagine…" Sheila blurts with a chuckle.

"In fact, he'll be furious if I ask him to apply for a permit."

"You've got yourself a grumpy husband, ha!" Sheila says.

"But he's a good man, Sheila."

"Why don't we take care of it then," Sheila replies. "Just tell him a permit is required, which may take awhile to process. After the ownership is transferred, you and I will go to the City Hall and apply for the permit. Alright?"

"I guess… This is better than telling him the whole truth and listening to his bitching for another month," Maggie replies with a tense giggle timidly.

Although Maggie censures the gist of the news, Salvador whines all night, "Shoot…! Shit…! Shoot…!"

"But, honey, it'll be all right," Maggie says after taking in enough 'shoots' and 'shits.'

"I told you she doesn't know what she's talking about!"

"But these things take time," Maggie insists. "She didn't know about the process, either, like us."

"She told us it's easy and she'd take care of it right away. Now the tree may still be there when we move in," he replies.

It is not a matter of 'maybe,' she ponders stealthily, timidly. It will definitely be there, but it would be imprudent telling him that certain cruel reality.

"She never said cutting a tree was straightforward," Maggie says. "She merely promised to help us and pay for the cost of taking it away. She'll still do that once the permit is issued."

"Why do you defend her so much? She'd promised the tree will be gone before we move in," Salvador growls and walks away. "That's exactly what you told me yourself, unless you were only lying to manipulate me…?"

The possibility of the tree cutters showing up one day with their awful electric saws after they move to their new home, on a day he happens to be at home maybe, haunts Salvador during the next four weeks. He has a few nightmares about a screaming tree, protesting, and slamming the side of the house by its long, heavy branches. He drives by the house twice, hoping that the business is taken care of and the tree is gone. Instead, it seems to be getting bigger very fast out of spite. Its branches wave at him in the mild wind as though dancing with jubilation and mocking him.

The tree stands proud when the Rombles move into their new home. It spreads murky shadows on the house all day as though avenging the doomed destiny planned for it by the insensitive new owners. The creepy shadows also crawl inside the house like black, ferocious anacondas and dragons. Salvador ignores their intimidating infringement in order to mitigate his sense of guilt and responsibility. And he ignores the tree's protests and clever pleas by shaking its branches and leaves—violently thumping on the roof sometimes, softly caressing the windows sometimes, or sneakily knocking on the front door now and then. It takes the Rombles awhile to figure out nobody is at the door, but only the tree tricking them repeatedly.

With the approach of the winter, the house is cold with the southerly sunrays powerless to penetrate into the house past the tree branches and leaves. The hiking gas and electricity rates lead to a larger utility bill every month. All this is the tree's fault and it must go for sure, Salvador swears. The matter is now beyond his control, anyway, but the tree is guilty of obstructing the view and dampening the ambience of the house, not to mention the number of times he has gone to open the door for nobody. He wants to hate the tree so much so he feels no guilt at all when it is cut. He just hopes that one-day he comes home to see it gone and all their problems solved. Meanwhile, he would not interfere or even ask Maggie why it is taking so long to get a simple permit.

Maggie has applied for the permit without telling Salvador the details and hassles involved. For the price of fifty dollars, a city engineer has to take the pain of visiting a tree and proposing a politically sound course of action. In the past, the media have made noise about hacking old trees; and the environmentalists have accused the bureaucrats in the City Hall of carelessness. Acting hastily could cost the Council a major embarrassment and perhaps their jobs in the next election. So even these simple cases require the Council's approval as well, which is another headache and time-consuming formality.

A city engineer informs Maggie that if she could embrace the tree trunk in full, it would possibly be all right to cut it; otherwise getting a permit could be almost impossible. Maggie hugs the tree for testing and fails miserably. She wonders why she had even attempted such an absurd experiment when the outcome was obvious just by looking at the fat tree. *Am I losing my mind or something, hugging a tree like an imbecile? I hope neighbours didn't see me and praise my sentimentality!* She tells Sheila about the engineer's ruling and her foolish, failed trial. Sheila promises to bribe a member of the Council she knows to get the approval somehow. So, at the end, Maggie just sits back, too, waits, curses Sheila, and wonders why Salvador is not asking any question or complaining about the tree anymore. He is not 'shooting' and 'shitting' around the house these days, which is so blissful and she thanks god for it.

The winter passes and the permit does not arrive, nor does Salvador mention the tree even once. Maggie keeps her mouth shut, too. The tree has become a big taboo that nobody wishes to discuss anymore, although they desire privately that the problem gets resolved soon somehow. Late in the spring, hundreds of cute little buds appear all over the tree branches and they grow bigger every day. The Rombles casually watch them turn into tiny round fruits hanging from long stems. Salvador wonders why nobody has told them all along what kind of a tree this is. One afternoon he notices Maggie's bewildering face fixated at the tree.

"You know what kind of a tree this is?" she asks.

"No… You?"

"These buds are starting to look like figs. Don't you think?"

"Yeah. You're right. They're figs, I guess!"

"Wow… millions of figs."

"This is just great, if it's fig. You know how much I love figs," Salvador says.

"I know… And all these years fighting your yearning, just to save our money for buying a house," Maggie replies mockingly.

"You know how expensive figs are!? One dollar each…"

"Only multimillionaires can afford it…! I know! You told me a few times before, I remember… But if these are figs, it's much more than you can ever eat. You're a millionaire at last."

"I didn't know fig trees can get this big and fertile," he says.

"Neither did I."

"Listen, Maggie, tell Sheila not to cut the tree."

"But I received the permit two weeks ago and gave it to her."

"Shoot! Go call her and ask her to wait for now."

Maggie calls Sheila and then addresses Salvador: "Her phone says she's gone to California for a week. I left her a message, although her recording says she won't be checking them."

"Shoot! What if she doesn't get your message?"

"I don't know. But I've nagged so much for the delay she may not even bother calling back."

"Shit!"

"She's really angry with us, but she has arranged everything with the tree-cutting company."

"You know which company?"

"No."

"Shoot! Shit!"

"Don't worry… Maybe she calls back soon…"

"I don't trust her. One of us must be around in case the tree cutters show up."

"But I have things to do," Maggie protests.

"Try to stay home when I'm at work; or leave a message on the tree… and one on the front door, too, if you really have to go away," he says in distress. "Why do you have to go out?"

"Why…? You don't want to cut the tree at all?"

"I don't think so… Not right now for sure…"

For eight days, Maggie and Salvador take turns guarding the tree and watching the figs grow. Sheila calls casually at last upon returning from California, surprised by the Rombles' change of heart regarding the tree. She had not checked her messages while in California to enjoy a quiet vacation. After hiring a tree-cutting company, she had no other urgent business to fret about, anyway.

"You're lucky the company had been busy before you guys figured out what you really wanted," Sheila says with sarcasm.

New problems emerge soon after postponing the tree execution. For one thing, birds attack the tree in large waves like a hungry army. They eat many figs and puncture many more inedible. The Rombles invent all sorts of gimmicks to deter the bad birds from approaching their lovely tree. They hang bells, pans, and spoons to branches to jingle upon birds' landing. They pinpoint the branches covered with ripe figs regularly and spread small nets over them with difficulty and utmost diligence to avoid harming the leaves and fruits. They also erect two scarecrows around the tree. However, all these tricks work only marginally, forcing the Rombles to think harder every day for better solutions. If the birds are not enough, neighbours and pedestrians become the added nuisance. They sneak around and help themselves to the ripe figs hanging temptingly all over the tree. Salvador staggers in the front yard regularly to parade his presence and often sits near the window in the dining room to watch for some passersby's intrusion. Many of these people seem to have known about the tree for ages and are showing up at the right time every year. When someone approaches and reaches for a fig, he yells, "It's not ripe yet." The intruder usually gets the message and scrams. Eventually Salvador hires a contractor to install a fence around the front yard. Still some people sneak in when the Rombles are not home, especially after dark, to snatch a few figs from the proud, tall tree that keeps tempting and daring everybody.

Despite the birds' feast and neighbours' fiesta, plenty of figs remain for the Rombles to enjoy. They eat relentlessly, give away plenty to friends and family, and make two dozen jars of jam. Salvador's digestive system has become too active and he visits the washroom several times every day compared to his regular constipation. Still, he cannot avoid all that delicious figs, even when his condition turns very close to diarrhoea, staining his shorts a few times, and Maggie making fun of him constantly for his greedy appetite and lack of self-control. The higher branches remain out of reach even with their twelve-foot ladder, yet he tries hard to reach them even at the risk of falling down and breaking his back. Plenty of figs rot on the tree or drop under it at the end of the summer. The immensity and fertility of the tree prove even beyond its vast appearance.

All the joy and commotion caused by the tree throughout the summer create a special bond between the Rombles and the fig tree. Now it is treated with a dignity parallel to its 'now-fully-justified' colossal size. For Salvador, in particular, the experience is somewhat divine, feeling ashamed occasionally of their plan to dismember such a fruitful member of the family. True, he had assumed that adopting a passive role about the destiny of the tree would diminish his responsibility for its demise. Yet, he despises his hypocrisy now. He had been guilty sitting idle and letting some idiots plan to kill such a magnificent tree just for the sake of the view, sunlight, or sales commission in the case of crooked Sheila. Now he abhors Sheila and her Mercedes even more.

The fig tree spreads its domain over the minds and hearts of the Rombles in addition to their house itself. It becomes the most sacred entity around the household. When a branch pokes inside an open window, they move it outside carefully and lay it against the side of the house before closing the window. Children are reminded repeatedly to refrain from breaking a branch or tearing a leaf. If the husband and wife disagree about so many issues, the safety of the tree, they agree, is a holy mission bestowed upon them from the heavens. Maggie enjoys Salvador's keen affection for the tree, since this romantic side of him has begun to affect their relationship in an unprecedented way as well. It seems the more figs he eats, the more passionate and horny he gets. *There must be some special potion in the figs,* she ponders with delight. *Just feed him more of this heavenly fruit every day and reap the rewards every night,* the devil inside her reiterates.

They upgrade the basement with major hassle. When a few walls and dead spaces are demolished to start the renovation, the fig tree's roots appear crawling over and around the foundation of the house. The sneaky roots under the ground are even curlier and scarier than the spooky branch shadows over and inside the house. The massive roots threaten the mere existence of the house, but also make the renovation project difficult and costly. Yet Salvador devises plans with painstaking diligence and directs the contractor to work around the roots to preclude harming them too much.

The fig tree keeps growing faster as if fuelled by the love of the Rombles. It expands its reign over the house by scattering its branches and roots leisurely above, under, inside, and around the house. By the following summer, some long, thick branches cover a good portion of the main entrance and everybody has to bend or lean against the patio wall to reach the main entrance. The higher branches push against the roof and some are putting dents in several parts of the outside walls. Still the Rombles put off cutting the branches since each one not only carries thousands of buds, but also is now quite strong and lively very much like the arms of a divine creature. *How could one bring himself to disfigure such an animate existence?* the Rombles often ponder. They remain apprehensive at the same time about the condition their eerie sentiment is gradually imposing upon them. The tree is slowly destroying the foundation and structure of the house. And the permit sits on the refrigerator collecting dust. The Rombles remember it as a delayed death sentence, yet avoid mentioning it, because they no longer have the heart or guts to act upon it. They hide their growing tension about the deteriorating situation, while hoping some miracle would resolve the matter automatically.

Two more fruitful summers pass despite the birds and beasts helping themselves relentlessly. Salvador and Maggie invent new methods of deterring the intruders, walk around it regularly, or guard the tree from inside the house. The heavy branches of the tree almost block off the front entrance and everybody uses the staircase on the side of the house to get in through the solarium.

Maggie asks Salvador one night unexpectedly, "Now that you've got your promotion, maybe we should look for a new house in West Vancouver?"

"Why? You don't like this house anymore?"

"Of course I do. But if we can afford a bigger house in a better location why shouldn't we go for it?"

"We could always check out the market."

Behind their seeming casual plans, the Rombles hide their real intention and their rising stress about the flourishing status of the tree in their lives—a looming disaster in the making. Although neither of them dares to express his or her true motive openly, they sense each other's silent desperation about the future of the house and the tree.

"Sheila can show us some houses then," Maggie says.

"Sheila again?"

"She got us a good deal last time. She knows about the history of this house, too. And…"

"What?"

"Nothing."

"Tell me…"

"She knows about the permit, too, and probably the need to renew it. If so, she's the only person who can do that, I'll say!"

"You mean the permit for the fig tree…"

"Yeah. A buyer may be found easier if the permit is ready, or, even better, if the tree is gone..."

"Maybe… Should we abandon this tree now?"

"I know it's hard… But we need a new house. We must think of ourselves as well," Maggie says timidly, still denying, even to herself, that the intruding fig tree is in fact the only motive behind her suggestion to move.

"I can never come back to this neighbourhood again if we sell the house. I don't want to know what might happen to the tree," Salvador says.

"Me neither."

"How can I live without figs after living like a king for five years?"

"They're probably two dollars each in the market nowadays."

"We'll never afford it again…" Salvador moans.

"You'd probably lose your passion toward me, too, right?"

"That'd be a big risk for you…! Do you still want to move?"

Maggie only sighs and walks away.

The sight of the fig tree blocking off the entrance shocks Sheila. She uses the staircase on the side of the house instead of the front door, but makes no comments in fear of annoying the Rombles. Avoiding discussions about the tree has become customary amongst all their friends and family. Nobody wishes to criticize the Rombles' bizarre attitude. Sheila promises to find them a good house in West Vancouver, assess the value of their present house, and check the validity of the five-year-old tree permit.

"I have good news all around," Sheila says when she returns one week later.

"Shoot…" Salvador whispers.

"First of all, the permit is still valid."

"Shoot! Don't they wanna check the tree again? It's grown a lot since we moved in," Salvador whines with disappointment.

"Yes, I've noticed that…! But I guess the City doesn't want the hassle of opening this can of worms again."

"What else?" Maggie asks.

"Your property can now be rezoned as a double lot."

"What does it mean?"

"It means you can build two houses on your lot now."

"Two houses?"

"Yeah. Two houses or a duplex."

"So we get more money for it now?" Salvador asks.

"Yes, if somebody wants to knock it down, cut the tree, and build two new houses."

Salvador forces himself to accept the inevitability of their situation and to stop feeling too guilty about his role regarding this matter. He really cannot do anything more about it, except alerting the buyer about the amount of figs and fun they have had every summer. Afterwards, it would be up to the new owner to decide about half a ton of figs every year. After five years of joy and torture, let the tree become someone else's responsibility and killing it be on someone else's conscience. Sticking to this house forever like a leech is nonsensical, especially under its present circumstance. The Rombles are ready to move.

In the following weeks, Sheila shows the Rombles several nice houses in West Vancouver and hints about a few developers interested in their house. The informal offers are not exciting, considering the sluggish housing market. But more importantly, Salvador insists on knowing the buyers' plans, although he had promised himself to stop fussing about the tree. He always finds out that the house and the tree would be knocked down to build two houses. Sheila reiterates that only developers are interested in their property and only because of its double-lot zoning.

The Rombles discuss the offers and fret over their indecision. They still hope to find a decent fig-loving family, quite naïve like them perhaps, to buy the house for dwelling as is, for the sake of the figs at least. However, deep down, they know they are only dreaming. They must get more realistic and decide soon before pissing off the brave developers willing to pay for the big lot and accept the headaches of demolishing the house and tree. *These kinds of adventurers do not grow on trees in millions like those figs,* Salvador ponders, but still cannot make up his mind.

The summer heat has lingered into the fall with no sign of rain. The dry weather and the daunting indecision have made the Rombles, especially Salvador, restless many nights. One night a dry storm approaches Vancouver and a hot wind blows outside the house as they toss and turn in bed. The burly branches of the fig tree rub angrily over the dead leaves and the cedar shingles on the roof, and against the house's cedar sidings. Some branches knock at the door hard with immense urgency, as if delivering an important plea or message. The thunder and lightning strike the house rampantly and the tree branches and leaves mimic horrific shapes and shadows outside the bedroom window. The house resembles an ancient, ghost-ridden manor. The branches slam the roof or the side of the house faster and harsher and create horrific sounds, like the screams of ghosts and goblins from a dungeon, as though the tree is tired of the turmoil it has caused the Rombles for so long.

Salvador smells smoke. He gazes with panic outside their bedroom window and notices a few tiny flames spreading fast over the trunk and branches of the tree. The noise and the sight of the fire alarm Maggie, too, and they run to the kitchen next to the solarium and the staircase. Salvador calls 911 before they all manage to escape the roaring flames that engulf the entire house quickly.

Standing in awe on the sidewalk, the Rombles watch the flames cover the tree with hurry. It appears to be saying goodbye to its faithful friends and apologizing for the agony it had caused them for years. And then its blazing branches and trunk faint on the house and together they turn into ashes soon after the fire trucks arrive. Only a pile of debris remains amidst a big lot as the Rombles still wait on the sidewalk in bewilderment. The shock from the loss of their house, belongings, and their beloved fig tree, all in a matter of twenty minutes, mixes with an air of relief about the tree itself solving the dilemma they had struggled with for five years. To Rombles, this dramatic ending actually seems like a glorious act of self-sacrifice by the fig tree—spreading its branches widely to help the flames move up its humongous trunk quickly, gain momentum, and burn that beautiful tree terminally.

The following summer, the Rombles move to their new house on the west side of the lot. With the insurance money and a bank loan, they have built two houses on the lot and sold the one on the east side. The profit from the project has covered the cost of their new cosy house with a good view of the city. Their only grim sensation is the memory of the old fig tree, especially the sight of burning itself down reverently for a divine cause, like Tibetan monks, before tumbling over the house. They miss its immense presence around the house.

"Salvador, come here for a second," Maggie yells while strolling in their cute new garden.

"What is it? I'm busy…" Salvador replies with impatience.

"Why are you so grumpy again today? Did you finish all the figs I bought for you two days ago?"

"Of course, I did. How long do you suggest I should take to eat two dozen figs?"

"Never mind…! I'll buy you some more when I go shopping this week, but now come here for a minute."

"What do you want? Can't you leave me alone for a second even?" Salvador asks upon approaching Maggie. She stands next to a three-foot plant sticking out of a heap of tulips.

"This thing… What is this?"

"Oh… that… Last year I took a few shoots from the old fig tree and planted them around the house. I guess this is one of them. The rest didn't survive the construction activities."

"So, this is the fig tree's baby?"

"Yeah, look at the leaves. This is our new fig tree. Let's make sure nobody damages it," Salvador says with excitement.

"Here we go again…" Maggie replies with a grin and great anticipation. She thinks she must work very hard to make the tree grow fast and start giving them enough figs to save their marriage before Salvador goes totally cuckoo!

*****

I am supposedly Salvador in this tale, with a grouchy personality, although I admire his sensitive side these days, becoming so much more passionate about plants and animals, while he learns more about, and regrets, humans' crude nature and naiveté every day! I enjoy all this enlightenment almost as much as I love figs. The prospects for a promising relationship with my wife during that five-year period had also felt delightful. Not having to whine too much awhile, thanks to my improved marital life probably, had been a big relief for me. Still, even then I often could not stop pondering the absurdity of the life I was leading. I wished I could quiet my brain more often as well, instead of only keeping my big mouth shut, mostly by shoving more figs into it, just in hopes of saving my marriage.

Sadly, the new fig tree did not grow and fruit fast enough to prevent my subsequent marital setbacks! Apparently, even figs could not help my mood much those days, while poor Maggie kept buying lots of them non-stop with great hopes!

Howe Sound

Atop a remote cliff overlooking Howe Sound, Jeremy Hamilton is suddenly inspired to become a professional painter, *for real this time,* as if struck by a jolt of awakening. Becoming a true artist at his age feels weird, however, although he had wrestled with this idea before on several occasions in the past for various reasons. When single, he had actually painted a few odd objects, like skulls, for fun and maybe even making some money. This was when he was new in Vancouver and could not find a decent job. He bursts into laughter recalling the comical, somewhat forced exhibition of his art pieces in a reasonably reputable gallery for ten days. What was the name of the gallery, he muses, cursing his lethargic memory these days due to aging and marital quarrels. *Oh, gosh, what's wrong with my memory? What was the name of the Gallery's owner!* Jeremy murmurs with a chuckle. *He was a lost soul as well, so pathetic around women, maybe like myself these days. What happened to me?*

Jeremy looks into the horizon once more and sighs when this swift freaky urge to paint the serene scenery before him agitates him again. He has never painted a landscape, not even a leaf, let alone a tree, never mind the whole forest; or an ocean as today's subject. But now this heavenly view has possessed him out of the blue, as though bestowed with a sacred mission. He wishes he had a pad and pencil to start sketching the view right away. Yeah, the notion of becoming a real painter feels so serious this time! It is nothing at all similar to those old whims.

More importantly, a mystical peace has replaced his daylong anxiety and he is not angry at the whole world anymore. Only two hours before, he had left home after a nasty row with Lorie. He had driven up Marine Drive, the winding road to Horseshoe Bay, and stopped at Whytecliff Park with the aim of making a decision about his mangled marriage: to leave Lorie and their children that he has always loved so dearly despite their growing snootiness, or end his life. It simply did not make sense for him or Lorie driving each other crazy with their vile accusations and too frequent clashes. Enough was enough!

Jeremy shifts his butt a bit to the left to give it a relief. He has been sitting on that rugged rock for an hour. He raises his head and glances again at Howe Sound that stretches majestically in the horizon. *Gosh, who am I kidding? I can never paint such an intricate mood.* Again, a perplexing inkling soothes his annoying old cynicism: *Maybe I can do it!* Jeremy ponders and bursts into laughter light-heartedly. *I must paint this scenery…*

A gloomy day… A big cluster of dark, loaded clouds crowds the cobalt sky. A shapely interlaced mountain formation in the horizon resembles a line of steppingstones over the ocean linking Bowen Island to Horseshoe Bay. A pinkish haze saturates the colours of plantations dressing the mountains. Another mix of glorifying hues diffuses some violet rays on the cloud tufts, and scatters a soft, soothing reflection over the Bay. A few glitters of purple and ultramarine mingle merely a touch above the water, making a vast area of the ocean appear solid like a china dish. Jeremy imagines a stone striking the surface of the water would only clink and bounce a few times before settling smoothly on the glistening ocean surf. Far out, near the horizon, a tiny sailboat stands still like a *white dot* in the middle of the vast universe. At that moment, Howe Sound resembles the whole universe to him, with the wee white dot further exaggerating its glory and enigma. Then again, the overwhelming ambiance, including the menacing clouds, is reverently romantic.

He wonders why the sailboat is out there in this weather and who is inside it. In a fleeting trance, he imagines himself all alone in the boat's cabin at the centre of the universe. The image surges another wave of serenity within him. A shallow breeze rustles the nearby leaves and branches, and he believes the clouds shuffled slightly, too.

Jeremy gazes at the scenery for another half an hour, until the daylight dies and gradually the horizon becomes a blur. He can hardly discern the formation of the mountains or the location of the boat. He hopes that whoever is in the cabin is safe and knows what he is doing out there this late with a storm possibly gushing in the Bay any minute. A fantastic thought enters his mind: Maybe a man and a woman in the cabin are so deeply in love they do not realize what time it is, how fast the light has faded, and how dangerous a sudden storm may be. Or maybe they know, but their love is so powerful they do not care about the consequences, not even if they die in each other's arms that very instant. He wishes he were the man.

But he is not the lucky man, and it is now time for him to go home, back to reality, in the bosom of his nagging wife. He moves away from the edge of the cliff carefully, as his body feels numb after sitting in one spot for so long. But his mind is clear now: Suicide is out of the question and arguing with Lorie must stop. He should simply learn to tolerate the situation even more than before. Now he has more energy and spiritual wisdom to control his ego and temper. He must also commit himself to paint the scenery he has engraved into the deepest channels of his brain so diligently. He must paint the scenery that seems to have changed his perspective so swiftly and made him feel alive again. But how? He is not a landscape painter, he reminds himself again in the car, driving home with a grin cracking all over his face.

Yes, yes, I must learn 'perfection' and I will paint that scenery when I am ready. I must do it to survive. I will.

Lorie looks anxious but fully freshened up with makeup, hot red lipstick, and brushed silky hair. It is so damn difficult to grasp this woman, one minute roaring like a tiger, then purring like a timid pussycat the next minute, as if I should not remember her vicious words and insults, Jeremy thinks while sizing her up. His relaxed mood and smirk feel peculiar and annoying to her, assuming the worst regarding his whereabouts the last four hours and looking so happy after such nasty argument between them earlier this afternoon. At last, she controls her itch to attack him again. She pretends to be busy around the family room and kitchen, making a racket, while Jeremy finds some food and eats it voluptuously during a boxing match on TV before turning in.

This afternoon's enlightenment has boosted Jeremy's sexual appetite, too. He believes he must firstly test his newly gained self-confidence and self-control. Second, he should train his fussy sexual drive to be more forgiving of his lousy relationship with Lorie and actually help him make love to her now *right away*. He succeeds under the sceptical, yet encouraging, response by Lorie. She believes all that makeup she had so meticulously put on her face that evening had done the trick. *I did it again... Am I smart or what?* she ponders proudly. *And gorgeous too, of course!* When she falls asleep with her regular loud snore, Jeremy muses again over the way a childlike urge to paint is boosting his mood and relationship with his family so quickly. What is behind all these mysterious feelings overwhelming him today? He ponders the possibility of Howe Sound's grandeur having swept his mind away to a sphere where one merges with the universe. The other possibility is that his mind had been desperately seeking a refuge, a means of coping with the harsh reality of his life, especially the nagging wife. He had thought only of separation or suicide, but then God had offered him a third option so unimaginable before this deep urge to paint artistically had emerged.

But now what? Despite the amazing awakening, he is still doubtful about his new mission. One thing remains certain though: He must maintain his good mood through meditation, to learn to paint, to paint the scenery that has boosted his spirits and shaken his monotonous life. The details of the seascape appear to have been etched vividly in his brain. Recalling such minutiae is a miracle all by itself for a person who seldom remembers even simple things, like, for instance, where he left his sunglasses or car keys. All these revelations today at Howe Sound are good omens, as if his hidden potentials were manifesting curiously at last. *Have I matured in a matter of minutes?*

Naturally, earning the calibre to paint such a breathtaking mood would be a huge challenge. But first, he must overcome an even more insurmountable obstacle: He must justify his urge to paint to his insensitive family and himself. He has always been a pragmatic person, only pursuing financially rewarding activities. 'Why would you like to become a painter?' people would ask. 'Aren't there enough hungry and heartbroken artists in this world already?'

Answering these rational questions, especially to his super demanding family, would be awkward. A main cause of their arguments has been family budget. He works hard all day and some nights, yet there is never enough money for the extravagant lifestyle his family demands of him. So how can he justify not only the cost of lessons and painting supplies, but also the time spent on painting instead of being out there somewhere making more money? This is a serious hurdle, a great potential for the next round of commotion as soon as Lorie finds out about his intentions.

So how should he approach the matter? Jeremy wonders in the darkness of the bedroom with Lorie's snore now reaching a new height. *This is the reward I get for making her so happy, twice, with my fresh emotions and sexual stamina.* He recalls his past 'positive thinking' schemes to keep his life bearable. Sadly, all those exercises and efforts to curb his niggling inner conflicts and outer demands of the family have proven futile. But now, suddenly, disregarding his family's raw judgment and believing in himself to learn painting at a master level are the most 'positive thoughts' he has entertained so convincingly in his entire life. Now he is electrified in the middle of the night, unable to sleep. Yes, he should paint Howe Sound even if it would be the last thing on earth he must ever do. He would die of depression and desperation otherwise; so why concern himself about his family's reaction.

Jeremy leaps out of the bed, reels to the kitchen, and drinks a glass of cold water. He lurches to the study, sketches the scene of Howe Sound as faithfully as he remembers, and makes notes about the colours, the boat, and his feeling in that divine moment. Writing about all those colours and his emotions that afternoon makes him feel so romantic and elated already. *Maybe I'm now becoming a poet too!* He hides all those sketches and poetic notes in his briefcase before returning to bed, thrilled that the painting mission is launched, and nothing and nobody can stop him now. Still, instead of confronting his family with the shocking news, he decides to break it to them diplomatically. He is not going to quit his job to become a painter, not tomorrow at least. So why not find a way to impose his desire gradually and indirectly one way or another. On this positive note, he falls asleep immediately, right after a short pause to ponder and purge his crazy urge to awaken Lorie to make love to her again.

To Jeremy's amazement, his yearning to paint is still intact in the morning. His mood remains upbeat all day at work to the surprise of his colleagues who have not seen him so buoyant for ages. He jokes with everybody and makes fast decisions, while musing over the idea and ideal of becoming a real painter. Actually, the matter sounds more exciting and tranquilizing every minute. Even more thrilling is the sly scheme he contrives for fooling his rigid family about his ultimate intention. He finds an art store near his office and buys a large supply of acrylic paints, papers, and brushes. He borrows some books from Vancouver library, too, and studies 'painting in acrylics' in the privacy of his office during lunch hours. All along, his enthusiasm to put his fresh knowledge into practice drives him nuts. 'Patience, patience, my friend,' Jeremy allays his animated spirit while playing with the dry brushes, moving them around the white paper as if painting a real picture. That is the best he can do for two weeks.

Finally, he brings the painting supplies home along with a book—*How to Draw and Paint*. He gives the package to Judy, his youngest daughter, as her tenth birthday present. She has shown interest in painting, which gives any devoted father a duty to nourish! Lorie supports the project, too, by assigning a corner of the study for painting. She buys an easel for Judy and finds a small table for laying out the painting supplies.

Occasionally, Jeremy sneaks over Judy's works on the easel and admires them, though they all seem still too crude to him, of course. He is developing a good sense of art after reading so many books and surveying the pictures of the Masters' paintings. He notices often that Judy has not cleaned the brushes properly or has dropped them in the jar with the bristles pressing against the bottom of the jar. So he washes them again and puts them upside down in the jar.

Despite his ulterior motive, Jeremy is excited about getting Judy involved in art. He hopes to use this opportunity to improve the father-daughter relationship, too, perhaps even paint together and motivate each other. Being a mentor for Judy, *supposedly,* would at least be a great excuse for him to start painting himself! Once he tries to explain a few pointers to her about painting in hopes of initiating their artistic bond, which might hopefully work better than their failing genetic connection so far.

"See Judy, I'm hoping that I…, I mean you, work with oil paints soon," he say softly with great enthusiasm.

"Okay… We'll see…" Judy murmurs edgily.

"But it's easier to work with acrylics first. It dries quickly, so you don't have to wait a long time or mess up your work by smudging the wet paint. Also, it's better that you need only water for medium, instead of smelly linseed oil and mineral spirits."

"Yeah, I know all that," Judy replies impatiently, examining the brushes listlessly.

"So, do you know how to take care of the brushes?" Jeremy asks, somewhat concerned about the brushes he would be using soon himself. He cannot think of any excuse to buy new brushes, either, if Judy keeps wrecking them quickly!

"Yeah…!"

"How?"

"I wash them with soap," Judy replies.

"Water is enough if you get the paint out completely. Soap will damage the brushes."

"Okay… No soap!"

"And then?"

"And then what?" Judy shrieks with frustration.

"Dear Judy, my beautiful daughter, I'm only trying to help. There's no need to get snotty," Jeremy says calmly with the kind of affection he believes Lorie has always neglected to recognize about him and maybe even publicizing around the family at least, too. Handling three teenage daughters and a son has been a big challenge for Jeremy. They do not even acknowledge his right of existence, let alone his authority. They have learned good lessons from Lorie about treating him so poorly and passively. Whenever he complains to Lorie about the matter, her response is even more infuriating: 'Because they don't see any affection from you. What have you ever done for them?'

"But, Dad… I told you I know all this stuff," Judy replies.

"All right. Instead of arguing with me, you could answer my question. I'm only trying to find a project for us to do together."

"I don't need help, Dad. I wanna do it alone."

"Okay, okay…" Jeremy says and leaves the study with angst. He knows that trying to convince Judy or waiting around another minute would only result in Lorie hearing them and rushing over to scream at him herself as well, 'Leave the child alone…'

For two weeks, Jeremy monitors the situation from a distance. Finally, home alone one Saturday afternoon, Jeremy believes his time to start some real landscape painting has come. He has two hours to awaken his neglected genius before his family returns. He fills two glass jars with water for washing the brushes and thinning the paint, and pulls the photograph he had hidden in his briefcase to use for practice at this point. It shows a dozen ducks swimming in the pond at Stanley Park, plenty of bushes, a couple of trees, and a line of daffodils across the bank. Although he knows that doing a sketch and drawing an outline on the paper are *supposedly* necessary, he decides to skip these mundane steps and go directly to the heart of the matter—putting paint on paper. Besides, he must hurry. He does not have too much time before the family returns. Jeremy struggles for two hours, then cleans up his mess and hides the painted paper in a safe corner for now, before somebody catches him in action.

The following weeks witness Judy's loss of interest in painting and Jeremy's tense sneaky attempts to paint when his family is absent. All along, he reminisces about those good old times when he, as a carefree young man, had fooled around painting stuff without answering to anyone about how he preferred to use his spare time and life, or worrying so much about money. Now he has to sneak around like an intruder in his own house and he must answer to a million people, just for making a living and engaging in an adventure as innocent as painting.

He senses some progress, but still nothing looks right or straight. He cannot figure out why his landscapes do not have proper dimensions or depth. He agonizes over the brushstrokes, mixing colours, and the volume of medium for developing each aspect of the painting. Thus, he reads more books and practises persistently with angst until his family finally catches him in the middle of one of his fervent shows of artistry when they arrive home one day rather unexpectedly. Actually, he is too involved and frustrated that afternoon to worry about getting caught.

"So now you're painting yourself?" Lorie asks mockingly as she passes by the study and notices him hard at work in a pitiable shape.

"I wanna motivate Judy more somehow."

"And this is the way you can do it?" Lorie asks with sarcasm.

"Yes… I want to show her that only perseverance pays off," Jeremy replies with a guilty conscience.

Lorie and Judy enter the study and survey his work. Lorie does not hide her contempt, witnessing a middle-aged man losing his sanity and wasting time on such a childish endeavour like a kindergartener.

"Is this the result of your perseverance, my darling?" Lorie says sarcastically, staring at his masterpiece with a smirk.

"Well, I'm just starting… But it's not too bad, is it?" Jeremy asks like a child seeking some form of approval from his cheeky mommy.

She only glares at him and his painting, before exchanging mocking grins with Judy.

Jeremy loathes the expression in her eyes, silence, shaking her head, and leading Judy out of the room, then staring at him again at the door pitifully. He is humiliated but happy that at least the genie is out of the bottle. No more need for secrecy, which means painting whenever he gets a chance regardless of his family's attitude. Yet, he is caught off guard a few days later when his family arrives home and finds him painting arduously again.

"You're using all of Judy's paints and supplies!" Lorie yells.

Jeremy is startled, but adheres to his novel wisdom to dismiss her absurd comment. Then two nights later, Judy notices him during another one of his painting struggles and yells, "Mom…, Daddy is using all my supplies again."

Lorie comes to the study, anchors her hands on her hips, glares at Jeremy, and awaits a valid response from him.

"Well, nobody else seems interested in using them. I've spent money on these supplies and can't let them go to waste," Jeremy replies innocently and convincingly.

Knowing Jeremy's obsession for waste management, Lorie leaves quietly. His response has indeed been more than valid and ingenious! It is a genuine excuse, in line with years of heartfelt performance. When grocery or leftovers are about to rot or reach their expiry dates, he eats them before Lorie discards them so ruthlessly. He believes nobody in his household realizes the value of money and the evil of waste. He works his ass off and listens to all kinds of nonsense all day from his arrogant colleagues and boss to make money and then his selfish, daft family wastes it as if he is photocopying those bills at the print shop. The lights, computers, and appliances are left on for hours needlessly. He must go around all the time to turn them off and eat the rotting fruits and food. He has also been getting fatter and angrier every day, while struggling with his obsession to prevent waste when so many people around the world are dying of famine daily. His complaints have proven futile, too, so he has stopped lecturing them about buying too much stuff in the first place, beyond their consumption capacity. He recalls an incident when Lorie caught him eating the rotting fruits dutifully. Instead of appreciating his sacrifice, she merely screamed at him mockingly, "What's the point, anyway... They're all coming out from you other end!"

That is how vulgar and stupid Lorie is, he ponders and giggles as Judy appears out of nowhere and stands stiff before him, after Lorie's provocation and warning apparently: that Judy's growing apathy to paint prevents her from arguing with Jeremy about his use of the painting supplies instead of letting them go to waste.

"What? What do you want now?" Jeremy asks tensely.

"I *should* paint now," Judy says with stress for being in the middle of this nonsense—getting pushed by her mom to paint, all because of her dad's obsession to avoid waste.

"Okay, I'm done," Jeremy says while cleaning the palette and brushes. He believes that Judy's sudden urge to paint is only a fleeting impulse. He would not have to worry about Judy ever getting serious and thus nullifying his excuse for consuming the painting supplies. He is ecstatic about inventing such a scheme—

a foolproof rationale. He would soon return to paint and nobody would dare to stop him. Nobody would suspect for a second that he is painting for a more divine purpose. He would paint because this family, in this case Judy, has no sense of discipline to pursue a worthwhile project, now forcing him to become a prominent painter just for the sake of avoiding waste. Actually, he keeps buying more supplies every few weeks and adding them to the existing pile stealthily, so it appears never running out. That is a tricky scheme he must now manage on the side smoothly without raising Judi's suspicion! *Gosh, what a tough project this painting has become for me!*

During her casual attempts, Judy paints a nice landscape in fact, which makes Jeremy both proud and perturbed. *She paints so effortlessly. She's surely inherited my artistic knack! So why are these kids so lazy and careless about their potentials crying for attention?* He is genuinely sorry about his failure to motivate Judy. Before his awakening, art had felt only a means of fooling around or indulging oneself occasionally, maybe painting a pot or a skull, wandering in a museum one afternoon, or possibly going to a concert. He had always pitied the poor artists wasting their lives away in pursuit of such futile purposes, the same way Lorie is feeling about him these days. So, he cannot really blame Lorie for thinking and behaving like a normal person that he himself had been until recently. Now, however, he honestly believes that art is the only source of relief and freedom; and that almost all other human endeavours are worthless, tainted, or unnatural. No wonder our primitive ancestors realized intuitively that they must somehow paint the pictures of all those animals and other stuff all over their tiny caves with so much effort. It was such a heartfelt thing to do, and not because they intended to leave us just some jumbled pictures of animals as their incredible discoveries. What other impulse, other than a divine urge, could have goaded them? *Here, I saw a cow one day. Here, I saw a deer the next day. Guess what? I saw an eagle last week too.* Nonetheless, only for this once, Jeremy is slyly happy that Judy is lazy.

Soon, Jeremy's prediction prevails. Lorie's efforts to motivate Judy fail, too, and soon the painting corner in the study remains amply empty. Not even any variety of Lories' waste-threats can curb Judy's resolve to fight back these sorts of nonsense. Enough was enough! In fact, she feels obliged to resist her silly parents' pressures despite her craving to paint. *I can always learn to paint later,* Judy muses slyly. *But right now, my main job is to teach these loonies that they cannot push me around. Now, fighting is more important before things get really out of control!*

Anyhow, Judy's smart thinking affords Jeremy the immense opportunity to paint without concern about his family's sarcastic remarks. His progress becomes tangible, yet it seems he could still climb Mt. Everest before turning into a true artist. He keeps painting the ducks in the Lost Lagoon at Stanley Park, but the ducks still look more like frogs and the blue pond resembles a swamp with dead smudgy colours supposedly representing the delicate reflections and lilies. *Why is landscape so hard to paint when I was so good with the skulls' paintings?*

Two months later, finally Jeremy thinks that his recent works are coming close to perfection. Nobody would notice the small flaws that his ultra-sensitive artistic mind detects here and there. So he feels ready to enrich the entire world with his artistry—a 16 by 20 inches canvas. All along, he has hidden his paintings from the family for the right moment and ignored their stares full of pity and mockery. They have believed all along that he was only fooling around with paint and paper. They simply hope all those supplies are soon consumed before Jeremy's sanity is. *Oh, what a bunch of morons, teasing my artistic gift, unaware what pleasant surprise awaits them,* Jeremy chuckles privately.

Jeremy buys an expensive frame and falls in love all over with his masterpiece after realizing how effectively a frame manifests the depth of a picture. The framed painting is ready for prominent curators to discover his genius and artistry, to see what they have been missing all these years, but first his family. Let them be bowled over pleasantly. He puts it at the foot of the fireplace mantle in the living room so that Lorie can decide about the best spot for hanging it in that large room. Actually, one or two of the existing pictures on the walls should be removed to open up a large space for a true art—the one sitting there ready for Lorie's amazement. It would actually be an insult to have those imperfect artworks even remotely near his masterpiece. Deep in his fantasy, admiring his creation from afar, Lorie steps in the living room through the dinning room and notices the painting.

"I hope you don't intend to hang this thing anywhere in this house?" she exclaims.

"Why? Isn't it good?" Jeremy asks in absolute disbelief.

"Don't you have any sense yourself anymore? What is this a picture of, anyway?"

"It's Stanley Park, and those are ducks roaming around the pond," Jeremy explains timidly.

"They look more like dogs running in the pasture."

"No, they're not running. Those aren't their legs. Those are ducks' reflections on water," he explains, almost bursting into tears by so much insult.

"Get Judy to help you," Lorie blurts with a smirk, then yells, "Hey, kids, come see your dad's masterpiece."

Jeremy's world collapses swiftly. All his dreams dissolve into a dreadful despair and shame. He hides the painting quickly and leaves the house after his kids get a chance to mock him as well. He drives aimlessly, but soon finds himself on the same cliff at Whytecliff Park where he had been initially inspired to become a real artist five months earlier. Like a guru returning to the sacred mountain to cleanse his mind and body after committing a sin, he stares at Howe Sound and recalls the memories of that fateful afternoon when he had intended to commit suicide, but instead had been inspired to become a painter. Now what? If he cannot even be a painter then maybe he must commit suicide, after all. Now he has even more reasons to do so. Not only his relationship with Lorie is still murky, but also he has proven again incapable of being an artist, not to mention the humiliation of confronting his family later after they saw that horrible thing. *What was I thinking? What is the matter with my mind and senses? Am I in fact going crazy?*

The sky is clear and the ocean in turmoil with the wind. There is no haze in the horizon or a sign of a sailboat floating in the middle of the universe in total seclusion. Jeremy notices a wild bush grown at the edge of the cliff. *How could this tiny, pretty thing grow out of such sturdy rock? Is there life and soil inside that solid surface?* As he touches its leaf, however, a thunderous thrill surges inside him and he feels attached to Nature with some unprecedented sentiments. He can suddenly feel, see, and smell the nature surrounding him in a much clearer perspective with full consciousness and respect. He can see colours and shapes he has never envisioned before. It is a real awakening this time by the way he sees the depth and beauty of Nature and feels his deep connection to it. The wide view of Howe Sound both enlightens and entertains his soul. A spiritual ecstasy floods his veins fast and he shivers with goose bumps needling his entire body. A heavy lump in his throat hinders his breathing, some tears slither down his face, and he bursts into bawling in the privacy of the cliff. The burdens of life and his failures sip out of his body and, in two minutes, he is empty of worries or haughty desires. He realizes the pettiness of his existence, thoughts, and values in the light of a supreme wisdom surging within him after touching the leaf of the wild bush.

There is definitely something special about this cliff, the one he has come to today for the second time. The first time, it had triggered his devout urge to become a painter. However, today's awakening has been even deeper, opening his mind and vision to an entire new world, where he can feel and perceive things with a pious passion. Five months before, he was inspired to become a painter, and today he is inspired as a painter. Now he realizes that no matter how good he paints the nature, he would never be able to portray the beauty he feels beyond his five senses this minute.

Nobody can paint what Nature means to him now or manifest for him. By the virtue of his new enlightenment, he is now as humble about his existence as he is eager to paint. Now he realizes and admits wholeheartedly how rubbish his paintings and efforts have been, as he can only now see at least some of the meanings and secrets of Nature. Now, only if he can somehow capture some of these values and perceptions, he may have a chance to paint something significant.

A soft blow of crisp air, moistened over the surface of the ocean, caresses his face while he lingers at the top of the cliff and observes the rapid mood transformations in the horizon of Howe Sound. Half an hour later, Jeremy starts toward home with great drive and designs. Under his curious family's astonished eyes, he burns all his paintings in the backyard and then piles up the paints and brushes in a plastic bag and throws it in the garbage.

Courageously and casually, he also announces to his family that he is not giving up painting, but rather getting too serious about it to fool around with low quality material or keep flawed paintings. Indeed, he does not need any supplies for sometime until he feels mentally ready. He would do everything properly from now on and possibly take private lessons, too. The family is too intimidated by his actions and tone of voice to protest or even peep. But deep down they believe he has finally gone berserk and nobody can save him now. Actually, they had sort of predicted this episode—Jeremy's utter lunacy if painting supplies do not run out fast enough! So now, they just have to wait and witness his final mental demise if he keeps disregarding the futility of his childish urges. Lorie wonders whether she has pushed this poor man too much over the years to cause this kind of madness. *Maybe we could've tried harder to show him just a bit sympathy before all this happened!* For a person so fussy about 'waste,' throwing all those supplies out is by itself a definite sign of his absolute sudden insanity.

Well, he is a goner, Lorie thinks with stress, and I cannot help the situation. I must worry only about myself and leave him then.

Jeremy feels that going to the cliff at Whytecliff Park every few weeks improves his vision of Nature. It also reinforces his resolve to become an artist despite his humble realization that he can never paint anything as perfect as his mind can perceive now. He photographs the sceneries evoking good painting compositions in his mind. After completing the planned period of meditation and erudition, he buys all kinds of supplies to start painting on canvas in oil. He paints a large cliff at Stanley Park, next to a desiccated tree, inhabited by seagulls. He remembers his vow to paint Howe Sound, which has been his initial source of inspiration. However, before tackling such an intricate subject, especially to incorporate the haze, dim light, and glorious colours of the mountains and the Bay, he must practise more with less complicated compositions first to improve his technique and confidence.

He puts the painting of the cliff and seagulls in the corner of the foyer to assess it under natural light, which shines abundantly through the skylight. It would be ideal to paint outdoors to render the true daylight colours, but that is too much hassle if one is not living in countryside. *Oh, how difficult painting is if one wishes to remain even partially faithful to Nature.*

"You did this painting?" Lorie asks as she stops in the foyer on her way upstairs. Jeremy is startled and rushes to collect the painting. He had not meant for anybody to see it yet.

"Yes, why?" Jeremy asks.

"It's nice. This one you can hang in the living room."

"Thanks, but I don't think it's good enough."

"Why?"

"It's still not quite together. The ambience isn't vivid enough."

"It looks very good to me."

"No… It's not yet an effective painting overall," Jeremy says solemnly, although he sounds constructive rather than moaning. "I should solve the problems and improve the ambience or throw it away."

"Throw it away? Do you always have to contradict me? Now that I say something nice about your painting, you reject my judgment and want to throw it away?" Lorie says with temper and leaves.

Filled with mixed feelings, Jeremy collects the painting and puts it back on the easel. He is flattered by Lorie's compliment, but flustered for his inability to tackle the problem in the painting. After his second inspiration on the cliff, he is now too sensitive about the tiniest flaws in paintings, especially landscapes that must reflect the grace of Nature. His new bottleneck is emerging: He detects more flaws faster than he can fix them. He does not have the technical expertise to rectify the problems easily, either. Sometimes it takes days and weeks before he is rather satisfied. 'Relatively' only, though, because when he revisits a completed painting in a few days, he finds yet more faults in it. He is also seeking a better effect in his next painting, in line with his deeper visions, which never seems sufficient on canvas in his demanding mind.

Ten months and twenty paintings later, his efforts to become a worthy painter only brings him frustration, yet he remains unable to renounce his passion. Worst of all, he does not still dare to paint the view of Howe Sound that he has been postponing to such time when fulfilling this sacred mission feels plausible. By Lorie's encouragement, he has framed a few of his paintings for hanging in the living room at last, including the cliff and seagulls painting after he fixed its mood. Friends and foes congratulate and encourage him to participate in competitions and art shows, but he rejects their compliments, sometimes rudely, on account that his paintings are still raw. He goes to galleries, finds many faults with those paintings, too, and then suffers because of it. He is often ready to start an argument with gallery staff or owners for allowing such displays of human self-absorption in the name of art, not to mention the insult to Nature. One time, in particular, he finds himself in the Edward's gallery and arguing with the owner, Edward, tensely about most of the displayed paintings. The frail, old Edward is shocked and humiliated, while struggling in his head to remember whether he knows this man—Jeremy—from somewhere. He looks terribly familiar to Edward and raises bad memories, too!

The only good thing about Jeremy's critical view of art is that now Lorie finds his sense of romanticism and vulnerability quite intriguing once more—something that she has been missing in him in recent years again after improving for a while. He is edgy sometimes with his critical mind and approach, but she enjoys his dependence on her to calm his roaring emotions. They feel closer despite their personal differences and annoying habits. Jeremy appreciates Lorie's indirect influence and support for painting— something he had not anticipated. Painting has become his true passion and Lorie's patience is invaluable. And they both are learning about art, too, which by itself has become a new source for enriching their souls and relationship. Lorie takes one of his paintings, without his prior knowledge, to a reputable gallery to solicit their opinion. They show interest in exhibiting it and in fact sell it within a week after Lorie asks for Jeremy's permission to do so. After this lucrative sale, in particular, Lorie has become a full-fledged promoter and supporter of Jeremy, and in return, he appreciates these new developments overcoming some of their earlier marital conundrums.

Overall, life is improving for Hamiltons and Jeremy is starting to believe in his talent as a painter, until the night they visit their friends. Vivian Marchon has been taking lessons from prominent painters for fifteen years and her paintings ornament their house walls. She has surely been working hard, but she does not seem to be inspired the way an artist must be blessed naturally. Hard work and practice are crucial, but, without a genuine juice within a person, all those efforts would be futile, Jeremy ponders grimly. *Only one absorbed in Nature can become a true artist.*

"Am I like her?" he whispers to Lorie with tension.

"No…Your paintings have soul," Lorie murmurs. "And also ambience," she adds quickly, since she knows how much Jeremy likes and uses the word 'ambience' these days.

"Aren't her paintings adorable?" Mike Marchon asks proudly. Vivian, leaving the room to fetch coffee, rushes back, anxious to hear their guests' verdict. Especially, respecting Jeremy's artistic and critical mind, his verbal and facial expressions would be too precious for her to miss.

"They're nice, Vivian," Lorie says hastily, fearful of Jeremy's cynical feedback devastating Vivian. Hearing the truth might be helpful for her or not, but she does not want to witness Mike's and Vivian's world crashing tonight on their account. She is quite certain that Jeremy would at least mention the lack of *ambience* in her paintings! *Now even she knows well what ambience means and how terribly missing in Vivian's paintings!*

Jeremy, anxious and about to deliver his honest opinion, gets the clue from Lorie and stops his big mouth in time. Vivian keeps staring at him, though, waiting for his verdict.

"Yeah, they're good. But I'm no expert," Jeremy says at last with gloom. "I have enough trouble judging my own paintings."

"I think this is her masterpiece," Mike interjects excitedly, pointing to the painting framed above the mantelpiece, at the prime spot of the living room. "Come check out the brushstrokes she's managed."

"Yeah, I can see them from here," Jeremy says impatiently. "I don't think I can ever do that." *I hope not,* he muses. He then turns to Lorie, who is also gauging the painting with pain. They exchange bewildered glances before returning to their seats with guilt and despair.

"You really think they're good?" Vivian asks with stress and everybody nods politely. She leaves the room reluctantly in baby steps to fetch the coffee she had promised them long ago. She remains sceptical about Jeremy's lacklustre approval and the low conviction in his words. A nagging voice whispers in her mind, *Maybe they are all teasing you, Vivian, especially Mike? Maybe Mike's trying to drive you crazy?*

Mike's motive to admire Vivian's lousy paintings appears suspicious to Jeremy, too. Yet even more depressing is the way it triggers Jeremy's own insecurity. His inner conflicts about the purpose of painting, even when others admire his works, explode that night. As a pragmatist, he must legitimize his pursuits in life; and now he does not have any for painting. Even the fact that some of his paintings were sold in reputable galleries does not give him the assurance he needs. 'What those gallery owners and buyers know about real art?' he wonders. Why should he paint when he is never satisfied fully with the outcome of his works? The rewards are still minimal, anyway, considering the amount of time and effort an artist puts into each painting and marketing it; especially after paying 40-60% commission to galleries. Then why should he struggle to paint a landscape, and then suffer from the thought of having insulted Nature, too? *Am I getting crazy or too romantic in my old age, or merely too uptight again?* Jeremy wonders.

Now that Lorie no longer nags about him wasting time on painting, he cannot stop torturing himself all alone. Despite his relatively quiet marital life in the last three years, his persistent cynicism prevents him from enjoying life. Obviously, Lorie's support is precious. Her praise, comments, framing his works for display around the house, all the tasty figs she keeps buying only for him, and bragging about him to their friends and family, they all seem genuine most often. *But maybe Lorie is contriving the same game that Mike is playing with Vivian. Maybe that is Lorie's way of driving me crazy if not merely my own uptightness molesting my poor psyche again?* Time has come for a serious meditation to make a final decision about painting. Maybe it is time to quit painting in order to revere Nature and the universe more closely and truthfully in some meaningful ways. Meditation would be a more direct and divine pursuit for any intelligent man, instead of imprisoning himself indoor and spending so much time looking at pictures and playing with paints. Maybe I should get out of the house more often to embrace Nature, instead of wasting my life hoping to replicate it on canvas. *Maybe putting those feelings into words and poetry is diviner than painting, too!*

One Sunday afternoon, Jeremy drives to Whytecliff Park and goes directly to the edge of the sacred cliff where he had been inspired twice before. Mesmerized by Howe Sound's majestic view, he believes another inspiration would help him make up his mind for good. That supernatural power that has guided him so far to pick up painting for soothing his boiling emotions should come to his rescue once more. *Oh, please, God almighty, tell me what to do now!* Jeremy whispers in a divine mood. He waits for half an hour, while gazing into the horizon with anticipation and admiration. He droops to meditate awhile and then touches the plantations surrounding him in hopes of recreating that special trance that had led to inspirations before. But nothing spiritual is happening to him today. He is puzzled and disillusioned now even more than he had been this morning before coming here.

The calm and quiet is precious, though, and he decides to stop thinking about everything for a while. He is almost dozing off when a voice startles him: "Nice day, eh?"

Jeremy looks around but finds nobody. The secluded cliff has supposedly been his secret place all these years. An intruder has penetrated this sacred spot, except that there is no sign of him. Is he hallucinating after many years of meditation? Was the voice his imagination? Was it the voice of God or an angel?

"I love the view of Howe Sound in a gorgeous afternoon like this. How about you?" the voice continues.

Jeremy peeps around before bending over the edge of the cliff carefully and noticing the legs of a man apparently sitting on a break in the middle of the cliff.

"How'd you get there?" Jeremy asks.

"There's a narrow path behind those bushes. You cannot see it from up there. It's *my* secret path."

"But now I know. I'm certain I'll find it if I go look for it," Jeremy replies teasingly.

"I don't think you can find the path easily… Even if you do, let's keep it secret."

"Okay… If that's so important to you."

"You wanna come down here?"

"If you don't mind showing me how."

"Return to the main path and go up for about two hundred meters until you see a pine tree tilted thirty degrees to the left as if coming off its roots. You must grab its trunk and turn around it carefully. It looks daunting because of the steep slope and the sight of the tree roots sticking out on one side. But the tree is safe, *I guess.* Just hold on to it tightly and turn quickly. You will see a narrow path under the heavy bushes below the tree. Jump on it carefully and it'll bring you here."

"That's too much hassle. I'm okay here," Jeremy replies.

"That's the whole point."

"What?"

"If you're comfortable there, it's time to try something more thrilling. Come on, I'm sure you can do it."

"Thanks, but I don't think so…"

"Come on… Once you learn about this place, you'll never want to be up there."

"Why?"

"Because this spot is absolutely sacred. You'll agree once you get here and then you'd always like to return only to this spot to meditate."

The guy sounds smart and the prospect of sitting on the lower ledge of the cliff and chatting with him entices Jeremy. Besides, if that particular spot is 'absolutely sacred' as this guy claims, perhaps it would facilitate his urgent need to get inspired today. A childlike urge overwhelms him in line with a sudden realization that taking risk is necessary for creating adventures and reaching the ultimate enlightenment.

Jeremy follows the young man's directions and finds the tilted pine tree. The sight of the steep slope, almost like a canyon wall, to and below the tree, scares the hell out of him. He freezes while gazing at the tree and contemplating the objective of taking such a foolish risk just for the sake of meeting this guy. He recalls his previous experiences with mountains and his promise to himself years ago not to ever come close to tricky mountains again. *Where was it? Yeah, Riverside, near Los Angeles. Stranded in fear and cold for two nights, I swore to never mess around the mountains again!* The view of Howe Sound is as splendid on the top or middle of it and the sacredness of the cliff cannot be any different, either. So why listen to a moron who probably has no responsibility or family to worry about if he plunges to his death? But, for him, with all his obligations and a nagging family, death is an easy way out and thus unacceptable. Besides, he is too smart to fall for these kinds of cheap thrills. Maybe this guy is a lunatic, trying to clown with him to his death and then laugh his heart out?

"Come on, don't be a chicken," the guy's faint voice echoes from a distance.

Being put in such a humiliating position agitates Jeremy. His dilemma at that moment feels almost as disturbing as his initial inner conflict that had brought him to the cliff today—to find the purpose of pursuing his painting passion. The risk of plunging to his demise is too grave for the thrill of sitting on the ledge of a stupid cliff even if he could trust this guy. He turns back to leave but hears the bushes rustling. Soon the young man appears out of the tall undergrowth and greets him. He stands below the pine tree and stretches his arm toward Jeremy, who is eight meters away. *What is this silly boy trying to do, offering me his hand like an idiot? Why is he trying to lure me to jump to my death?*

"No, thanks. I'll go back to the top of the cliff. You keep your scary sacred spot to yourself," Jeremy says with irritation.

"I don't blame your caution. Until you get the hang of it, maybe you need a safety net today," the guy says.

"What safety net? You have a rope or something?"

"No. But I'll stand here ready to catch you if by any chance you lose your grip over the tree. Just come down in my direction and try to grab the tree trunk."

Jeremy chuckles nervously for facing such a stubborn person who behaves like an old, intimate friend. He has an honest look and voice, too. But would not all crooks and morons? He gauges the situation again and again. The canyon is at least three hundred meters deep and those sharp rocks down there fashion a horrific sight. He trembles. These kinds of adventures are absurd for any sane person, especially a man of his age and stature with such a horrific history with mountains. *Can't we humans ever learn a lesson even from our own mistakes?* The guy's teasing smile is not helping his ego, either. Nonetheless, he feels committed to go down there and meet this fool who has kept his arm stretched toward him all along; like a mother encouraging her child to take the first step.

Since the guy is promising to catch him in case he misses the tree, maybe the risk is rather acceptable. But what if he is lying and merely stands by and watches him glide all the way down the canyon? *On the other hand, I'm nearing the end of my useful life, anyway!* He thinks of an additional safety measure: Instead of jumping for the tree, he can slide to it on the gravel slowly. After another minute of contemplation, finally he sits on the ground, opens his legs and arms, and aims them toward the opposite sides of the tree, to embrace it with both hands and legs. Slithering slowly would also help the guy catch him if necessary.

"Okay then, get ready to catch me…" Jeremy says.

"Alright, go ahead."

"Are you ready? You're sure you can catch me?"

"Yeah, I promise. Come on, man!"

Jeremy still hesitates, feeling quite foolish to trust a stranger, but also spellbound somehow—perhaps another symptom of the sacred cliff beckoning him? *Stupid Jeremy!*

"Heeeerrr Iiiii commme…" Jeremy stutters and slithers at last. He grabs the tree with his arms and legs. It feels horrifically fantastic to be safe when death is only a wrong motion away. The guy laughs light-heartedly from the way Jeremy hugs the tree like a leech. He offers Jeremy his hand to turn around the tree and jump on the narrow path. But Jeremy's grip is frozen stiff around the trunk, embracing it tighter the more he thinks about turning.

"Come on, turn before you lose your grip," the guy says with a genuine concern.

Jeremy is paralyzed. The idea of turning around the tree is too ridiculous and revolting now with the horrifying view below him more ominous than before. Moving even one finger feels too risky, but he agrees with the guy's point that he must act quickly or lose the opportunity to do it right and thus plunge to his death. He curses the guy from the bottom of his heart and turns around the tree slowly with the aid of his toes pushing the ground around the tree.

"Great job... Now hold my hand," the guy says.

Jeremy accepts the hand and jumps on the path. His blue jeans is ripped when sliding on the hard gravel and hitting the tree. The guy notices it and they giggle about it while climbing up the cliff and settling on the ledge. The sight of the canyon below is both breathtaking and horrific, but Jeremy feels safe sitting on a solid rock after his haunting terror of clinging to the tilted tree with shaking arms and legs.

"You did a great job," the guy says.

"I still think it was silly taking such unnecessary risk."

"Life is only risks and uncertainty."

"But some risks are pointless."

"But they help us see life in a clearer perspective. All other questions and quarrels of living become less significant when we face the immediate danger of demise."

"Maybe you're right philosophically, but still the idea of a tiny error plunging us to our death is absurd. That pine tree did not look strong to me, either. It's coming off its roots, it seems," Jeremy says.

"I think the same way whenever I aim to grab it. What if it's diseased and rotten from inside?"

"You ask me?" Jeremy shrieks.

"No, that's what my boring brain often asks my adventurous spirit..."

"But you still keep doing it against your logic?" Jeremy asks

"Yes… I know I'm a bit irrational about existence."

"I won't come down here again."

"We'll see. The next time you come around here, you'll think differently, especially if you believe you must put a part of your life in a finer perspective. Bring a rope with you if you're scared to jump or like to respect your brain as well."

"Any special snag or thought brings you here?" Jeremy asks.

"Some, but mostly I come here to cleanse my soul. It merely gives me energy to go on."

Soon Jeremy feels at ease with this mysterious stranger who is putting radical ideas into his head and seems to be wrestling with many dilemmas of his own. Jeremy recounts his bizarre story of discovering the cliff three years back and returning to it whenever he faces a dilemma.

"But painting has already served many purposes for you," the guy suggests.

"Such as?"

"First of all it saved your life. You were contemplating suicide just before being inspired to become a painter… Right?"

"Yeah, it's true."

"In fact, it made you love your life now, to the point of being so paranoid about taking even a small risk."

"Yes, I guess so. I love life now!" Jeremy replies pensively, as if discovering something very bizarre about himself for the first time in his life.

"Then it saved your marriage. You were depressed about your marriage. You were thinking about abandoning your wife and children. Instead, you've now learned to tolerate them better and your painting is a device for you and your wife to communicate as well. You're now enjoying your family."

"Yeah, that's true too."

"And painting has apparently enriched your soul as well. You had no clue about your existence and connection to Nature. And now, you whine about suffering for feeling too attached to it. In addition, you have found your hidden potentials and creativity.

And remember that your passion in general might've never been stirred up in other ways."

"These are all true…"

"So what else you expect to gain from painting?"

"Nothing from painting itself, I guess… but what next?"

"Do more paintings and explore the depth of your passion. You'll find a lot more about yourself and art, all through Nature while satiating your spirit, too. Didn't you say you were inspired initially to paint Howe Sound?"

"Yes."

"Then perhaps it's time to fulfill your vow."

"Yes, that's a great idea. I should paint Howe Sound next. It's finally the right time to do it!"

"Good. I bet your anxiety in recent months relates to your constant procrastination to paint the Howe Sound."

"Yeah… Maybe you have a point…"

"So, now you know what the problem is, right?"

"Yeah, I guess you're right. Now I seem to have the courage to do it at last."

"And don't worry about your inability to paint the glory of Nature adequately. Forget about being perfect and focus on being spiritually intact. Painting may be the only way to raise your spirit and express your passion, to grasp the essence of your existence."

"You speak weird but sound smart and free," Jeremy says.

"Thanks. I guess it happens when one delves into spiritual moods and readings on top of daring to come to this spot."

"Who are you?"

"I'll tell you when I see you here next time. I have some good stories to tell you but now I must go," the guy says and jumps on the path.

"Thanks for the advice and causing my pants rip," Jeremy yells as he watches the guy's departure. Suddenly he realizes his likely difficulty returning to the main path. "Hey, wait a second."

The guy turns and waits with a smile.

"How'd you think I could get back up there on my own?"

"I'm sure you could manage it."

"I'm not so sure. I would've been stuck here for a few days and died of hunger and thirst," Jeremy says half-teasingly.

"Yeah, maybe when I returned in a month, I would've found your skeleton sitting on the cliff, staring intently at Howe Sound."

"I should've not come down here in the first place."

"Maybe you're destined to die on a deserted mountain one day," the guy says with a smirk. "I bet somebody will find your skeleton sitting on a cliff someday at last, still wondering about the meaning life."

Jeremy is shocked by the guy's magical comments, as if he knew not only about Jeremy's uptightness about existence, but also his scary ordeal on a mountain for three days many years ago. He stares into the guy's eyes with bewilderment, while he smirks at Jeremy with passion. The guy helps him climb up a line of tiny tractions to the main path by clasping to sturdy plantations along the way. Then he disappears promptly.

Jeremy drives home, ecstatic about the idea of finally fulfilling his sacred commitment to paint Howe Sound. That would be the true measure of his mastery. It would attune his soul to attain true freedom, to abolish self-doubt regardless of people's reactions and intentions. Then, he would become the ultimate judge of his life, which is now deeply delineated by his passion for painting. Oh yes, Howe Sound will present the final frontier to prove him a true artist as much as it has been the gateway to his awakening.

The breathtaking mood of Howe Sound three year before manifests itself in Jeremy's mind in full details. Still he returns to the cliff one afternoon to do the under-painting of Howe Sound onsite on a 20 by 24 inches canvass, to ensure the mountain lines are sketched properly, and to gather the courage needed for this overwhelming mission that had changed his life three years back. The main work, including twenty-six layers of glazing, takes him seven weeks to complete in his home studio. He would have kept doing more glazing if necessary. However, his sacred mission now appears fulfilled. The tableau is perfect, manifesting a divine setting, just the way he had envisioned it in one glorious instant in that fateful afternoon at Whytecliff Park. Jeremy puts down the paintbrush and stares at the painting of How Sound with awe. He cherishes the superb ambience. The slow evolvement of such a heavenly scenery and now in its final form with such delicacy has transformed him into a real artist at last, and he now believes it wholeheartedly. He is satisfied with a painting unconditionally for the first time. *I'm not going to ever sell this one.* What an epic masterpiece:

A gloomy day… A cluster of loaded clouds crowds the cobalt sky. A shapely interlaced mountain formation resembles a line of steppingstones across the wide ocean linking Bowen Island to Horseshoe Bay. A pinkish haze saturates the colours of varied plantations dressing the mountains. A few glitters of purple and ultramarine mingle just a touch above the water. The bay glistens like a china dish. A tiny sailboat stands still near the horizon like a white dot in the middle of the dark universe. A man and a woman are kissing in the cabin of the boat. They are so deeply in love they do not care about the consequences of a fierce storm, not even if they die in each other's arms that very instant.

In that very instant, more than ever, Jeremy wishes he were the man.

*****

Well… this is the *almost* true story of how I became a devout landscape painter.

Villain in Vivian

In the massive darkness of the bedroom, Vivian Marchon cannot make out the numbers of the old digital clock. Filled with angst, she decides to ignore Mike's dislike for their glaring fluorescent clock in the bedroom and re-plug it in the morning out of spite, anyway. She reels to the window, tugs the drape slightly to let in some street light and check her wrist watch. It is 2:26 a.m. and some seconds that tick away torturously slowly, every one of which surges her rage to strangle that son of a bitch, Mike. *See how casually he is sound asleep when I am feeling so restless in the middle of the night! He would sleep even through a big flood sweeping the whole goddamn neighbourhood!*

This madness must end one way or another, she reckons, but killing him tonight may not be such a wise option. *I must not act hastily and be sorry about it in the morning.* Besides, she is not a cold-blooded murderer, after all, contrary to her sudden baffling urge to put the pillow on his stupid face and sit on it tight until he suffocates and stops kicking the air. *Yes, I will face him tomorrow once and for all.* She puts the pillow down.

The only obstacle is, of course, confronting him when he looks into her eyes passionately and listens with patience. He seems to have a strong hold over her, although it might appear the other way around in the manner Mike always humours her.

Whether it is love or fear, psychological or real, it prevents her from betraying him. Actually, she panics and pants horribly whenever she considers leaving him—the man she has mated for eighteen years and made four children together. On the other hand, her rising frustration with this whole situation further fuels her lifelong desire for assertiveness—to free herself from his hold. Alas, she does not know how.

Vivian decides to spend the rest of the night on the couch in the family room. Under the present circumstance, in particular tonight, she cannot sleep in the same room with this hideous jerk, let alone in the same bed. With a swift, rough thrust, she pulls her pillow and a blanket from her side of the bed. At the door, she takes another contemptuous glimpse at Mike who is still sound asleep *so casually*, unaware of all the negative vibes in the room and the sudden impulse of his beloved Vivian to strangle him only two minutes earlier. The sight of his gross flabby belly partly revealed from underneath the blanket, his homely but kind face perked up by a vivid grin, and his wide-open mouth emitting a foully fused odour of garlic, alcohol, and partying bacteria, is etched in her brain before she leaves the room. "Shit," she moans.

She takes an aspirin from the medicine cabinet and swallows it down with a glass of cold water before lying on the couch. Her throbbing headache relents a little despite the last image of Mike in bed still enraging her. She recalls his subtle grin in sleep and gets still madder over the possibility of him enjoying a nice dream in his relaxed world, totally ignorant about her fidgety nights on the couch instead of slumbering on their *BeautyRest* mattress. No wonder she is so *Rest*less often and her *Beauty* is slipping away fast, too!

She is right about him dreaming: He is sunbathing alone on the beach in Honolulu, where he had taken Vivian for vacation recently and had a good time together. Two Hawaiian goddesses flirt with him from a distance, showing off their slender, tanned bodies, and teasing him with their enticing smiles. He smiles back and soon the girls and Mike are chatting and flirting in his hotel room, ready to roam into intimate territories. But Mike gets up abruptly and leaves the room in search of Vivian, whom he imagines must be somewhere in the hotel. He looks everywhere with no luck, getting more agitated and depressed by the second, yet he cannot give up. For a second, he ponders returning to his room and resting in the arms of the Hawaiian girls, at least out of spite for Vivian—always hiding herself from him and torturing him so much for no apparent reason that he can think of. Yet, the idea of cheating with the Hawaiian girls feels only appalling rather than appealing. Instead, he searches even more keenly for Vivian's chubby body, dying to make love to her passionately that very instant, but she is nowhere to be found. He screams "Vivian…" with a rowdy tone—like Marlon Brando (Stanley) in *A Streetcar Named Desire* yelling, "Stella…"—so forcefully, in fact, that he awakes in distress with a light sweat dampening his face.

Still drenched in his weird, melancholic dream—the ecstasy of flirting with two Hawaiian goddesses, and the stress of missing Vivian—Mike reaches out to the Vivian's side of the bed to touch her and bring her in mood for love. But she is not there. He assumes she has gone for a glass of water or something and soon he is back in deep sleep.

In the morning, Mike Marchon marches into the kitchen, still cheerful from the effect of the last night's weird dream, despite missing the opportunity of intimacy with either the Hawaiian girls or Vivian. *Why in the hell I reject gorgeous women and look for Vivian even in my dreams? And still Vivian always accuses me of flirting with other women! What is wrong with both of us? We're both simply crazy for different reasons—me, for not doing it, and she, for imagining I'm always doing it.*

Vivian glares at him from the corner of her eye with her usual suspicion of whatever he normally does or says, and now his cheery mood this gloomy morning.

"You look happy!?" she blurts with agitation.

"Why not? Another day to live with a gorgeous artist like you, why not be happy?"

"I bet you had a dream about a slut again, didn't you?"

Mike bursts into laughter: "Two actually, this time... How'd you know?"

"I saw you..." Vivian asserts with tension, quite happy about her premonition last night watching his wide grin in deep sleep.

"You can see me even in my dreams?" he says with a giggle.

"Yes, you better believe it... I can see everything you do even in your dreams," she replies.

"In that case you must've seen me looking for you even in my dream. I must be crazy."

"That's for sure... But who was in your dream this time?"

"Later, later... I must run. Tonight I'll tell you if you remind me, and if all these women chasing me don't kidnap me by then."

"Yeah, sure... There's a race to steal you from me!"

"See you later, honey," Mike says, admiring his haughty daughters arriving for breakfast and getting busy with food fast without acknowledging him. Vivian yells at the boys, making a racket upstairs still, to hurry up.

Vivian gasps a sigh of relief or despair—she cannot say which—when the kids leave, too, and she is finally alone in the quiet house. Now she can take the nap she needs so badly. She gauges the option briefly, but then calls Lorie Hamilton instead and they plan to meet in Capilano Mall in one hour. It is time to pour her guts out to someone about her torturous life with Mike. She can no longer keep this nerve-racking secret all to herself.

"You look pale," Lorie says after sipping her coffee in the food court.

"It's all Mike's fault," Vivian replies. "You can't imagine what I'm going through."

"What's wrong?"

"Everything..."

"Like what? Does he have an affair or something?"

"Probably not, although he behaves suspiciously sometimes."

"How?"

"Well, like this morning, for example. He confessed having a sexy dream last night with two girls. Then tried to fool me that at the end he came looking for me instead of making love to them."

"So? That's not bad. It shows he loves you," Lorie says with a hint of jealousy.

"Well... What was he doing with those whores in the first place? Why should other girls—two at a time—be in his head at all and come to his rescue in his dreams. I bet he's looking for another woman to fool around with or maybe even ditch me."

"Oh, Vivian... You have such an active imagination. If these are your only clues, I suggest you go see a shrink. Do you have any evidence he's after another woman?"

"No."

"Actually, I envy the way he always adores you. I wish my husband were as passionate as Mike," Lorie says while touching Vivian's hand with sympathy.

"No... I don't think he loves me enough," Vivian blurts and bursts into tears.

"Oh, come on Vivian. Don't cry. I know he loves you. I've seen the way he looks at you and admires your paintings."

"But I don't believe him. I think he's fooling around about my paintings, too."

"Why do you say that? Don't you like your paintings?"

"I do. But I think Mike is either exaggerating or mocking me in the way nobody can see it behind his charming looks."

"But as long as you believe they're good, who cares..."

"Sometimes I wonder... Are my paintings good, really?"

Lorie keeps quiet, searching for words. In the past, she has always praised her paintings whenever the subject has come up. But the truth is that her compositions are dull and her choice of colours dreary. Now that Vivian has herself raised the subject, maybe Mike is in fact teasing her, so subtly that no one realizes his sarcasm except for Vivian perhaps! At last, Lorie collects her thoughts and courage to give Vivian a hint.

"Maybe you should try another instructor, too."

"You think so? I still need more lessons?"

"There's no end to learning. You can always improve your technique and colour selection," Lorie replies timidly.

"Oh…?"

"Let's forget about your paintings for a second. What's your real beef with Mike besides his sexy dreams?"

"He snores a lot, like a giant," Vivian replies with gloom.

"Are you serious? You're mad at him because the poor man snores?"

"Yeah, plus the way he admires my paintings. Maybe he has a mistress too."

"Wow… What a real jerk he is, I should say…!"

"You see what I mean?"

"Are you out of your mind, Vivian? Now that finally a man understands his wife, you despise him because he snores? Maybe men are right about women being—"

"Don't dare say it…"

"What?"

"Crazy? Were you gonna say 'crazy'?" Vivian asks.

"No. I was gonna say 'a bit cranky' sometimes."

"I'm not cranky… Anyway, I still love this bastard. But I can't tolerate him anymore, especially his snores. I don't know what's happening to me."

"I've heard about relationships like this, which are usually hard to figure out."

"Like what?" Vivian asks.

"Like when you love and hate a person at the same time."

"Still I hate him so much for snoring, more than I like him for everything else."

"Use an earplug at night or sleep in a different room…"

"We don't have a spare bedroom. Earplug didn't work either. I tried it. It irritates my ears and I hate him for it even more."

"Then tap his shoulder to shift his position. It'll work."

"Yeah? You think so?"

"Well, try it…"

"I will… But tell me, honestly, what do you think about my paintings?"

"I told you…" Lorie replies carefully.

"I understand. I'm not good enough," Vivian says with a sigh.

"But you can always get better. Look at Jeremy. He's really improved a lot in three years."

"What'd he do? Who's his teacher?"

"He learned by himself."

"Come on, tell me the truth. How could he learn so much by himself in three years and paint better than me already?"

"I don't know. Except that he often goes to Nature and sits on a cliff for a while to get artistic energy and inspiration. Then he comes home and paints like crazy."

"Where does he go? Maybe that's his excuse to get out of the house and meet his lover. All men have their secrets, you know. I bet he goes for private lessons from a lover…"

"Vivian… You really have a wild imagination. He goes to Whytecliff Park and sits on a cliff that he believes is sacred… That's all… That's his only secret… And only for becoming a better artist."

"And you believe him?"

"Of course. In fact, he just did an amazing painting of Howe Sound from the same cliff. You should come and see it."

"Yeah… I like to see it. When should I come over?"

"Next weekend. We have a party; you and Mike come too."

"I've had it with your snores," Vivian confronts Mike at bedtime after pumping her nerve to become a bit more assertive with him. "I'm gonna tap your shoulder tonight anytime you snore, to shift your position. I haven't been able to sleep for ages."

"Okay, honey. But you snore a lot yourself."

"I never snore like a giant."

"Yes, you do. If you could hear yourself, you'd be amazed how good you're at it. Do you want me to tape it for you?"

"No, it's not necessary. You just wake me up, too, and I'll switch my position," Vivian says irately. *So he now thinks I am a giant, too? Is he trying to say I am fat?*

They try the new scheme and the situation gets more out of hand. When Vivian awakens Mike to shift his position, he either rolls over and starts snoring again soon enough, which forces Vivian to wake him up again and again, or he is unable to sleep for a long while, until Vivian finally dozes off and starts snoring loudly herself. Initially, Mike feels guilty to interrupt Vivian's deep sleep. But after Vivian's persistence to wake him every few minutes, he decides to give her a taste of her medicine. So he taps her shoulder and she rolls over with a groan. After a few startles every night, however, stress and anger besieges her, though she tries to hide her frustration.

The nightly war continues as Mike fails to convince Vivian that the tapping scheme is impractical. He plays along, though, hoping she would finally get tired of this game. He keeps tapping her to hold his ground and ascertain Vivian receives her share of torture throughout the night, equally afraid to fall asleep. Yet, the stubborn Vivian strives hard to hide her agony and never accept defeat. Instead, she intensifies her tapping frequency on Mike: every few minutes, as soon as his exhausted body breathes a bit deeper—way before it turns into a legitimate snore.

Vivian views her persistence a sign of gaining assertiveness, at last. The joy of witnessing Mike's pain more than compensates her suffering from the shock of being awakened by Mike and inadequate sleep. Sometimes she takes a nap in the afternoon to make up for her sleepless nights. But poor Mike has to get up early every morning and go to work with a blank mind. A few times, he attempts to sleep on the couch in the family room, but it is too short, narrow and spongy to avail a good night rest. No end is in sight for their dilemma and nightly drama—Vivian getting meaner with lesser sleep than before, and Mike on the verge of a heart attack from Vivian's tapping shocks, sleep deprivation, and his frustration about Vivian's lack of logic or consideration.

"Whose stupid idea this tapping business is, anyway?" Mike asks Vivian after six nights of agony.

"Lorie. She remembered her parents did it and it worked."

"Lorie? Her parents? You're torturing us based on Lorie's memory of her parents' bedroom melodramas?"

"Yes... She's smart. I trust her opinion."

"You trust everybody else's ideas except mine, don't you? Don't you see it's not working? Let's find a better solution."

"It works fine for me," Vivian replies, enjoying Mike's pain, which is a good enough reason for her to continue the tapping scheme despite her own suffering.

"I'll get Lorie for this," Mike snarls.

"We're going to their house for dinner on Saturday, by the way. I must get Jeremy to tell me where he goes for meditation."

"Why do you care about his meditation?"

"Because that's how he gets painting inspiration."

"What painting inspiration?"

"Lorie said he goes to a secret place, gets divine inspiration, and creates his beautiful paintings. I'm gonna ask him to share his secret with me."

"Your paintings are better than his. What're you worried about?"

"That's another thing... Don't ever mention anything about my paintings again!"

"Why? You think I'm lying about your paintings, too?" Mike asks with astonishment.

"You wanna drive me nuts, admiring even the paintings I hate myself. You wanna confuse me and send me to a madhouse."

"Vivian, you'd better go see Dr. Mulholland already, instead of all this nonsense. Maybe sleep deprivation is killing your brain cells?"

"You go see him. You're the crazy one," she snaps and leaves with agitation.

At the Hamiltons' party, Vivian stares at Jeremy's new painting in awe, with utmost jealousy: "Wow, Jeremy, this is a terrific work."

"Thanks. I'm finally pleased with a painting of mine, too."

"It looks familiar; where's this place?"

"It's a view of Howe Sound from Horseshoe Bay."

"Is it the place you go for meditation and inspiration?"

"Who said that?" Jeremy asks with anxiety.

"Lorie did."

"Lorie and her big mouth! It's just a place I go to be alone and think. That's all."

"Where exactly is this place?"

"It's a remote spot off the Whytecliff Park. But it's not a safe place to go to, anyway. You can see the same view, more or less, from most spots in the Park."

"But I want to go some place special and quiet, like the place you go. Can I go with you next time you go there?"

"Well… perhaps…" Jeremy replies with gloom. Rejecting a friend's request is rude, but revealing his secret hideout to others feels vexing. His privacy would be jeopardized and the cliff he has considered his sacred temple may lose its magical power if everybody learns about it and wants to climb it for inspiration. Just imagine thousands of desperate artists in Vancouver trying to climb up and down that tiny cliff every day! Many people are so desperate for some relief and inspiration these days, they might really start to believe even in the sanctity of a cliff. Soon, artists all over the world may hear about it and arrive in busloads for pilgrimage.

"When?" Vivian interrupts his train of thoughts.

He stares at her with bewilderment: "What?"

"When can we go?" Vivian asks with a childlike enthusiasm, her eyes glistening from the thought of mounting the cliff that has transformed Jeremy so rapidly. She cannot take her eyes off his new painting. *Just look at his marvellous paintings after only a short period of self-teaching. And I still suck, even after devoting my entire life to painting and spending all that money on lessons.* It must definitely be the blessing of the sacred place he goes to for inspiration. She must discover the cliff at all cost.

"Soon I hope. I can't say now…" Jeremy replies.

Lorie notices his frustration and comes to his rescue.

"Hey, Vivian, how's Mike's snoring?" she asks teasingly.

"You should be ashamed of yourself, Lorie," Mike shrieks. "She's not letting me sleep anymore, waking me up every five minutes to roll over."

"You see what I'm dealing with," Vivian snaps and then turns to Jeremy: "Then I'd better call you during the week to arrange a time for the next weekend perhaps?"

"Well… Okay."

"Do you do any sketching or painting there?" Vivian asks with zeal, ignoring Mike's and Lorie's—let alone Jeremy's—frustration with her persistence.

"No… I just go sit there… That's all."

"I really like to go sit there, too, and get inspired like you."

"I hope you won't be disappointed when it doesn't work," Jeremy says with a giggle for his subtle sarcasm. Vivian gets it, however, and despises him for it, plus his gorgeous paintings.

Jeremy lurches away to chat with other guests, hoping they have not overheard his conversation with Vivian. The idea of a particular cliff being sacred—and the secret behind all his sudden success—and now another woman being haunted by it as well, is embarrassing. Of course, he believes in the divinity of the cliff and admits his occasional inspirations on it. But explaining it to others is a mistake and a possible cause for ridicule by this bunch of rational friends. Thank Goodness, the loud conversations and music have filtered Vivian's chattering. Vivian, thrilled with the promising developments, reels to the kitchen for a glass of water.

"What's happening to Vivian?" Lorie asks Mike.

"I don't know, but she's acting weirder every day. The way she wakens me by shaking or pinching my shoulder is absurd, and now this obsession with a cliff to become a saint and master painter. I'm totally lost."

"I hadn't seen her so distressed and desperate," says Lorie.

"She's getting out of control. Do you know an exorcist to suck the devil out of her?"

"Oh, Mike, don't exaggerate. The situation mustn't be that bad!" Lorie says.

"Oh, yes. It's very bad."

"Maybe she is a *real* artist then, after all?" Lorie asks.

"What do you mean?" Mike asks with surprise.

"Well, real artists are often somewhat crazy or paranoid. Even Jeremy gets restless and useless sometimes."

"Then maybe she's a real artist, or too obsessed about it."

"Yes, one of them for sure…" Lorie says with a chuckle.

"She keeps accusing me of having an affair anytime I talk with a woman for a few minutes. We must be careful chatting so friendly now."

"Are you serious?"

"Yeah. Let's go mingle before she spoils your party."

The following week, during her sleepless nights, Vivian basks in the upcoming miracle of inspiration by visiting the sacred cliff. She calls Jeremy but cannot get a definite commitment from him. Meanwhile, her nightly bedtime rivalry with Mike and tapping each other to roll over continue ruthlessly. They toss and turn in bed for hours unable to fall asleep, while also remain fearful of being shaken out of sleep again and again. Under the old routine, when Vivian escaped to the living room in the middle of night, at least they both got some sleep. But now they fight tenaciously throughout the night to hold their grounds.

On Friday night, particularly, Vivian can hardly sleep while persisting with the tapping scheme. She finally dozes off at dawn when for some odd reason Mike is not snoring or waking her up. Embracing the joy of the rare silence, just before dipping into a sweet dream, she ponders that maybe Mike is dead in the way he is not moving, snoring, and perhaps not even breathing. *Oh, who cares!* Even if he has rolled over and died, she is too tired to worry about him now. *We will check it out later in the morning,* she muses. She just has to get some sleep… yes… thank God. But two minutes later the phone shrieks. She leaps out of the bed and loiters in the middle of the room like a zombie, uncertain about her senses and whereabouts.

She gazes around in confusion, focuses on Mike's motionless flesh, dead quiet, and finally notices the phone ringing at low tone.

"Hello…"

"Vivian?"

"Yeah…?" she says with a wide yawn.

"Are you alright?"

"Who's this?"

"It's Jeremy, Vivian."

"Oh, Jeremy, hi," Vivian exclaims with a sluggish, hopeful excitement.

"Did I wake you up? You don't sound good."

"I'm fine. What's up?"

"I'm going to a club near Horseshoe Bay. So I thought maybe I'll show you the cliff you're so keen to explore before joining my friends."

"Yeah? When?"

"Right now. If you wanna go, you should come over right away and follow my car."

"Right now?" she asks, exhaustion numbing her fully.

"Yes, right now. I have only one hour to meet my friends. But if you don't feel good, let's wait for another time."

"No, I'll go. I'll be at your house in fifteen minutes," she says, hangs up the phone and rushes to get dressed and go.

Mike is still soundlessly asleep or dead, she cannot say which, nor can she care at this moment, either. *We will check it out after I return.* She rushes to take advantage of Jeremy's unexpected generosity.

Vivian follows Jeremy's car to Whytecliff Park where they walk on a bushy trail for ten minutes before Jeremy stops and shows her a hill on the left side of the path.

"Here it is. Follow the footpath to the top of the cliff," Jeremy says and leaves.

Vivian lingers, her heart pounding at the sight of the sacred sanctuary and the possibility of getting inspired any second. For a while, she feels too exhausted to climb the hill; maybe she should return another time? Then she wonders whether this is the right cliff. Could Jeremy have taken her to a different cliff just to get rid of her? *Nah...* He knew where he was going and his face seemed honest. So this must be it, the sacred cliff she has been yearning to climb and become a real painter. *Once up there, I'd be inspired into a different being,* she forces her mind to believe while chuckling light-heartedly. Perhaps she can take a nap up there as well, if it is not too breezy. All these hopes fire up her last grains of strength to climb the mountainside to the top of the hill. It is a hard undertaking considering her dizziness, but she feels ecstatic upon reaching the summit with newfound determination and confidence.

The mountain breeze, drenched with the fishy odour of the ocean, hits Vivian's face as she lolls on the top of the cliff and exalts the view before her. This is the right cliff, she imagines immediately, remembering Jeremy's painting of Howe Sound. The breathtaking view energizes her, but no tingles of inspiration. She stares at the bay, the mountains perked up with the morning light, and seagulls flying close to the water and shrieking. She ponders painting the same view. But the idea does not excite her. *Why am I not getting inspired?* She closes her eyes and tries to meditate for another thirty minutes, hoping divinity fills her any minute if she concentrates deeper. Again, nothing happens. She stares into the horizon with anger and desperation, begging god for any sign of inspiration.

She delves into deep depressing thoughts and almost dozes off when the sound of branches rustling alarms her. She had not expected anybody to be around, according to Jeremy that this was a secluded spot, and hopefully no animals. The sound of bushes rapping and branches snapping grows stronger, though no creature is in sight. Her heart thumps and she leaps to leave or at least get ready to defend herself. The sands under her sneakers loosen and some drip over the ridge.

"Jeremy? Is that you…?" a voice says from below. Vivian is startled, but relieved that all those noises had been from a human instead of a bear or a racoon.

"Hello… Where're you?" Vivian shouts.

"I'm down here."

"You know Jeremy?" Vivian asks, looking down the cliff and noticing a man sitting on a break about six meters below her.

"Yes… Jeremy, the painter?"

"Yeah."

"Is he your friend or husband?" the guy asks.

"He's my friend. He showed me this place today before going to a club," Vivian replies.

"So what're you doing here?"

"The same thing Jeremy has been doing last three years."

"Which is?"

"To meditate and get inspired like him."

"You're a painter too?"

"Yeah. But I'm not good like him yet."

"What's the matter with this world?" the man asks with a mournful sigh. "Everybody wants to be an artist nowadays, among many other things…"

"Can you guess why?"

"Maybe it's because we're fed up with our regular lives and relationships, so we try to lose ourselves in art. Maybe we also hope to find an easier relationship at least with Nature or God."

"Exactly… Our lives are so shitty and artless," she says.

"I agree…"

"Are you an artist yourself…, for the same reason, perhaps?"

"No, I'm not. I don't even like to think or pretend I could be."

"Why not? Because your life is not shitty enough?"

"Well, maybe…" the man says. "But mostly because I always thought artistry was a divine gift that erupts naturally without so much efforts and lessons."

"What do you mean?"

"Not everybody is cut out to be an artist, I mean."

"Why not?"

"You should have the right spirit for it in the first place."

"What's the harm in trying anyway?" Vivian asks with angst.

"Nothing, if it soothes people's suffering. However, even art has nowadays become too weird and tainted with greed and the urge to compete. Some even get nervous breakdown when they don't succeed."

"Has Jeremy told you that?" Vivian asks with surprise and paranoia, wondering whether the guy was talking about her, and perhaps even repeating the words Jeremy had said about her.

"No, he seems to be blessed with the right spirit."

"Did he tell you about me, too?"

"No… Why do you say that?"

"Because you sounded like him about my chance of getting inspired here like him."

"All I know is that not everybody has the right spirit, but more importantly, only few have the passion and patience a real artist needs to express his or her feelings selflessly."

"But we don't know that unless we try!"

"True, but as I said it happens naturally to a real artist. Taking lessons and going to colleges and universities to learn how to become an artist sound really weird to me," he says.

"So you think I shouldn't waste my time here?"

"What are you doing exactly?" the guy asks.

"I told you… Meditating to get inspired like Jeremy. He told me that this was a sacred spot."

"The exact spot he got his real inspiration was actually down here. But the main point is that he was probably blessed at birth, and then became an artist only after he discovered *why* he wanted to be a painter."

"Down there?"

"Yeah, but that wasn't my point."

"Jeremy didn't mention anything about *down there*. That sneaky bastard! That's why I'm not getting inspired sitting up here all morning. How can I go down there?"

"You can't."

"Why not?"

"Because getting here is dangerous. Besides, this spot doesn't inspire everybody automatically, as I told you."

"Are you trying to stop me, too?"

"Don't be cynical. Stop competing with Jeremy. Go do your painting the way you've always done only as a hobby. There's no inspiration here for you," the guy says with compassion, though it sounds like an order and pity to Vivian.

Angry and humiliated, Vivian looks around and below the cliff to find a way to the lower ridge where the guy is sitting, but she fails and gets even more flustered.

"How'd you go there, tell me?" she says and blasts a load of dirt from the top of the ridge over the guy's head with the tip of her shoe.

"I can't. I won't have anything to do with this," the man says and jumps off the cliff on a path hidden by heavy undergrowth.

Vivian calls him repeatedly, but he disappears swiftly without responding to her pleas. She can detect his movement through the undergrowth and realizes that there must be a certain path leading to the lower break on the cliff. She surveys her surroundings for a way to the lower ridge again to no avail. She descends to the main path and walks up the trail to find the guy coming out of the bushes or the path he had used to get to the cliff. She finds neither even after charging up and down the trail a few times nervously. The effect of sleeplessness, hunger, and now the humiliation of abandonment heighten her dizziness. Eventually, she decides to hit back home and try to explore the secret path later, perhaps the following day. She curses both Jeremy and the young man for being secretive. All men are jerks, she whispers with anguish on her way to the Park.

At least this morning's exploration has already had a useful outcome. Now she knows the exact spot for inspiration, and that, in fact, the cliff inspires people, since that guy had also confirmed it, aside from Lorie's and Jeremy's indirect hints. Anyway, there must definitely be some truth about it. Now, her hunch about that sneaky Jeremy showing her a wrong location this morning is also confirmed. He would surely get angry and jealous when she tells him that she has discovered the right spot. She is sad and angry, but thanks her luck about the guy showing up and telling her the secret. As if not humiliated enough already when she reaches the parking lot, her car also looks bored and laughing at her, like a live creature bewildered by all these nonsense about inspiration. All these hallucinations are the result of her insomnia, too, she thinks while sitting behind the wheel and slamming the car door with rage. *Stupid car!* She screams as she swerves out of the parking lot. *At least you shut up!*

After preparing a fast, lousy supper for the family and taking a hasty shower, Vivian calls Jeremy.

"I knew you'd try to fool me," she blurts with rage.

"What do you mean, Vivian?"

"You tried to hide the exact inspiration spot from me, didn't you?"

"Of course not. Why do you say that?" Jeremy replies, feeling sorry already for his efforts this morning to take her there.

"Why didn't you tell me there's a lower ridge on the cliff?"

"What are you talking about?"

"Stop your game, Jeremy. I already discovered the exact spot where you get your inspirations. It is not at the top of the cliff, but on the ridge in the middle of it. You made me waste the whole morning at the top of the cliff and nothing happened."

"I told you nothing will happen."

"But it'll happen if I go to the right spot on the lower ridge."

"Who said that?" Jeremy asks with agitation.

"A guy sitting down there"

"Who? Benjamin?"

"I don't know his name, but he knew you very well."

"Then it must've been Benjamin."

"But he refused to tell me how to go down."

"Good."

"Why's everybody sabotaging me? Why are you so mean?"

"I'm not mean, Vivian. I showed you the right place. That guy is probably pulling your leg. Believe me."

"No, I don't believe you. Just tell me how to get down there."

"I cannot."

"Why not? Don't be so mean," Vivian shrieks.

"Forget it, Vivian. I just don't want you get hurt or take this inspiration business seriously."

"Well, I want to try it anyway. What can I lose?"

"Your life... As I said, getting down there is dangerous."

"What're you talking about? I saw the guy walking there."

"That guy is probably crazy or suicidal, believe me." Jeremy regrets not denying his knowledge of the lower ridge, although the guy might have told her that Jeremy knew how to go there.

"Just show me the damn path instead of worrying about me."

"No. I can't be responsible for it," he says.

"For what? Getting pricked by the bushes?"

"No. The problem is getting to the path."

"Why?"

"The path starts under a pine tree that is hard to reach."

"I wanna go and see it anyway. If you did it, I can do it too. I want to check it out myself at least."

"I think it's a lousy thing to do for no logical purpose."

"Let me worry about my affairs. You just tell me where the lower path is."

"Sorry. I must go now...," Jeremy replies.

"Wait, Jeremy. If you don't tell me where it is, I'll tell Lorie how you always flirt with me."

"What? Listen Vivian…" Jeremy says nervously. "Please put Mike on the phone."

Vivian hesitates awhile and then calls Mike reluctantly.

After two minutes, Mike hangs up and shouts at Vivian, "Are you crazy?"

"*You* have made me crazy," Vivian yells back impatiently. "What'd Jeremy say?"

"He said you want to climb a rock or something dangerous. Are you out of your freaking mind, Vivian?"

"No, I just want to be an artist like Jeremy. I must."

"But why are you haunted by this mumbo Jumbo, climbing rocks, and hoping for inspiration. Just take more classes and keep practising. You'll become a master without putting poor Jeremy in such an awkward position."

"What poor Jeremy," Vivian says and grabs the receiver. "I must call him back."

"He won't give you the address of this shit rock unless I tell him so."

"Okay then. Tell him so," Vivian says, extending the receiver toward Mike's face.

"But Vivian—"

"No buts. Just call him."

"I really like to know what's gotten into you."

"You must let me go; otherwise I'll be even snappier around the house."

"I'm lost, totally. Let's wait awhile until we talk about it some more first," Mike pleads with desperation.

"There's nothing to talk about. I want to go there tomorrow."

"May I go with you at least?"

"No. I must be alone for meditation. Just call Jeremy."

Desperate and defeated, Mike calls Jeremy and gives him his consent. Then he passes on the receiver to Vivian.

"I still think it's a bad idea, Vivian," Jeremy says with gloom.

"Let me worry about that myself... You just tell me where the damn tree is."

"On the main path go past the cliff I showed you this morning for about two hundred meters. If you look down the canyon, you will see a pine tree sticking out at a sixty-degree angle. You must somehow get to the tree, grab it, roll around it, and then below it is a path you must jump on. It'll lead you to the cliff. At least take a rope with you."

"It doesn't sound so difficult and I don't need any goddamn rope," Vivian snaps.

"You'll see what I mean when you see that steep canyon and the tree you must jump to. I'm sure you'll change your mind once you get there. Be smart, Vivian."

The excitement of the next day's adventure mixed with the agony of Mike's snores keep Vivian up almost the entire night. It has been a long time since she has had a decent sleep. But tonight especially, with the anticipation of the next day's challenging quest churning her mind, Vivian struggles in bed restlessly and wrestles with a bunch of emotions. She wonders how inspiration feels and how it changes people. That must be a great revelation! Among many mixed sensations, she is hopeful about inspiration, sceptical about the risk of jumping to the tree, impatient about fooling around with ropes that she does not have, concerned about her sanity being questioned by her family and friends and perhaps even deep down by herself. During the long torturous night, only the joy of waking poor Mike repeatedly relieves her rowdy mind and sleeplessness. Tonight, life means different to her, although the feeling is weird, something like an intriguing confusion—an urge too mysterious in itself. It is an odd, mystical sensation that just roams inside her without stirring any recallable emotion. *I bet I'd sleep sound at nights, too, once I get inspired!*

Two cups of coffee in the morning, looking calm and collected, Vivian leaves under the concerned eyes of Mike and children, all witnessing the villain erupting from inside Vivian. Has *it* been hidden deep inside her all these years and nobody known about it, perhaps not even herself? Has she always been so uncaring and selfish, but somehow in control of *it* within her until now? Maybe a part of her brain has been gradually damaged! Contact with all those paint pigments, mediums, and solvents might have poisoned her, Mike ponders. Yet Vivian does not care about their dire stares, pleas, or thoughts. She drives determinedly toward Horseshoe Bay, as if embarking upon the most urgent mission of her life—maybe not exactly like the feelings of a soldier going to the battle zone, but very close to it. Despite her erratic scepticism about her mission, she strives to fight off the tension pent up within her and to redeem her damaged pride. She must prove herself to everybody once and for all.

In half an hour, she is at Whytecliff Park, her heart thumping faster every minute at the thought of the challenge ahead. After all the wrangling about the purpose of finding the secret path and refuting everybody's advice, she senses a gush of hesitation once she gets out of the car and hurries toward the cliff. She questions her sanity and motivation for going to the edge of the cliff where that young man had been yesterday. She doubts her logic about a particular part of the cliff bringing her tranquility and inspiration like the one Jeremy had acquired. Why is she so naïve to assume her artistry would improve upon conquering the sacred cliff and sitting on a hard rock for a while? How could a cliff inspire or help her any better than all those painting lessons she has endured during the last fifteen years? Then, the next minute, she assures herself again that this sacred mission would solve all her misery and problems. She would be a good—no, a great—painter after meditating on that sacred ridge. Then everybody would pay her the respect she so rightfully deserves. Finally, after fifteen years of struggles and hopes, people would witness and acknowledge her immense talent the way she had known all along. She would be somebody at last. People would admire her the same way they praise Jeremy and his stupid paintings.

The sight of the cliff revives her strength and resolve. Swiftly, her irritating doubts vanish, which she attributes to her mission's divinity in itself. No more negative thoughts, she promises herself and marches forward on the path in search of the pine tree. *Yes, Mrs. Marchon, just keep marching on to victory,* she muses with tension. She counts her steps to calculate the two-hundred meter distance. Roughly, about three hundred of her long strides, she estimates and keeps counting. After two-hundred-fifty, she looks down the canyon wall more closely for a sign of the pine tree. Soon it appears; a pine tree with a thirty-degree slant to the left. Upon a quick glimpse, she thinks it must be the tree. Her second peek at the deep canyon below scrambles her nerves. Swiftly she steps back, fearing that a startle or some unexpected movement behind her plunges her down into the canyon. She waits twenty second to gather her breath and courage before reeling forward cautiously to take another peep. *Oh my God, what a horrifying sight.*

What a horrific sight indeed and, even worse, what an awful position for her to be in. She has promised herself to get inspired one way or another today, to prove to those arrogant bastards, Jeremy and Mike, that she is more capable than they presume. Perhaps this is not the right tree. Carefully she surveys the tree. Yes…, it is pine at a sixty-degree angle, coming off its roots, about to collapse—exactly as Jeremy had described it. But at this part of the world, especially around the cliffs and canyons, so many trees are slanted. She decides to pace the path some more and hopefully find a more manageable tree. But her search only confirms her initial discovery. *Now what?* Now go back home and forget about ever contemplating such a silly act again, her terrified brain cells order and she accepts their sound suggestion wholeheartedly. *Or go buy a rope at least!* one of her sneaky brain cells whispers into her ear. She stops and thinks briefly but then keeps walking. She is not about to do something so foolish merely to prove a point, or get famous, all on a dismal hope of getting inspired. *Inspiration is baloney, anyway.*

Instead, now only perspiration and agony engulf her as she struggles with her erratic emotions, while she walks sluggishly in haze toward the parking. She feels rueful and agitated recalling the absurd notion of getting inspired if she gets to the ridge. Yet, all these perspiration and agony today have by themselves been a good lesson, she ponders, which she may use to improve her life. Let us go back home, she whispers to the devil inside her and keeps lurching down the path toward the parking lot, very much like one of those defeated Napoleon soldiers fleeing Russia. *Maybe I should tell everybody that I did it?* But that would be the biggest lie of her life and they would detect it in her timid eyes. They would laugh even harder behind her back, especially when they look at her new paintings that she should do after her alleged inspiration now. It would be impossible to lie regarding such a sacred experience. Such an achievement would be apparent in her eyes and spirit for everybody to witness readily without her having to mention or show it off or even doing a new painting.

Then again, reaching the tree would by itself be such a brave act and potent triumph. A whole world of spiritual sensations would surge from such a feat. *I hate defeat.* The inspiration would happen naturally the second she embraces the tree and steps on the path to the cliff—the path to her enlightenment. It would change her perspectives of life and 'self' forever. Now these tempting bold thoughts besiege her conservative brain cells again and she halts in her tracks only a few meters away from the parking lot. She glances at her parked car that seems ashamed for driving her all the way here only to see her chicken out in the last second. *Stupid nosy car! Shut up! Shut up! Shut up!* But if the car alone sends such a pitiful message, just imagine other people's, especially Mike's and Jeremy's, perceptions and reactions after she returns home and announces that they were right and she was a chicken. *She should never admit to being wrong or let others witness her defeat,* the villain inside Vivian is now commanding her with a compelling voice again. It is trying hard to inject some positive thoughts into her slow brain. Then instantly, *it* is out there on the path before her now, no more content to stay inside her to control her emotions and motions from within. Now *it* manifests in the open predominantly away from Vivian's flesh. Now the villain must be stronger if Vivian is losing her nerve. Now *it* must guide her more cogently from a palatable platform. *It* stands before her and blocks her view of the parking lot with a humongous flame of agony and self-pity. She must return and finish her mission, the villain orders and Vivian obeys. She turns and charges up on the path toward the slanting pine tree, now fully determined to disallow silly doubts deter her sacred mission of reaching the cliff through the secret path. *No way…! Defeat is not an option. What is my life without inspiration? What is life without positive thoughts and firm actions? March on, Vivian Marchon! March on for a complete victory…*

Suddenly, Vivian has the courage of a cougar and the vigour to jump like one, too. She glances behind her and observes the devil and flames following her on the path rapidly, threatening to push her over the ledge or burn her on revenge. She glimpses again down the canyon beyond the tree, which now resembles a soothing swimming pool, refreshing and safe, and she just leaps toward the tree with her arms wide-open to grab it. Instead, her left shoulder hits the tree and the impact thrusts her off the target, her arms dangling in midair. She merely takes one last glance at the bottom of the canyon and the devil awaiting her down there with a cocky smile.

*****

I hope I am not responsible for Vivian's demise in any manner—though I feel guilt and remorse sometimes, anyway, and wonder why! Perhaps Mike's snoring and Vivian's insomnia could be blamed for this tragedy—unless Vivian had been sick or suicidal and nobody knew anything about it! If so, we could not even condemn her obsession for inspiration, achievement, and fame! We would never know what drove her to such level of insanity!

Mike blamed himself for letting me give Vivian the address to the doomed cliff. He also blamed his failure to find a common interest with Vivian to amuse her and alleviate her obsession for becoming a renowned artist, at the cost of devastating her family, instead of trying to be a loving wife and mother. Yet, in the end, only the villain in Vivian had driven her toward the edge of the cliff and caused this catastrophe, plus so much grief and guilt for the rest of us.

Lorie and I felt sad and sorry that our acquaintance with this family, along with my own sudden obsession for painting, had triggered Vivian's sense of rivalry and self-pity. Lorie appeared even guiltier than me after she mentioned her old advice to Vivian once, about improving her technique and colour selection.

Also surprising and bizarre was Benjamin's reaction when I saw him again on the cliff and told him about Vivian's accident. He showed plenty of guilt and pain for opening his mouth to her about inspiration on the lower ridge instead of up there. I told him how we all felt sick and sorry for our words and small actions leading to a wasteful death and lingering gloom for a shaken, confused family. All along, I have been baffled often when many small incidents and coincidences lead to outrageous outcomes, sometimes for the better and sometimes for the worse according to some kind of a mysterious, settled predestination. In this case, however, everybody had regretfully seen and blamed that horrific Villain in Vivian.

Trumpet Man

Prelude

The daily commotion around the intersection of Burrard and Dunsmuir streets in downtown Vancouver is quite colourful if you truly get into the scheme of things. In three corners of the intersection, major office towers draw a big flow of foot traffic. Accordingly, in the southwest corner, adjacent to the Hyatt, the Burrard station accommodates a large volume of public transit for this busy part of the city. At the street level, various bus routes transport people or provide transfer facility to Skytrain, which operates in the lower levels of this prime station. The so-called 'Skytrain' actually runs on and under the ground, as well as on raised platforms across the city. From the street's bus stop, the stairs descend to a large, glass-canopied hall that connects two small malls on the opposite sides. This grand solarium provides ticket dispensers and entry to the lower levels for access to the trains.

Especially during office rush hours and tourist season, the Burrard station is one of the busiest parts of Vancouver, offering an ideal location for panhandling enterprises of all kinds. Some of these vagrants are aggressive and pesky, as if only exercising their constitutional rights to claim a fair share of the pedestrians' fortune. Their daunting stares, pleas, and even random profanities

—when ignored—intimidate most people. Some ultra polite ones are eager to share their long stories with you first to support their subsequent heartbreaking pleas for food, job, or bus fair to return to their hometowns, as *they claim* they have lost their wallets or something and thus stranded in Vancouver out of bad luck!

In contrast, some are too lazy or proud to beg directly, thus use cardboard signs to declare their demands with their crooked handwriting, *although they seem to have put a lot of thought and diligence into it!* They usually parade some coins in a cap or a cup to exemplify the generosity of the public and the going rate. A few years back maybe dimes or quarters were acceptable, but these days more loonies and toonies are in the loot. Some specify the amount explicitly on their signs in case an idiot is unaware of the going rate or likes to get funny: 'Please pay fifty cents,' which sounds like a real bargain considering the competition for a spot around downtown core. You must really appreciate the hassles of securing a prime location for this lucrative business, while also staying vigilant for law enforcement officers rounding them up from time to time. On the other hand, some vagrants do not really mind a short break in jail with a couple of free meals perhaps before returning to their work the next day rested and ready.

By the way, *please* note that their meticulous mannerism for using the word 'Please' on their cardboards is merely a generous, conditional courtesy to the public, as they reserve their rights to resort to profanities, as required, if you disregard their patience or refuse to be a well-paying customer! Just beware of their patience if you try to be or look funny.

Most panhandlers have, however, adapted themselves to the sophistication of the new era by offering some creative services for change. A hierarchy of decency is evident in their approach and level of services, too. Some resort to business tactics, such as finding unexpired, transit tickets and selling them for a fraction of the regular fare to greedy commuters, especially to unfamiliar tourists. Some even attempt, idiotically, to expunge the stamp marks of the expired tickets for resale.

Then there is this squeegee bunch who strives to clean the cars' windshields at the four corners of the intersection. Their speedy manoeuvres around the halted traffic and synchronizing their minute time to clean a windshield diligently and convince the driver to pay up before they leave the traffic lanes are quite intriguing. Their artful dexterity to elude impatient drivers when the traffic lights turn green must not be underestimated, either. In fact, they resemble danseurs in the way they tiptoe and zigzag slickly in and out of three lanes amidst the cars, especially when they also turn topless during hot summer days.

Another group of panhandlers offers some kind of newspaper, which specifies, 'Price by donation.' It seems to provide a very specialized type of news about street life, vagrants, and similar local dramas. Apparently, a parent company prints the paper for them for a fee. One particular guy, usually in a grey heavy coat, has persistently occupied a specific spot near the bus station for the last ten years. He offers a small paper called 'Street Corner.' He stands near the street corner, too, perhaps in his cute attempt to stay faithful to the paper's title.

Then there are street performers, some of whom are indeed decent musicians that enhance the spirits of commuters. Like gypsies, they come and go, except for Harvey Gilbert, the fiddler, who has occupied a spot exclusively at the Burrard station mall level next to the escalators for the last seven years.

Harvey discovered this thriving spot after canvassing the neighbourhood and gauging its potential in terms of foot traffic and income. A large crowd passes through this corridor from the two adjacent malls, the stairs descending from Burrard Street, and the stairs in the west corner leading to Dunsmuir. Overall, Harvey's prime location was logistically unparalleled. Moreover, it was relatively warm and secure from the wind and rain that erupts in Vancouver even in the middle of summer. Initially, he had eyed a few spots inside the Seabus terminal at Waterfront, where a ferry service transports passengers between downtown Vancouver and the North Shore. That location is substantially

warmer in winter and fall and enjoys a bit more foot traffic as
well. But since a few performers had already established their
tight territories over those areas, Harvey had settled for the next
best location in the neighbourhood. Indeed, he was proud for
having discovered that particular place at the mall level of the
Burrard station all by himself. And, surely, like any explorer, he
had grown a strong sense of ownership over his discovery to the
point of privately calling it Harvey Music Hall. In fact, the echo
of his music in that expansive solarium with such a high ceiling
resonated serenely, like playing in a concert hall with significant
acoustics. In particular, for his fiddling of Bach violin pieces,
Harvey Music Hall had proven to be more functional than the
other locations at the Seabus terminal.

Harvey's passion for fiddling had always exceeded his talent
and opportunities. He had never contemplated a life without his
daily musical performance, despite his failure to flourish due to
inadequate formal training. Not for the lack of trying, he had been
unable to play with a band, teach violin, or find any substantive
means of making a living out of fiddling. For many years, he had
sporadically tried to live off odd jobs. But failing in all of them
had only raised his passion to fiddle further to soothe his sorrows.
Fortunately, his unremitting dedication had all along fuelled his
optimism about being discovered as a virtuoso someday. Yet, he
was getting old with no break coming his way.

Harvey had lived with his father in a small house in Burnaby,
which he had then inherited and sold eventually due to its high
maintenance costs and taxes. He had bought a tiny apartment and
spent the rest of the money over the years. His engagement at
Harvey Music Hall was his last resort to stay afloat in society and
sell some of his CDs, of which he was so particularly proud. His
performance at Harvey Hall brought him around $350 a week in
donations, which was not bad at all considering his eagerness to
play, anyway. He went to Harvey Hall midmorning almost every
day and stayed around until six p.m. before returning to his suite
and amusing himself somehow if he had no nightly engagement.

Occasionally, he landed a job at some bar or with a band and made an additional ten or twenty dollars and a meal for the night.

Harvey's life dragged out quietly. Other than a few artless neighbours he knew and met occasionally, he was doomed to a life of solitude. Yet he felt responsible for maintaining the mood of the Burrard station after many years of performing at Harvey Hall. The transit inspectors, who monitored the area and checked passengers' tickets occasionally, knew Harvey and let him stick around. Many regular passers-by also liked Harvey and his music and helped him make a living. Some of the nosier ones who liked his music and enthusiasm, like me, spent a few minutes with him when an opportunity arose, or when he simply stopped fiddling to acknowledge his regular patrons. He was such a polite person, you always felt obliged to indulge him and enquire about his life when he interrupted his performance just to thank you or talk with you. I had grown fond of him and made a point to chat with him without interrupting his business too much. In fact, I had felt some special curiosity about him for some unknown reason, but perhaps wondering how such a relatively decent, artistic person seemed doomed—like myself, probably worse than the rest of the world!

Everything was fine and dandy for hopeful Harvey though, he thought, considering the turmoil of growing up motherless with a lousy father who was hardly ever home. He died eight years ago at the age of sixty-five, which made Harvey feel even lonelier. What a life, then and now, Harvey pondered often when fiddling in his apartment for his own soul and sobbing sometimes.

Main Story

Near four p.m. on a fine, sunny day in May, Harvey resumed fiddling after a break in preparation for the rush hour frenzy, which lasted around two hours and brought him the bulk of his income. His thoughts were sporadic about life a few years ahead when he would not have enough energy to spend so many hours fiddling in the streets. The low soothing tune of his violin echoed serenely, moving the big flow of commuters to search their hearts and pockets for empathy and spare change. He was not Itzhak Perlman, but did a decent job of lifting people's spirits by his evangelic recital of Bach music.

At a long high note, when Harvey was pouring his guts out into that smooth, soothing stride of the bow, a horrific and loud intermittent noise shattered his daydream and concentration. He strived to maintain his composure like any professional artist, while checking from the corner of his eye for the source of such outrageous intrusion. On his right, north side of the escalators, a tall young man was playing trumpet fervently. However, the noise he made could hardly be considered music. He might have learned to blow some notes into a trumpet at some point in his life, but he definitely could not play any music, Harvey mused in bewilderment. The trumpet case was open before him with a half dozen loonies and toonies in it. A black magician chapeau shaded his bloated face while he tried to connect some broken pitchy notes as musically as he could muster. Harvey gazed at him with awe and anger, witnessing the most bizarre scene in his musical career. Somebody dared to emit such offensive, loud noise and expected to get paid for it, too, not to mention his inconsiderate interruption of Harvey's performance. Going only by his normal sense of humour, he would be laughing his heart out right now watching that idiot. But it surely was not a laughing matter when a moron was ruining his concentration and business.

The soft tune of Harvey's violin could hardly echo amidst the trumpet roar, though he persisted fiddling. Finally, he lost his patience and froze in shock with his violin and bow hanging in his left and right hands. The clamour and the coolness of the trumpet player were simply amazing, as he seemed immersed in his appalling presentation even more deeply than Harvey had been two minutes earlier.

Harvey studied the situation and his options for a minute. Fury shattering his body, he approached the possessed fool. But the guy was merely lost in his noise-making endeavour with such exuberant passion beguiling the lucky public. He was simply too absorbed in his mastery to check out why Harvey was standing so close to him and not even contributing to his loot. He even ignored the violin that Harvey swung before his eyes a few times. For fifteen seconds, Harvey watched the trumpet player disregard him totally, felt angrier every second, and finally shrieked, "Are you out of your freaking mind?"

The trumpet player did not respond, though stared at Harvey in bewilderment. Harvey got closer and yelled louder, until the trumpet player finally took the trumpet away from his narrow foamy lips and began shaking his head in disgust and disbelief about some hardheaded jerk daring to halt his art.

"What? What?" he cried before wiping his mouth with the sleeve of his blemished blouse in distress.

"What do you think you're doing?"

"What do *you* think I'm doing?"

"Making a lot of noise, driving people mad."

"I'm making noise? Who do you think *you* are? Beethoven?"

"At least I'm playing something."

"So what am I doing? Dancing?"

"You don't even make the right notes. You're just blowing into that damn horn and deafening people."

"What's it to you?"

"You're killing my music."

"Then go play somewhere else."

"You go play somewhere else."

"I like it here. If you're unhappy just hit the road," the trumpet player said, raising his trumpet to continue his recital.

Harvey pushed the trumpet away from his face and screamed, "Listen man, whoever you are... This is my spot and you better leave."

"You leave... I feel just fine right here."

"No, you can't be here, I told you. This is my spot."

"Show me your deed."

"Here, here…" Harvey shrieked, shaking his fist near the guy's face, "Here is my deed, you asshole."

"Shove it in your ass, stupid son of a bitch," the trumpet player yelled back while grabbing Harvey's fist, squeezing it within his big palm, and pushing it away from his face.

The pain in Harvey's squashed fist aggravated him enough to kick the trumpet case fiercely into the air, all the coins flying out and rolling all over the place. The trumpet player posed to punch him in the face, but stopped just short of hitting Harvey. Harvey stepped back, realizing the punch could have broken his nose and a few of his teeth. Gradually, he retreated to his spot on the south side of the escalators, feeling somewhat sorry for scattering the guy's coins. Nonetheless, that was a good punishment for him for now, and necessary, Harvey thought. Hopefully, this moron had learned a lesson and would leave soon.

Under Harvey's curious eyes, the trumpet player scavenged within a large perimeter and salvaged his coins, counted them twice, and laid them in the case randomly again. He then grabbed his trumpet and resumed his recital as if nothing had happened and Harvey did not exist. Harvey could not believe this jerk's arrogance, so casually taking over Harvey's place of performance and business—the presumed Harvey Music Hall. *The nerve of this mad moron, playing one hefty note at a time so loud without any rhythm or harmony! But who's gonna pay him?* This swift, sweet inspiration brought him a quick sense of relief to the point of laughing at his own stupidity. *Why did I get myself worked up about a bum pretending to be a musician?* He would go away soon enough when nobody gave him any money. Why did he even bother confronting such a weirdo whose fate as a performer would end in an hour, anyway? *Then commuters would actually appreciate my romantic violin tunes even more. It must have all been God's design.* Indeed, it would be an insult to all musicians around the world to think of that idiot as a 'trumpet player.' *At best, we may call him the tramp 'trumpet man.'*

Harvey leaned against the wall and monitored the situation with a jubilant smirk, counting the last minutes of that tramp's musical adventure. Fiddling amidst the hideous trumpet noise was futile, anyway. He just had to wait for Nature taking its course of letting the stronger, in this case the more talented man, prevail. Deep in his thoughts, giggling privately regarding the trumpet man's silliness and dismal fortune, a young woman dropped a few coins in the trumpet case and then gave the guy a flirty grin before going away. *Oh shit,* Harvey murmured. He had not considered the trumpet player's young charming face in such droll magician hat crowning his tall slender body and a head full of curly brown hair bursting out of the corners of his chapeau. A cold sweat and gloom besieged Harvey.

The stream of commuters gushing toward the trains in the lower levels was increasing. They seemed drawn to, or at least curious about, the trumpet player's loud intermittent noise that resembled the abstract paintings of Picasso in the manner they attracted people only for their absurdity. So maybe these people believed his music was terribly innovative and fresh. After all, Harvey had witnessed Rap's popularity amongst youth despite its musical daftness. Maybe this trumpet man was up to something special, too. Maybe he was about to create a fad and put him out of business, Harvey thought in haze, while a rash of insecurity overwhelmed him.

Some of his depressing life experiences flashed before his eyes—like the time he had tried to follow his father's footsteps as a carpenter. However, both his father and he had conceded after one year of apprenticeship that he was hopeless, and finally his father had fired him with fury. Perhaps he had been concerned subconsciously about any kind of labour damaging his fingers and jeopardizing his fiddling dreams. He would never sacrifice his chance of becoming a virtuoso; never—he had already made that commitment to his delicate soul. He would never amount to anything, his father had remarked a few times when he had strived to be a salesman or a music instructor, or tried several other professions. Yet, his sudden loss of confidence today felt too deep and bizarre. Why should he doubt his initial judgment regarding the foolishness of the trumpet man and his music?

Meanwhile, the tramp played his pitchy patchy notes, and people, in larger numbers than ever, paid him before Harvey's bewildered eyes, *maybe even out of spite for Harvey who seemed so tense and useless today,* Harvey imagined. Or perhaps the commuters took his silent scrutiny as a sign of his humiliation and awe in the presence of the trumpet man, amazed and amused by such artistry pouring out of that shiny trumpet. Before, they usually nodded or smiled when approaching him, but today they passed by him quickly with pity or a smirk. Harvey's violin case was still wide open with the violin upright in a corner and a pile of coins in the main compartment of the case. Commuters peeped at his retired violin and the coins pitifully, and cursed his guts for still expecting them to pay him even though he had evidently given up fiddling. A few actually took the trouble of going out of their ways to drop a coin or two in the trumpet case with an odd grin. *What a horrible, crazy world! Why is everybody mad at me and, instead, so supportive of a stranger who has ruined our lives and the serene mood that my Bach music always spread here?*

Harvey's life was shattering and he felt more depressed than normal. He watched the trumpet player's booming business, took in the commuters' passive ridicule, lost more of his dignity and confidence, and finally decided to close shop and go home.

Harvey was tense even in his sleep. In his nightmares, the trumpet player's teasing, cool face glowed amidst a cheering crowd, record producers competing to sign contracts with him and offering him large stacks of cash. Everybody enjoyed the trumpet man's gibberish music while mocking Harvey for his tacky taste of three-century-old tunes. 'Who cares about melody and harmony anymore, man,' the crowd cried in his dream. 'You must be creative at all costs even if it means making repulsive noise with your instrument that only scars one's soul.' He was flustered and furious even in his dream about the way a tramp had ruined his relatively stable life. At dawn, he entertained the possibility of the trumpet man not showing up today, which helped him sleep a couple of hours without any more nightmares. He ate some cereal, cleaned and tuned his violin, and departed for his regular spot in the subway station.

Approaching the Burrard station, Harvey trembled from the trumpet noise audible from afar. His heart thumped and ached of anger from the idea of confronting that arrogant tramp again, in particular if he had also occupied Harvey's spot on the south side of the escalators. The foot traffic was much higher in that corner, as it provided the shortest distance from Burrard Street to lower levels for access to trains. He charged down the stairs nervously, and then exhaled a sigh of relief when he saw the trumpeting tramp in the same area as yesterday on the north side of the Hall. At least he had showed the decency of acknowledging Harvey's claim over that prime piece of real estate. This relative victory—probably the result of yesterday's confrontation—calmed his nerves a little. Still, the fact that the trumpet man was sticking around and spoiling his business remained disturbing, of course.

Harvey rushed to his spot with furtive excitement, set up his violin case as a gesture of securing his territory, and then glimpsed at the trumpet man with a timid expression of triumph. Now what? His fiddling would be futile while the sound of the trumpet besieged the Hall. Nor could he give up his spot and go play somewhere else, not even for an hour. That would be a sign of defeat and giving up his claim over the territory nobody had dared to penetrate for seven years. No, leaving was not an option. Confronting the trumpet man was risky, too, because he could get nasty.

Harvey left the violin case open, staggered to the west side of the Hall, and sat on the cement platform of the flowerbeds. He felt desolate and helpless. Gradually, however, some rational thinking made him accept the reality that others had a right to perform in the prominent Harvey Music Hall, too, despite his monopoly all these years. He really did not own the place nor was his deed valid! Maybe he could consider the trumpet man a 'guest performer' for now—as a comedian instead of a musician, though. He had lost control over the situation, but maybe he could trick the trumpet man move away. Convincing him to leave would be tough, however. He really hated that tramp's guts and the idea of speaking with him again.

Harvey's deep contemplation broke when the trumpet noise halted abruptly. The alleged music was so bizarre nobody could anticipate its ending or beginning. Harvey watched him put his trumpet in the case, take off his chapeau to wipe the sweat off his forehead, stroll a little, and then go inside the mall, careless about leaving his trumpet and the open case with a good bunch of coins unattended.

Harvey gathered he was taking a break. So he ran to his own spot, grabbed the violin and began fiddling while there was an opportunity. Like a naughty kid taking advantage of his mother's absence, he showed off his tenacity with vengeful enthusiasm. He played frantically, basking in the precious moment, while also loathing the humiliating stance imposed upon him. All along, he watched the mall entrance tensely for the trumpet man's return any second and spoiling his performance. Now, he did not even care how much money he made, but how long he played. He was tempted to run over and smash or hide the trumpet. Yet he could not gather the guts to do such an outrageous act.

For fifteen minutes, Harvey played anxiously, often in a faster than usual tempo. Then he noticed the trumpet man emerging from the mall with a cup of coffee. He smirked coolly at Harvey fiddling fervently, then peeped toward his trumpet case to ensure his assets were safe. He moseyed to the far end of the Hall and sat near an azalea bush planted in the flowerbed. He took a sip of his coffee, lit a cigarette, and blew out its smoke intermittently very much like his trumpet playing. He peeped at Harvey occasionally and swung his head rhythmically along with Harvey's music. He showed his enjoyment shamelessly with no sign of arrogance or hostility. His open support and appreciation of classical music felt just amazing, but also infuriating to Harvey! If this moron really understood music, he must naturally recognize the absurdity of the noise he made with his trumpet. Did he know any music at all? Was he only pretending to enjoy classical music, just for mocking Harvey again, now in a different way?

During the trumpet man's half-an-hour break, Harvey fiddled frantically and collected some change. Maybe the situation was not out of control completely, he thought, while he would wait for the guy to scram in a day or so. On the other hand, all that trumpet noise was driving him nuts all by itself. After all, he was the one exposed to that racket all day more than anybody else was.

Soon enough, the guy returned to his trumpet and blew into it forcefully as if chasing the last note hanging in midair since he had left thirty minutes earlier. The beginning was as nonsensical as the ending in his last recital. Harvey stopped playing since his efforts seemed pointless under the pressure of the trumpet noise. Maybe it was a good time for Harvey to take a break himself. He grabbed his water bottle from the corner of the violin case and took a sip. Despite his rage, he giggled privately regarding the masquerade—the scene of an idiot playing his gibberish music, and the way commuters could be judging the situation, especially Harvey's seemingly solemn defeat and resignation.

For the rest of the day, Harvey and the trumpet tramp took turns playing their tunes or resting, even more conscious of each other's presence and routines as the day drew closer to the end. Subconsciously, they even felt obliged to watch over each other's assets when one of them left his unattended to go to washroom or buy a cup of coffee. A reserved sense of empathy was developing between them, although they still felt the need to compete for playing time and maximizing their income. At the end of the day, Harvey had made less than half his usual income. That was tough and unacceptable in spite of his growing tolerance for the tramp and his nauseating music.

At his tiny apartment, Harvey paced the living room in search of a solution and finally succeeded in cooking up a scheme by bedtime. In the morning, he had a bigger load to carry to work, but that was okay, and necessary for implementing his devious plan. Approaching the Burrard station, he heard the sound of the trumpet again echoing in the Hall. He giggled this time, though, thinking of the gimmick he was about to play on the poor trumpet man and ruin his day. *How sweet revenge always feels!*

At his regular spot, Harvey laid the big bag and the violin case. Slyly, he glimpsed at the trumpet man watching him with suspicion, probably guessing what was in the bag by the way he glared at it and Harvey in disgust and distress. His angst delighted Harvey already, as he opened the bag slowly and pulled out two speakers, an amplifier, a battery unit, and a tiny microphone that he attached to his violin. He connected all the wirings and turned on the power.

Harvey had bought this sound-amplifying unit long time ago at a bargain price from a desperate performer. He used it on some occasions during the weekends when he went to Granville Island and played in the midst of noisy crowd and several performers offering all kinds of music. Carrying the heavy bag was surely inconvenient since, together with the violin case, at least the task of getting on and off the bus became awkward. Nonetheless, it had been a good investment for performing in Granville Island when the weather was good and he was in the mood to go there. The Burrard station and downtown Vancouver were relatively quieter and it made no economical sense to use the amplifier unit. However, today, all the trouble of carrying it and attaching all the wirings and paraphernalia was absolutely warranted.

Harvey strummed the violin strings and adjusted the amplifier for the sound level. The initial humming noise and the short blast of the speakers had already pissed off the trumpet man plenty. Harvey launched his attack with the loud sound of his violin swiftly overpowering the trumpet noise. A wide grin brightened Harvey's face, as he fiddled with amazing vigour and excitement even baffling him. Obviously, the trumpet man had instigated his childlike enthusiasm and sense of competition. He enjoyed every bit of it now, while the trumpet man seemed quite agitated by the sudden trap. Yet, he strived to defy defeat and disallow Harvey ruin his resolve. He blew faster and harder into the trumpet and played as many high notes as he could in order to maximize the noise. Since he was not playing any particular tune, he had the luxury of choosing any note he desired randomly and playing it as long and often as he wanted. This was a major advantage, which Harvey lacked, as he had to follow a sequence of notes to play a particular piece of music. The best he could do was to think of some Bach music with higher notes than his average compositions. He searched in his head for screechy tunes to play. The trumpet player was fast discovering and perfecting many innovative tricks of his own, mainly timing the blowing of his high and loud notes with Harvey's slow romantic bowing. A noise making war had begun. *Poor Bach; if only he knew he was now in the middle of such an idiotic war of noises!*

Harvey's remedy for the trumpet man's ploys was to increase the volume of the amplifier by another notch. And the trumpet player simply blew harder and moved a bit forward randomly to get closer to Harvey. Furthermore, he kept inventing better ways of intercepting the critical notes that Harvey played as a show of mastery. Their musical war continued, while they also enjoyed their own stamina and ingenuity to discover creative means of irritating the other. The commotion stunned the commuters as the Hall's soothing ambience had suddenly turned into a ridiculously noisy corridor to pass through. Both Harvey and the trumpet player were also concerned privately about the masquerade they had created. They realized how their childish war and incoherent music was spoiling the atmosphere of Harvey Hall so rapidly. The situation was particularly depressing for Harvey. The game these two presumably artists were imposing on themselves was ruining his hard-earned reputation in the Hall. Yet, neither of them cared to give in, as they exchanged ferocious glares and performed doggedly with anxiety. Only when one of them took a short break, the Hall became tolerable for the lucky passers-by and they threw some coins at them—mostly as a token of their appreciation for the relative peace and quiet. Their day income declined by more than forty percent, which translated to fifteen percent of Harvey's regular daily takings before the trumpet man's appearance.

Despite the joy of a tentative victory, Harvey remained quite distressed about the situation. He did not have any other plan to look forward to for the next day, while the trumpet man seemed equally stubborn and nifty in inventing irritating schemes. Then how should he defeat this mulish tramp for good, to bring his own life back to normal, and to rebuild the reputation of Harvey Music Hall? Harvey spent another restless night weighing his options: Without the amplifier, the trumpet man would be in charge of the situation most of the day. But using the amplifier would reduce his income even further, though it would at least give him the pleasure of pissing off that jerk, and possibly forcing him out. At last, he decided to carry the heavy amplifying set a few more days. He just had to find better ways of annoying that tramp to scram.

The next day, Harvey set up his sound system and connected the tiny microphone to his violin again. He increased the distance between the two tiny speakers a little more than yesterday, too, so that his music covered a wider domain. He glared at the trumpet player and began playing. The trumpet player increased the force of his blows, too, and used the sneaky tricks he had learned the day before to intercept Harvey's music. Harvey increased the volume by a notch. Immediately, the trumpet player leaned and pulled something from his own bag, and then smirked at Harvey who seemed curious and agitated already. He attached it to the end of the trumpet, which enhanced its loudness by fifty percent. The small extension also enabled him to aim the sound of the trumpet more precisely toward Harvey. He emitted his blaring, intermittent, high notes with even higher artistry and vigour this morning, as if he had been practising his new tricks the whole evening the night before.

The spite, anger, and desperation manifested in both their blushed, sweaty faces, while they tried to hide their hideous war from the commuters, too. They knew they had already pushed the limits. Any further competition would definitely intimidate commuters and result in even less income. On that ground per se, they had reached a very fine, implied understanding to keep at least their appearances normal, which then put extra pressure on them to remain both irritating to each other and conscious of the commuters.

Occasionally, the trumpet player tried to play his random notes in harmony with Harvey's music. This would show his mastery in mixing and orchestrating the overall music in the Hall while reducing the overall level of the niggling noise. Yet, his sneaky meddling irritated Harvey even more. More maddening than cluttering Harvey's music was that it could appear cute and creative to the commuters in the way he accompanied and teased Harvey's music. People might imagine he deserved more credit than Harvey did, for his ingenuity again, thus the person to get paid. The animosity intensified all morning with no sign of relief in sight. Only when one of them took a break, a tentative calm returned to the Hall.

Around noon, a transit inspector showed up for his rotating duty of checking commuters' tickets going down the escalators to the trains. He stood near the escalators between Harvey and the trumpet player, each about six meters away from him. After ten minutes, he felt tense from the horrendous noise bombarding him. He was used to loud music echoing in the Hall, but today it was too excessive and lousy. He gauged Harvey and the trumpet player competing callously not far from him. He tried to maintain his patience and pity for a minute, but then shook his head and flung his arm to Harvey with a gesture of confusion.

Harvey realized the inspector looked upset, but what was he expecting Harvey to do? He just could not care about the transit inspector's gesture or its alleged meaning since the situation was out of Harvey's hand. He then noticed one of his main patrons emerge from the lower platform escalator. This guy was always friendly with Harvey and often dropped two quarters in his violin case while nodding or waving to Harvey as a sign of appreciating his music and efforts. If Harvey were not playing, the guy would actually stop and talk with him for a couple of minutes as well before dropping the coins and going away. Sometimes, Harvey himself stopped playing merely to chitchat a bit with the guy who seemed interested in Harvey's life story, as if he were a reporter or writer of some sort. Maybe he could write his story and get him some recognition in this lousy world, after all. Today, the guy lingered near the inspector and monitored the trumpet man and Harvey awhile before bursting into laughter. He then chatted with the inspector for a minute, pointed toward the trumpet man, and laughed again and again, before they walked toward Harvey together.

"What's going on?" the inspector asked Harvey, while the other guy stood by and stared at Harvey with a friendly grin.

"Nothing…" Harvey replied after he stopped playing. "What you mean?"

"All this noise… Why's your music so loud today?"

"I'm using an amplifier," Harvey replied timidly.

"I can see that. But why? Your music always sounded good without all this mumbo jumbo. With all the echo in this place, you don't need an amplifier."

"I thought so too, until that jackass showed up."

"Your friend here says this has been going on for three days now," the inspector said pointing to the guy standing next to them.

"Yeah, he's right. That trumpet noise has been ruining my business for four days actually."

"But this isn't working out. There's too much noise around here. I cannot work like this and you are disturbing the people walking around here, too. You better turn off that amplifier."

"No, I can't. Why don't you go deal with that asshole? Can't you throw him out?"

"No, I can't throw him out. He's not using any amplifier."

"But that's not music he's playing…"

"Whatever… If you want to play here you better cut off that thing."

"No, I can't while that jerk is here."

"Sorry pal. If you don't, I'll have to call my supervisor and they may send the cops to sort this out. I don't want to cause problem, but be reasonable."

"I don't care about the cops or anything," Harvey said with anxiety, raised his violin, and began playing fast again to catch up with the trumpet man who was enjoying the chance of galloping alone for a while. Harvey liked the inspector, who had always been friendly and empathetic, often making a point to chat with him when he was not fiddling. But now suddenly he seemed like another jerk, blaming only him for all the noise.

After a long staring duel, at last, the inspector returned to his post to control both his temper and commuters' tickets. The other guy dropped three quarters in Harvey's case and waved goodbye to him before going away.

You might have probably guessed that this other guy was me again. I was surely curious what would happen next, but I was late for a meeting already, all thanks to the recent masquerade besieging the Harvey Music Hall making me linger and possibly even chat with Harvey. Anyway, I learned about the rest of the story when I spoke with Harvey a few weeks later.

The inspector pitied Harvey, knowing him for such a long time as a funny, friendly man. So why was he a jackass today? He waited another ten minutes, while the music felt more horrific by each. He considered talking with the trumpet player, but he was not committing any objectionable offence. Of course, his trumpet was too noisy and the music he played sounded too messy, the inspector conceded. What the heck was it that he was playing, anyway? He strolled toward the trumpet player.

Harvey had been observing the inspector's mood all along and considering disconnecting his amplifier while he was around. Then, he noticed him approaching the trumpet player and talking to him for half a minute. Promptly, the trumpet player collected his assets and left the Hall. Harvey could not believe his eyes. How could this tiny inspector make such a tough-looking asshole flee so hastily? But why should he care as long as that moron had left? After playing the last piece and making sure the trumpet man had gone for good, he disconnected the amplifier as well, feeling victorious and vivacious. Everything returned to normal, including the contributions to his loot.

Later, Harvey approached the inspector, "Thanks for getting rid of him and sorry for my loud music."

"No problem, Harvey."

"How'd you get rid of him so quickly?"

"I don't know... I didn't do anything special..."

"I'd been trying to run him off for three days and he was stubborn as a mule, and then you talk to him for a second and he scrams."

"Just be happy he's gone."

"Of course... But the way he ran off was weird."

"I told him the same thing I'd told you; that I'd have to call my supervisor and maybe the cops, unless you two made some kind of a deal."

The return of his calm normal life delighted Harvey dearly, until the following Monday when the trumpet player appeared before him like a ghost. Harvey trembled at his sight and assumed the worst. He was perhaps returning to resume spoiling Harvey's life, again, now that the inspector was not around. He kept fiddling and ignoring him, anyway. Yet, the trumpet player hung around, grinned at Harvey kindly, and nodded along with his tune so keenly Harvey felt he might even drop a coin into his loot any second. Finally, Harvey lost his patience and stopped playing.

"What the hell do you want now?" Harvey screamed.

"Here…" The trumpet player held out a capped paper cup toward him.

"What's this?"

"Coffee… For you..."

"What for?"

"For saying I'm sorry. Come on, take it."

Harvey took the cup from him hesitantly with suspicion, wondering what kind of a gimmick he was playing now. Only because he was not carrying his trumpet case, Harvey decided to be patient for a minute. He held the cup of coffee away from himself, however, as though it might explode any second. He just watched the trumpet player eat French fries out of a small bag.

"You want some?" he asked Harvey, offering the bag of fries.

"No."

"So, how is business?"

"Okay… What do you want?"

"Nothing… I just came by to say hi."

"You're planning to come back here to play?"

"No. I'm not here to play. I was just walking by and thought I should say sorry for teasing you a little. I was fooling around but didn't mean to bug you, man."

"You were rude, not to mention all that noise."

"Forget it man. I said I'm sorry. Go ahead, drink your coffee before it gets cold… What's your name?"

"Harvey," Harvey replied with impatience.

"Nice meeting you, Harvey. I'm Sam."

"Yeah…!" Harvey murmured tiredly, still suspicious of his intention. Maybe even the coffee was poisoned or something, especially the way Sam looked at it and kept asking him to drink it.

"Was this your own coffee?"

"Yeah… But you can have it."

"Where's your trumpet?" Harvey asked.

"I pawned it."

"Why?"

"I'm running out of cash to pay for the place I sleep."

"Why don't you find a real job?"

"Well… I don't know… I can't."

"Why not?"

"I just can't," Sam replied with distress.

"What happened to your hat?"

"I sold it… for eight bucks."

"It was a funny looking chapeau; I liked it on you," Harvey said with a smirk.

"It is getting hot to wear that chapeau these days, anyway."

"You want me to lend you a couple of bucks?" Harvey asked, relaxing about Sam, and actually starting to like him by the way he looked so lost and lousy today. He took the cap off the cup and took a sip.

"No, thanks man. I got to do something more serious."

"Like what? Rob a bank?" Harvey asked with laughter.

"Yeah… sure!" Sam replied with a teasing tone. "I don't know yet. But I'd better go."

"Are you sure you don't want a couple of bucks?" Harvey asked, taking another sip of the warm, tasty coffee.

"Yeah, I'm sure. Thanks." Sam began walking away.

"Come by sometime," Harvey said.

Sam turned, "Maybe…, if I'm around." He then waved his hand and stepped on the escalator up to the street level.

Harvey raised his violin to play, but was swiftly swamped by another one of his emotional surges that usually led to disaster for him. He knew he would be sorry for what he was about to do. But he could not help himself. An impulse was blurring his brain. In ten seconds, the logic lost. He turned toward the stairway and shouted at Sam getting off the escalator.

Sam stopped and Harvey beckoned him. Yet, as Sam began descending, Harvey already felt anxious and sceptical about his idea. He struggled with his inner turmoil until Sam was back downstairs, staring at him with his prying puppy-dog eyes.

"Listen. I thought if you don't have money for a place to sleep, you can stay with me for a couple of nights until you find a job or decide which bank you gonna rob."

"Do you have room for me?" Sam asked.

"Yes, for a couple of nights…"

"How much?"

"Nothing. But you must sleep on the couch."

"Thanks, man. You do that for me?"

"Yeah."

"You ain't weird or a pervert, eh?"

"No, no. Forget it, man," Harvey replied with stress, already sorry for inviting him. On the other hand, it was good that Sam himself had cleared the air. "So you want the couch or not?"

"Yeah, of course. I really appreciate it, Harvey."

"Come back around six and we'll go home together."

"I'll be here," Sam said, his eyes showing a combination of appreciation and suspicion.

Harvey raised his violin again and resumed playing, musing over his promise to Sam, and why he has always been such a softy. Why would he want to invite a stranger—who would probably eat his food, too—to his tiny apartment, all for nothing? How could he forgive that jerk so fast after all the agony he had caused him for four days? Even more depressing was realizing his apparent vulnerability due to loneliness. His sudden urge to invite a stranger to his apartment came from such depth of his psyche he had no power to control. Who was this man he was letting sleep only a few feet away from him tonight? All he knew about him was his cool face and arrogance almost destroying his income stream and Harvey Hall's reputation. And then he had disappeared, pawned his trumpet, sold his magician's chapeau, and come by to say hi to him and apologize with a cup of coffee as peace offering. Maybe he was a lunatic or a thief. His music alone could be construed a sign of his lunacy. Or maybe he was a charlatan, plotting all along to soften him to do something stupid; *stupid like inviting him to my place.*

With disturbing thoughts cluttering his mind, Harvey fiddled idly before a sudden realization crushed his nerves. He stopped playing abruptly to deliberate the notion carefully. The reason Sam had left the Hall after four days of tenacity had just been the inspector's ultimatum about calling in the police. The possibility that Sam was running from the police had not occurred to him until now. The reason he could not find a job was probably also due to his criminal records or something. He must confront Sam this afternoon. Then again, if he were running from the police, he would not confess it, would he? Agitated and sorry for getting himself involved with a suspicious lunatic or criminal, he kept fiddling passively with tension.

Just before six p.m., Sam showed up with a suspicious grin of his own that made Harvey even more nervous.

"Are the police after you?" he asked Sam rashly.

"No, why?"

"No reason. Forget it… let's go."

"Let's go to McDonald's and I'll buy us a burger first. My treat," Sam said.

"You're sure?"

"Yeah."

They walked to the McDonald's in the next block and Sam bought two burgers, but no drinks or fries. Harvey's stress settled a bit by Sam's generosity and charm, and also the fact that he would not have to offer Sam any of his bread and hotdogs he kept in the fridge for super.

"Will you give me an honest answer if I ask you something?" Harvey asked.

"About the police again?" Sam replied with anxiety.

"No, about your music."

"What about my music?"

"Do you really understand the meaning of the noise you make with your trumpet? It sounded horrible to me, more like a donkey braying, if you ask me."

Sam burst into laughter, almost choking on the piece of dry bread in his mouth. He gulped some water before replying, "I think it is music. If I believe it is music, everybody else thinks so, too. You saw it yourself. People paid me."

"But do you actually understand what you play? Be honest," Harvey asked with humour but deep curiosity.

"I know I like to play like that and it sounds good to me. It sounds like music to my ears and apparently to others, too. Why do you want to deny the obvious fact?"

"Stop fooling around. You probably don't even know how to play a trumpet, do you?"

"Are you nuts? Didn't you hear me playing?"

"No, I mean, do you know any notes or had any lesson?"

"I had lessons in grade eight, but afterwards I only played for myself sometimes. I had not played for a while… Maybe I'm a bit rusty."

"No, man. It is not just a matter of rust. You play one note or another at a time without any melody or connection. You're only fooling around with that trumpet and people."

"I'm not fooling anybody. They pay me because they like my music."

"What music?" Harvey blasted into laughter again.

Sam stared at him a moment and burst into laughter, too.

"Well, thank God, at least you gave that trumpet away."

"I'm gonna get it back now that I can stay with you free."

"Oh Gosh, what you need that thing for? You can't come back and play around me again."

"Why not? Aren't we friends now?" Sam asked.

"Not if you wanna return and ruin my business…"

"I'm just kidding. I ain't coming back here. But I'll try to find another spot to play and make some money."

"Okay, my crazy friend. But you got some nerve playing that horn the way you do," Harvey said with another burst of laughter.

"I love that trumpet and the sound of it. It's the only thing I have and care for," Sam replied with a childlike innocence.

Sam's bizarre passion for music—like a younger but much less talented image of Harvey himself—made Harvey relax some more about letting him stay in his place for a couple of nights. He could not be a criminal with such sad eyes. So, no need to upset Sam even more with his insensitive questions about the police and his past, at least not tonight. He should just sit back for now and maybe Sam would tell him everything about his life himself.

"Let's go, Louis Armstrong," Harvey said and they both chuckled again.

"It's a wonderful world, eh?" Sam asked.

"Once in a while…" Harvey replied. "But it's mostly a world of wandering fools like you and me, if you get my drift."

"Yeah, you're really smart, Harvey…"

"Don't tell me you can sing, too, like Louis?" Harvey asked.

"In fact, I do. That was my next move if you and that stupid inspector had not conspired to kick me out."

During the following days, Sam proved to be a funny, carefree guy, after all, laughing casually along with Harvey's continuous teasing. Harvey's normal sense of humour had also returned after torturing himself for a week about Sam. In fact, he now seemed eager to make up for all the time he had wasted worrying about Sam the prior week. The whole episode felt too comical now, and he could not get over the great humour in Sam's innocence and boldness, playing such moronic music with his loud trumpet in the streets. Sam's crude artistry and arrogance had turned into a real laughing matter now that he was not a threat to Harvey's business. So he used the occasion any chance he got to make both of them laugh like crazies. He tried to imagine Sam singing in the Burrard station, too, and laughed even harder.

Subsequent to the planned couple of nights, Sam did not show any sign of leaving and Harvey did not feel like pressing this matter, either. He was starting to like Sam's cheery, charismatic presence, yet a nagging voice about having a stranger in his apartment bothered him, nevertheless. Sam's reluctance to talk about his past, not even in response to Harvey's direct questions, was annoying. On the other hand, Sam was a generous man. He kept buying hamburgers for them at McDonald's or paid for the groceries that he cooked in the apartment rather tastefully. The arrangement was a big improvement for Harvey both financially and emotionally. After four days, Sam braved to ask Harvey for a $75 loan to top-up his own money and release his trumpet and Harvey agreed. Sam played in different parts of downtown and then they found each other around Granville Street at the end of the day, strolled to the underground station and took the train to Burnaby, usually without buying tickets, mostly out of spite for the transit inspectors. They laughed about that particular inspector who had kicked Sam out and the possibility of encountering him together now as two pals.

Their relationship flourished as Sam enjoyed a steady stream of income from trumpeting, Harvey's loan was repaid, and their cooperation for harmonious cohabitation worked nicely to their advantage. Harvey's trepidation about Sam's past had settled, too, or it seemed.

One month later, they were chatting and laughing on the down escalator in the Granville station. Suddenly Sam lost his composure when somebody yelled his name from the ascending escalator. He charged down the stairs toward the train and the guy chased him like a greyhound, after rushing up and getting off the escalator first. Harvey watched the incident in bewilderment, wondering whether he should start running after both of them, too. The chase appeared like those fast action movies he watched on TV every night. But now suddenly his heart thumped with apprehension about the possibility of Sam being in some kind of trouble and perhaps even dragging him into it; the kind of trouble he had been trying to avoid all his life; the kind of trouble one could expect from harbouring a criminal perhaps. Sam rushed toward the end of the station, planning to get out from the other exit. But he changed his mind when the train's chime rang the departure alert. He jumped into the nearby wagon just before its doors closed. The guy chasing him leaped into the last wagon and the train zoomed out of the station before Harvey's baffled eyes.

Harvey was now perplexed about Sam more than ever, since the guy chasing Sam could not have been a policeman in the way he had recognized Sam and called his name casually. Therefore, Sam was eluding both the police and some people, which made his case even more mysterious and unsettling. Harvey took the next train and reached his apartment half an hour later, but no sign of Sam. Another hour passed and when Sam did not show up, he began to worry even more, now fearing that Sam might never come back. He was already missing him, which was weird, considering his concern about Sam causing him trouble with whatever crimes he might be involved in. More than anything, he now feared the possibility of losing a good companion, someone he could relate to despite his weird sense of music and possible criminal background. He missed his cooking as well, which had already spoiled Harvey's sense of independence. He worried about losing the chance of teasing Sam about his music, which he regularly raised as an amusing topic, only for humour and never for hurting Sam. He actually enjoyed and encouraged his guts. In fact, he really liked the guy now regardless of who he was.

He fried two eggs and three sausages in a grease-smudged frying pan, while checking outside the window impatiently for any sign of Sam. Along with two pieces of toasts and ketchup, he ate the food with difficulty as his tension clogged his throat. While chewing the last loaf painfully, the familiar knock on the door revived his spirit. He leaped toward the door and let Sam in. He looked exhausted and in disarray. His shirt was wrinkled and his face and hair were messed up with dried sweat.

"What's going on Sam?" Harvey asked with agitation.

"Nothing," Sam replied tensely. "May I take a shower?"

"What you mean nothing? Who was that man? A police or something?"

"No. I told you it's nothing. That guy knows me but I don't wanna talk to him. It's personal, man. Let it go."

Harvey resented being nosy like a nagging spouse. But he liked to know more about Sam and whomever he associated with. He delved into deep thoughts while Sam took a shower. His hunch had been right about the man chasing Sam. At least he had learned that some personal matter was haunting Sam. The police was probably hunting him, too. That was probably why such a healthy-looking young man would not look for a job. Now his secrets were out and Harvey felt like a detective having pasted all the clues together. Something was certainly wrong with Sam's situation, and maybe it was time to ask him to leave. But the more he pondered this option, the more he felt sorry for Sam and himself regardless of Sam's guilt in the chaos surrounding them. Maybe he should give Sam another chance and question him later when they both felt calmer. Perhaps it did not matter at all who he was, anyway? He liked him too much to care anymore.

For two days, Harvey kept his emotions in check. They kept their routines of taking the train rides together in the morning and evening, making dinner, and watching TV. All along, he was getting more curious to know the truth, but hated losing Sam for what he might learn or by agitating him. Late one evening, while watching TV, some heavy knocking on the door broke the calm.

"Police... Open the door."

Sam jumped out of the couch and whispered to Harvey, "Please don't tell'm I'm here. I'll explain everything. I promise."

"Open the door. Now..."

"Okay, okay. I'm coming," Harvey replied, staggering toward the door. Two police officers and the building caretaker stood in the hallway.

"Is Joe Hanson living here?" the tall officer asked while the caretaker tried to peek inside the room from the crack of the door.

"I haven't even heard the name," Harvey replied.

"You're sure?"

"Yeah I'm sure. Who'd you say? Hanson?"

"Yeah, Hanson. You know him?"

"No. I don't know any Hanson."

"So who's the guy I've seen staying with you recently?" the caretaker asked.

"He's a friend; sometimes comes over for a visit."

"Is he here now?" the officer asked.

"No… Tonight he hasn't come by."

"What's your name?"

"Harvey… Harvey Gilbert."

"Harvey, you'll tell us the truth if you know this guy. Right?"

"Right… Of course…"

"Because we're gonna find out and you'll be in trouble, too. You understand?"

"Yeah."

The police officers surveyed Harvey's eyes and inside the empty room, with the TV on at the far end corner, then they left. Surprised at his courage and conviction to protect Sam at all costs, Harvey reeled with shaking legs toward the bathroom and opened the door. Sam was hiding in the tub behind the curtain. He burst into laughter and pulled the curtain.

"If the cops had come in, you think they would've hesitated to pull the shower curtain?" Harvey said half-teasingly with a chuckle again.

"I knew it was silly, but I couldn't think of anything better," Sam replied.

"So, you're Joe Hanson?"

"Yes. I'm Joe Hanson."

"Well?"

"Okay, I'll tell you everything. Let me get out of here first." Harvey started toward the living room and Sam followed him timidly. "Sorry for all the trouble. But now I'll get out of your hair."

"You will? But I don't want you to leave."

"I guess I'd better go away, perhaps tonight."

"Why? Why you have to leave?"

"Because the police might come back with a warrant and find me. They shouldn't find me, for your sake and mine."

"What've you done, Sam, or whoever you are?"

"Nothing. I told you."

"It can't be nothing! All these people and policemen looking for you…"

"It's simple when I tell you."

"Okay, I'm listening."

"The guy that chased me the other night is my wife's cousin. He—"

"You're married?"

"Yeah… Will you shut up and listen?" Harvey drooped and Sam continued: "I fled home two months ago. This guy who saw me by fluke is a lunatic. He chased me for a long time that night; maybe he managed to follow me here and tipped off the cops. That's all."

"So that's why you can't get a job?"

"Sorta…"

"Why'd you run away from your wife?"

"That's a long story…"

"Okay… Tell me."

"Let's go to the park or somewhere else before the cops come back."

Harvey nodded and left first to check around the building. Then they sneaked out of the building and strolled amongst the dark shadows toward the park.

"I'm from Red Deer, you know… in Alberta?"

"Yeah?"

"My father died when I was fourteen. He left me a small farm, a few sick animals, and a big debt. My mother had already abandoned us and nobody knew where she had gone with her boyfriend. Four years later, I married the daughter of a neighbour who had helped me run the farm. I was supposed to pay him back after making some money on the farm or selling it. I was young and knew nothing about farming or marriage. Two kids later and twelve years of torture by the witch I had married were enough for any man to go berserk. But I also had to work almost free for my father-in-law. I could not see any hope for that kind of life and my future. All I could do was to play my trumpet and suffer quietly, wondering why my wife was such a bitch, always nagging and blaming me for her misery. She insisted I would've died of starvation and loneliness many years ago if her father had not been so generous to me. The more I thought about my life and options, the less I could find a way out but to cop out. One night I took my trumpet and headed for Vancouver. I knew they wouldn't leave me alone and that she'd eventually find me, but I didn't expect it to happen so soon. I was hoping Vancouver was large enough to hide me for a year or so at least."

"Why are you afraid of the cops?"

"They'll probably force me go back to live with that bitch… I'm sure they've cooked up a lot of lies and criminal charges against me, she and her stupid dad."

"Maybe you should go back and divorce her, and then come work in Vancouver."

"No. It's gonna take a long time even if they let me do it."

"So what're you gonna do?"

"Maybe I'll be safe in Seattle or California if I change my name. I got to get a fake id somehow."

"So, you rather be a runaway wanderer for the rest of your life than going back to your wife and kids, at least for the chance of divorcing her?"

"Yes, absolutely… I'd rather die than bear another day with her and her family."

"I'll lend you two-hundred bucks to get around and pay me back later."

"You sure?"

"Yeah, I'm sure… You want more?"

"No thanks. You've been the best friend I've never had," Sam says while extending his hand to shake Harvey's.

"You go walk around a couple of hours and then come back after midnight to stay the night in my place and start your journey in the morning."

"You think so?"

"Yeah, I think so. If nobody shows up by midnight, you'd be safe for one more night."

"Yeah, you're right and very kind. Thanks, man."

"In fact, if this plan works out tonight, maybe we should try it awhile and see if it is still safe for you to stick around with me."

"You think so?" Sam asks pensively.

"Yeah, we can always try it safely for a while... Why not?" Harvey replies with joy as if enjoying a chance of keeping Sam around as long as possible.

"Or maybe we can go away together if you want," Sam says.

"You think so?"

"Yeah... Maybe we could go to Toronto or another country."

"Well, we'll think about it later... Now, I like your point about us living in this world like wandering fools even better..."

"Yeah, it's just not a wonderful world at all," Harvey says tensely. "Now go away for a couple of hours."

Sam disappears in the dark and Harvey returns home with tears gathering in his eyes and wondering whether he could bribe the caretaker to leave them alone. On the other hand, he is not sure that is a viable plan. We two fools cannot even wander in the world together!

*****

My commuting route changed when my office moved and I did not go through the Burrard Station for a couple of years. The hoopla at that intersection appeared to be intact though, anytime I happened to be in the neighbourhood and made a point to find Harvey in his regular spot and say hi to him. But then suddenly, since four years ago, Harvey is no longer there anymore, nor is the guy who sold the paper called 'Street Corner.' Maybe Harvey and Sam ran away from Vancouver together, I wonder with joy sometimes.

Sometimes, I think I should have asked Harvey for a way to contact him, although I had been trying all along not to pry in his life too much, more than what he had already preferred to share with me so generously himself. It feels so refreshing when we meet some odd humans with pure hearts by accident once or twice in our lives and forget, just for a minute at least, how the majority of us have become such horrible human beings.

It is too depressing and disturbing to witness so much poverty and misery all over the world, especially in affluent countries. In recent years, downtown Vancouver, especially around gas town and near the historic 'steam clock,' where tourist frequent, looks very much like a third-world country with lots of panhandlers roaming around and pestering pedestrians every step of the way. Despite the humour and the chance for learning humility, the scene of so many vagrants in this day and age in our so-called civilized nations is embarrassing for us at all social and personal levels.

Then again, you go nuts witnessing some young beggars just sitting there casually with their idiotic signs and playing with their cell phones, texting or talking with somebody so seriously. You certainly wonder whom the lucky call recipient is—a lover, colleague, friend, pizza parlour for ordering food, or maybe even their young children—just making sure they have arrived home safe and sound and are doing their homework, so that they do not end up like their parents with a similar strenuous career.

By the way, some panhandlers' touching signs are getting longer and more illegible. Therefore, it would take you at least thirty minutes for every city block, especially in crowded tourist areas like gas town, if you wished to read them carefully before not only deciding about the legitimacy of their varied pleas, but also choosing the ones best satisfying your criteria and qualifying for your limited charity budget for a particular day.

The End

RESIGNATION

Pink Dove

Entering Stanley Park through an elaborate archway, which I am noticing for the first time, a mysterious surge of serenity besieges me this morning. It is an odd feeling considering my chronic melancholy—like a sudden relief from a persistent migraine. Only some obscure flickers of daunting dilemmas flash in my head—merely resembling the fading residue of that imaginary migraine. *What is so different about the park today? Besides that peculiar archway, of course, which seems to have come from nowhere overnight!* Ecstatic by the esoteric experience, muttering *life is a very splendid thing* in tune with the old song, I proceed toward my favourite spot where I often relax on a bench near the rose bushes and admire their colourful variety and mesmerizing fragrance.

But the echo of ducks quacking and flapping their wings near the water lures me toward the lagoon where my freaky friend, the black swan, sometimes swims along the bank searching for food. The bad big bird usually hides inside the tall undergrowth and only seldom sneaks out to startle me by its appalling appearance. Its glossy black down stirs a sense of darkness and death in me. Yet, obsessively, I crave its arrival and exquisite cervical dance— the long narrow neck twirling around rhythmically and steering the bright red beak on the water surface to munch flower debris floating over the lagoon with an endless appetite. Its timid eyes betray its brave, showy manoeuvres near eerie humans like me. The poor bird must have felt enough of my fury recently, about to erupt and engulf everything and it.

Gazing over the lagoon for a sign of the wily black swan, I spot the two regular white ones that sail around and across the banks, caressing all day. With their velvety white statures, reeling peacefully in unison over the cobalt waters of the lagoon, they seem in love. They appear friendlier toward people, too. Still I look around and behind the shrubs hypnotically for the black swan. Like a possessed fool, I feel restless when I cannot locate this dubious bird, wondering whether its doomed existence has finally expired. I somehow relate to its fate, which seems full of bleak episodes similar to mine; and no companion to soothe its suffering and loneliness, either. Oddly enough, this curious bird sometimes appears to appreciate my anguish, too, maybe even better than my beloved Jasmine.

But why am I insisting on finding this black loner now that my mood has rejuvenated so miraculously this morning? Why not instead befriend those elegant white lovers inching toward me intently with their long necks erecter than ever? A premonition strikes me swiftly: That my fate will change today, as confirmed, or symbolized, now by the black swan's absence and the graceful approach of the white ones... Yes, some wonderful revelation will perpetuate my sudden jolly mood today and eradicate my worries forever... *Forget the damned black swan.*

I watch the vivacious white swans reaching me boldly, as if carrying a sacred message for me; or maybe because nobody else is around to feed them. They are now used to people bringing them bread or fruits regularly, though they often have to compete quietly with the greedy ducks and geese for their share of the loot. They linger near me patiently but curiously, which is a novel, perplexing gesture all by itself. Their sudden interest in me, or mere curiosity even, is precious this special day, though I feel guilty for not having any food for them. They are always polite and calm unlike those noisy, vulgar ducks and geese. I murmur, 'I am sorry,' as they keep gazing at me fixedly. I wonder again if my guardian angel has dispatched them as a sign, to affirm my premonition. So I keep nodding to them appreciatively and they start bobbing, too. All along, I wish the ominous black swan would never show up to spoil the serene mood and my growing friendship with the loving white swans. I promise to myself to bring them food next time and murmur my pledge to them, too.

Musing over the good omen and amused by the birds' amazing life in the park, I notice a Dove on a broken branch of a Japanese maple by the lagoon. Not a bird 'dove,' but rather a 'Dove' soap. I am not moved merely by a measly bar of soap, but because it rekindles nostalgic bachelorhood memories—the best years of my life, nevertheless, filled with riveting adventures and youthful hopes. Now in my fifties, a small pension starting in a few years, so little is there to show for all those dreams and efforts. But I am happy today too… Everything is wonderful, except… except for the creeping inkling of the damn layoff and my struggle to find another job. What a niggling nightmare… But forget the layoff… *Forget the black swan…*

Because I am happy today, even about marrying Jasmine after years of indecision for choosing a companion. She was elegant and pretty with blond hair and gorgeous body; smart too, at 25, I 37, at our wedding. Especially, I cherish her hindsight about the possibility of financial distress, always economizing, then getting a job herself ten years ago when our kids reached school age.

Approaching the Dove with caution, suddenly I crave to grab it and bathe with it, maybe even in the lagoon right now, despite the risk of people mocking me and possibly getting arrested, too. Whose Dove is it, anyway? It seems perfectly new, judging from the glossy, cute little box with the tiny image of a flying dove. I imagine a nicely curved soap inside the tight pink wrap, yet I hesitate clasping or opening the package to examine its existence. Nobody is around the tree to stop me from taking it, either.

The smooth ripples in the lagoon keep patting the bank. A goose shrieks and the two white swans swiftly swerve in synchrony. Again, I survey my surroundings and the Dove on the Japanese maple, thinking that I can snatch it because nobody is watching me. However, oddly enough, the Dove reminds me again more urgently of Jasmine and her sacrifices for me and our children. Suddenly an urge to surprise her—to take her to lunch and admit how much I appreciate her devotion and foresight—besieges me. The idea of charming her with my *'I love you'* intrigues me even beyond the sensation that had beset me earlier upon entering the park, beyond the sense of lightness after crossing through the mysterious archway, beyond the thrill of finding the Dove, and beyond all that weird yearning to steal it and bathe with it. Yeah… I must go embrace my loving wife and tell her the funny and freaky story of the Pink Dove, right after telling her that I love her, of course.

Glimpsing one last time across the lagoon—the loverly white swans swaying away cheek-to-cheek and still no sign of the lonely black one—it is all definitely a clue about the good omen approaching. Yeah… it has all been about finding Jasmine and thanking her. *Forget the black swan… Forget the pink Dove…*

I charge toward Jasmine's office only fifteen minutes away from the park. She has been content with her job as an equity analyst at Allied Investments except for too much seclusion in her office all day without any contact with clients. However, we agree that her present research job is less stressful than dealing with edgy investors in her previous position. Now she sits in her quiet office all day, crunches some numbers, creates financial charts, and prepares rosy reports. I feel like a hero for rescuing her today, for at least an hour, from the dungeon that she often complains about. Her tenacity to call her cosy office a dungeon may be a kind of whining if I wanted to criticize her. But I love her anyway, especially today, especially this very minute. I wish I could land a job like hers and work all day in a dungeon like hers, instead of wandering in the streets and parks. I am not jealous or anything; only sick of feeling idle and aimless. Though, today I am happy and all I want is the company of my gorgeous wife for lunch; that is all. Is this too much to ask too?

I take the elevator to the 18th floor and smile to the unfamiliar receptionist. I have met most of Jasmine's colleagues in company picnics and parties, including the regular receptionist who is not around today.

"Hi," she says.

"I'd like to see Mrs. Jenkins, please."

She consults the list before her, "Mrs. Jenkins isn't here right now. Can somebody else help you, sir?"

"Is she coming back soon?"

"Not today... Did you have an appointment?"

"No, thanks," I say and turn toward the elevators, wondering how she has escaped her dungeon and where she has fled to!

I am flustered going down in the elevator and staggering back to the park. I feel down about the good omen I had anticipated in surprising Jasmine and taking her to lunch not materializing. I do not know what to do with the big 'I love you' I had so keenly prepared to give her. I am beginning to lose my confidence again after feeling so jolly all morning. My mood is deflating fast, though my spirit still strives to survive. I try to refocus on the good omen supposedly promised me upon entering the park this morning and reaffirmed by the black swan's absence. *So, what is the good omen?* I meander in the park aimlessly, totally confused about Jasmine's absence, still struggling to contain my nerves and sustain my earlier magical serenity: *Forget the black swan... Forget the pink Dove... Forget the yellow Jasmine.*

Suddenly it dawns on me that merely discovering the pink Dove must have been the good omen—that is all. Whether this revelation has any other significance remains an enigma at this point. However, the pink Dove is the key. A glimmer of hope rejuvenates me to rush toward the lagoon where the pink Dove is. I will grab it this time without hesitation, even if people are around and witness my thievery. Then I will hurry home to bathe with it, which would evidently cleanse both my body and soul to feel alive again.

Recognizing the maple tree from afar, I squint to spot the pink box on the shaded tree branch. Unable to detect any pinkish hue, I presume my skewed angle of view is concealing the pink Dove. My heart thumps rampantly as I hurry and approach the Japanese maple with no sign of the pink Dove. It has vanished. However, I proceed at full speed and touch the broken branch where the pink Dove had dwelled. I peer all over and under the tree and survey my surroundings with stress. I stare at people around the lagoon watching me suspiciously. I am myself quite suspicious of them. One of them must have stolen my Dove. But which one? I cannot accuse anybody or claim the ownership of the Dove even if I knew the thief. I just glare at everybody intently, hoping that the culprit steps forward voluntarily and returns my Dove with an apology. It belongs to me! I had found it first. *Which one of you idiots took my pink Dove? You bastard thief...* Nobody shows any remorse or sympathy, though. They disperse after glaring back at me awhile. I lurch to an empty bench by the lagoon and delve into deep thoughts: *So, where is the yellow Jasmine? Where is the pink Dove? Where is the black swan?*

A faint munching sound on the surface of the water disrupts my daydream. As I turn, the bad big bird emerges swiftly out of the dense undergrowth that sprawls along the bank near the bench. The sight of the sneaky black swan swimming forward fast and glaring at me curiously is horrific. We gaze at each other frantically, like two estranged lovers inept to interpret the purpose of their accidental encounter. Maybe the cranky bird is furious about my flirting with the white swans earlier. Trembling from the intensifying glare in its fiery red eyes, I wake up swiftly in sweat with distress.

Loitering in the twilight zone, my sluggish mind suggests that I have overslept through another nightmare. Almost noon. Feeling dreadfully lonely. But what is the point of getting up early and being depressed a longer day? Before the damn layoff, I rose regularly around seven a.m. even if I retired late. But then I have been sleeping a little longer every day to elude the erratic world. Nightmares awaken me frequently enough already throughout the night to ponder my derailed destiny for many agonizing hours. I read romantic novels or watch comedy shows on TV late every evening, hoping to avoid insomnia or nightmares. But this scheme seems to have only exacerbated my sleeping pattern.

Musing over my bizarre dream makes me giggle, particularly about the mysterious pink Dove resting on the broken branch of a Japanese maple. Luckily, it is also sidetracking my recurring morning melancholy. Exploring its meaning, and inventing a positive message perhaps, may help mitigate my inevitable morning depression. *Maybe sun would shine merrily upon me today if I go buy a pink Dove and bathe with it? Maybe the angel of mercy blesses me upon changing my lifestyle, when I cleanse the old wounds, after rubbing Dove's leathery foam on my body and sniffing its familiar fragrance again, finally after so long.*

Despite the childish interpretation of the dream, I welcome the opportunity of entertaining a positive premonition: That a wonderful revelation would change my life before the sun sets today, like the omen in my dream. Yes, I remember that similar premonitions have never materialized in the past. But, today, the novel idea of partying with a pink Dove is intriguing—an urge more potent than ever. Anyway, I must force my cynical mind and uptight personality to remain positive for one day at least by anticipating a good fortune approaching. Even a crazier notion makes me giggle—about rushing to the park and finding that maple tree in my dream with a Dove possibly sitting on its branch. The silly idea brings me a surge of energy, erases the residue of my snooze, and I leap out of the bed after laughing silly awhile about my dreams getting sillier every week. I wonder if that maple tree really exists in that exact part of the park! Maybe I check it out someday, but not today!

Frowning at my frazzled face in the mirror, I wash my hands absentmindedly for three minutes. I feel an unusual appetite—perhaps another symptom of the premonition and my deepening optimism. Cheerfully, I fry three eggs and half a dozen pancakes, while a fresh pot of coffee percolates. After breakfast, I reel to the study and survey the morning paper casually. A mixed feeling tempts me toward the ultimate destination—the daunting 'career opportunity' section. Still hoping for a surprise job opportunity in today's paper, the dire outcome of all the previous meticulous matches saddens me. So, what is the point of trying? During the last eleven months, I have mailed over hundred job applications and received eighty-two rejections so far. Invited for merely two preliminary interviews, only rejection letters have ensued with ludicrous excuses—total bullshit if you ask me.

Sports section lures me with a frustrating picture of Canucks' disastrous loss the night before. Getting hooked on hockey within only a few years, for somebody with my background—raised in a country with no sense of hockey—is absurd and amazing at the same time! But before getting agitated, my mind swiftly ponders again the possibility of my premonition pertaining to a job offer I would receive today. Feeling ecstatic, I dash to the silent phone just to ensure it is in order. I am sceptical about Jasmine and the kids these days. They are quite careless regarding my needs. The receiver is in place; I check the dial tone as well. Back in the study, I scan through the career pages while anxiously anticipate a phone call for a job offer or an important interview at least.

Three job advertisements are clipped and placed tidily next to the computer to prepare cover letters later in the day—perhaps after the mailman makes his doleful deliveries. Maybe a job offer arrives any minute now and eliminates the need to send out more applications. The telephone rings.

I rush to the phone only to discover that the Diabetics Society will dispatch its van to the neighbourhood on Friday, wondering whether Jasmine has used clothing to donate. Yeah... Jasmine donates many clothes. So maybe she is spending too much on herself already while curtailing other expenses! Keeping herself so pretty and fashionable is surely expensive, though she justifies all that extravagance as a job requirement. Why do you need all that fashion and makeup when you are sitting alone in a *dungeon* all day then, ha? Anyway, I do not wish to dwell on this quandary today, either.

Hearing someone on the portico, I lurch toward the foyer's narrow window and watch the mailman doing his tedious job. I can never do this kind of work… I admit I have become too fussy about jobs and organizations. Many of them would kill me faster than unemployment. So I am doomed one way or another. I have become a bum! Maybe that was why I lost my job in the first place? The mailman notices me, too, and nods timidly with a hint of pity, and perhaps a sense of guilt for bringing all those rejection letters that only increase my despair and his workload. I grasp the meaning of his gawky glance, which reminds me of the teasing, dreadful eyes of the black swan in my dream. I shudder with tension and wait for him to scram before rushing to the mailbox and retrieving four more rejection letters amidst a load of junk mail. Still I am hopeful that my premonition for some positive revelation in my life would materialize *today*. Though, perhaps I must bathe with a pink Dove first… and then…? *I do not know… But one worry at a time… Let me go buy a pink Dove right away.*

Quickly I slip into my jeans, mosey to the grocery store, and buy a pink Dove, which is even more costly nowadays. I hurry back home and bathe with it buoyantly like a naughty kid doing some crazy stunt behind his mother's back. Not the act itself, but rather the tyranny of doing something against Jasmine's desire is making me tickle. I wonder if I should hide the soap afterward and perhaps even spray some air freshener in the bathroom to prevent any chance of Jasmine discovering my mischief. On the other hand, I feel a craving to challenge her. I wonder whether she might really make a big fuss about my impulse to buy the Dove, but I do not care about it today, anyway. I decide not to bother hiding the proof of my defiance, either. I am prepared even for her usual ludicrous lectures about the merits of thrift. Today is a special day. It is my day! So I dry myself cheerfully and exit the bathroom, as though I have just come out of a coma, somewhat enjoying my new rebellious self.

And then…? Nothing is changing, yet, except for getting so terribly confused again, while I wait patiently. *Now what?* For ten minutes, I fret pensively, then exclaim with excitement, "Yes, 'and then' I should call Jasmine and make a date for dinner." It is all very clear now! The plot is unravelled at last. The nightmare, the pink Dove, the urge to buy one, and the urgency to bathe with it, they have all been precious clues conspiring to stir my rusty subconscious regarding Jasmine's devotion to me and the family. At dinner tonight, I will divulge my dream and my desire to buy the Dove. And maybe later she would insist on smelling my smooth skin. We will surely enjoy a romantic evening—first an exquisite dinner and afterwards in the bedroom. *She is a good wife; gorgeous too. Maybe a little careful with money, but so what? She is loyal and she loves me; I guess she does! Does she?*

All these years, I have hardly called Jasmine at work just for chitchat considering her normally busy schedule and rather rude impatience a few times I had called her at the office. I bet she will be surprised to hear from me today so unexpectedly. I hope she welcomes my invitation for a dinner date instead of saying it is an extravagance during my unemployment. Her phone rings five times before the voice message comes on. However, I press zero to speak with the receptionist instead, while my premonition starts acting up again, too.

"Allied Investments," the receptionist says.

"May I speak with Mrs. Jenkins?"

"She isn't in today."

"She isn't?"

"No, sir."

"So you can't pass on an urgent message to her?"

"No, sir… Did you—"

"Do you know when she'll be back, so I can contact her?"

"Not really... Can anybody else help you, sir?"

"No, I'll call tomorrow. You think she'll be in tomorrow?"

"I really don't know, sir. She has been sick two days now. Hopefully she'll feel better tomorrow."

"Thanks..." I say with absolute confusion, *wondering again how she has escaped her dungeon and where she has fled to!*

I replace the receiver sluggishly, not grasping the meaning of this weird development. I feel awful and restless, especially for waiting a few hours until Jasmine arrives and explains herself. Then again, is her sudden, mysterious disappearance related to the premonition haunting me all day and the story in my dream? Oddly enough, the outcomes of calling on her in both instances had been equally confusing and frustrating. Oh, gosh, is this the omen destined to manifest upon bathing with the pink Dove? Why are the minutes dragging so long today?

Jasmine arrives just before the sun sets and I strive to deliver a cordial smile despite my unsettled emotions, almost suffocating. "Hi honey. How was your day?"

"Good... The usual..." she replies.

The *'I love you'* I have been pampering for her in my head all day is dying to jump out, but luckily the lump in my throat is crippling my tongue, too.

Instead, I ask her at last, "You feel okay, dear? Is everything fine?"

"Yeah... of course. Why?" she asks irately, blushing with a suspicious smirk.

"No special reason... Just thought you work so hard these days at the office. Especially yesterday and today you looked so exhausted, arriving home later than usual, too?"

"Yeah... I'd been preparing some reports yesterday and today for an important meeting next week. I really hate being cooped up in my windowless dungeon all day, every day. Do you know what I'm saying...?"

"You bet…" I say blankly, drooping to avoid her frisky eyes.

"Sometimes I feel you don't really care," Jasmine says with tension. "You don't even care to look at me now when I ask you a straight question."

Still unable to raise my head and meet her demanding eyes, I feel like dying, about to burst into tears.

"You've always been so unromantic," Jasmine murmurs with agitation and leaves abruptly for a shower.

I stand awestricken for fifteen minutes wondering about her last comment, while reminiscing my daylong dreams and plans to tell her that I loved her, plus all those other good things I had being pondering about her all day, and then all those running around to find her. At last, I decide to go out to a fancy restaurant for dinner, after all, alone. Today is my day, for sure, and I must celebrate it. Drying her hair, Jasmine yells from the bedroom, "Hey Brian, where'd this pink Dove come from?"

However, I am already halfway out the door even if I cared to explain anything. I just keep walking in a haze, not quite aware of my present state of consciousness or being, dreaming or thinking, feeling or forgetting…

Back to square one: *Forget the black swan… Forget the pink Dove… Forget the yellow Jasmine.*

*****

It has been torturous for me, for so many years, to suspect, feel, and try to forget that my beloved wife might not be as loyal and loving as she had pretended to be too ludicrously. All along, every time I have prepared myself to use the phrase 'I love you' on her, she has only given more reasons to stop being so liberal with such silly expressions and my ideal impressions of her.

Now, things are getting out of control, unfortunately, as you can imagine!

Accidental Affair

Lingering in his large, quiet office at 5:10 p.m., Zachary Blanch rubs his temples tenaciously, as if pain could be squeezed out of one's skull. *Is this madness ever going to end?* He checks his Rolex again tensely and decides it is time to go.

Days feel long and gloomy at work. Though nights are also equally murky, at home or in the streets, in particular during the autumn and winter when night falls so early and rain pours like crazy in Vancouver. His headache is from the stress and useless arguments with his colleagues over office trivia they insist on as matters of life or death. Not him. He only looks forward to the end of office hours, even though life at home is merely another big source of headache. Equally stressful arguments erupt there as well whenever Connie and he start a conversation. Therefore, their communication is at bare minimum nowadays. They hardly talk face-to-face, let alone eye-to-eye; sometimes unaware of each other's existence for days, even when watching TV together or sharing a ride home. Usually he occupies himself with repair chores around the house, while humming a love aria, imagining the life of a carefree bachelor tenor. He muses and giggles, *How innocent and hopeful the lovers in those operas are about their passion, promises, and future together, if only they could resolve that one single obstacle that usually prevents their union.* Later in the evenings, Zachary usually retreats to his own bedroom, reads a book, and falls asleep two pages later.

Tonight, he leaves the office three minutes earlier than usual to avoid Connie's bitching again about his tardiness. He is the one always compromising, waiting extra minutes in cold, dark streets in storms, just to keep her quiet. 'No Stop' signs and pesky traffic patrols agitate her and he ends up getting the blame and a tone of abuse.

He mixes with the rushing crowd and the cars trying to avoid one another and rain puddles. People are waiting in bus shelters and some, like Zachary, linger near the curb for a ride with a spouse or a carpool. Waiting patiently at the regular rendezvous for two minutes, the wind prickles his eyes, despite the outsized umbrella somewhat protecting him. Still, the decision to arrive early seems justified when the black sedan stops at the curb. He closes his umbrella with difficulty against the gusty rain, opens the door, settles in his seat, and the car pulls away swiftly.

Zachary leans back and looks out the side window at the wretched people rushing in the storm or waiting anxiously near the curb for their rides. Thank God, he is now warm and safe. The ride home is always quiet save for the music on the radio. Sometimes he takes a short nap while Connie drives recklessly, as if they were late for their leftover dinner, routine arguments, or monotonous life at home.

He closes his eyes to relax his mind and muscles awhile. The whipping wind has aggravated his headache while waiting for Connie. The strong scent of her perfume is not helping, either. It smells different, too, though it is not abnormal considering the amount of money she spends on dolling up herself. It burns his sinuses as usual, but he would never complain or even open the window, especially in a night like this, with so much wind and water pounding the speeding cars. Keeping his mouth religiously shut, he squeezes his eyelids together as well, as though trying to lock out all the negative thoughts and the sources of his stress. If he were brave, he would hold his nostrils tight, too. Alas, he is too chicken to agitate Connie. He wonders about all the courage he had before marriage. *Yeah, we use up all our courage just to decide about marriage,* he ponders amusingly. *Marriage kills our courage for good!*

Sometimes he envies his friends who enjoy going to bars and wasting their lives and livers on alcohol. His only amusement had consisted of occasional gatherings with his friends to watch hockey on television or go to the Rogers' Arena for a match. Thanks to the damn lockout, this only source of his entertainment is now abolished, too. Even his buddies seem aloof this year, keeping busy with futile stuff, already replacing hockey with football and drinking at bars, both of which he abhors. Now life is a real drag, with all kinds of financial and emotional problems on top of nasty office politics and quarrels. *How could so many egotistical assholes assemble under one roof by sheer accident and call it an organization, while scheming all day to screw up one another?* What is the point of working so hard all our lives for no tangible purpose? Though the idea of being unemployed again is also torturous.

Behind his itchy, shut eyes, Zachary imagines the car passing through Stanley Park and entering the Lions Gate Bridge with its distinct road bumps. She is speeding even more than usual, quite recklessly indeed, especially considering the pouring rain and poor visibility. In spite of the high risk of whining, he considers uttering his discomfort about her heedless speed and swerving in the middle lane next to the opposite traffic. Yet, before turning his throbbing head, she screams, "I can't take this anymore!"

He stares at her in bewilderment, "What the heck…?"

"Who the hell are you?" she shouts back after a glance at Zachary and veers the car to the left swiftly as though trying to elude him. A looming, intense light blinds Zachary and he barely witnesses the big bang.

The glaring light and the ear-piercing sound of the speeding and screeching vehicles fade as Zachary imagines standing alone on a train track terminated by a gigantic billboard blinking the blazing red message 'The End' in fast intervals.

Connie is furious when Zachary is not at the rendezvous. She drives around the block once, waits one minute with fury, then decides to go home without him. Apparently, he has retaliated for her complaint yesterday about his tardiness and disregarding her frustration to wait in a no-stop zone. *The hell with him and his childish attitude! He needs to learn a lesson about retaliating against me, asshole.* She drives only two blocks on West Georgia Street, though. "Oh God, not again…" she murmurs to herself. Often an accident on the bridge brings traffic to a halt for hours. "What a lousy husband I'm stuck with… so much worse than even this commuting mess I must bear day after day…"

A ghastly ghost stands by 'The End' sign and stares at Zachary, "Were you looking for the end?"

"What's this 'the end of?'"

"Your miseries…"

"Can I go home?" Zachary shouts in the midst of a train's roar approaching with immense light and speed. As the train smashes him into million pieces, he comes to in the hospital.

"What happened?" he mumbles.

"You were in an accident," a nurse replies. "You've been out for two days after doctors fixed you up."

Zachary stares at her blankly.

"Your wife said she'll return in an hour," The nurse says.

Later that afternoon, while Zachary regains some strength and memory, a woman comes around.

"Gosh, I'm so glad you're okay…"

"Who're you?" Zachary asks.

"That's the question I asked you before crashing into the van. I am sorry for hurting you. But you scared the hell out of me."

"I don't understand how I ended up in your car?"

"And I assumed you were George until you spoke."

"I guess you and George don't peep at each other, either?"

"Not really… For ages, it seems… Have you and Connie reached the same milestone?"

"Yes… Long time ago! You know Connie?"

"We met soon after they brought you to the hospital. But she never came back."

"She's always busy…"

"I think she imagines we knew each other already before the accident."

"Oh…? She does?"

"Yeah… Both Connie and George suspect we're having an affair."

"An affair...?" Zachary shrieks.

"That's what they think."

"It's funny… The nurse thinks you're my wife, too."

"Because I've been here the last two days. Connie came by only once, cursed you and me, and left."

"So why have you stuck around all this time? Were you also injured?"

"No, I was concerned for you. I'm sorry… But darn it, you really startled me."

"I was frigging shocked myself," Zachary says.

"It was really weird…"

"Have you read Allan Poe's *The Angel of Odd*?"

"No… Why?"

"It's interesting. It is weird all these strange things happen in life to people all the time…"

"I'll read it sometime," she says.

"Besides my weird marital relationship with Connie in recent years, I'm upset-minded more than usual these days, anyway."

"We all get confused at our ages, especially after our marital experiences," she says.

"Last week I strolled to the kitchen in the middle of the night to drink a glass of water. I've been sleeping in my own bedroom for three years, while Connie uses the king-size bed in the master bedroom. When I went back upstairs, I staggered to her room by mistake, like an old habit, I guess. I made love to her, too—as another bizarre habit, also, I guess—and slept there until morning without realizing the absurdity of it all. I had forgotten I had not slept with her or in that bed for months. In the morning, I asked Connie whether she'd kidnapped me, since I didn't remember anything. But she preferred not to believe me and instead kept complaining about raping her and then snoring a lot, too."

"Well, your story sounds unbelievable to me, too," she says. "Though many things we consider normal these days feel totally bizarre, anyway, especially our marriages."

"Now if she thinks I'm having an affair with you, she might even complain to the police about raping her as well!"

"That'd become a tough argument for her and court to sort out... Don't worry..."

"I bet she'd convince the judge, too. Don't you worry... You don't know her and her charming tenacity."

"You're cute..."

"A clown, you mean, ha?" he asks and Connie chuckles. He continues, "Life turns us into clowns or jerks just to survive... But my marriage has been hilarious enough in itself, anyway."

"That's a good way of looking at our marriages nowadays in fact—as funny affairs."

"Last four or five years, Connie and I have often ended up making love to each other when we'd been drunk, half-sleep, or with closed eyes every few months or so, mostly by some kind of fluke in an odd place."

"It's a symptom of modern lifestyles, my friend..."

"The nurse told me that my injuries aren't too bad despite the concussion."

"You'll survive... At first doctors thought your spine might've been damaged, but later they said you'll recover fully soon... except for the trauma of encountering another crazy woman, of course!"

"He told you personally about the crazy woman causing my trauma?" Zachary asks with a chuckle.

"Yes, he stared at me suspiciously when I told him the story."

"I'm sure he didn't believe your story, either."

"He didn't... They all believe our passionate affair has caused the accident as well. They all think we are lying to our teeth."

"How about the police? Did you tell them the story, too?"

"Yes... They also only stared at me and looked like trying hard not to laugh. Nobody believes us!"

Zachary chuckles and peers into her eyes with pity for both of them.

"We've both been traumatized somewhat by this incident."

"You're probably right and things might even get worse..." Zachary says with a chuckle.

"You're probably right, too..."

"What's your name?" Zachary asks.

"Sabrina..."

"Thanks for sticking around, Sabrina..."

"That's all right, confused stranger. I feel responsible for you now..." Her soothing words and passion feel both bizarre and refreshing to Zachary after years of hearing merely obnoxious marital arguments.

"You're very kind. But maybe it has also raised our spouses' suspicions about us having an affair?"

"I'll stop being kind then!"

"Just straighten them out..."

"In fact, I've avoided explaining anything to either George or Connie after my initial attempt and their persistence to disbelieve me," Sabrina says casually.

"Why not?" Zachary asks with surprise.

"What's the point?"

"What do you mean?"

"Do you think they care or understand?"

"Probably not..."

"So maybe we should let them guess as wildly as they wish."

"You wanna let people guess, have fun, or suffer… just by keeping them in dark?"

"Why not? They like it that way, it appears. Even Connie and George seem to be enjoying the situation."

"Yeah… They'll never believe our story." Zachary concurs. "That's another funny fact about marriages these days due to so much mistrust."

"So let's not insist on the true story," Sabrina says. "We just keep our mouths shout. That's all!"

"That's easier at least… Telling the truth won't help anything, anyway."

"In fact, maybe I should stick around a bit longer then, so that we have someone to talk with for a change. Maybe we should get over our traumas together?"

"That's a thought!"

The doctor arrives and checks Zachary for ten minutes. "You can go home in three days," he asserts and leaves with a wide grin, as if confirming his earlier suspicions about the silliness of Sabrina's story by the looks of it—the way the couple seem so cosy plus the nurses' gossips, they all add up.

"At least this stranger has been a good moral support for you last few days," he says mockingly, pointing to Sabrina standing by Zachary as he leaves the room with a telling smirk. Their story has made him laugh all along, but now he is still eager to reaffirm its childish falsehood for himself and the people in the room. *How do they think they can get away with these kinds of silly tales?* The good doctor thinks and giggles before leaving.

"I think the doctor was trying hard again not to mock us," Zachary says.

"Yes, I noticed it too. He's a nosy and witty doctor," Sabrina replies with laughter. "I wonder if he's married…"

"Let nobody believe us…!" Zachary says.

"Absolutely… Let people have some fun and laughter at our expense!" Sabrina replies.

"Let's hope they write the story in the papers, too, and the whole world laughs at us for inventing such a ridiculous tale."

They burst into laughter. "But we've laughed a lot ourselves after so long, too, right?" she says.

"Yeah, they probably think we're either total idiots or just too arrogant with our attempt to fool them," he replies.

"It doesn't matter to me what they think. At least we both were lucky, especially you, considering that the car was totalled," she says with a giggle. "Let's go celebrate and cherish our rebirth instead of going back to our tedious, lousy marriages?"

"I'm not sure about being lucky; what's the point of surviving just to drag along the same shitty life. I'm not sure about anything out there worth celebrating, either..."

"Gosh...! I really like your cheeriness and enthusiasm!"

"Sorry... But do you still remember shouting, 'I can't take it any more...,' just before the accident?"

"Yes, of course... I was supposedly yelling at George about our relationship."

"Exactly my point! I can't take it any more, either, the whole life, in my case, I mean!"

"So what now?" Sabrina asks.

"I wish I knew... You should've finished the job..."

"Maybe next time. Give me another chance, please."

"Actually, Connie may not even take me home now that she thinks I've been unfaithful in addition to everything else."

"Then I must take care of you myself," Sabrina says with a teasing grin. "Maybe we should elope then, after all...?"

"Where to?" he whispers.

"Let's go to a remote cosy island first, for a while at least, where no one can find us."

"So we're gonna have an affair, after all?" Zachary asks in a serious tone.

"We might as well..."

"Everybody has already given us the credit for it, anyway."

"So what do you think?" Sabrina asks. "Should we do it?"

"Why not? We both have permanent problems with our spouses anyhow, now more than ever."

"We need a break from all this nonsense as well."

"I'm game…"

"You better rest now. I'll see you soon, maybe tomorrow." Sabrina starts to leave. "Listen… Will you tell the insurance company that you startled me and caused the accident?"

"You want me take the blame, the way Connie always does?"

"It's better this way. Besides, you did startle me… Right?"

"They won't believe our story, anyway," Zachary says.

"I guess… But tell the insurance people the truth. It may help a little after they laugh at us like everybody else…"

"Now everybody takes our story as a big excuse for insurance company, too, on top of a cover up for our affair."

"That's a valid point as well, I guess…"

"Are you in trouble with the insurance company?" he asks.

"Yes, I smashed another car just last month."

"It's odd nothing happens to you. Who'd you kill that time?"

"George got injured slightly. It's all his fault that I have these accidents. He makes me mad all the time… I can't stand him anymore. I'm losing my mind."

"Are you the one responsible for all the accidents on the Lions Gate Bridge?" Zachary says teasingly.

"Not all of them!" Sabrina replies.

"Still, I guess, it's safer that I do all the driving from now on when we go somewhere together," Zachary says.

"Fine with me…"

"I'll tell the insurance company the truth. I bet they welcome hearing the truth and enjoy its huge benefit for them."

"What truth?"

"That the accident happened since we both hate our spouses! But the insurance company might save tons of money now that we've met and you'd think more about me from now on instead of only hating George and crashing so many cars on the bridge."

"Stop being a clown…"

"I'm not kidding. They'd be happy if they believe our true story and realize how much money they'd save after this bizarre accident."

"Will you just tell'm straight that you startled me real bad and being in George's seat all along without me noticing it?"

"You really need my help, eh?"

"Do you want us get into a fight already, even before starting our affair?" Sabrina asks with a cute chuckle.

"But you're already bossing me around, too, like Connie!"

"I'm not…! Besides, you'd better prove you're different from George, in fact."

"I don't know how, but I'll help you. I'll be fine anyway."

"You shouldn't file a claim with insurance company then."

"I guess I can't if I admit having caused the accident…"

"Thanks Zachary. Then I'll see you tomorrow perhaps…?"

Two months later, Zachary Blanch is lingering in his big, quiet office at 5:10 p.m. and rubbing his temples tenaciously, as if pain could be squeezed out of one's skull. *When would it all end? The end of the world or my life at least, whichever,* he murmurs to himself solemnly. He stares at his Rolex hoping to relax just by following the rhythmic, smooth jumps of the seconds' handle, but even this trick does not calm his nerves. What a confusing, useless existence, every damn second of it! He checks the time again and again, before finally taking the elevator to the lobby. It is quite dark and cold in the street as he walks in the rain under his big umbrella toward the rendezvous at the curb. A black car hits a rain puddle and splashes water all over his pants before stopping before him. He looks inside the car and smiles to the pretty driver before getting in—just making sure he is not getting into another car by mistake again!

*****

Many coincidences in our lives feel like mysterious, divine clues to force us delve deeper into ourselves for solace, find plausible meanings for our feelings and actions, and perhaps even enrich our dull lives randomly. At the same time, these blissful, random experiences have mostly convinced me that, in the end, I would always remain a lonely human forever, though blessed with the mercy of a conscious power out there ready to help my growth, right in the middle of the messy or miraculous events recurring erratically. Meanwhile, I naturally sense and keep enough faith in both the validity and vanity of human existence per se. I hope you get my drift, although I realize my inability to be precise at this point without sounding too mad or ridiculous. *Of course, if you read my essays in other places, you'd probably get a better clue about what I'm talking about!*

Many of us struggle with a rather philosophical or religious notion regarding the viability of a divine reason behind the scene for everything happening in our lives. It is difficult to overcome this rational doubt. Yet some of us would finally get enough clues to recognize this reality with all our hearts and minds. That is the moment we resign rationally with conviction and embrace the sad truth about our existence, although we feel both helpless and needless to explain this raw personal realization of ours to others.

In particular, when a passionate affair erupts accidentally in the middle of our routine lousy lives, often in a bizarre manner, we get both mesmerized and carried away too fast, thus usually end up in peculiar circumstances with perturbing thoughts that only raise our sense of guilt and anguish. The big mystery is that not all coincidences are divine or blissful, either. Sorting them out thus remains another source of pain and pondering.

Aliens

Out there are many of them—those eccentric inhabitants I was commissioned to research in year 2000. The objective was to study their temperaments and motives. We already knew that many of these quiet and creative creatures live among us rather peacefully, although they may seem odd to most of us, especially when they get emotional or critical, sometimes with fury and frustration. We also knew that their population has risen rapidly, almost in line with progress in computers and the internet. They have applied these tools more diligently every year to research and prepare a massive amount of facts and fictions. They also use computers and internet to exchange their thoughts and products among themselves and with the people they have been aiming to influence for their ultimate goals. Although they live a life of semi-seclusion, they have a keen eye for trivia and a profound curiosity about human nature, interests, and lifestyle. They are observing us keenly with huge curiosity and are quite meticulous in their fact-findings and analyses.

Luckily, the project was not given a high priority and nobody had pushed me for a report before collecting adequate data. My boss also confirmed that the project was assigned to me merely due to my background as a private detective for ten years, before becoming a journalist at the *Time Magazine* for thirteen years.

Anyway, I had promised him to unravel this social phenomenon and substantiate my findings with sufficient evidence.

Yet, sadly, I found it harder every day to finish my research and produce reliable statistics, not even in terms of the population and the growth rate of this curious group in society. This aspect of the study had been most important and rather difficult, too. The main hurdle was finding the subjects and a proper research methodology to perform valid tests and analyses. I could not put an ad in papers and ask the people with certain characteristics to come forward for an interview. Nor could I ask the public to identify these peculiar people based on a raw profile. This would only bring me a big headache and a long list of rudimentary hunches, too cumbersome to follow up across the continent. Even if I found the subjects, they would definitely refuse to see me. They would surely suspect my intention from the first minute of interview, anyway, especially if they learned how I had used their neighbours and friends to betray their privacy. Furthermore, investigating all these leads would be a nightmare. So, I needed a more reliable tactic without giving these creatures an impression of infringing their privacy and divulging their secrets. However, developing such a delicate scheme had proved cumbersome.

My preliminary research indicated that these odd inhabitants are actually more civilized, sensible, and passionate than most ordinary people. They live and behave like normal people, too, most of the time. Yet, we can see how peculiar and perplexed they are on some occasions. Many of them have normal jobs like the rest of us, while behind the scene their intricate interests and activities remain totally serious and secret. I have come across a number of these intelligent creatures and made basic interviews with them, leading me to believe that they are more harmful to themselves than to others. They seem to be quite introvert and show no sign of malice and animosity, at least not beyond what we might already expect from an average human, anyway.

Obviously, the public knew very little about these people's existence, the large volume of work they did quietly, and the amount of intelligence that remained unnoticed in our society. Nobody could imagine how much time and effort they spend in seclusion, secretly focusing on their main mission and objective of being on this planet. I was shocked myself by the speculations about their drive, fast growing population, habits, and motives. Anyhow, I kept the assignment in the backburner and did only some perfunctory research casually when I encountered people who matched the profile of these mysterious inhabitants or had firsthand information about them. Nothing came of this creepy assignment and I was not pressed for it, either, until I asked for retirement in year 2002.

My daughter had married a Canadian and moved to Vancouver in 2001. Therefore, my wife and I agreed to retire to a quiet community close to our daughter's family. Especially, we were eager to see our grandson who was already nine months old. My early retirement request was approved on the condition I continue my investigation of the two-year-old assignment. The Magazine agreed, of course, that I work on the project leisurely according to my own timetable and retirement priorities, as long as I finished it within two years. The timeframe appeared reasonable to me and the fee, payable at the time of submitting my report, could help immensely with the high cost of living in an expensive city like Vancouver. The prospect of securing similar commissions from the Magazine and collecting handsome fees for the type of work I liked to pursue anyway, without time pressure and nagging, was another incentive to do a good job on this assignment. Therefore, I accepted the challenge.

Within a month, we bought a nice house in Silverdale Street in North Vancouver. The neighbourhood drew us by its serenity and seclusion from the city traffic and commotion. By sheer fluke, it appeared also quite fruitful for my research and finalizing the assignment for the Magazine. I met a bunch of genial people and we felt welcome in our new home. Eight families also came by, introduced themselves, and informed us about their frequent get-togethers. But nobody from 356, the house opposite ours, showed any interest to acknowledge us. I bought a case of good BC wine and sent a bottle to each of the neighbours along with a thank you card, my phone number, and other vital neighbourly information. They all called and thanked us except for 356.

The 356's apathy annoyed my sensitive wife, Phyllis, the most. I worried of her wicked way of reacting when someone pushed her nerves and starting a war before I got an opportunity to explore these curious people. To me, 356s actually seemed to fit the attributes of the profile I had developed about my research subjects. I also believed that odd events and encounters usually revealed information beyond the routines of social wheeling and dealing. Those days, especially, people's odd behaviour quickly picked my curiosity about them as likely subjects for my study.

Having a profile developed about the subjects seemed like a significant accomplishment all by itself, I presumed. It helped me identify my subjects rather promptly at least. Actually, most of my spare time and analyses since the project's launch had been devoted to preparing this working profile, while developing a research methodology and some plausible hypotheses had proved rather challenging.

The subjects' main characteristics were quite vivid, anyway: They were quiet, intelligent, introvert, impatient, mature looking, secretive, males usually wearing a goatee or full beard as if trying to hide their true identity, very observant despite their timidity and pretences of apathy, always carrying a small pad and pencil and making notes about humans' motives and attitudes, looking slightly disturbed emotionally, generally avoiding eye contact and communication unless amongst their own group, maybe snob and apprehensive about the common way of life on the planet Earth, etc. etc.

Overall, the profile contained over hundred traits and clues in four pages, but I hardy needed to consult the list to pinpoint the subjects. By now, I had developed a sixth sense on this matter. Any small hint nowadays raised my radar about the subject due to my subconscious affinity to this odd topic for so long, not to mention my detective background. Yet, befriending the subjects under some civilized pretences, after finding them, had always been a challenge for studying their secrets, lifestyle, and motives. Again, I must stress that these people are extremely intelligent, private, and impatient.

Anyway, after two weeks of surveillance and gauging the neighbours' gossips, I believed that at least one of the occupants in 356 fitted the profile. So now, I needed a plan to confirm my hunch, although finding some clues alone would not help without a full-fledged private interview, perhaps when the subject was drunk or hypnotized. The house was usually empty during the day when the couple worked and their kids were at school. Thus, I had only two weeks, before the schools closed for the summer, to sneak around or into the house to find some preliminary clues. Yet, the risk of breaking in and getting caught felt unwise and unproductive. Neighbours might also notice my snooping around and get suspicious. Maybe the house had an alarm system, too, although no warning tags were posted on the windows or around the house.

Finally, I decided to find some preliminary clues indirectly first before inventing a plot to interview those snob people. One option was to rummage their garbage for evidence, or examine their recycling material, which was easier and cleaner to handle. The recycling bags—blue for newspapers and yellow for other stuff—were put out once a week at night for pick-up first thing next morning. Late in the evening, the next three weeks, I took our blue and yellow bags outside only after the neighbours' bags were all lined up in the street and they seemed to be asleep, or busy having sex. I put the blue bag in front of the lawn, rushed to 356, and switched the yellow bags swiftly, praying nobody saw me. I returned to our garage, closed the door, and emptied the 356's recycled papers. For two weeks, I could not find anything suspicious. But then my luck struck in the third week and my ingenuity was proven to me once again. I stumbled upon the torn pieces of an incriminating document in the yellow bag. After a quick review, I hid them in the drawer of the small table in the garage. I refilled the yellow bag, put it in front of our house, and went back inside to the family room.

I gazed into Phyllis's bewildered eyes for ten seconds, trying to hide my mischief. She seemed suspicious of my behaviour in recent weeks and spying on neighbours' affairs. But she did not say anything. Spending so much time in the garage, so late some evenings, had by itself appeared quite odd and suspicious to her already. I often worried that she might catch me sifting through the waste papers of a yellow bag, which did not resemble our recycled material, either.

I plummeted onto the couch and wondered for one hour if there was a better way of doing this research and completing the assignment without all these dirty works, hassles, and secrecy. *How we do these humiliating stuff merely for money is appalling and ridiculous!* Then again, I knew these creatures were very private, intelligent, and impatient. They would not volunteer any information or leave any trace for me to peruse directly. More importantly, it was the matter of getting inside their heads that constituted the essence of this assignment. So I had to befriend the people in 356, find out who they really were, and how their minds worked. *Why were these people so aloof? Assholes!* All my previous attempts with similar subjects had produced limited information, since I had failed to befriend them or penetrate their private lives. Therefore, I was determined to use the opportunity wisely this time, supplement all the previous data, write the damn report, and end this masquerade, even if I could not provide a scientific proof, exact statistics, or a definite conclusion. If the *Time Magazine* wished to do a more in-depth study, they should sign a new contract with me or hire someone else.

The next day, I retrieved the torn document I had hidden in the garage. Fortunately, the numbered pages were casually ripped into eight to sixteen pieces. It took me only two hours to attach them with scotch tape and get my thirty-two-page evidence. It was a draft copy with corrections and editing marks all over the pages in red ink. Some parts were crossed off and some illegible handwritten notes were added in the margins. It was not easy to read the draft document and make sense of it quickly. Moreover, the writings seemed more like a fictional recount of some events and places too peculiar to interpret, especially about the writer's mental state and motivations. Many questions still remained, yet the document was an excellent first crack of the case. I prepared a summary of my understanding of it, only as a basic interpretation of its value in literal terms as well as the strength of its content. Experts may wish to examine the original document later for more clues. I also wrote the following storyline evident from the document and put it in the binder:

'During the summer of 1963, a dozen spaceships had arrived from the outer space to explore the Earth and exploit the human race. The intruders have been successful in infiltrating the whole globe and brainwashing politicians and business executives to help them build ultra-sophisticated facilities for nuclear fusion. This project has been one of their main purposes for traveling to Earth. Although the nuclear sites of their desire have not yet been conceived and approved by the congress, the plot is proceeding as planned in terms of planting the seeds for the development of facilities and justifying the huge cost of pursuing the project. The aliens have masterfully created a race among modern nations for mastering the technology first. Therefore, the governments of advanced countries are facing added pressures to justify the costs and risks quickly. Apparently, some form of combined helium and hydrogen fusion has a potential to create energy million times stronger than the nuclear energy presently mastered by the humans' limited technology. Building such nuclear facilities would provide the fuel needed for all aspects of life, especially for extraterrestrial travel. Some pockets of resistance to this type of revolutionary fusion have slowed down the progress, though. Especially environmentalists consider this technology dangerous at this point. Most scientists acknowledge the risks, too, but also value its vast potentials. Various interest groups push for more studies and justifications, which is frustrating the aliens who have cleverly integrated themselves within the world population. The aliens have also used the state-of-the-art genetic engineering to resemble humans, but with the intelligence and mindset designed for their mission on Earth. They orchestrate various schemes and conspire continuously to destroy resistances and get the project underway promptly. If they cannot achieve their goals peacefully, they might resort to violence. They need urgent access to the Earth's relatively abundant helium and hydrogen resources and nuclear facilities for fusing them.'

That was all I could gather for depicting the storyline. The names and locations mentioned in the document were irrelevant for my purpose at this time, yet some of them made me chuckle a little. Some suggestions felt outright childish and too fantastical for my simple mind. But I ignored all these literary details. I had more important things to worry about and spend my time on. Yet, the preliminary information was sufficient to pursue this matter more urgently and directly at other levels more in line with my commission.

With my early suspicions confirmed, the next phase was to find a way to penetrate the hearts and minds of the people in 356, maybe with Phyllis's and the neighbours' help.

"We must meet the Vatandoost family…" I told Phyllis one evening casually.

"Yeah…? They don't seem interested and I don't care about them, either."

"Don't be so spiteful…"

"They are aloof. Why do you want to meet them, anyway?"

"I'm just curious about them."

"Curious about what?" she asked.

"Just in general. They seem to be very curious people."

"Since when you're curious about curious people? Especially since they've ignored us all along?"

"I'm always curious… I'm a journalist. You forgot?"

"But you never snooped into neighbours' affairs before."

"People who're different always intrigue me. Besides, these people fit the profile of the subjects I must find for my study."

"What study?" Phyllis asked with stress.

"I told you, I've been working on an assignment for the Magazine…" I replied, wondering whether I had really told her about the assignment.

"No I don't remember. What's it about?" Phyllis asked.

"It's about…" I suddenly realized that revealing the details of the study might jeopardize my plans if the neighbours find out. "It's about… aliens… in general," I blurted mockingly, hoping she would leave the matter alone.

"Aliens? Are you fooling me, Tony?" she shrieked.

"Shshsh…, you want the whole neighbourhood hear us? They may think we're crazy or something."

"You're acting like one these days, anyway!"

"I don't want anybody know about my project. I'll explain it later. But for now, just forget it. Okay…?"

"You're losing it. No wonder the Magazine let you go…"

"I quit myself. Besides, I'm still working for them. So just leave me alone. Instead, see how we can get friendly with this Vatandoost family, will you?"

Phyllis nodded with distress and left the room, murmuring some words to herself. Three days later, she reported the neighbours' testimony regarding the Vatandoosts' apathy for socializing. The only people in Silverdale they met occasionally were the Dogwoods, mostly due to their children being friends and old classmates. Charlie Dogwood was a charming, humble, and friendly man—the first person to come by to welcome and inform us of the neighbourly affairs and events.

During the next couple of days, I occupied myself in the front yard and strolled in Silverdale leisurely. I was hoping to find Charlie casually or see a member of the Vatandoost family to go introduce myself. Only once, the Vatandoost's car turned around the corner. I waved to Mr. Vatandoost, he nodded politely, and drove away without stopping the car. He went inside the secured garage and closed the door swiftly. Later that afternoon, however, Charlie appeared in his front yard, four houses away from ours, and we waved to each other. As I had expected, he started toward me, making my ingenious scheme to catch his attention casually successful.

"Hi Charlie... Nice day, huh?" I said.

"Hi Tony... Beautiful day... What're you up to, neighbour?"

"Not much. Just cleaning the yard a little."

"It's a good exercise too..."

"I saw Mr. Vatandoost driving by. He looks like a nice guy."

"Yes, he is. I don't care what people think about him."

"Like what?"

"They think the whole family is weird."

"What does he do?"

"He's a chemical engineer... genetics engineer, or something like that."

"How well do you know him?"

"Actually we're good friends. You should come to my house and meet him sometime."

"Yeah... sounds like a great idea. I like meeting him if you guys wanna get together to watch a game or something."

"He's not much into sports. But we can play billiards and drink beers."

No interest in sports... another good clue, I thought, recalling the subjects' profile. "Yeah... I like that. I'm free this weekend."

"All right, Tony... I'll ask him..." Charlie replied sceptically, rather bewildered by my over-enthusiasm.

As I had suspected, Ralph Vatandoost was a reserved, quiet man, though his smile and humble tone of voice appeased me when we met at Charlie's house on Sunday afternoon. His odd accent made it hard to understand him, although he spoke English rather fluently. His mannerism, grey goatee, and white hair, matched the profile of the research subjects perfectly. We played billiards and drank beers. I felt I was penetrating their hearts, especially after their appreciation of the Cuban cigars I had brought, hoping Ralph was a smoker like me. I was putting a lot of thoughts and dough into this friendship, so I became ecstatic every time the bits and pieces of my plan fitted together smoothly. I lit my own cigar triumphantly and Charlie added black Smirnoff to our beers to make our afternoon more relaxing. I was a bit anxious still, but tried to stay sober for my planned heart to heart with Ralph later.

"I guess we're all about the same age? Maybe Charlie is a few years younger than the two of us," I blurted, mostly addressing Ralph, hoping to get him open up and strike a friendship. Deep down I knew we were different kinds of creatures, unique in our own ways, with distinct interests. But I had to find good reasons for us, especially Ralph and I, to be close friends. He should be convinced I was a trustworthy person.

"I'm fifty-eight," Charlie said. Ralph only nodded agreeably.

"I retired early to enjoy the rest of my life," I said.

"Good for you. I'm thinking about the same thing," Ralph said finally with some effort.

"But what're we gonna do with all the time on our hands," I asked innocently with a devious hidden agenda.

"Play billiards and go hiking or camping," Charlie said.

"But that's not challenging enough… Are you thinking about retiring, too, Charlie?" I asked.

"Maybe in a few years… I don't want to be the only one in this neighbourhood working."

Charlie excused himself to go start the barbeque. He had promised us his special burgers that he was so famous for in the neighbourhood. We had stopped playing billiards and focused on drinking and smoking our cigars around a small round table in the far corner of the rec room.

"Do you have any hobbies, Ralph?" I asked, hoping to hit the jackpot.

"I have a few interests, you might say," Ralph replied without conviction, clearly hesitant to divulge his secrets.

"Like what, if you don't mind my asking," I asked.

"Hmmm… Nothing especial…" Ralph said blankly, looking at his watch with agitation as if I had touched a nerve.

He was still not drunk enough to trust me. I felt embarrassed for putting him on spot and the possibility of losing him sooner than expected, perhaps even before the hamburgers were ready. According to the profile, these people have a strong tendency for departing prematurely or pooping the party. I had to salvage the afternoon somehow and refuel the prospect of becoming his friend. I almost came up with an idea despite my normal lack of spontaneity. But before opening my mouth, Ralph peeped at me intently with a shallow grin to soften the awkward silence.

"So, Tony, what'd you do before retiring," he asked politely.

"I was a journalist and editor at the end. I worked for the *Time Magazine*," I replied with pride.

"You did?" Ralph asked giddily as though a miracle had just occurred. He was swiftly rejuvenated and smiled with the kind of affection I had imagined possible only after a few months, if at all. My sixth sense also hinted that his sudden jubilation fitted the profile nicely. Anyway, the opportunity was precious and I had to build on it quickly to take our friendship to the next level.

"Listen Ralphy, would you like to come to our house next Saturday for dinner with your wife; what's her name?"

"Maxine… Is it a special occasion?" he asked with a soft tone that showed his growing respect for me.

"No, nothing special… We're planning to ask the Dogwoods and it'd be wonderful if you and Maxine joined us, too."

"Sure… I guess it'd be okay with Maxine as well. I'll confirm with her and let you know."

"Of course," I said while jotting down my phone number on a piece of paper for him and then got his number. The situation was improving fast, much beyond my imagination.

"So why'd you give up such a wonderful job and come to Vancouver?" Ralph asked with genuine interest.

"I'd worked long enough and needed some time to myself. In addition, our daughter married a Canadian guy and moved to Vancouver. We came to be around my grandson, too."

"Yes... grandchildren could be fun. I'd like to have some of them someday, too."

"I have only one so far..."

"Are you still in contact with your colleagues?" Ralph asked.

"Yeah... Leaving them was the hardest part of moving here."

"You're doing any writing now?" Ralph asked.

"No. Not really. I'm tired of writing after all these years."

"Perhaps you need a break... We need it once in a while..."

"Maybe..."

"I know it helps... I'm a writer, too, or try to be one at least."

"Oh?" I faked my surprise. "Have you published anything?"

"Not yet... But it should happen sooner or later, I hope."

"What do you write about?" I asked innocently.

"I work in genetics engineering, so it's natural for me to write fiction with some kind of twist caused by genetic manipulations. Always unpredictable things happen when we pursue intriguing innovations."

"That sounds very interesting. I'm surprised you haven't been published yet, though," I said, ashamed of my hypocrisy. I knew the difficulty of being a good writer and, even tougher, getting the attention of publishers nowadays with such stiff competition.

"I bet you know many editors and publishers?" Ralph asked.

I had been expecting this question from the moment of his sudden interest in me. I was thrilled about my foresight, although I normally resent dealing with people who mean to use me. But his question fitted nicely with the profile of the research subjects.

"Yes... I guess so..." I replied casually and hoped we would not get into too many details today. I must get the information I needed from him first before telling him the truth. I did not want to lie too much in one day. Thank God, Samantha showed her head from the crack of the door to say hello to us. Charlie was still in the backyard barbequing.

"Hello, Samantha," I said with enthusiasm and walked to her. "Phyllis asked me to invite you guys for dinner next Saturday."

"Yeah… sure…" she said and left as Charlie arrived with a large plate of hamburgers.

We enjoyed Charlie's juicy burgers, drank one more beer and Smirnoff and then left. Both Ralph and I seemed to be savouring the milestones we had achieved that afternoon, each for his own secret purpose. We loathed risking the possibility of ruining the deep friendship we thought we had built in only three hours. So we did not ask each other any more questions that day.

I did not see Ralph until the following Saturday when they all came to dinner. Leaving the research and Ralph alone awhile was a better strategy than showing over-enthusiasm. I was on the right track and that was sufficient for now. The gathering at our house progressed smoothly—the drinks, light music, dinner, coffee, and more Cuban cigars I had bought for the occasion. However, I noticed a twinge of discomfort in Maxine's eyes and behaviour throughout the evening. I ignored it, while wondering if she was also another subject for my studies going by her edgy mood. On the other hand, she seemed to hit it off nicely with Phyllis. She helped with clearing the dinning table and serving coffee and dessert, before the ladies got engaged in their private gossiping.

"I'm really happy for moving to this neighbourhood and meeting nice people like you guys," I blurted my sentimentality, trying to be a gracious host.

"I'm sure!" Maxine interjected irately as if I had hit a nerve. "Especially since you've been telling people that we're aliens…"

I froze in my seat in shock. Everybody remained quiet while pondering her absurd accusation. She peered around with a timid annoyance before gazing at Phyllis and me with a grimace, like demanding an explanation.

"Are you serious?" I exclaimed with a chuckle at last, eager to break the long silence killing the ambience in the living room very fast. "Who said such a funny thing?"

"Neighbours told me, of course, but I don't want to mention any names," Maxine replied. "Apparently, Phyllis has started the rumour."

I was flabbergasted, recognizing the severity of the situation, and cursing Phyllis's loose mouth. She must have repeated my silly comment about the aliens before a neighbour for humour perhaps, but most likely to take her revenge on the Vatandoosts, too. I knew she had this knack for wisecracks sometimes. Yet she looked too embarrassed to speak suddenly and only stared at me for help. Anyhow, her remark had been insensitive and now causing such a lousy commotion. Our fragile friendship with the Vatandoosts was in jeopardy unless I found a solution instantly. My brain had to invent an explanation quickly.

"Whoever the gossiping neighbour has been, she's certainly misunderstood Phyllis, or Phyllis misunderstood me when I told her that Ralph writes fiction about aliens." I realized Ralph had not mentioned anything about 'aliens' to me, but I had to rectify Phyllis's blunder somehow first before worrying about Ralph's reaction to my lie. Things could have gotten completely out of hand and I might have lost my chance to befriend Ralph if I had not jumped in fast with an expedient lie.

"I don't remember mentioning anything about 'aliens' stories to you..." Ralph said with surprise.

"Sure you did... in Charlie's house last weekend when you mentioned being a writer and using subjects related to genetic innovations. Remember?" This was my second *expedient* lie in a matter of thirty seconds, but I imagined it was a calculated risk. At our ages, Ralph and I are bound to doubt our conversations a week earlier. Especially by supporting my lie with an event—discussing his writings—I imagined he would most likely be confused enough for my legitimate purpose. Fortunately, people my age are quite susceptible to the power of suggestion, unless they have already turned into relentlessly dogmatic creatures who deny even their own words a minute earlier if they so decide for any reason. According to the profile, the subjects of my research are usually of the former type, though.

"Maybe... I guess so..." Ralph murmured. His response and reaction relieved everybody, but more importantly, it proved the predicting validity of the profile.

"Lend me some of your 'aliens' stories to read," I asked Ralph diplomatically to seal the deal. Phyllis looked relieved, too, and took advantage of my success by adding her own diplomatic lie to support me.

"I like 'aliens' stories too..." she said tactfully. "Maybe somebody took my comment the wrong way or wanted to pull your leg, Maxine. That's real funny."

I appreciated Phyllis's effort to mend the damage, yet her tone of voice lacked enough sincerity and conviction to me. It usually takes a long time before she can change her mind about people, if at all. Her spite is usually too deep and irreparable.

"Yeah, just imagine having aliens living in our backyards," Charlie said. "Though, your last name sounds weird. Where'd you find 'Vatandoost'?"

Everybody laughed and fooled around a bit and then the guests left. I had an argument with Phyllis about her big mouth that had almost ruined my plans. She fought back and blamed me for putting these silly ideas in her head. In the end, we had a lousy sex and fell asleep, after I wondered enough about the purpose of our attempts to feel sexy at our ages and bear the humiliation of fulfilling this ludicrous habit in line with some faltering urges.

Two nights later, Ralph called to thank us for the party and then asked me over for a shot of cognac. That was the best invitation I had received in a long time. I rushed to his house and we went to the study with our cognacs. The shelves were filled with books, papers were scattered everywhere, and his computer was on, as though he had been busy working.

"About the comment your wife had made... about me being an alien—" Ralph blurted half-teasingly.

"I'm sorry, Ralph. It's been a terrible misunderstanding. Please forgive her..."

"No, no. That's all right. She's right. And if you said it too, you're right as well..."

"I'm right...?" I asked, wondering if I had stumbled upon a real alien from outer space by fluke, after all!

"Yeah..."

"You're an alien?"

"Yeah, I guess so..." he said with despair. "It's all there in my essays. People can see it and feel it about me, anyway. So I might as well admit it."

"So what planet and galaxy you come from?" I asked with a mix of humour and confusion about his absurd confession.

"I really don't know... All I know is that I don't belong to this planet. I do not understand anything that goes on around here and it is obvious that people do not understand me, either. Not even my wife understands me after living together for thirty years."

"But you're a human, right?" It was getting harder for me every minute to judge his being or state of mind.

"I doubt it."

"You doubt it?" I shrieked, totally at sea by now.

"Yeah... I really do..."

"Oh...? Why do you feel this way?"

"I've done many wicked things, especially when I was young. Even now I can't control my rage sometimes. I'm spiteful and jealous toward those writers who've become famous for no valid reason. I really feel like an alien in this world. I wonder how much idiocy we people like to live with and spread around."

I believed Ralph was getting too philosophical on me and perhaps even lost his sense of reality due to old age and writing too much about weird characters that I had found in his writings.

"How much time do you spend on writing?" I asked.

"Five to seven hours every night... writing and editing my stories. I work like hell for nothing!"

"How long did you say you've been writing fiction?"

"Fifteen years…"

"And you've not been published yet?"

"Maybe I'm not talented, but I guess I'm not lucky, either."

"So why don't you quit? What's the point of wasting so much of your life on some adventure that seems to go nowhere?"

"Because I can't help it. I just love to write and edit and read."

"How can you keep going and sacrificing your life this way?"

"In the end, I don't care about getting published, anyway."

"How come?" I asked with confusion.

"Because what I write and the characters I create give me the ultimate satisfaction, anyway. I am having a ball living with my characters. They get me better than anybody else in this world."

"So you're happy regardless of getting recognition for your efforts or not?"

"Of course, I am. But I also imagine the chance of some smart people grasping the gist of my writings; and maybe even being known as a creative and original writer with fresh perspectives to make the readers think, laugh, cry, or relax for a few minutes. Nobody can deny his or her need for recognition. But ultimately, I need a hobby to amuse myself before going totally nuts."

"Why? Do you have work or family problems?"

"Not more than everybody else. But I'm really sick and tired of handling people in our supposedly normal life. Our hypocrisy, stupidity, and delusions are ruining all our senses."

"Maybe you need another hobby instead," I said.

"Well, I have done a lot of painting, too."

"Are those paintings on the walls yours?" I asked, staring at so many rather nice paintings hung throughout the house.

"Yes, Tony, they are…"

"Oh, they're really nice… Do you sell them, too," I asked.

"Yes… In fact, I used to sell a bunch of them in galleries," Ralph replied.

"So why have you stopped painting?"

"Because now I feel I must focus only on writing. It feels like an obsession. I seem unable to stop my urge to write."

"Why don't you go back to painting to curb your obsession for writing and get over this seeming hurtful addiction?" I asked.

"No, painting is out of the picture for good, it appears."

"Why?"

"Painting, even after I was successful, couldn't satiate my soul enough anymore, the way words and those characters do now."

"I think I know what you mean…"

"Now, words are way more soothing to me than the glorious Nature itself, including a mood, scenery, or colours on canvas."

"How about music?"

"I'm not a musician, though I love and listen to good music a lot. I think, not even music can match the effect of words…"

"These are strong sentiments," I said, while making a mental note to use his peculiar sentiments in my report, as they sounded like the main purpose of doing this research for the magazine.

"But they're true and natural, although it sounds weird to say that writing is more potent than other arts."

"No, I don't think it's weird. As you said yourself, some kind of truth surely exists behind this feeling at least for many people."

"It is true and has been an eye-opener for me personally after being a fanatic Nature lover and a successful painter."

"Why do you think they don't publish your works then?"

"Maybe they hate my guts and cynicism. Besides, editors and publishers are swamped with submissions and it's easier for them to rely mostly on referrals and books' commercial potentials. You know all this shit, don't you? They also prefer to publish garbage, for propaganda, business purposes, and supporting some special groups' interests."

"Yeah, that's probably true. And yet you keep writing and sending them to those hypocrites, anyway!"

"I might as well keep trying," Ralph said with a sigh. He left the study abruptly. I thought he went to cry a little bit in private, but he returned with the bottle of cognac and poured another good shot in our glasses.

"Have you shown your writings to your friends?"

"I'm not convinced their opinions can help. But yours may... Do you want to read a short story about aliens I've just finished?"

"Sure. I'll read it and give you my honest opinion," I said with a grin. I could not tell him that I had already read a draft of that ridiculous story after stealing it from their recycling material. I believed he was talking about the same story. On the other, what I had read had been only a draft with too many corrections. Maybe his final edits were actually decent writings.

"Maybe you could then introduce me to your colleagues and editors for consideration?"

"Okay... Maybe..."

"Thanks..."

"Ralph, may I ask where you're originally from?"

"Iran... I was born and grew up in Tehran."

"Oh... So when did you come to Canada?"

"Twenty years ago. But I lived in Los Angeles for ten years going to university and working before escaping to Vancouver."

During the next two weeks, I read a bunch of Ralph's essays and short stories and enjoyed them a great deal. He was a good writer and storyteller indeed. Therefore, the fact that he had not been able to attract someone's interest after so long was amazing and heartbreaking at the same time. I promised to help him with some editing and perhaps find him a publisher if he in return helped me complete my research. I had to study his work habits, personality traits, objectives and aspirations, mood swings and reactions to rejections and so many other factors. I gathered a large wealth of information from him for my project in the following weeks and was ready to write the report. Instead, I sent the following note to my ex-boss.

Dear Alex:

For three years, I have worked on the assignment you had given me about the traits and lifestyle of unpublished, old writers. You know almost everything I can tell you after such a long research.

I cannot add much more to that. These people are a bunch of hardworking, heartbroken, creative artists who simply enjoy pouring their guts out onto paper to release their tensions, forget about their lousy lives for a while, or challenge their minds. I will prepare a short report on this subject, anyway. But instead of spending more time on this project, I am going to write a novella about one of these creatures that happens to live in my neighbourhood. His life story is quite intriguing. It depicts some perplexing events that have turned him into a philosopher more than a writer now. It will be interesting to delve into his life while he feels like an alien on this planet and believes he should not be considered a 'human' also for all the nasty things he has done and maybe still doing. I believe he is misperceiving human nature, anyway, although he often shows his cynicism about humanity and his inability to relate to common people. I must somehow clarify this matter for him, if I can. He must at least stop worrying about not being a human on top of the agony of feeling like an alien on Earth and not getting a single story published. Anyway, after hearing his story and associating closely with this guy, now I am going to be an old fiction writer, too. Now, I am hooked myself. I am now at the verge of becoming a subject of my own research—an old unpublished writer. Let me know if you like to buy the publication rights for my great novella, or if you know someone who might be interested.

Gosh, I already sound old and desperate, don't I; like all these unpublished old writers!

I never received a response from Alex or the payment for my lousy report, which I prepared and sent to him a month later. I did not care to pursue the matter with a jerk like him, either. Instead, I have become a close friend of Ralph to the point that Charlie sometimes appears jealous and sorry for introducing him to me. Apparently, Maxine does not like Ralph's hanging out with me so much, either. She does not like anything the poor guy does, anyway. Their marriage seems to be in big trouble as well—like mine—and it is making Ralph even sadder these days. Phyllis and Maxine hate each other secretly, too, but mostly are angry and distressed for not knowing how to handle their husbands and their growing affinity! They simply loathe seeing us a bit happy. What a mess! What a world! Wow, I talk a lot like Ralph already, too! Maybe we should move to a different neighbourhood. I bet Phyllis would be thrilled to hear this idea.

*****

My neighbours are most likely right about my family, especially myself, appearing rather aloof and odd, like aliens. Life turns many of us into this bizarre position. In particular, when spouses feel trapped in a dysfunctional relationship and lose their spirits for living, people around them see them as aliens as much as the husband and wife themselves feel like aliens to each other. We just keep living in the abyss with a crabby mood in some form of resignation. In the end, however, we are the ones who choose this rather stoic lifestyle, as a survival mode, when it feels like the most peaceful and fulfilling means of 'being' available to us.

In English, foreigners are called aliens in a special context with a different intention *apparently*. But how do we foreigners know why English started calling us aliens to begin with or why they have not yet distinguished us from those ugly and nasty creatures possibly living in outer space that would come only to hurt us horribly when they do? This is just amazing, at least for cranky or sensitive foreigners like me! Thank goodness, at least we do not have this confusion or misunderstanding in my native language, Persian.

By the way, I liked both the novella and the above essay that Tony wrote in relation to his research about 'Unpublished Old Writers,' and asked me to read and edit them for him. So, you may wish to go back and reread this essay now that you know who the presumed aliens in this story are and what it might be all about. The second read is often a lot more fun for smart people.

Prank Calls

All those anecdotes about couples' difficulty to understand each other had only made me laugh. I honestly believed they had not really tried hard enough and they did not know how to go about it properly the way I could as a diligent scientist. "Studying any subject with passion would lead to more understanding for sure," I had assured my married friends who had tried to warn me. They just mocked my inability to learn a lesson even from my own previous relationships. However, deep down, I had always blamed myself—as a reckless, immature person—for not caring or trying enough in my past relationships. With such an innocent heart and juvenile confidence, I had married Sheila with great intentions many years ago after exchanging our blazing passion. We just could not stop kissing or caressing each other or live without the other even one more day.

Then, the bizarre reality knocked me on the head like a sledgehammer within a year. How was it possible? Why was I getting more confused the longer I lived with Sheila? Why was it getting harder every day to understand her? This painful puzzle hurt deeper year after year, not merely because it affected our marriage, but mostly how it offended me as a top-notch scholar —especially after all that bragging to my friends. We learn more every week even about the behaviour of these monstrous cancer cells. So, why in the world would not these basic principles of scientific deduction work in this special case with this particular subject?

I discussed this bizarre anomaly with my confidant, George, many times during our weekly hikes. He is a famous psychiatrist, but could not offer a straight answer to my simple enquiry, either. He only smirked at my flustered face as if I were mad or joking. He said he appreciated my intention to boost my ten-year-old marriage. However, he still seemed unable to grasp the gist of my curiosity, although I did not mind boosting my marriage as well, if possible at all by a miracle. Instead, he seemed mostly amused by my naïve persistence to understand Sheila.

"Just let it go," he said with impatience. "This phenomenon is beyond human intelligence or scientific laws."

That was easy for him to say. He did not really appreciate how these types of mysteries could throw a *true* scholar. He was only a psychiatrist, after all.

"But, George—"

"No buts… Why are you so uptight?" he said with empathy. "Your obsession is going to kill you…"

"My obsession?"

"Yes, you're too damn sensitive."

"I can't help it, I guess," I said with resignation, feeling sorry for myself. I always knew I was being wasted in this ungrateful world.

"All couples face the same conundrum," George said, as if his prophecy had any technical merit or could cure my curiosity.

"Then there's need for research even more than I'd thought," I emphasized.

"No, there isn't. Merely gender differences and hormones are responsible for everything. That is all! And nobody can fix that!"

It took me several years to grasp George's wisdom and admit I could not solve this particular puzzle. It was just a big enigma that no amount of science could ever unravel. I tried to curb my ego and stop being a neurotic scholar for this once. "It's a part of marriage," I reminded myself whenever Sheila and I argued about silly stuff—about sixteen times a week. I believed I was reinforcing my resilience. Still I was not prepared for the shock Sheila gave me with her decision to leave me.

"But why, Sheila?"

"Because you'll never *understand* me."

My heart tore apart in my chest, as if she had just plunged a big dagger into it and twisted it round and round and round.

"Is it my fault that I don't understand you?" I asked in total disbelief.

"Isn't it? You're so *insensitive*, you deny even this simple fact!" Sheila shrieked. "You never really tried to understand me, did you?"

"I'm insensitive?! What more could've I done?"

"Oh, gosh! Where should I begin?" she exclaimed after a heartbreaking sigh that made me feel guilty for five seconds, but then I remembered my sincere desire and intense labour all those years to figure her out.

"Just give me an example," I implored, almost certain I had cornered her cleanly this time.

"Just look around you…"

I looked carefully all around me for twenty seconds like an imbecile, but could not find any clue about my wrongdoings. Only expensive furniture and paintings, which she had bought herself, mocked me. I had never questioned her taste, despite all the money I believed we were wasting on interior decoration.

"What?" I asked. "I didn't buy any of these!"

"What're you talking about?"

"What're *you* talking about?"

"I feel jealous," Sheila yelled.

Startled, I was at sea, on a fast sinking ship. Had I been too sociable with another woman for two minutes again? After our marriage, I had always been stiff around women just to keep Sheila 'un-jealous'—my dear angelus. Actually, I even behaved like a snob idiot sometimes to avoid other women's careful or casual flirting. The big irony was that Sheila's face showed how well she knew her dear friends were usually guilty. Yet, not all that knowledge ever stopped her from judging and blaming only me. These women are always playing some kind of a game among them, I tell you. They just do it so cleverly to tease one another and we men are only the means—and for getting all the blames.

"What've I done now?" I asked her with desperation.

"Go learn something from your friends!" Sheila said.

"You must be kidding me! Please tell me you're joking," I said with an idiotic chuckle.

"They spoil their wives all the time."

I was numb for twenty seconds. After my brain decided to come back to work, it took about fifteen seconds to connect the dots and sort of guess the possible cause of her jealousy. For the next ten seconds, I was relieved that at least she was jealous about something I had not done, which was hopefully a lesser crime than having done something deliberately, such as flirting with another woman. Then again, I wondered for another ten seconds whether the opposite were truer these days. Just recently, she had suddenly stopped caring about other women's joking with me, which made me wonder why. Maybe I had improved in her eyes on this specific flaw at least—in which case she was certainly wondering why, of course! Or she did not really care anymore for some reason—maybe total loss of interest in me, or gaining deep interest in someone else instead. These delicate revelations take us men a long time to sort out, if at all. Anyway, after about one minute of numbing confusion, still undecided about the real source and extent of my guilt, my injured pride pushed me to say something about my moron friends, whom she was expecting me to *go learn something from*! I had had it with both their hypocrisy and submissiveness, always covering up their affairs with gifts or sucking-up.

"I don't care what my lousy friends do… They're a little weak, if you ask me."

"Oh, yeah? They're weak because they listen to their wives?"

"Absolutely... What's good about being scared of your wife, anyway? I've always wanted us to be friends. Don't I support you with your career and other stuff?"

"That's not enough. You never spoil me," she said.

For Heaven's sake! This 'spoiling' business was just freaking out my finicky brain, which had already threatened me to go on a long strike this time. Was I missing a big point here, again? I'd be really insulted if someone thought I was spoiled or if he or she tried to spoil me! Of course, I have nothing against spouses being romantic and all. However, how could any intelligent person who demands to be spoiled not be rotten already? How does it fit all those gender equality slogans, anyway? This was in fact another bizarre phenomenon, but I decided not to dwell on it as a new research topic. I had just had it with all these relationship riddles and my futile efforts to research these weird mysteries. I believed George would not have an answer for this new dilemma, either. *What the heck these psychiatrists are good for then?*

"Your nagging alone shows how spoiled you are already," I told Sheila anyway, even though I really tried hard to keep both my big mouth and scientific conscience in check. But these kinds of refined deductions cannot be easily swept under the rug.

"You think so, professor?" Sheila blurted.

"Don't you see that even expecting it shows how spoiled you are?"

"You just don't get it... Forget it."

"True! I do not understand anything anymore! I'm absolutely astonished!"

"Don't be! Now it's your chance to get rid of me."

"But why? How about us?"

"Life's too short."

Here we go again... Another hollow jargon screwing up so many marriages nowadays. Just another excuse to look for new imaginary soul mates, adventures, and more orgasms.

For three days, I tried to change Sheila's mind. But it was like talking to the Great Wall of China. I even promised to try harder to understand her, while my conscience kicked and screamed that it was an impossible mission and a big lie. Her impatience finally convinced me that she either had an affair already or was dying to start one right away to avenge her *insensitive* husband's tyranny. She seemingly needed someone so badly to spoil her to death immediately!

Anyway, even if I could forget all her insults, I just could not get over her comment about my insensitivity, especially since George had already accused me of being too sensitive. On the other hand, perhaps her conscience (or whatever in her case!) was bugging her a little about a possible affair or plan she did not want to confess to. Separation would relieve the burden I could see in her gorgeous eyes. These conclusions seemed plausible to me. My extensive research about, and personal experiences with, relationships had made me an expert already, maybe one even more so than George. I reckoned a time comes in everybody's life eventually when he or she is too ashamed of his/her lies and infidelity, thus separation becomes his/her only solution to calm his/her inner conflicts (and *conscience* for some people) a little perhaps. So, I let our lawyers prepare a separation agreement to her liking. I did not want to delay her happiness in her lover's cosy bosom; or keep her worried any longer on my account about 'life's shortness'! *I'm such a great guy, aren't I?* Within two weeks, she was gone.

George tried to cheer me up and a few other friends made efforts to see me now and then, too. Yet, their friendships seemed even less real than ever. I reckoned their wives had warned them against spending too much time with a loser like me. I was a bad role model, too, after all—not only as a fresh, carefree bachelor, but also because Sheila had keenly told everybody that I deemed my friends too submissive to their bossy wives. Nobody had quite appreciated my blunt observation. The whole world now avoided me as if I had become a leper overnight. They blamed me also for the separation, even though Sheila had buoyantly bragged to everybody about my pitiful pleading to reconsider her decision. What a crazy world! The women who had always flirted with me in front of their husbands and Sheila now just stared at me blankly, as though I had turned into a hopeless jerk overnight. Now that I was free and available, they did not want me anymore! Women's games are certainly too complex and confusing, I tell you! I was invited to only a few parties, out of pity perhaps. My lifelong friends probably felt obliged to invite me now and then, until they found an excuse to oust me for good —I could see how hard they were working on it by the way they got anxious around me.

I travelled in Europe for two long months after the separation —in search of what, I never understood. The whole time, I kept asking myself what I was doing there anywhere I went! Later, a bachelor colleague told me that I should have gone to Cuba or Thailand instead. Travelling was George's suggestion to get over my gloom. My boss also agreed. He let me use all the vacation time I had saved as part of my plan to surprise Sheila and take her to Europe—an idea she had suddenly become obsessed with in recent years. I had been working quietly behind the scene to spoil Sheila very soon, anyway, if she had not been too spoiled already to screw up her own chance of being spoiled even more by me! At the same time, maybe my Europe's lonely excursion had been merely a subconscious drive, out of either romance or spite. *I talk a lot like a psychiatrist these days, don't I? Well, somebody must do the job George seems incapable of doing properly!*

Once I was back in town, I started receiving a few prank calls at home every week. When I answered the phone, the caller hung up. Soon I believed it was Sheila. She had realized her enormous mistake at last, I reckoned with pleasure and pride! Perhaps she was even in love with me again! *Did this mean that I had to go to Europe again, maybe next year, with her? Damn!* Maybe she would confess to her affairs, too, if we ever got back together.

How convenient! Commit adultery, ask for separation, have some extra fun, complete your experimentation with the other fellow, realize your BIG MISTAKE, and then manipulate your estranged spouse to take steps for reconciliation. Could anyone have been more spoiled? Is not separation such a novel scapegoat nowadays, to satiate your sexuality just in case you are a bit shy to demand an open marriage? Just a hiccup before moving on. Forgive and forget without fuss. Anyway, the fact that she missed me boosted my spirit and it felt like a major victory—a piece of good news to cling to after three months of agony and depleting self-esteem.

Yet I wondered why she would not speak out at least—to admit her mistake and desire to come back home. Her stupid pride and arrogance stopped her like always, I bet. However, I was tired of justifying her misplaced pride and spoiling her even more. Expecting me to initiate a contact with her was just another type of her manipulation—that spoiled broad. I had a bit of pride too, after all, you know! I was not even sure about taking her back, even if she begged me. Or even bothering to listen to her lies about how and when her affair with some jerk had started. *Okay, now tell me about all your other affairs before this one, if you don't mind, my rotten wicked wife!*

Of course, I could trace the prank calls through the call-back feature. Or I could get the caller-id option added to my service and then go buy a new telephone with display screen, too. Too much hassle for nothing, I thought. Sheila knew I seldom used the phone or cared about adding these fancy options. I never cared to have a cellular phone, either. Yet she had hoped I would figure out that she was the one making the calls and then also do something about it. It was odd and annoying—and confusing in itself—how she sometimes trusted my intelligence too much and sometimes not at all. She never let me know where she stood even on this rudimentary matter—although I must say, in her defence, that she had more often tried to prove my stupidity than not, especially about my poor grasp of her needs. Anyhow, she was proven right, as I was ninety-nine percent sure that Sheila was the culprit behind the prank calls. I did not need to be certain, anyway, because I was not going to call her. Period.

I told George about the prank calls and my hunch that it was Sheila. He noticed and loathed my pathetic thrill, yet never made any comment. I resented his pitiful peeps and apathy. He asked me only once whether I wanted to mend fences with her and I said, "Are you kidding me?" He took my answer the wrong way and said nothing else. In fact, I had hoped he would explain the purpose of his question and then perhaps offer his suggestion for a possible intervention or something. Naturally, if he had been a good psychiatrist, he would have figured out my meaning fast the same way I had! He would have then followed up the matter to get to the bottom of things, but he had just kept his silence.

Three more months passed and I still received the prank calls. What perseverance! I chuckled with pleasure. Sometimes they were more frequent, and sometimes there was a gap between the calls. Whenever the calls stopped, I got nervous. I worried she might have forgotten all about me and moved on. But then she called again. And I bragged to George about it, too, while he shrugged off my enthusiasm. His mysterious indifference was infuriating, while my curiosity about Sheila's real intention was growing. How could he be so cold about such a sensitive and entertaining matter? Yet I took his apathy as his way of goading me to forget all about Sheila and move on. I liked to give him some credit once in a while when possible. One day, however, he mentioned a story that rattled my nerves. I guess he had become fed up with my juvenile joy from the prank calls and bragging about them to him.

"You know something, Jim?" he asked me with stress.

"What, George?"

"You can't be sure it's Sheila making those calls. Besides—"

"I'm sure it's Sheila…"

George kept silent as we continued hiking and thinking. My mocking, confident tone had obviously irritated him again.

"Besides what?" I asked. He ignored me.

"What else were you going to say?" I insisted with a soft tone, hoping to make up for my rude interruption of his usually useless advice.

He sighed at last and said, "Somebody mentioned to me that his girlfriend has picked up a habit of making a prank call right in the middle of sex. She presses the speed-dial and disconnects when the person answers. Then she resumes sex as though she'd needed a boost to reach an orgasm."

The story had totally disgusted me. Even worse, I could not believe George telling me this horrible account of some idiot's life when he knew I was not in the best condition these days. Hearing about people's freaky perversions with any resemblance to my case was poison for me. But it had raised my curiosity too.

"Is he one of your patients?"

"Not really," George replied.

"Who's he then?"

"Just a friend… Forget it. I'm sorry I mentioned it."

"Someone I know?" I insisted with tension.

"Let's drop this conversation, please."

Two more months passed while the prank calls still kept amusing me. One night, a close friend visited me. We drank beers and smoked pot while watching hockey and barbequing.

"So, are you having fun without Sheila, like the good old times?" Sam asked.

"Not really… I am busy. I'm not in the mood for any kind of affair, anyway."

"Why?"

"I don't know…," I replied.

"What do you miss the most about Sheila?"

"Umm…," I stalled while sipping a large glass of beer slowly and hoping he would drop the subject.

"Nothing?" he asked and kept staring at me.

"Our sex…," I blurted at last.

"Yeah...?"

"Yeah... It was always special if we were in the mood."

"But now you should move on."

"I wished it were easy," I murmured with a sigh.

"It's probably easier for women..."

"I don't know. Is it?"

"Sheila sure handled it better than you!"

"How's that?"

"I've heard something about her too," he said as if gloating.

"Like what?"

Sam covered his mouth with his hand, burped, then muttered, "About Sheila and Jack..."

"Jack Mather?"

"Yeah... You guys're still friends?"

"I don't know... Haven't seen him lately."

It took me about ten minutes to think straight again. *How much must we torture our poor brains, really!* Then I decided it was time to open that expensive bottle of cognac I had brought back from Europe—probably my only proud triumph from the European tour.

"Care for a shot of cognac?" I asked Sam, while wondering whether I could have brought back a livelier and more useful souvenir for myself if I had gone to Thailand or Cuba instead.

"No, I'm smashed already... I better go soon," Sam replied.

"What's the rush?" I poured a shot of cognac for myself while Sam stared at the beautiful bottle. "Stay overnight then, if you're smashed."

"No, Debby won't go to sleep until I get home."

What a wonderful, devoted wife, I wanted to puke. She used to flirt with me often, sometimes under Sam's eyes, when I was married and now loathed me for..., I do not know what! Maybe Sam had sensed it then and was now finding the right opportunity to take his revenge on me finally. I had really tried not to betray my friends, despite their wives' tenacity to either lure me or test my power to ignore their charm.

"Then I'll drive you. Don't worry."

"Why? Wanna kill us both?" Sam groaned. "Least give me some of that pretty cognac, after all."

The next day, I woke up still lying on the sofa, with the TV on, the bottle of cognac two-third empty, and no sign of Sam.

The following weekend, George and I were hiking again with little breath left in us. Me especially, I had in fact had difficulty breathing the whole week since Sam's slip of the tongue. I had felt lousy all week. I no longer wished to talk with George about my depression, either. I was sick of them all. What friends! George noticed my exasperation and abnormal silence, so he tried to boost my spirit by teasing me.

"Did you get any more prank calls last week?" he asked, his annoying smirk pinching my nerves.

"Yeah... Thanks for reminding me!" I mumbled, thinking about ending my life. "I got three of them, actually!"

Wow! I wondered with envy. *We hardly did it even once a week in the last years of our glamorous marriage. She had surely found the right kind of lover to spoil her so often with sex, plus many other gimmicks or jewelleries perhaps. Is Jack Mather the guy and so good?*

"So why's your mood so messed up?" George asked.

"May I ask you something, George?" I said.

"Ask..."

"Were you serious about the woman making prank calls in the middle of sex?"

"Of course..."

"You aren't teasing me or lying, are you?"

"No... I wouldn't tease you in your present condition."

"Thanks." We continued hiking and thinking for a couple of minutes in silence.

"Was it Jack Mather who told you the story?"

George froze in his tracks and stared at me with wide-open eyes. He knew that his startle had already answered my question.

"Y…e…a…h…! How do you know?" he muttered finally.
"Just a hunch…"

Maybe I was an *insensitive* husband who never *understood*
Sheila, nor could *spoil* her to death. But I surely understood it
was time to spoil her insensitive fun. I had the caller-id option
added to my service and bought a new phone set with the display
screen. Instead of only counting her number of orgasms per
week, I am now wondering how many she is losing because I do
not pick up the phone. Her calls continue at the same rate,
though; some weeks even more aggressively than before—due to
her frustration, I bet. Hearing my depressed, defeated voice on
the phone had certainly been satiating her obsession for spite and
boosting her ecstasy. That was how vengeful and vulgar I had all
along figured out Sheila to be and I was thrilled at least for being
a great psychologist to figure out all these complex stuff—so
much better than this lousy George had proven to me to be. I feel
a wicked ecstasy myself watching her number on the display
while the phone rings and rings and rings. What perseverance!
What spite! I pick up the phone occasionally, anyway, just to
keep her hopes high, as though I did not have a caller-id. Or
maybe I am hoping subconsciously she would speak out one day!
She really makes me giggle, more than she ever did when we
were married. I *understand* her now better than ever too! Too late
for me though, I guess…

*****

So now you also know about the appalling ending of my morbid
marriage, although it brought me right to a blissful beginning for
a self-searching regimen and exploring the essence of existence,
especially mine with all its peculiarities and perturbing mysteries.
Naturally, only some odd individuals, like me, might feel blessed
with this kind of bizarre lifestyle and enjoying it, too, contrary to
common perception. Surely, solitude is not a sane option for most

people, thus humans' obsession to be sociable at such humiliating cost, merely to avoid boredom and loneliness, is understandable. One must develop a taste for it, which can happen in many ways. Mine grew and was perfected over the years mostly as a general life path, while my aversion for modern lifestyle, personalities, and values rose, but also because people eluded me for their own reasons on top of my seemingly aloof, pensive attitude.

Naturally, my life of solitude after divorce has had its own upheavals as well, some of which might become apparent in the future stories, but overall it has proven a thrilling adventure and preference for my taste. It has not been only enlightening, though, but rather useful at many personal levels for handling my daily routine, thus worth all the hassles and pains of loneliness. For one thing, it made me realize I would not care to know about Sheila and Jack's love affair that had driven me to explore other realms of existence or about my creepy friends who left me, so rudely and arrogantly, to rot in my empty house with my weird thoughts.

Ironically, and to say even more about human nature, this large group of disloyal friends have still insisted on proving their arrogant nerve by calling me sporadically only for getting my advice on many topics when desperate and entangled within their own messy existence around their lousy, demanding spouses. It appears their revered lifestyle would never give them some peace of mind, either, even in this late stage of their pathetic lives. Of course, I cannot care less about their welfare, but am just amazed of their guts to still bother me with their idiocies, and then even expect me to empathize with their pains as well!

The Man in Charge

Killing your lifelong pal is a difficult deed indeed, *even* in spite of his treason and rising malice. Yet, it seems like the only way to free my soul and find peace. This dilemma has haunted me now for sometime, although I am sure I would not get into any trouble with the law for having him eliminated. Actually, I think nobody would really care even if the whole world found out about my eerie revenge. People would probably call me a lunatic and laugh a little, but nobody would fuss about the death of my partner in so many crimes. "All that solitude and despair finally drove him to this point of total madness," they would say, while congratulating one another and gloating for their joyous premonition about the outcome of my rising idiocy in recent years.

Therefore, it is just a matter of convincing myself to carry out my spiteful, but liberating, act or somehow forgive this Monsieur Rishard for the thousandth time despite his growing malice.

It was during my trip to San Francisco, in the summer of 2011, that I truly realized how Rishard has been fooling me all my life after puberty. My pitiful willpower to elude his wicked influence felt too embarrassing and frustrating, yet I seemed trapped. I have never had enough self-discipline to resist his cheesy charm. Last week, however, I thought I had really had it with this devil when he startled me with another one of his daft ideas and I lost the control of the car. It swerved to the right and then left, nearly crashing into the oncoming traffic. Luckily, I turned the steering wheel at the last moment and brought the car to an abrupt halt near the curb. Then I confronted Rishard the next day as my final ultimatum before fixing his fate.

"Do you know how much pain you've caused me every day, you sex maniac?" I yelled at him.

"I can say the same thing about you, you lover boy."

"Who do you really think you are?"

"The devil apparently," he replied casually. "The same devil you used to cherish every day, mind you."

"You think you're funny?"

"Not as much as you are!"

"We could've died last night because of your outrageous, silly suggestion!"

"Is it my fault you can't even drive a car anymore, old man?"

"Yes, yes… You're just driving me nuts with your attitude. This is not acceptable," I said.

"Not acceptable? Oh, I'm afraid!"

"You should be…! Don't make me do something crazy that we both might regret later!"

"Like what?"

"Like… You'll never find out until it's too late…"

"What do you want from me?" Rishard asked.

"Just a little cooperation. Stop humiliating me so much in front of women. How dare you?"

"Again, it's your own fault, always gloating, as if you were still a teenager."

"Is that right…?"

"Absolutely," he murmured.

"So, now you wish you could go find yourself a younger buddy, ha?"

"Just stop bugging me. I'm getting old too."

"So what're we supposed to do now?" I asked.

"How the hell do I know? You're the one with the brain!"

Talking to Rishard has always been a waste of my breath. I am merely amazed at my own stupidity to imagine for a moment that he might understand even a single word I say. No point feeling sorry for him anymore, either, or even reminding him that he cannot survive without me for a single day. Simply time has come to gather my guts and cut him loose despite the inevitable pain and bloodshed. What is the best way to do it? Is it a wise and practical decision? I should find and pay an expert to eliminate him, anyway. But, by God, it seems like the only solution left. Indulging him feels more embarrassing every day.

I promise to recount the sequence of events in the summer of 2011, leading to my outburst. It is an enlightening story to make your own judgment about this devil. First, let me say a few words about our history, though. After all, he deserves some credit for our embarrassing joint ventures that brought my best experiences and lots of fun, despite all the crimes he pushed me to commit. I simply cannot forget our youthful mischief around the city, how tough he was, and how he stood up for me, pushing and shoving together for our common interests, although we usually ended up screwing another person, anyway. We used to work quite nicely together indeed. Alas, those good old days are forever gone! And now my life feels like an endless, wearing war with Rishard.

In the Beginning

Rishard and I literally grew up together, although we became best friends after puberty when he kept barging in on me and raising my interest in sex and girls more every day. His thrill-seeking attitude and audacity impressed me. He got stronger and bigger every day, although I have always remained much taller than he has been. I was not jealous, but his importance became obvious as we thought about girls urgently with desperation. His influence over me increased, too, as I kept playing with him and submitted to his erotic suggestions.

Rishard's agility and persistence to go out and chase girls was so cute. Actually, he was just interested in finding a pussy, no matter whose or at what cost. When it came to pussy, he was also quite generous with my money. He did not even care if I was right in the middle of some serious work or had planned to go somewhere for business, grocery shopping, or whatever. I got upset particularly when he interrupted me every time I tried to read a book or do something useful with my life.

"What're you doing?" Rishard often asked.

"I'm trying to learn something," I replied.

"Forget about that. You're not gonna learn anything from reading books. Come on, let's go have some fun."

"But…"

"No buts; get up, let's go do something wild."

The way he just got crazy, jumping around and teasing me, was too innocent and amusing, which made it impossible to say no or resist his sneaky manipulation. This kind of his childlike attitude made me laugh and forgive him all over. I never really learned to discipline this pervert. I do not think it was possible, anyway.

Of course, Rishard's vivacity and tenacity to explore the beauties around the city was inspirational. It encouraged me to keep a rather positive outlook on life and share his passion for sensual pleasures. Only because of Rishard, I did not commit suicide after realizing life's vanity so early in my life. As a token of my appreciation, I indulged him too often and followed his lead. I let him pull my strings and play me like a puppet, simply because I liked him too much. I did everything for my own good, I guess, for chasing and entertaining women. Naturally, I was the one picking up the tab when we went to restaurants or movies. He just enjoyed the free ride. I was the handsome one, too. He was actually rather ugly with his large, lumpy figure. Most girls were initially startled when they met him for the first time. And yet, he was the one eventually getting all their attention and being showered with kisses like a sweet Popsicle. Ironically, he usually screwed them in the end and still those girls never complained about his pushy attitude. Instead, they blamed me for everything later, even about the painful things Rishard had done to them.

No doubt, Rishartd's charisma was enviable, although he could never build a character. He was just a useless dick spending most of his energy on sex, then suddenly losing his interest in everything and sulking in a corner like a snail. His moodiness showed from the beginning, as he cowered in his small world for days. You would wonder what he was up to! **BUT** when he emerged from his seclusion, he was too vivacious and vulgar, especially around women. Still, they seldom got offended. In fact, we all enjoyed this side of Rishard much better. Except that showing off his perfect erection seemed too hedonistic, as if he were the only one in the world who could do that. *Big deal!* That is how I felt then, until we got old and realized that in fact it had been a big deal!

Anyhow, as much as I tried to live like a gentleman, Rishard embarrassed me more often in front of girls by his vulgarity or aloofness. While I tried to be a man of principles and etiquette, he remained a mindless narcissist. This contrast obviously caused regular frictions between us. His demands on some occasions were simply too appalling, like the times he wanted us to seduce a woman regardless of the consequences, whether she was up to it or not. It sounded more like rape, and I said no, which made him tense and wild. The throbbing veins bulged all over his body as he shook hysterically, so much so I thought he might explode from blood pressure any second and kill me in the process, too. Monsieur acted like those snob Frenchmen who roam the streets of Paris casually and believe they can, or have the right to, seduce any woman they wish.

Stopping him from causing a commotion or committing a crime took a lot of my energy. In return, he retaliated at worst possible times when I needed his support. "Let's go, let's go… Get up…" I yelled while pulling him from his neck. "Let's check this out, you lazy devil." I begged him or shook him with rage, to no avail. He pretended to be asleep or deaf, merely to enjoy my frustration. I wanted to smash his bald head when he became so loose and insensitive. His retaliations have always been critically timed and terribly annoying. A few times, he actually pissed on my legs, shoes, or brand new trousers.

Before continuing with more bitching and badmouthing this idiotic dick—Monsieur Rishard—I know that a similar character runs and ruins every man's life. We all enjoy our cosy friendships with these devils, but they eventually make us lose the control of our lives. Even worse, we feel abused and abandoned at the end. No point denying the main source of our agony, my friends. That is exactly what I am doing here by exposing Rishard to justify my final decision about his fate. This long essay may convince some women, too, to forgive me after realizing my innocence for all those vulgar things that Rishard forced me do to them. In fact, I am hoping to prove, and defend, men's eternal helplessness just due to our natural attachments to these devils! You gauge my grievances, too, and be the judge. Especially, read the incident in San Francisco, under the heading of *Main Story* below, and then rule on Rishard's fate. Actually, go read that story now or at any point you get tired of listening to my whining; because I have so much to say about this devil's effect on my mind and destiny all along. I really wish to get this big load off my chest, if you do not mind.

In the Middle

I had always hoped to live peacefully with Rishard despite his moral defects and waning loyalty. Our random rows had felt natural, too, for two inseparable buddies. I tried to cope with his needs and moodiness, as a normal way of life, while running his errands all along. God knows how often I felt obliged to deceive pretty girls just for his benefit! He was the chief and the expert, yet I had to do all the lying and conniving because he is dumb. Once, he even made me seduce the fiancée of my close friend.

All those years, I never realized I was spoiling Rishard while he became less reliable. Instead, I felt guilty for not following his lead as much as he wanted me to. On the other hand, if I wanted to listen to Rishard, I had to quit my job and forget about all my other life responsibilities just to go around with him and chase women. When I reminded him of my job and other obligations, he ridiculed my logic and humiliated me again in front of women —to make me feel useless without sex.

I often tried to explain to this maniac that sex is not the answer to all human problems. But he just stood stiff, stared straight into my eyes, and eventually hypnotized me to follow his orders and seduce other girls. He kept goading me to have sex with different women to forget all the nonsense about love. Even then, he still shed tears and sulked at the end—to make me feel guilty for what we (mostly he) had done.

Of course, he still interfered with all my love affairs, anyway, while insisting that sex was the main part of any love story, too. Our quarrels about love and sex always led to more arguments and finger pointing whenever one of my love affairs went sour. I blamed his sudden apathy toward my lovers. And he mocked my romanticism with his regular words of wisdom. In particular, he kept saying, "Love means shit when sex is lousy!" You see how arrogant and vulgar he gets sometimes? He wanted to be my mentor and a philosopher, too. Stand back Socrates!

I wrote poetry and love letters for my lovers, all along hoping Rishard would not find out. I imagined my feelings would stay private in my head and heart without Rishard always butting in. However, he usually emerged out of the blue and began pushing my lover during our romance. He just stood between us with a hard stance, thrusting her, and trying to find a hole in one of her positions. Without even grasping our conversations, he got wild and attacked her the minute he heard some romantic words.

As you might imagine, Rishard always mocked my idea of getting married to some decent girls I met at university and work. Every time, he just repeated his old lecture and enumerated the merits of chasing girls every night and having casual sex. "Forget the damn marriage, will you?" he yelled. Then one day, suddenly he insisted that I should marry a particular girl. I was stunned. Pamela was a sexy girl but very conservative. She refused to have sex, although she said she loved me. Rishard was initially shocked and confused for a few weeks when Pamela and I dated. He got angry with her a few times, too. Then, he was intrigued that this kind of girls still existed in our sexually crazed society. At last, he got obsessed to solve this mystery at any cost. So he started encouraging me to marry her as *the* final resort for having her—as if she were merely a piece of cake that a child wants to grab at any risk.

"Forget about her. Let's move on," I insisted.

"Move on? Are you crazy? This mystery is not a matter you can ignore and move on," Rishard persisted.

Pamela and I had different lifestyles and mentalities, though. Yet Rishard promised that sex would solve all marital conflicts. "Don't worry," he kept saying. Again, I was stupid enough to believe him. He insisted it was time to marry, since I was way past thirty at the time, and almost the whole city had heard about my irresponsible lifestyle—all thanks to Rishard, of course. Anyway, he pushed me to settle down with a wife who ruined both our lives, as well as Rishard's perhaps. Pamela and I lost the opportunity of finding suitable companions when we were young and attractive. Still I forgave Rishard again, even for forcing an agonizing marriage on me. I did all these forgiving because I was under his spell and had so much patience. Not anymore! Sorry!

The irony is that Pamela left me right after I finally learned to cope with her malice, while I was also getting old and vulnerable. Yes, that bastard Rishard caused our separation, too, if you were wondering. For one thing, he had been insisting for five years that I could (and should) find a better partner. But, I am sure now, he had been only interested in freeing me up for casual sex with girls; to get me involved again with his erotic fantasies around the city like the good old times. I bet Pamela's pal (ɪ) was goading her to ask for separation, too, for similar reasons.

Besides his guilt to force me marry a nutcase like Pamela, and his sin to push me leave her, the way Rishard often sabotaged my marriage had been too humiliating. He simply refused to stick up for me when I needed him to make me look good and strong in front of Pamela. Instead, he embarrassed me enough until she lost interest in me—as well as in Rishard himself. The manner he did it was most bizarre: he simply sulked a lot when we were around her, which tainted Pamela's image of me as well, for being so helplessly attached to such an instable mound of flesh.

"What the heck is the matter with you?" I yelled at him often. "Life is tough enough already without you sulking erratically as well."

"Talk to God about it, not me," he murmured casually.

"About what, you devil?"

"About your tough life… Actually, complain about me, too, while you're at it. He created me this way, after all."

"He already knows everything regarding your vulgarity and pushing me around all my life."

"Then also tell Him how much you've smacked and squeezed me when I was tired and just wanted to loosen up," Rishard said.

In the End

I noticed I had changed a lot soon after Pamela's departure. I had become too grumpy and lost my trust in love, as if Rishard had been right all along about the futility of seeking compassion and passion. Rishard was himself frail and lazy for adventures. Now that I agreed with him to focus only on sex, he refused to play our old foolish games, such as sneaking into our girlfriends' private places unexpectedly and startling them. That was his favourite game in the past actually, although some women considered our intrusion vulgar and threatened to file criminal charges, including rape against me again, as much as I insisted it was Rishard's idea.

"So what happened to all your promises to be adventurous and energetic once I was a single man again, you lazy dick?" I yelled at him. "What's so good about this single life then, you idiot?"

Pretending innocence again, he drooped without answering me, as if I were speaking in Spanish. His moping was a familiar scene I remembered and resented, but now it just happened more often after my separation from Pamela. I had to beg, scream, or reason with him, to no avail.

Rishard was right about one thing, though. Many desperate women around my age looked for a companion. The situation seemed ideal if we stuck to Rishard's basic guideline and focused only on sex—if we had any energy to focus, of course. Naturally, these women were all damaged, like me, by our past affairs. Yet, they all insisted we were perfect together if only I changed my attitude drastically to match their lifestyles and learned how to spoil them. They demanded romance and commitment now that I wanted only sex. The same old dilemma regarding sex versus romance still haunted me, now in a reverse manner. I struggled to convince those women that I could never learn all those talents they expected of me. I loathed indulging even my good old friend, Rishard, let alone all those snobbish women who lived in some fantasy world. It usually took them a long time to realize I was hopelessly unchangeable and left me with anger. All their tenderness and friendship claims turned into hostility in a minute. Accordingly, the more I noticed the phoniness of most women's show of passion, the more I mistrusted love in general as well, beyond women per se.

"Now you get my meaning about love and women? Now that you're gonna die soon, you're starting to believe me at last, ha?" Rishard kept whining, which made me feel more stupid and sorry for all those years of wasting on love, contradicting Rishard, and wrestling with my dilemma about love and sex. But then, my new philosophy and attitude to stick to Rishard's guidelines was not helping me, either.

From my understanding of Freud's theories, my rising anxiety and depression relate to both Rishard's obsession for sex and his sudden sulking right in the middle of our adventures. Yet Rishard does not want to accept even this obvious Freudian proof of his guilt. His tinkering with Freud's theories is maddening, but also amusing. In fact, he suggests various scientific reasons for his tantrums, while mocking my stupidity, too. Mainly, he blames me—my own quirks and stress—for his indolence. He claims the war between my twisted mind and romantic heart causes my anxiety, which then affects him, too. He is now a psychiatrist, too, besides being a philosopher. Stand back also Dr. Sigmund Freud! Here comes Professor Rishard. Both my brain and heart are guilty according to him. Which part of me is all right then? Am I that complex and defective the way Rishard always wants to make me believe? Is Freud really wrong? I wonder how Freud would respond to Rishard's insults and bizarre theories.

Anyway, sensing the final stage of my life, I have strived to accept my fate and live the rest of my life quietly with no hope for ever finding my soul mate—back to the basics of survival, with less greed for pleasures. My soul-searching and resignation have caused me new dilemmas every day, however, while I have been mourning the fall of my relationship with indolent Rishard, too.

Maybe I deserve all the blame for spoiling Rishard, but he is totally out of control now. He has become lazier and made me lose my confidence completely. He embarrasses me regularly around women by his sudden sulking. Simply, I cannot trust him anymore like before. He refuses to participate even in a normal intercourse that he would definitely enjoy, if only he put his silly head into it. Some friends have suggested that this type of erratic moodiness happens to many people and maybe Rishard needs some medication, a pill called Vigora or something like that, to deal with his depression. In my opinion, however, his problem is much deeper than any medication can cure. He is possessed, if you ask me. He just enjoys torturing me.

Of course, he still encourages me to chase women merely as an old habit and then mocks me in front of them with tenacity like an eternal obsession. This is the ultimate level of humiliation for any man, which gives Rishard infinite joy. Sometimes, we meet women who are quite horny and cooperative, but still do not *come* with us despite my efforts and their desperation, all because Richard starts sulking in a jiffy too often. Like a mad sadist, he enjoys my defeat and pain in front of women, instead of trying a bit harder to make them come with us and share a pleasant time together. He simply cannot anymore, I guess; poor guy! He gets bored or exhausted quickly. This is a frustrating situation and funny, too, sometimes. But I just feel horrible for the way I look so pathetic to women and the way Richard appears so useless. So tell me, what is the point of living if I cannot keep even Rishard happy?

Main Story

In the fall of 2010, I received a surprising message from a girl I knew at college. Sherry was three years younger than I was and she still looked great in her recent photos. She had found me on Facebook and decided to check me out. She was divorced, too, and lived in San Francisco. Our communication became more intimate as we exchanged funny stories about our past glamorous marriages! She invited me to San Francisco, but I was reluctant to travel so far to meet yet another desperate divorcee. I invited her to Vancouver, but she declined with her own lame excuses. I let it go. She sounded sophisticated and artistic, though. Then again, she was probably pretending to be like this and that, the same way I did to impress women. At our age, bragging is all we have and do to hide our cynicism and past mistakes.

Rishard was more excited than me to meet Sherry, however. The more I said no, the more he pushed the idea of dating Sherry on me. After failing to convince me to do it for sex, he resorted to my romantic side.

"She may be the goddess you've been waiting for…"

"I don't think so. Thanks for your interest, pervert," I replied nervously. He had really turned into a full-fledged sadist in recent months. He just wanted to prove my stupidity for the thousandth time—that my quest for a stable companion was doomed forever. The only possible outcomes of going to San Francisco would be my humiliation and maybe some sex—the two most precious obsessions of Rishard.

"Why don't you wanna go?" he asked.

"Don't we have enough troubles with women in Vancouver already?" I replied. "They all sound nice until we meet. Then we face the same facts."

"What facts?"

"That we cannot deal with each other's quirks at our age."

"Stop being so finicky then!"

"I can't. Besides, it's mostly your grumpiness these days that makes it impossible for me to dig a woman or impress her in bed the way I did before!"

Rishard shut up after my sarcasm possibly insulted him a bit. Good! At least, he sometimes seemed to realize his guilt and role in causing me so much pain. But the next day, he brought up the subject again. "I really think you should go check Sherry out…"

"I think I already told you that I'm not going to San Francisco just to test my luck again!"

"But I can't let you make such a big mistake!" Rishard said so innocently I almost believed his sincerity. Swiftly, however, I remembered what a wicked dick he is.

"No, I'm not going… Leave me alone," I shrieked.

"What're you gonna lose by going?"

"I don't want to waste time and money to go to San Francisco just to check out another chick. We have enough headaches here in Vancouver already."

"But Sherry will be different…"

"How would she be different? The women we're dating in Vancouver are prettier than she already."

"She looks and sounds very sexy though…"

"So?"

"So…? She might be extra special in bed… Maybe she's also romantic, who knows! Perhaps she's your dream girl, after all."

"You're such a jerk, only thinking about sex…"

"What else is there?"

"You're not even good at it anymore," I said.

"Give it a try anyway… Maybe Sherry can rock your world!"

"You want me take all this hassle just for a pussy, you devil?"

"Why not?" Rishard replied so coolly I wanted to grab his thick neck and strangle him.

"Because, to me, pussy is pussy…Why are you so shallow?"

"Pussy is pussy!? Are you crazy?"

"Spend so much time and money just for a new pussy?"

"Of course… How can you even think about time and money *at a time like this?*" Rishard said mockingly, standing stiff and arrogant, like our snotty college professor, Dr. Dickson when he got excited. *At a time like this…!* Rishard's stance was simply amazing, I should say, while I kept staring at him. So tough and excited, he reminded me of the old times. For a lazy parasite who has not earned a single penny in his entire life, he was again so generous with my hard-earned money, not to mention his usual disregard for my time and emotions.

"I'm speechless. I don't know what else to say to you…" I yelled at him.

"But I know… Just say yes and call the travel agency. Let's go to San Francisco."

I went to the bathroom, instead, for a cold shower to ease my tension. However, soon, I was taking a hot bath and picturing sexy episodes with Sherry, under Rishard's influence, no doubt.

I ignored Rishard's nagging for two weeks and he snubbed me in return whenever we went to parties. He refused to partake in any intercourse or fool around with other women. I flirted with Susan, Julie, and Gloria, but he ignored all of us. The pressure Rishard was putting on me was spoiling my sleep, appetite, and sex life. I just could not bear Rishard's sulking, I guess. So, in my subsequent conversations with Sherry, I showed some flexibility about visiting her. She said she might take a few days off if I liked to travel along the Pacific Coast all the way to San Diego. As usual, I was just fed up with Rishard, but I had to keep him happy to avoid loneliness. Maybe he had a point about my chance of discovering Sherry, after all. Of course, disregarding or killing Rishard has been a tough decision also because he has been my last hope for a limited contact with people after I have abandoned my friends and focused on solitude a great deal.

I took three weeks vacation to visit Sherry, enough time to measure our compatibility. She welcomed my decision, while Rishard was ecstatic about my submission to his whim again. He would be tagging along with me to San Francisco, naturally—a new place for both of us to visit. We have surely been inseparable even when we have been mad at each other. I had not spoken to Sherry about Rishard, but believed she would not be surprised or upset when she saw him. She would probably be startled initially, but soon would start enjoying him like other women. Besides, it would have been quite silly to announce that Rishard was going with me to her house and why. There was no point to explain the details of what he would be doing there, either!

Sherry was a nice, sexy woman. We had a good time in San Francisco sightseeing and going to restaurants. We also visited Fisherman Wharf and Sausalito. We had great sex three nights in a row. Rishard kept bragging about his role to bring me so much pleasure, and for convincing me to go to San Francisco in the first place. I agreed privately with this bastard for being right again. Sherry had many fine qualities I sought in a woman. She was elegant, artistic, and easygoing, exactly as I had envisioned her. Except that she was much sexier than I could have imagined! Still another fact that this arrogant Richard had predicted, pressed on me, and now bragged about. So, we were hitting it off quite nicely, thank God. For once, my encounter with a woman had exceeded my initial optimistic impression of her. I was looking forward to the next couple of weeks that we had planned to travel together and learn a lot more about each other. Maybe I could have a sexy, sophisticated soul mate, after all.

But no sooner than my life appeared to be improving after so long, I noticed Rishard's sulking again.

"What's the problem now?" I asked him with a nervous grin.

"Nothing…"

"Isn't Sherry great?"

"I guess…"

"What do you mean, 'I guess'? She's very nice indeed."

"I agree, I said. What else you want from me? An affidavit?"

"Then, what's the matter with you?" I asked tensely.

"Let's go back to Vancouver…" Rishard murmured.

"Go back to Vancouver? Are you mad?" I yelled tensely, trembling, totally frustrated. "We've been here only four nights, and now you wanna go back? What's wrong with you?"

"Well, it was fun. But I'm bored now."

"But Sherry and I have planned to travel and spend more time together."

"I didn't agree with any such plan."

"What's the rush suddenly?"

"Don't you miss Gloria, Julie, and Susan?"

"Don't you remember how much you insisted that we come to San Francisco? All those nights you didn't let me sleep…! And now you're sucking my blood, again, this time for going back?"

"Well… I miss my life in Vancouver… And don't you have any meditating to do in solitude?"

"You're really amazing! No, you're crazy," I yelled. "We're going to travel along the coast and that's final. Leave me alone."

I got out of the bedroom, wishing I could just tell that moron to go back without me: "Just go, you crazy monster!" But I knew it was impossible, even if I gave him all the money he needed for travelling. Sadly, certain things in life cannot be changed easily and painlessly.

I started down the stairs toward the kitchen where poor Sherry was making our dinner. I hoped she had not heard my loud voice in the bedroom upstairs arguing with Rishard. If she had heard my screaming, she had probably thought I was a lunatic. Perhaps she had already figured that out in the last few days, anyway. *Am I really a madman?* I wondered as I descended the stairs. *Would a madman realize his madness and acknowledge it as well so willingly? Probably not! In which case, I am most likely as sane as any other person who believes to be rational. Which means what?* Anyway, if I happen to be a lunatic, it is all Rishard's fault, too. Just trust me on this one if you also think I am a maniac. Blame it on Rishard.

Sherry delivered a blank grin to me as I entered the kitchen. I could not gather from her impression whether she had heard my yelling at Rishard or not. Then she asked if I had been speaking on the phone upstairs. I said, "No," which probably made the matter worse. I kept gazing at her gorgeous eyes, but it was hard to guess what she was thinking about me. I drank a large glass of cold water to calm my nerves a bit. I embraced and kissed her, but did not feel sexy toward her anymore, as though hugging a cold, rugged log. I was mad at Rishard for making me lose my senses. I kissed the soft skin of her neck... Nothing! She moaned, though, which only made me feel guiltier.

Long story short, I felt obliged to revise our plans. Instead of travelling along the coast, we went only to Carmel for two nights and drove back to San Francisco. All along Rishard remained sulky, even though I promised him to return to Vancouver sooner than planned. Sherry and I had no notable intercourse during the remainder of my stay with her, all thanks to Rishard. My mood was terribly spoiled, and Sherry was wondering what had gone wrong so suddenly. I kept reassuring her and apologizing for Rishard's misdemeanour. His incredible spite and lethargy was just maddening.

Of course, Sherry could see for herself that Rishard was not feeling good. He was not the same vigorous self she had seen and enjoyed the first few days. The difference was like day and night. She tried to cheer him up. She even massaged him and kissed him repeatedly to get him moving again, to no avail. I somewhat appreciated her open affection for Rishard. It was mostly for my own good, after all, I reckoned! She was hoping to prevent a lousy ending for my trip. On the other hand, it was disheartening and humiliating to watch her solemn struggles to resuscitate this rude Rishard, who seemed dead to me for all practical purposes. I was angry with her as well, for assuming she had a superhuman power to make him reconsider. She was adamant to succeed on a matter I had failed miserably and felt so helpless about during the last five or six years. Rishard's cool indifference to her affection was even more intimidating and infuriating. Anyway, they both appeared determined to prevail over each other, no matter what. Their tenacity was driving me nuts, though the whole shenanigan looked commendable and amusing, too. Just try to imagine my embarrassment, stuck in this formidable situation between two selfish and stubborn friends—Sherry struggling to revive him and Rishard adamant to ignore her.

Sherry was so kind to suggest we take Rishard to a doctor immediately and get him some of those Vigora pills to mend his mood. But I said no. Absolutely not! Because I was pissed off with both of them despite the idiotic grin on my face. She seemed concerned, all right. But more so for Rishard and herself. She was obviously unhappy about my visit ending sooner than planned. To me, however, she seemed too worried about Rishard at the time I was playing seriously with the notion of getting rid of him altogether, even if it meant killing him—even if I ended up dead myself. Maybe she assumed Rishard was important to me, which, you could say, would be a reasonable assumption by her. However, to me, her keen attention to Rishard only revealed her shallowness. Now, she appeared more erotic than sophisticated, contrary to what I had assumed only a few days earlier. I bet she would have only laughed hard if she could read my mind, or if I had just told her, about my brilliant idea of cutting Rishard loose.

I tried not to be jealous and angry. But it was hard not to be, considering the way Sherry took Rishard's side and peeped at me with suspicion. As if it were my fault Rishard behaved that way. As if I was the one making this devil depressed, and not the other way around. I hated the way she appeared ambivalent of my helplessness. She, too, was judging me according to Rishard's mood, but also blaming me for his moodiness. This was just too ridiculous. I had received similar vibes from other women in the past, too. In this particular case, however, I had expected Sherry to be more intelligent and considerate. Instead, she seemed quite disappointed in me, as if I had committed a crime. I was sick and tired of being the villain instead of the victim in this never-ending charade caused by Rishard. Having to keep my idiotic grin all along, to hide my frustration, was the added agony.

Anyway, I put my foot down and said 'no doctor' for Rishard in San Francisco. I promised Sherry to think about her suggestion more seriously in Vancouver.

"I promise," I kept telling her, but still she stared at me with cynicism like watching a useless flesh—a lost cause.

I was not sure about keeping my promise to her, either, in fact. Maybe I would help Rishard get the right medication. Or maybe I would not. The hell with him. Just let him die in his sleep from depression. Just to show Sherry! I know you think Sherry was doing everything for my own benefit, anyway. But still...! She appeared rather shallow for not grasping my pain and its cause or showing compassion properly. Instead, she simply dismissed all the humiliation that Richard caused me.

Suddenly I was facing at least five dilemmas: First, I could not have sex with Sherry because of Rishard's attitude. Second, Sherry looked rather disappointed in me, because she blamed me for Rishard's sudden sulking. Third, I was disappointed in her myself, since she made me feel bad because of Rishard. Fourth, I was not sure what kind of a relationship I could have with Sherry, because of Rishard's inevitable role in my relationships. And fifth, I kept thinking about Rishard's vulgar comment not long ago, "Love means shit when sex is lousy." It indeed sounded like a profound philosophy by this asshole all of a sudden. Sherry's attitude, like a sudden change of heart about the strength of our relationship, was a clear clue about love's shittiness without sex. Ironically, she was then probably even thinking I did not love her enough merely going by Richard's mood!

Despite her dubious disappointment in me, Sherry still tried to find out where our relationship stood. It was a nice gesture on her part, I thought! Or maybe only a trick question! I did not know how to respond, though. I really liked her, but it was silly to make a commitment to her about starting a more serious relationship. The distance was, of course, a major obstacle and we both worked in different cities. But the main problem was obviously Rishard, as usual, plus the related five dilemmas I counted above. He would never let me build a relationship with Sherry or any woman for that matter. What kind of a man was I? Who was the man in charge of my life? Who has actually been in charge of my entire life all along?

Back in Vancouver, life resumed as usual. Some evenings, we courted different women, including Julie and Gloria. However, I was still sad about my experience in San Francisco and all the questions echoing in my head about my identity while Rishard remained attached to me. We went to parties as usual out of habit, while I was torn in two pieces with major conflicts burning inside me. A part of me was happy, I must admit, while Rishard kept enjoying himself again! He seemed quite jovial and rejuvenated since we had arrived in Vancouver. But what about my romantic sentiments that I kept suppressing? When would all this craziness end? How can it end? My helpless situation felt pitiful, especially when witnessing Rishard's revived firmness and gloating.

The days and weeks passed and I loathed my lousy life. Just the same old phony routines to get some shallow, and sometimes sickening, sex. Then, lots of squabbles with women to prove our incompatibility. It was a lot of hard work for nothing, especially when Richard kept sulking rather erratically and adding to my sense of cynicism about life and women. Nevertheless, I decided to plough on and forget about Rishard's increasing fussiness. Heck, I was willing to forgive him even for his big lie about my chance of 'finding a more suitable partner if I divorced Pamela.'

Last week, I was driving solemnly after we left a party late in the evening. Steering the wheel as carefully as a semi-drunk could, I was lost in my thoughts, wondering about the purpose of living such a lousy life and how much longer I could go on like this. What was the point of living now, anyway, if Rishard and I kept arguing so much regularly? Could I get my pride and honour back at least now, at the end of my life? Suddenly I felt Rishard was talking to me.

"Are you deaf?" he said.

"What? What is it now?"

"Why don't you answer my question?"

"Sorry... I didn't realize you were talking to me."

"Is anybody else here in this car?"

"No... Sorry... What's your question?"

"I was just wondering when we're going to San Francisco to see Sherry again?" Rishard said with his childlike enthusiasm. He sounded so natural and innocent you would imagine he were a saint or a baby born yesterday.

Swear to God, I had never been so agitated by this devil or anybody else for that matter. My head started spinning fast from anger; I lost control of the steering wheel and almost crashed into the oncoming traffic on my left. Luckily, I turned to the right and pressed the brakes fast. The car finally hit the curb and came to an abrupt stop. The speeding drivers honked their car horns while narrowly eluding my car's erratic swerving. One driver showed me his middle finger and I showed mine to Rishard.

*****

Now that you have learned enough about Rishard and his role in my life, my whining and detailed descriptions of our relationship would make more sense and feel sadder every time you go back and reread this story. I guarantee you would enjoy it and laugh more every time as well, at my expense, of course! You would realize how even a relatively wise and educated man, like me, might reach a point where daily routines and demands become torturous, especially if his erratic relationship and memories with Rishard—this ungrateful dick—still spoil his existence even when he tries to bask in his solitude.

Yes, I have made my decision now! I will kill both Richard and myself in ten days, on Tuesday night, after talking to my lawyers and completing some papers. That is my final decision. That will be the best ending for my lousy life.

The Final Plan

Ten days seemed like ample time to arrange my early departure to eternity. I called three lawyers I knew to consult and give them 4-5 days to prepare the paperwork. One of them was on vacation. The other one was on edge, sounding hesitant or unprepared for *my queer type* of estate planning. "I don't know!" he kept saying. The third one was on cloud nine, already assuming he had the job. "I know, I know. Just leave everything to me," he interrupted me and insisted every ten seconds. Leave *what* to him? The job, the details, or all my helpless money? Even worse, "Sixty-one," he replied with irritation after a pause when I tactfully asked his age. A badly bald, bulky, heavy smoker with a big belly, he has always overcharged me, too. He surely deserved to come along with me for an overhaul instead of working so hard and hustling for more business still. I agreed to meet him, anyway, lest being rude or hasty. Maybe one of us could convince the other, though I preferred to prevail and take him with me! I made appointments also with the estate planners at the Bank of Montreal and TD Bank, which at least eliminated my concern about a particular lawyer's age for my elongated will administration.

Next, I pondered my scheme for stealing Gary's revolver to use later in a private place, either at home or in a forest perhaps.

Dying at home had some glitches, of course. For one thing, it could take weeks before somebody discovered my rotting body. Ironically, I had once expressed my concern about this matter to my son who is a smart graduate student.

"The way you guys are always busy and hardly check on me worries me about something," I said with stress and hurt feeling.

"What's that?" my son asked impatiently.

"I'm afraid it might take months before somebody finds my body if I happen to die in my sleep."

"What difference does it make to you?" he replied coolly.

How could I even argue with such a profound and meaningful response? Yet it saddened me. His casual *cool* reaction to the idea of my body rotting in the bed felt depressing, but what really killed me was his *surprise* and response with such sarcastic tone to my comment—as if I were too dumb to appreciate the finality of death. It was altogether too much information for any father to absorb and still wish to leave any inheritance for anybody.

Of course, the stench would eventually seep out of the big house, I presumed, and the neighbours would call the police. Yet, at least the inevitable gossips would be degrading. Selling the house could get difficult for my impatient kids, too, even after the stink and its spooky story faded away.

Another option was to go get lost in dense forests and die of hunger or in the paws and jaws of wild animals. This alternative, however, had the risk of my corpse not being found soon or ever, especially if animals ate the whole thing and threw the bones all over the place. Without solid evidence, I would remain a missing person for years, even if I left a note. Neither the authorities nor my family would take the note seriously. My kids would think I have gone on the long journey I have threatened everybody with frequently for drawing their sympathy. "He's fooling us again, crazy old man," they would say. "He isn't giving up his clowning even at this age!"

Then again, my kids would most likely try to use my note as a solid proof to convince the authorities issue my death certificate, so they could get their dirty hands on my money quickly! This would be a more likely scenario, even if they still believed my note was only a fake claim of suicide for fooling them. They would probably kid around amongst them and say, *Too bad if he returned and found out his death certificate has been issued and his assets distributed.* Ironically, they would not realize until much later that even getting my death certificate would not settle their legacy for ages!

All these ancillary analyses, plans, and paperwork for dying —after years of pondering the 'life' decision itself—felt absurd. Reading my lousy life stories has surely alarmed you about my obsession to find the right reasons for living, although it has been a tough and time-consuming job. Yet, the validity of a decision to die felt imperative, though proving difficult to formulate as well! Caring even about people's impression of my suicide method or mental state was ridiculous. Except, I loathed giving anybody a reason to think I were mad, desperate, or thoughtless about any of my deeds. *I believe my chronic uptightness would follow me to my grave!*

The most critical decisions, however, related to my money— who should get it, and why. Sadly, my scrutiny over this matter during the last four years had been depressing and inconclusive, while delaying my departure as well. With a set deadline now, however, all those annoying dilemmas needed fast resolutions one way or another. Enough thinking and wondering! Finding a reliable administrator for my estate also cluttered the process, although it mattered mostly if I decided to give my kids only a monthly allowance instead of a lump sum, immediate legacy. Most people make these touchy decisions easily merely out of false emotions or spite, but this approach felt sloppy to me. Of course, 'charities' was another option, although they also seemed inefficient and ineligible for the whole shebang for sure.

Of course, being only a multimillionaire is not a big deal these days, which makes my fussing appear rather ridiculous. Yet, the destiny of my hard-earned and well-preserved money in the hands of some undeserving or irresponsible people—be it my grown kids or greedy lawyers—required serious consideration. Even worse, I knew my kids would give a good chunk of it to their greedy mother, who had grabbed and wasted tons of my money already. This notion alone drove me nuts! Especially, the image of these people partying lavishly, while mocking my logic and frugality impishly, has always haunted me. This dreadful image had actually stopped me many years ago from making more money intentionally, as its future had become questionable and vexing. The tales of lottery-winners and celebrities losing their fortunes due to bad advice or personal laxity made my kids' sloppiness with money even more predictable and bothersome.

Anyhow, after long contemplation and soul-searching under time pressure, I decided to stay logical and fair, despite my kids' relentless tyranny. So, as a first step, I prepared the following list of potential justifications that any sane caring parent could think of regarding his or her kids' eligibility to inherit anything:

My children *might* deserve an inheritance because (*or if*):

1. I love them
2. I have given them my bad genes
3. I need them now
4. I need them when I die
5. I feel guilty for not giving them enough love or attention, or whatever, when they were young
6. I feel guilty for bringing them into this chaotic world
7. I feel guilty for treating them badly
8. I cannot think of anything better to do with my money
9. I feel responsible for their welfare
10. I feel obliged to help them
11. I want to empower them
12. I want to feel good about myself and my generosity
13. I care about their and people's impressions of me
14. I feel responsible for marrying their mother who passed on her own crooked genes to them

15. They are my best creations
16. They love me even though they do not show it
17. They take care of me and ensure I do not need anything
18. They help me with my plans and projects
19. They show a lot of respect, compassion, and love
20. They trust me and listen to my advice
21. They call me regularly to ensure I am alive
22. They ensure loneliness is not killing me
23. They are desperate or destitute
24. They are unable to work
25. They are handicapped mentally or physically
26. They are good humans in general
27. They are geniuses
28. They can do great things with my money
29. They think they deserve it
30. They expect me to pay up
31. They will hate/curse me if I do not leave them a legacy
32. People will hate/curse me if I disinherit my kids
33. It is customary in society and among friends and family
34. My parents did it for me

My objectivity was crucial at this point, especially, because my relationship with my kids remained vague and a barrage of dilemmas convoluted my sentiments. A balancing act has always been crucial to cope with their lousy attitudes without submitting to their demands too much. Dealing with their subtle suicide threats has been tricky all by itself. What could I do? Just leave their fates in God's hand or distract them again with yet another big chunk of money, a new car, or words of wisdom that they did not seem to value or able to digest? Sadly, the right options in life are getting more obscure every day. At the same time, I think my kids also have a right to be the way they are (or like to be), not to mention the effect of hormones and genes on everybody's needs and choices in life. In particular, I could not stop blaming myself and my ex-wife for the bad genes we had passed on to them.

Accordingly, I have swallowed my pride all along and kept my mouth shut even when they took my silence and compassion as my gullibility or weakness to detect their manipulation and apathy. Actually, I could make a longer list of reasons, around 260 points, they *should not* inherit anything. However, I decided to remain my usual gentleman and skip that negative side of the equation, at least for my own sanity's sake. I was also accepting the big risk of assuming they were definitely my kids, although we had never done a DNA test to be sure. Then again, at the very least, their indisputable mother and I had raised and loved them a lot, anyway.

I created a rating system, too, with the intention of grading my beloved creations rather leniently on the noted 34 potential eligibility factors. Furthermore, I decided if even one of them got the passing mark, they all became eligible for inheritance, though the amount and payment method may depend on their individual scores and personalities. Have you ever known a more liberal and forgiving person than me, not to mention my diligent objectivity?

I called Gary, my semi-retired friend, who lives mostly in a cabin near Sunshine Coast. He had shown me his revolver last year and I got a hunch he wanted me to feel free to use it if necessary. His timing to reveal its hiding place to me without making a direct suggestion—after hearing enough of my whining about life—was impeccable. I appreciated his discretion. He was probably unhappy also about his handgun not being put to any good use so far. I wanted to help him, too, while making sure he got it back afterwards—just in case he or any of our common friends wished to follow my example.

Anyway, after our long chitchat, I offered to visit him on the coming weekend and he agreed giddily, probably thinking I had finally come to my senses, built my nerve, and was now ready to borrow his gun for a sacred mission.

Later in the afternoon, I went for my usual walk at Mosquito Creek, which is a wooded area only three blocks away from my house. I like the seclusion and serenity on the trail next to a big river that is usually loud with crushing water rolling down North Vancouver Mountains. Along my route, I still kept pondering the best suicide method for me. As I approached the entrance to the trail, I could not believe my luck when I saw a new sign warning visitors of a cougar sighting along with plenty of precautionary advice. In fact, while amazed of my fate, swiftly I realized I was not merely witnessing my luck or just an ordinary public notice, but rather a divine sign in relation to my dying options. God was telling me that I did not even have to drive out of town and look for a dense forest to fulfil my option of suicide in the hands of wild animals. He was also sending me a direct message to choose this option in order to make myself useful at least in my death— by letting a cougar gain some strength, too, against all the selfish intentions of the Conservation Officer trying so hard to make the poor animal die of hunger. All I had to do, when I was ready on the tenth day, was to just stroll on this trail as long as necessary until the cougar and I found each other.

Since I thought nobody would believe my luck, the sign, and God's intervention in such timely manner, I decided to at least take the picture of the sign the next day when I returned with a camera. It is printed on the next page.

That day, however, I walked only a short distance on the main trail very cautiously, while contemplating my plan of action in line with the sacred omen. I went home with plenty of excellent ideas about preparing myself for the cougar on the last day of the Final Plan. Thanks to the Officer's comprehensive warning sign, I could simply do all the necessary things to draw the cougar's attention and interest and hope for the best. The main premise of my foolproof strategy was to make the cougar's job as easy as possible by defying the Officer's advice. As an additional trick for helping the daft cougar, I decided to skip showering during the last 3-4 days as well, so that my stench penetrated the woods for kilometres and alerted the lazy cougar if it were slumbering somewhere in despair. I just prayed that the cougar had enough patience and food to wait for me another nine days or so, ready to go head to head with me with all its might.

I listed the following crucial steps, in line with the meticulous advice on the sign, to be prepared: I would approach the cougar and try to block its escape route with absolute tenacity. If it did not work, I would turn my back and wait a while to see if it gets my drift and excited. If not, I would start running away, but make sure not too fast or far. If still alive, I would cringe as much as possible to look as small as the cougar might like. If the damn animal is still standing there and only yawning, then I would go hide behind a rock or a tree to stir its curiosity or frustration about all the silly games that I have been playing uselessly to get its attention and entice its appetite for an old man's flesh. Sadly, my children are not small enough anymore and I do not have a pet to take with me as baits or maybe even as hors d'oeuvre. If none of my elaborate gimmicks works, then the stupid cougar deserves to die of hunger and I must go find a dense forest, after all. *I did not know these wild animals are so fussy or it is so difficult to get their attention!*

By the way, I truly admired Conservation Officer's priceless concern, foresight, and advice! I have been meaning to call the good officer and thank him/her for *everything* on behalf of people using that trail every day! The only reason for my hesitation has been that he or she may get confused or misunderstand my words or think I had sounded sarcastic. But do not let me stop you from calling him or her yourselves and expressing your gratitude for his/her scrupulous life-saving efforts. Tell her/him I said hi, too, without mentioning my sentiments. Of course, I would definitely call him/her myself to complain about the warnings' impotency if the cougar refused to move a finger to eat me after I disobeyed all those instructions to the dot.

On day two, I studied the 34 items on the Justifications List and scored my kids diligently. Six hours later, their eligibility looked quite shaky even after making vast concessions everywhere. Only six items remained on the list—though none of them still resembled a fully convincing justification for my horrendous generosity all their lives. Nevertheless, that was the best I could do without lying too much. Although not a new revelation, all these sad realizations were quite painful. Anyway, the following shortlist reflected life's reality and my pitifully soft personality—the absolute best way I could justify my benevolence.

1. I love them
2. I have given them my bad genes
3. I feel guilty for bringing them into this chaotic world
4. I cannot think of anything better to do with my money
5. I feel responsible for marrying their mother who passed on her own crooked genes to them
6. They are sort of geniuses

I was listening to Billie Holiday bitching non-stop about her man this and that—*I'm a fool to want you*. Her dire simplicity always captivates me, but she was not helping much today when I was labouring on the eligibility list and wondering where I had gone wrong as a parent or someone's man. Her voice and my reminiscing of the old memories had aggravated my gloom. So I watched an episode of *Curb Your Enthusiasm* before turning in.

The next morning, I reviewed the long list one last time and mourned over every crossed-out item. All those compassionate, potential justifications so easily dropped, despite my deep liberal deliberations two days, was both enlightening and disheartening, whichever way you viewed the matter. But I let it go. At least the six items on the shortlist still had merits—barely. To be honest and fair, however, I believed my kids should actually pay me for my patience and love, rather than I paying them for nothing.

The irony is that they are (or pretend to be) nonchalant about inheritance, anyway, as the elimination of items 29-31 on the long list also suggested already. They are not rich or even reliable money-makers, but merely too engaged with their sexuality and artistic dreams to worry about inheritance or me. This is in itself an irritating, insulting, and confusing quandary—like pouring vinegar over my wounds. At least a dozen reasons could exist behind their seeming cool apathy; and not knowing the real one complicated my decision further. For instance, it could be another means of humiliating me, a well-orchestrated tactic, a genetic malfunction, a sign of their pride and self-confidence, their total trust in my soft-heartedness, their lack of appreciation for money, their idiotic absorption in their sexuality, artistic ambitions, etc.

I would be proud if they really had so much willpower and self-reliance, but their dubious composure and show of autonomy feel like another type of naiveté. I abhor shoving money onto their faces when they seem not so enthusiastic about it. "Come on, pretty please, take it! And please don't forget to waste it, too." I could not raise the subject and my concerns with them, either, while they insisted on being cool about the whole matter. Had they been married, things could have been different, though, I am sure. Suddenly their spouses might have made them show more interest in my money. Yet, that prospect (their eventual marriage) actually added another daunting dimension to the whole puzzle. I abhor any part of my assets going to strangers after they divorce my kids, which is a highly likely scenario nowadays. I worry too much about so many things, I know; but whose fault is it?

The fourth day was unproductive, except for putting a general plan together before meeting the greedy lawyer and banks' estate planners. Under the deadline pressure, at last the six reasons on the shortlist seemed sufficient to leave everything to my kids. The third item got 80% weight, while the others got 4% each. In fact, I was getting hopelessly softer by the minute after realizing the importance of the third item on the short list. On that ground, I actually reckoned that our innocently spoiled kids should not only inherit everything automatically, but also have a right to sue their parents anytime after legal age. Parents must face the music, for bringing them into this chaotic world so selfishly merely to satisfy their own egos and loneliness, or by repeated accidents. They should think hard before making feeble humans left and right, and even worse spoiling them beyond repair. This reality needs a few centuries to stick, though a class action lawsuit against governments might expedite the matter. Actually, maybe kids must have the right to sue governments if their own parents are too poor to pay for their mistakes. Meanwhile, parents can learn to hide their assets from their kids. Well…, enough moral gibberish for one day!

On the fifth day, the estate planners and I reviewed a few options. Involving them seemed risky and costly. So, I decided to give everything to my kids in lump sum and get it over with, which required only a simple will and power of attorney. Furthermore, no reason existed to give more to any of them, either, especially considering the crude nature of the justifications on the shortlist. Enough fussing, although my decision looked too perfunctory compared to my initial intentions. I was just tired.

I decided to donate my paintings, with a suggested pricelist, to BC Children Hospital to auction according to certain guidelines or leave them for my kids. An art curator had recently valued them at one million dollars at least. My other valuables, including my unpublished writings, would also go to my kids. What they would or could do with those presumed literary masterpieces, only God knew! It would be only on their conscience, because they are mostly about family affairs and love. *Well... that's all for the inheritance then.*

Plenty of time remained to finalize my simple will and give it to the lawyer. Thus, I tried to relax, which felt like an awkward duty for someone with nothing else to do in life, ever. The damn seconds ticking slowly on my Rolex made relaxing impossible, while I worked on my will's details sluggishly. An appreciative viewing of my paintings and reading a bunch of passages from my own books occupied my mind somewhat, while those words rekindled the memories of my intellectual endeavours in line with my pathetic predicaments with my kids. Still, waiting in limbo was a nasty and exhausting business.

Of course, you may so duly ask why bother with a deadline, or live even one extra second when the decision at hand was so well measured and deemed necessary. Why fret so much over some paperwork or who gets what, anyway? Well..., for one thing, I believed my final plan should be tidy and purposeful, too, like the rest of my life endeavours. Not that I am proud, or sure about the value, of doing everything so meticulously, considering the lousy outcomes of my diligent life decisions. But at the very least, I could not change my personality and methods in the last days of my life, could I? Any hasty or emotional act only serves the devil anyhow, no matter how sound the decision appears. On the other hand, without a deadline, even a methodical person like me might procrastinate a few more years again with a bunch of other lame excuses. Setting a solid timetable was a matter of principle and discipline, to deem my decision final, assess all the facts, and get everything organized quickly.

Merely out of curiosity perhaps, you may also wish to know my reason for suicide, anyway. First of all, we need a good word for what I meant to do, which is a mindful act when living proves permanently senseless. Repeating pointless routines like a robot is silly, yet I had hoped, like most people, to gain certain wisdom that justified my persistence to stick around. I had imagined God had hidden some clever clues somewhere to broaden our brains, until it became clear that He has made no such bid or else would have not made it so obscure even for an obsessed guru like me. It seemed I had procrastinated long enough already, while watching people's humiliating struggles to live just another day pained me, too, as though they had an obligation to God or their spirits to live merely for suffering. That was something positive about society, I reckoned, to keep people hopeful to continue. I liked this social knack, although I have never been able to grasp or relate to this type of bizarre lifestyle, especially now at old age. Sorry...!

'Suicide' implies copping out, despair, and weakness. For some odd reason, God has apparently made it a sin, too, going by religious propagandas. To me, however, mere 'living' is an even shoddier option without having legitimate reasons for it after, let us say, sixty or seventy years of seeking one's mission in life. Any reason is good enough as long as one is **honestly** convinced. Otherwise, persisting to live merely on various hopes, out of fear of death, or for flimsy pleasures shows one's lack of initiative and foresight. Many people reach that milestone eventually and find their perseverance demeaning and embarrassing. Besides, you do not want to wait for all kinds of ailments and pains make your meagre existence even more humiliating, especially when you imagine the possibility of (god forbid) incommoding your busy family with a lengthy disability. Some of us cannot live just for the heck of it, as if existence were an endurance contest. Not that we are wiser or madder, but only more cynical and proactive. We are wired weirder. Our mentality is perceived unnatural, spiteful against God, and an unforgivable sin. Yet, that is the criticism we can live with too—or actually die for. We are merely martyrs for humans' dire failure to define their being. The only question is if suicide is itself an upshot of one's fate or a personal initiative against fate. Which one of these conflicting options holds water? I wish I knew this one at least before I go!

Anyway, let us not dwell on these philosophical nitty-gritty.

The risk of remaining a missing person instead of dead officially, and my kids cursing me for keeping their inheritance in suspense for many years, at last convinced me to do *it* at home. However, to avoid a long delay, while I decay, I decided to leave my son a message in the last minute, to come over and arrange things through the police and undertakers. Their telephone numbers would be in a note, along with my instructions for a very simple and fast funeral. No memorial of any kind. Just put me in the cheapest box they could get—possibly even a cardboard box, if long, or at least sturdy, enough to hold my corpse during the transport without dropping it and breaking my neck, too. Then dump the damn thing in the hole and put up the tombstone with my spectacular words of wisdom on it. I was working frantically on a two-liner that would mesmerize, or traumatize, my family if they ever came to visit me. Maybe someday it makes them feel guilty for ignoring me so much. The way it read at the time was,

> *'Had you visited me more often,*
> *My heart had not so quickly rotten.'*

I wished there was *room* to add many more words of wisdom, such as, *'And the absurdity of human dreams and worries had become clear to you, too!'* Alas, these headstones are too small for my vengeful, literary needs.

Yes, the music. Choosing the right tune for the last minutes in my deathbed felt also essential. After long deliberation, testing, and sobbing, I settled on Saint Saens' *Requiem*. I would wait and enjoy it until the last movement, which has always given me the biggest chill and thrill at the same time, before pulling the trigger and meeting my dear mysterious creator.

On the sixth day, I bought my grave, ordered my tombstone with the current year on it as my expiry date, and met the undertaker. I mentioned my illness was terminal, without specifying he would hear from my jubilant survivors on Wednesday. His efforts to look sad, while appreciating my business as well, appeared like a tough undertaking even for him—a professional undertaker—*until* I stressed on doing everything as modestly and cheaply as possible. "Just take me under quietly," I joked as he smirked. The way he stared at me was both insulting and funny as if stressing in return, 'Why do you hesitate wasting some money at least now that you surely have no further use for it?' I abhorred dying still wondering why people think so foolishly only in one dimension about everything, especially our intentions and actions in life.

Gary and I shared the weekend drinking quite a bit of alcohol, arguing, wandering in the wilderness, and bickering about our trite friendship that had fallen apart when we both got entangled with family issues, divorced our wives, and he fled the turmoil in Vancouver. Maybe I should have done the same, rather than basking in luxury and philosophy—a bizarre mix anyway! He seemed to know what I was up to, but spared me from his trite lectures about life or similar bullshit. We just enjoyed ourselves too much, which felt embarrassing whenever I remembered why I was there and my misjudgement about a dying man's appetite for fun. I indulged myself, although it did not feel right when we laughed light-heartedly like kids! I let it go as another life's eerie imbecility. While Gary took a shower, I found the handgun in the dresser beneath his underwear and replaced it with my prewritten note. It alone would exonerate him from any wrongdoing even if the lawyer lost the sealed envelope I would give him regarding the borrowed handgun. The handwritten note said:

Garry, I borrowed your handgun for an emergency—to end a useless creature's life. Sorry for not getting your permission, because I didn't want you try to dissuade me! You'll get it back right away.

The storm on the way back, Monday morning, depressed even a meandering corpse with a pass for only two more days. This time, it was my soppy gloom that seemed misplaced rather unexpectedly! Naturally, I had never been in this position before. Especially, after all that clowning over the weekend, my sudden melancholy felt too heavy for my spirit, but also rather natural! Well, who knew how an elderly martyr should feel!

I went to my lawyer's office on Tuesday morning—the destined day, finally. I collected the papers and dropped them in my bank's safety deposit box. Although my son had the authority and key to access it, I decided to remind him in my long message just before pulling the trigger later in the evening. He usually does not answer his phone, but if he did, I would tell him to come by the next day and collect an important document (my diligent instructions) from the mailbox. I had to prepare myself for his small resistance, though, since he would most likely ask, "Can't you mail it?" He lives only ten minutes away from me, driving the brand new car I bought him a few months ago.

I plummeted onto the edge of the bed, stared at the loaded handgun ornamenting the bedside table, and mused pensively. Yes, I had covered all grounds. *That's it,* I sighed.

But it was only seven o'clock. I could use a couple of drinks and a colourful meal before finishing myself, I reckoned. So I got dressed quickly and drove leisurely to my favourite restaurant in West Vancouver, took a window seat, and watched the wet storm twisting and tumbling the tree branches. *No more decisions or plans after tonight,* I imagined with delight. People peeping at me with pity alarmed me, though—sitting there alone with an idiotic self-gratifying grin. They probably guessed it was my last meal, too, from the way I voluptuously sampled the half-dozen dishes I had ordered, like feasting in a Chinese restaurant. I waved my wineglass to a pretty woman who insisted on checking me out furtively for whatever reason—most likely out of pity as well! She turned her eyes swiftly and reported my bold gesture—the big atrocity—to her husband. "How come it's okay for her to stare at me with pity persistently, but then I'm a pervert just for raising my wineglass to acknowledge her empathy?" I planned asking her husband if he came over to put me in my place.

Staring out the window again, I chuckled about the possibility of the husband kicking my ass just before I go home kill myself. "No, those bruises were not self-inflicted. Somebody beat him good just a few minutes before shooting him in the heart," the coroner declares adamantly to rule out suicide. That could surely cause another mix-up and mystery I preferred to avoid.

I wished it were not such a stormy weather, imagining the slush around my prepaid grave at such a prominent spot, and my kids' hassle of getting there, with their clothes wet and their shoes muddy, just for those few minutes of paying their phony respects. Maybe they would not show up, anyway! I could not say! But I decided there was certainly no point flossing and brushing my teeth tonight. The idea thrilled me, like a rebellious kid finally savouring his last opportunity for self-expression. My lifelong uptightness, especially toward my teeth, felt commendable but tiring. It had not mattered how late, drunk, and exhausted I had come home some evenings, the damn teeth had been brushed diligently. Tonight, however, I would just slip into my pyjamas, lie in the bed, aim the handgun toward my heart and bang... My brain was spared, considering its loyalty all these years, not to mention its cute obsession for cynicism and criticism. Surely, it was unfair to shoot it as a token of my appreciation. Besides, if something went wrong, living with an angry, damaged brain sounded terrible. My heart, though, I could easily punish it for making me too romantic and soft so often. It has been a nuisance all along and made my brain's job difficult, too.

At home, I reviewed my final steps—to get into my pyjamas, call my son, etc. But no dental hygiene, I kept reminding myself to prevent my cute sneaky brain tricking me into doing it—the same brain I respected so much and spared from the bullet. I went upstairs, turned on the bedroom light, and froze by the ugly sight before me. A big puddle bubbled in the middle of my beautiful bed as water dripped from the ceiling. What the heck! Only a year earlier, I had replaced the roof with designer shingles that came with a fifty-year warranty. The possibility of a leak in my expensive, state-of-the-art roof was infuriating. Fast, I fetched the ladder from the basement, used the flashlight to walk carefully on the beams in the attic, and deflected the light on the area above my bedroom. A big branch from my neighbour's tall pine trees had punctured the roof like a spear. This was the second time in the last two years. With a bit more momentum, it could have ripped the ceiling, too, and gone straight into my heart, had I been lying in my bed listening to Saint Saens Requiems' beginning movements! The branch was too thick and heavy for me to push out as a first step. Nobody could do anything about the situation this late at night, it seemed. And the rain kept pouring from the sky without mercy. *I'm cursed for sure.*

Mother Nature sabotaging my meticulous 'final plan' was frustrating, besides the sign that God did not want to let me off the hook easily yet. Obviously, completing my plan by lying in the middle of that mess was unsightly and humiliating. My damn uptightness was a big pain even at the moment of death. Shooting myself in another room could raise new odd questions, though, including the idea of the roof leakage stirring my final breakdown and hasty reaction. I believed my departure deserved a proper appreciation and due credit, although I was not planning to spell it out for people. And in case the idiots did not get it, I hoped it would at least cause them big confusion about the reasons behind my suicide. Besides, I could not leave my kids with two major messes. My departure would cause them enough inconvenience already without the burden of calling the roofers, arranging other repairs, cleaning, etc. They would never forgive me for dying before having the roof repaired, anyway, no matter how much inheritance they got. Their job of sifting through and disposing an awful amount of junks I have collected over the years, or fighting over them, would give them enough hassles already, which they would curse me for as well.

The roofer sounded testy for calling him so late, but promised to send someone in the morning to cover the hole for now. He said the right shingles might take ten days to arrive from the States. Totally disenchanted about things getting so fast out of control in the very last minute and missing tonight's scrupulously orchestrated deadline to meet Azrael, I seemed stuck, forced to live a bit longer and to start planning again meanwhile. Brushing my teeth with tension, I pondered killing my asshole neighbour instead, or in addition. *What difference did it make to me?* as my wise son might have asserted cleverly. *Merely one or two fewer idiots in this wacky world!* I had told that imbecile a few times to cut those rotten branches of old pine trees in his yard to no avail.

Gary called the next day and asked glumly if I still needed the revolver. He sounded as if totally disappointed to hear my voice.

"I'll return it on the weekend," I said "I needed it for getting rid of the raccoon that ransacks my garbage bins every night."

"Did you do it?" he asked.

"No. Either it's on to me, or a neighbour beat me to it."

"Well, I got worried this morning when I saw your note. It sounded as if you intended to end your own useless life," he said in a teasing tone, but he still sounded disappointed. I bet he had even seen my note earlier, instead of this morning, yet had waited a day to give me enough time to complete my plan! Only now, merely for this divine purpose, my good old nosy friend, the last one still humouring me, had decided not to intrude in my affairs!

Something felt amiss again after I hung up: Fun, gloom, and now spite—toward my haughty neighbour and a hungry raccoon —felt confusing and embarrassing again! They all felt unseemly for an enlightened philosopher resigned and ready to depart.

When I met Gary again, he renewed his offer to sell me a three-million-dollar life insurance, which I declined for the hundredth time during the last thirty years. As a pesky broker, he has made himself a fortune, but never got over the fact that I was his only friend he could not convince to buy life insurance. The idea of leaving behind an extra three million dollars only made me laugh hysterically. I kept saying, "What's in it for me?", but he ignored me, looking worried only about his fat commission before it was too late. *What difference does having life insurance make to me?* I asked him again as I was leaving.

"How about one million then?" he asked with tension, totally flabbergasted now about losing his last chance to dupe me as well before it was too, especially if I still felt like killing myself sooner or later. I had proven to be the biggest challenge in his career.

"I may have to borrow your handgun again," I told him.

"If you really have to kill this nasty creature, be my guest...," he replied. "You can borrow it anytime, but I still suggest you buy life insurance, too."

"Whom are you leaving all your money for, Gary?"

Startled, Gary stared at me in shock awhile before shrugging. My comment was rude, I knew, but also hilarious if you got the gist of it. At least I still had some kind of a lousy relationship with my kids, which made my generosity look rather normal, and I had also worked out some justifications for myself—albeit after a great deal of pain and contemplation—regarding my generosity. What the heck was poor Gary supposed to do without even a simple contact with his children during the last nine years or a single justification to leave them anything? They had dumped him ruthlessly for divorcing their bossy, rich mother. And now he was stuck with all that dough and nobody to give it to. However, he still could not stop himself from selling more life insurance to people and earning more commission. Old habits are hard to kill, too, I presume, maybe even harder than killing oneself.

I was not proud of myself for leaving Gary agitated and gloomy, but he had it coming with his persistence to sell me life insurance. The image of his sullen expression amused me all the way back to Vancouver, while I suddenly felt proud of my…, my relationship, or whatever the hell one may call it, with my kids.

The roof and ceiling repaired, the carpet and furniture replaced, a fresh coat of paint has brought everything back to normal. So technically, I could now reschedule the 'final plan' that was halted abruptly ten Tuesdays before. But during this seemingly fateful interruption, a legitimate reason for living had suddenly presented itself like a divine awakening. It appeared so obvious I was surprised of my stupidity. Anyway, better late than too late. The sacred justification that now hinders my misperceived 'final plan' is that my early departure would certainly thrill so many people, including friends and family. The sheer satisfaction of preventing their jubilation, while also keeping them in suspense about their inheritance, makes up ten times for the deep agony of living. I guess I am not so softhearted, after all, which, if true, is just another good reason to celebrate and live for all by itself!

My talent to make so many enemies is commendable, much beyond all the credit I deserve for being successful and rich. They are related matters, though. For instance, you can imagine why even my last friend, Gary, does not think so highly of me. Other people's reasons for hating me are just as silly, I promise. What an embarrassing collection of friends and family! Anyhow, my final plan befell the same fatal fate that my 'big plan' did over forty years ago. When I recall the kind of life Father and I had envisioned for me then and how it had actually turned out—so fully out of whack—I just laugh my heart out. That is all we can do with this world! Except…

Well… The other thing I do in this crazy world, sometimes I go picnic near my grave with the gravestone erected and all. Gary has come along with me a couple of times, too. We drink quite a bit of liquor and eat plenty of figs as well, as I reminisce about the times my wife filled me with figs to enrich our marital life. What a pity, it did not work! The *ambience* is quite relaxing up there with fresh air and a nice view of the city. Actually, I could paint a nice landscape from that spot if I still had my urge for painting. Anyhow, I reckon I might as well visit my eternal resting place regularly and enjoy the view and eternal serenity awaiting me, instead of letting this pristine ambience sit idle for so many years I am eagerly planning to live. Too bad, I still hate waste even at my age and all that pampered wealth going to waste somehow, anyway.

Naturally, it appears pathetic to keep living merely out of spite for friends and family, especially considering my misgiving for ploughing on aimlessly forever and struggling with the dilemma of existence uselessly. However, I feel thrilled now for having a lasting, plausible reason for living finally, even though it is built around spite. Surely, finding a purpose for living in such a bizarre notion after a lifetime of curiosity and research is a revelation! I may also get a chance to write a few more books, meanwhile. Accordingly, I am taking all kinds of vitamins nowadays, have become extra careful with my diet, and exercise every day in a gym to live forever. Of course, this rigid regimen is consuming a great deal of my time and energy, which feels counterproductive in some moments of self-appraisal and reflection. *But, sometimes, a man must also do what his silly ego tells him to do, even if it only proves his own foolishness.* By the way, this urge for spite as a matter of principle reminds me of an incident almost fifty years ago when I was hoping to become more assertive and teach a lesson to my Jewish roomy, Sid, while he was plotting to stay a few extra days with me without sharing the rent. It all shows how ironical and funny living is if we really get the gist of it. *Well, that's life, isn't it?* It feels as if we never grow up!

My strenuous new plan to keep living merely out of spite has a gigantic glitch, however: My wealth is growing too fast while I refuse to kick this heavy bucket of shit. Even worse, this matter of waiting has provided a great deal of time and opportunity for more create thinking and spiteful planning that ordinary people might perceive only as a sign of senility.

(Two Years Later)

This damn 'Final Plan' has become so dynamic and progressive, almost like a creepy creature. It has gotten bigger and sadder than all serious, sensible schemes I have devised and pursued all my life, and I feel ashamed of being the sly mastermind behind this notorious project. Clearly, this has been contrary to my initial intention and the meaning of any 'plan' to be fixed with a definite timetable. However, this final plan seems highly susceptible to new initiatives and adjustments as things change, I keep on living keenly, and revolutionary ideas keep striking me so magically and mysteriously out of the blue. Accordingly, I might have to update the last chapter of *My Lousy Life* when these revelations warrant the insertion of additional information for curious readers until I die, at last, by accident or change of plans yet again.

While the outcome of my experiences and deliberations in the last two years are noted below briefly, details and reasons behind these conclusions are offered at the end of this chapter under the heading of *Touchy Research*. It is for curious readers looking for more ironic, humorous points about family affairs nowadays and my repulsive, secret analyses of this topic.

First of all, a divine inspiration struck me only a few months after I had signed and filed my will with the lawyer. I decided to add a clause that stipulates with great emphasis and pleasure that my kids get their inheritance in whole (in a big lump sum) ONLY after their mother's passing. My lawyer made the changes with pain, complications, and complaint, which I took reverently along with substantial added costs. The new clause has several great merits, which I leave the task of guessing most of them to you—my dear, faithful readers. Yet, its main merit now is that my ex-wife's obsession to outlive me for a few decades would not prove as restful and fruitful as she had been hoping. Her daily anticipation for my departure to get our kids pay her rising debts would turn into a colossal disappointment when my ingenious will is read to them. My only regret is my absence to witness their surprise and flustered faces when my lawyer reveals this new delightful deal to all of them. The image gives me a big thrill, except that I am afraid they might go piss on my grave, which is probably better than not going there at all.

Accordingly, my kids' stress and guilty conscience for seeing their mother as their sole obstacle to retire rich right away would drive them nuts, as they suffer in their meagre jobs day after day! All along, my ex-wife's rage toward my soul, while feeling guilty for living, would be a deserved long torture for her. Then, they all would feel guiltier and gloomier every day, as their consciences also get messed up about all these vile feelings. All those senses of guilt, desire, dreams, shame, spite, resentment, mostly toward each other, would probably drive them nuts. The way they would stare at one another with mortifying thoughts and hopes would be just precious. I enjoy imagining these likely dreadful sights and sentiments, thinking that a somewhat fairer correlation is at last established between my kids' attitude toward me and my lifelong generosity and sacrifices—all for nothing, not even a simple show of gratitude. Sadly, time has come for me to stop being so flexible and caring, in spite of my blissful good nature and my worries about their likely financial hardships or deprivations without my assistance.

I believe I have now accomplished the greatest milestone any human can attain—to fathom equally precious reasons for both living and dying—compared with the common situation when people, including myself until two years ago, have no legitimate reasons for either living or dying! Naturally, the sooner I die and the longer my ex-wife lives, the more stress and longer torture my kids must endure in line with the new clause in my will. Still, I am adamant to live as long as possible for its own sacred merits noted before! Ironically, both my life and death now have divine purposes, I reckon with *reserved* delight.

Yes... the delight of this accomplished milestone is reserved, because I feel both obliged and crippled to choose between these two equally rewarding options of existence on my own sooner or later! Indecision is torturous when loving both living and dying so much has become too annoying and agonizing suddenly. I had always imagined humans' biggest dilemma erupts when they cannot find a good reason for either living or dying. So, they just procrastinate and suffer all their lives. Now, the agony of having so many excellent reasons for both living and dying rivals the humans' common source of pain, if not exceeding it. I seriously doubt anybody has ever been in such a bizarre jam and felt so ridiculously confused even in such a seemingly enlightening time of his life! I guess God is playing an extremely masterful and mysterious game with me!

This damn Final Plan has surely found a philosophical dimension while still evolving in many directions. Especially, the following four new developments have necessitated some adjustments.

1. My kids' attitude toward me has deteriorated recently, as if they have mysteriously learned about the new tough clause I have put in my will. Maybe they are getting tired of waiting for my death, while I look stronger and healthier anytime they happen to see me. They have also been rather nasty about my refusal to give them more money nowadays like before. Besides, I believe their mother's badmouthing and blaming me for her lonely, depressing life has been ruining the last grains of my kids' feelings for me. They have hardly visited or called me to say a simple hello. Their rooted apathy two years ago has now turned into disrespect and some kind of spite. So, giving them so much inheritance, even after their mother's death, has felt stupid quite often, *again*. Thus, I felt I must do some more thinking! *Sorry dear readers…! I guess I must apologize for my erratic emotions and busy brain.*

2. I realized the two-liner poem on my gravestone would soon seem ludicrous if I kept living past eighty. Claiming that my heart had rotten would sound quite silly in that case! Thus, it seemed I needed a new gravestone with a factual poetry to

express my boiling sentiments without blaming my happy, strong heart for my belated death.

3. Visiting my prepaid grave alone or with a friend has been tough and rather restricted due to so much rain in Vancouver and the lack of privacy to talk, smoke pot, drink, and laugh when other people around us had been only mourning, moaning, or meandering with their respectful silence.

4. I have suddenly realized that I would like to be buried, *when I succumb to death at last,* in a raised concrete tomb rather than under the ground surrounded by worms and wet soil.

Accordingly, I am working seriously on an idea that might sound a bit odd or a lot crazy to you dear readers. But I would like to assure you that this new amendment to the 'final plan' makes absolute sense to me and so many of you, if you were in my place and shared my sentiments about life, death, and family. The plan is to spend most of my money to build an expensive mausoleum for myself as soon as I find a proper site in West Vancouver cemetery or another place nearby. I would like to make it as a warm resting place for me both after my passing and during my remaining years of living and fooling around. It would be around 200 square feet with heating and cleaning facilities, stove, and a fridge full of beers and other goodies. I think I would put a table and a few chairs in it to entertain myself and special friends occasionally. I might even use the raised tomb as a bed if I happen to stay overnight to test and enjoy my eternal resting place. I think it would be both enlightening and fun to use the mausoleum also as a casual meditation spot, meanwhile! I could play some serene music, which might delight the dead, too, if I leave the windows open occasionally. Sleeping among the spirits some nights would also be a bold, refreshing experience, to test my guts and curiosity. *They might even start making their weird requests for the kind of music they'd like me to play for them!* Besides, I might luckily die one night when I am sleeping over, thus eliminating the need and hassle of carrying my body. Of course, I would keep the mausoleum door perfectly locked and the alarm system armed when sleeping there—just in case! I wonder if an alarm system is allowed in a cemetery, or deemed a nuisance for the dead! I would also like to keep some of my paintings and books in that cosy mausoleum for posterity and possible appreciation by future generations. *I am starting to think like Pharaohs now!* Well, since I cannot take my wealth with me, I should at least rest on it for eternity away from other people's access. *That had most likely been those Pharaohs' motive, too!*

I confess this 'final plan' has become quite freakish. I wonder if anybody in the recent history has pondered these kinds of crazy and likely sinful ideas, let alone acting upon them. Yet, these new ideas sound most appropriate and necessary for this occasion, for someone with no regular worries or amusement. These ideas may also be the symptoms of my solitude in recent years.

Anyway, my ridiculous final plan now includes a major secret project that will be completed within the next two years. I am hoping to do a few more scientific explorations, possibly with the roaming spirits in the cemetery, too, while annoying many people in the process. Besides flabbergasting my kids and ex-wife when they finally learn about my expensive tomb—instead of being merely cremated and disposed in a nasty storm as they wish—my big tombstone would have enough room to include the lovely fresh poem I have written now that the old poem does not hold water. Meanwhile, I will just look forward and try very hard to live past eighty.

> *Against all the odds and many evil thoughts,*
> *Behind your clever acts and concealed spites.*
> *At first, it was hard to bear all your silly apathy,*
> *But, soon, learning the truth made me very happy.*
> *What didn't kill me, made me many folds stronger,*
> *As a result, I was able to live very much longer.*
> *And I became more careless, too, like you!*
> *So now, we're even, though I'm not a yahoo!*

I think I have done it now! I hope my kids read all this poetry at least once, although I am almost sure they would hardly ever come around anymore to read the profound confession on my tomb over and over. Nevertheless, the gist of my words would be etched in their pitiful brains forever, anyway, I imagine.

Naturally, I will make all these investments without changing my lifestyle or even selling my expensive house. Instead, I will borrow for building the mausoleum, while wasting money also on other silly stuff that I can think of. My lawyer would convey the terms of my kids' inheritance, but neither he nor anybody else would know about the extent of my liabilities and measly net worth. Only my accountant has this confidential information until the day my assets can be distributed to my kids, right after their dear mother joins me in eternity—although I would not be able to see her in that hot region from my cool castle in heaven.

To make up for my kids' small inheritance, I might give them a choice, under certain conditions, to be buried—after many good years of living and working hard—in my mausoleum below my big tomb. I guess I cannot stop being a softhearted person, at least a bit, even when I am totally disheartened by people. However, maybe this idea merely reflects a subliminal urge in me to have my kids separated from their mother as much as possible and closer to me at least when everybody is happily dead eventually!

By the way, a plaque at the entrance will read TJ Mahal, since TJ is my native name and Mahal means 'place' in Persian. The big difference with Taj Mahal in India is that Shah Jahan built Taj Mahal for one particular, precious love, while I am building TJ Mahal out of lovelessness and spite for some devils, as well as a tribute to my wise, vengeful spirit.

Again, I must stress that I feel embarrassed watching myself turn into such a spiteful old man wasting so many precious years of his dwindling life on these silly schemes. Then again, the truth is that my family made me this way—so thoughtful. More awful and depressing than my childish idiocy and comical retaliation, however, is the kind of persons my kids have turned out to be for their own welfare at least—so spiteful and uncompassionate. Of course, a slim chance of changing my mind about everything and readjusting my will again also exists. *Am I crazy or what?*

Touchy Research
For Very Curious Readers Only

I hate to bore you with more whining about my family saga and my determination to leave this world according to a well-crafted plan—if I can finally make up my mind about how it should look like and what it should accomplish! *But what else do you expect from an uptight person set to resolve as many of his dilemmas as possible before succumbing to death?* Maybe some good points have come out of my varied family relationships and researches for others to ponder as well, even if my analyses have felt too personal or tedious. If you are tired of reading more depressing confessions in the following pages, you would probably not miss much by considering this book finished right now and skip the rest of it, or go read the Epilogue.

Certainly, being driven by the devil to this extent and forcing me revise my will repeatedly, when felt so rational and necessary as well, has not been a fun project or easy on my own soul, either. Things have simply gotten out of my control, as if a mysterious hand, or this devil, has kept throwing new ideas and dilemmas at me, the same way it forced my kids on us in the first place! This devil has probably been responsible for my lifelong uptightness, which may be causing my ultimate insanity now. Still, I have felt rather obliged to document my latest gloomy discoveries about life and my family affairs for posterity—the way any true scholar would. Especially, two events I did not fuss about before require a quick mention here to further support my latest conclusions and decisions reiterated above: **First**, the sudden flow of large royalty cheques for the sale of my books and paintings has introduced new concerns despite the huge costs of building that mausoleum. **Second**, a curious, divine urge to gauge my son's level of apathy besieged me as his birthday approached. My chronic obsession for scientific exploration goaded me a lot all along as well.

The clever plan—a pesky itch—to test my son's empathy for me occurred to me one evening swiftly, as if the devil got bored or adamant to hammer the last nail into my coffin personally and get the matter over with. My son and I have always got together or at least called each other on our birthdays to show our general civility. For his last birthday, however, I decided not to call him, not only because he had not contacted me for three months, but to see if it would worry him about the possibility of my illness or death without anybody knowing about it. Then I waited. I waited for his call—and sounding quite anxious indeed—to ensure I was well or still alive. In fact, I wondered if he would *dare* to ignore even this major clue about the chance of my demise or needing help, or to at least avoid a show of absolute apathy on his part for ignoring to check on me after such a suspicious occurrence. He did *dare*! I waited for days, weeks, and months! Hoping and praying. But nothing happened! Not a damn thing... Nothing whatsoever! None of my kids called, of course, but my son had always shown some degree of logic and compassion. He had been my last hope for a bare minimum family attachment. So, should I really be worried about these people's welfare, at all, you be the judge!

Past my own heartbreaking discovery, I also tried to imagine what reasons my son might have contemplated for my neglect or refusal to call or see him for his birthday for the first time and the way he must react in such an unprecedented and confusing case. Again, I must stress that I felt obliged to do these analyses not merely out of heartbreak and despair, but mostly for scientific research. Accordingly, the possible thoughts I imagined could have gone through my son's head were:

1. I was dead and he did not want to have anything to do with the hassle. Even worse, he was not keen to even verify his

hunch—just in case I was well indeed and he felt obliged talking to me a few minutes for no reason whatsoever!

2. I was sick and he hated the hassle of helping me.
3. I had forgotten his birthday due to mental issues or general life pressures.
4. I had hurt feelings about something, yet he still did not care, or see the need, to clarify and rectify the situation.
5. I had realized his lack of interest in maintaining any kind of relationship with me, like his siblings, for whatever reason.
6. I had not called him out of spite or for showing my anger about something or his general attitude.
7. I had been having such a good time and life, I had forgotten all about him.
8. I had tried to challenge or test his feelings for me (the truth).
9. He had wondered why I had not called him, but decided to show no reaction, hoping that the more he ignored me, the faster my heart would rot and the sooner he would collect his inheritance—as my first tombstone had declared!
10. None of the above or any thought had crossed his mind and he had not even bothered to worry why I had not called him.

Any of these possible thoughts reflect my son's callousness one way or another, since he had at the end ignored to check on me to learn what was actually wrong and whether I was even alive. The only rather positive, but unlikely, thought could be # 7, but even that is not a valid reason for him not to check on me merely to stop my impression about any of the other possibilities. The likelihood of # 8—my true reason—occurring to him would have been slim. However, even that option required a reaction by him. As another unlikely chance, we could imagine he had been too preoccupied with his own problems or simply indifferent about my call, so no single thought had crossed his mind about my deliberate or valid reason for not calling him for his birthday.

By the way, the reason # 9 reminded me that one of these days I should go to the cemetery, where they were still keeping my old gravestone and pay someone to destroy it, unless they had a use for it—maybe even willing to buy it back from me for a younger person dying from a rotten heart.

The idea of deciding which one of the above ten thoughts my son had most likely entertained and accepted was too frustrating on top of heartbreaking. Then again, his guess of my possible conclusions from his reaction (or lack of it) would be even more fun and funnier to speculate on and know. But I spare you from all those extra mind-blowing analyses. This loop about the father and son's imaginations of each other's actions and reactions in line with vast amounts of thoughts and feelings can continue for a long time. I can write a big essay, if not a huge novel, in itself, about his and my thinking, reacting, and ignoring each other. The only depressing, ironic result of this experiment was that I have now become more careful to call him on time for his birthdays. I think, and probably he thinks, he thought me a lesson, after all!

Despite all these possibilities, the bottom line and my general conclusion about the way he had reacted (none whatsoever) and what he might have thought were rather clear and interesting. I also pondered my options of sending him a corny email to say; 'I heard you loud and clear, my son!' or simply ignore the outcome of my doomed experiment totally myself! The latter made more sense at the end.

A likely conversation between my son and his mother made me laugh a little, though, which felt like a good potion for my torn heart. It sounded like the following:

"I've lost lots of money if he is angry with me now," he says.

"Don't worry, he won't disinherit you, I promise," she says.

"I hope you're right, but why?" he replies.

"What do you think he can do with all that money, a person who hates both waste and charities so much?"

"I don't know! Maybe build a huge mausoleum for himself," my brilliant son replies. He is in fact smart enough to guess even this crazy project, although I've never mentioned it to anybody. I give it at least a 60% chance that he would think of this project or an equally silly one and states it brazenly for kidding his mother at least.

"Nah, even I don't think he's that stupid," she replies giddily.

Ironically, my ex-wife and I had never planned to have kids as a necessary step or duty, anyway. They just happened like some kind of uninvited guests, despite our precautions, maybe showing up merely out of spite for our lack of parenthood enthusiasm. She just surprised me with the news and we simply let them come crowd our lives and cause frictions between us indirectly. I have always been against abortion, so we kept them, despite their mother's seemingly laxer attitude about this option. Then we both had to work hard and suffer for raising them, right after we fell in love with them forever the second with met them. So, my sense of vanity about all my efforts, worries, and time wasted for decades on making and saving money for the ultimate benefit of a bunch of ungrateful souls feels legitimate, especially when I see how they are now entangled with their own futile struggles and thoughts about existence and society. Then the agony of finding something useful *and logical* to do with all my extra money feels even sillier. At least I feel somewhat liberated now, at last, for the rest of my life—many good years ahead, I hope—and maybe even feeling so careless about everybody on some days.

Oh, how delightful it has been, after forty years, when some days I have felt much less worried and responsible for my kids' welfare. At last, an occasional chance to think more selfishly! That dire sense of parental obligation that had crippled me all along, right after my first child's birth, has been alleviated at last and I have felt free again. Except for a nasty dilemma haunting me sometimes when I wonder whether my kids are nonchalant about inheritance due to their pride and self-reliance, or I am such an unbearable devil they rather forgo all that money than humour me just a bit. My best and happiest guess is that neither case is true. They are merely lost, like most young people these days due to the chaotic world they have inherited on top of the crooked genes of their parents, in particular their mother's, even if I am their father! This is surely worrisome for every parent nowadays. Then again, I am ultimately proud and happy that my kids do not care about my money, despite the sadness of their apathy toward me.

It appears I must think, feel, act, weep, and write novels and essays until the last minute of my life just to endure the big load burdening my chest. No moment of relief has been meant in my fate! I have hardly had a peaceful day in my life since the day Father pushed the Big Plan on me in vain and now ending with this horrific Final Plan.

Apparently, talking about and laughing at life's realities are the only remedies to endure the endless anguish of living and dealing with human stupidities and dramas. But then, ironically, so much of these realities and thoughts involve money, at least as means of revenge in my case, and thus brought up repeatedly despite my loathing for discussing it so much, especially as a retribution tool. Please believe me. Then again, I cannot overcome my fear about my assets growing faster even in my death, especially due to my insightful books' growing popularity and royalty income. Sadly, as I noted with shame before, I have felt obliged to invent new measures in line with the intention and spirit of my dynamic will to address all perceivable monetary headache. *Yet, I have run out of ideas!* Pondering and pursuing so many idiotic projects so far, such as building a large mausoleum, merely for wasting money are in fact getting too awkward and making me sick*er*.

I hate my inability to justify charity as a seemingly universal way of distributing our useless wealth after ruining our lives to accumulate it so greedily and ruthlessly within inhumane notions of capitalism. Sadly, despite so many needy people in the world, my research shows that at least 90% of people in general, both rich and poor, are terribly damaged and malicious—with little fault of their own—to deserve any assistance. They have been born or become this way—so wicked! Accordingly, the idea of getting rid of one's money through charity feels absurd, even if human nature was not so horrific and charitable organizations were efficient and trustworthy. So far, only one university is on my list to get some money for research in family education.

As an alternative, I had in fact been contemplating all along to give a part of my assets to a family member, friend, or even a stranger if only he or she proved to be a decent person with some high qualities. Yet, I have so far failed in that regard, too, in spite of my sincere, keen appraisal of many potential candidates. I have not found one human who does not lie rather systematically, if not also holding a big assortment of direr impieties. Especially, I have been monitoring my young nephews and cousins who had seemed to be nice despite their parent's sloppy and wasteful lives. Yet, unfortunately, they also failed to prove their compassion and intelligence. Instead, they made me more cynical and depressed about human nature. Of course, in their defence, they had no idea about my intention; otherwise, they might have behaved more civilly and respectfully. Poor souls! Perhaps my relatives' views of me had confused their grown kids as well and contributed to their crude demeanour. Actually, my retard relatives seemed to detest my efforts to befriend their sons, perhaps worrying that I might try to buy their affection now that I had lost the love of my own kids. They also fretted about my influence over them in terms of social principles and life philosophy.

I hope you agree I have been suffering the most personally for my failure to find a decent human being these days to give him or her some money. I have done my best to be as useful and decent as I could be, all in vain. Instead, I still live in limbo at my age with lots of doubts and dilemmas I seem unable to sort out. Not knowing what to do with your wealth is excruciating, I tell you! Poor guys' envy of rich duds only shows their naïve assumptions. The suffering that rich people must endure even for wasting their wealth, not to mention the hardships of making and preserving it, is just unbearable. You poor creatures, please be thankful for all the pains you are avoiding so nonchalantly and unappreciatively.

Anyhow, now my two toughest challenges in future years are:

1) To keep improving and ornamenting my mausoleum, maybe even with a golden dome and then setting up a rich trust for maintaining it for eternity. This appears to remain my only option if I cannot find a decent human by fluke soon to unburden me from the damn extra money pouring in from various sources, including my paintings that a curator took away with a great offer and arrangement just before I could donate them to the Children Hospital. So, the chance of those gorgeous paintings also starting to sell at outrageous prices, at least after I die, is now suddenly worrisome, too. Oh, God, please send me some new ideas soon, before I die at last; hopefully ending the life of this crazy 'final plan' as well!

2) Try much harder and more diligently to fathom sneakier gimmicks to fool around with my kids at least after my death. Suggestions and nomination are accepted!

Deep down, however, I still hope a big miracle revamps my relationship and perspective of my beloved kids and I can change my will for the last time to make them the sole beneficiaries. My pathetic or wise hope stems from my strong belief that an outer force drives humans to seek and possibly gain some level of enlightenment. I can say this from personal experience and gloat when I recall the kind of devil I used to be myself. Therefore, there is a chance that my darling children, all three or some of them, would also be blessed with this divine opportunity at last.

Oh, how depressing it feels to be a vengeful and meticulous maniac during one's last 10-20 years, instead of focusing on one's salvation and becoming a bit less cynical about people and the world. I had imagined (and stressed in this book as well) that the third phase of one's life should be devoted to, and reflect, one's resignation, yet here I am too active with no willpower to let the whole thing go. Then again, I must reiterate that my kids started this exhausting game. I am only trying to invent a good ending for their game and my lousy life.

Epilogue

Life is a lousy, lame endeavour and enduring it is tough despite our eagerness to show our resilience and pretend how successful and happy we are. Deep down in our sad souls, past our idiotic positive thinking, we feel that our struggles to find a meaningful purpose for living have failed. Even those luckier people, who enjoy a rather comfortable and rich life, often feel this way. In the latter stage of our lives, especially, we realize how pointless our fears, efforts, and hopes have been. In the midst of it all, of course, some joys and pleasures, music and theatre, love and sex, art and literature, spirituality and enlightenment, tranquility and wisdom, and blissful incidents keep us amused and hopeful and fuel the engine of our existence. Sometimes, we get or take a break, maybe for a week, a month, or even an entire year if we are really lucky and able to stop fussing too much while taking life in our strides. However, soon we somehow get entangled with some new hollow challenges and bewildering thoughts over and over. We face merely more disappointments, while we cause plenty of hardships and stress for others and ourselves.

It is easier for most people to shoot for, anticipate, or pretend a flourishing life and they might have the right idea for taking life in their strides and losing themselves in the prevalent world of delusions instead of whining like me. I wonder sometimes myself if I must envy the mainstream and apologize for my cynicism pervading this book and some of my other writings, although I hope the humour in them has alleviated the burden of sad truths about existence.

The stories in this book highlight our spirits and craving to achieve certain goals, overcome the obstacles, stay positive, solve problems, have pleasures, amuse ourselves, love someone, create something interesting, find a soul mate, sustain our relationships, etc.—all in response to our inherent need to grasp the purpose of our lives. Our priorities and the nature of our conundrums change as we wander and learn a few things, too, yet our fundamental doubts and dilemmas never end. We just plough on aimlessly through life's journey, hope and pray, and keep looking for that elusive happiness we believe we deserve and imagine is out there for us to grab. That is all we can do, since there is nothing else in this wacky reality we have created around our illusions.

The interpretations of the above fifteen stories are obviously left to the readers, and hopefully the subtle points scattered in each story come out clearly to most readers. For example, the last couple of stories reflect the agony and frustration of the ultimate defeat most of us feel near the end of our life journey, if not sooner, and even then, we remain trapped despite all our wisdom. Unfortunately, it simply gets harder, as we age, to distinguish our inherent madness from the crooked wisdom that might come with living. Our wisdom and madness somehow converge, as though humans are doomed even if they reach the height of their intellectual capacity. The outcome, our existing chaotic world, is obviously a symptom of all that madness and wisdom mixed up erratically. It is the creation of our shoddy choices and untamed desires, because we are such a weak species, unable to figure out a more meaningful and longer lasting values for ourselves, and then collectively for our societies and relationships. Whether our wisdom or madness makes us do all these horrible things to one another and ourselves, it is getting difficult to trust humanity to survive such deepening social and personal turmoil.

All along, we must also face our inevitable sense of loneliness and accept the humiliation of learning that nobody would ever understand or care about us, even when they pretend that they do. Not even wealth and recognition prove or help our real identity, —which we might feel only tentatively sometimes—nor do they provide a way of finding the connection we painfully seek with the universe and other humans.

Is not God Himself cruel when so much wicked genes are so prevalent amongst humans? Reflecting merely on the facts noted in this book, especially the last chapter, we can fathom the true nature of humans and God's game of life. For example, my kids' lack of compassion is heartbreaking, but their reluctance to even pretend some sympathy at least to inherit plenty of money is downright bizarre, more than naïve and insulting, if you get my drift! As I said before, I would be proud if my kids' apathy was a reflection of their autonomy and positive pride. However, I am more inclined to attribute it to their naiveté, which makes me worry about their future as well as humanity to ever find peace and commonsense. Fortunately, I often entertain the chance that my son's seeming show of autonomy is a precious sign of his rising spiritual enlightenment, which I believe is quite tenable for a genius person he is. Accordingly, another delightful conclusion here is the possibility for a person being both naïve and a genius at the same time, like my blessed son perhaps—maybe even me, as I find myself sometimes! My daughters have a lot of potential to be enlightened humans, too, on top of being geniuses in their own rights.

It is a big consolation for us to realize that 80% of humans' apathy relate to their crooked genes and their parents' horrible influence on them since their childhood. Still, that 20% residue applicable directly to their naivety and inability to see some of the fine points about compassion is unforgivable and a major crime, enough to contemplate comical retributions I have enumerated in the last story with both delight and guilt—and lots of intention for humour. At the end, humans have the responsibility and ability to redeem themselves and become better beings despite their inborn and earned defects.

At the same time, of course, all the silly thoughts and plans in the last story, instead of just forgetting about my kids' characters and choices altogether or forgiving them, makes me look like another vengeful parent. This is so unbecoming for an allegedly enlightened spirit that I have claimed a few times to have become and also considered possible for all humans eventually mostly through resignation and humility.

Recalling those earlier years when I suffered to figure out my purposes for either living or dying makes me feel stupid enough. However, now having valid and potent reasons for both being and dying represents my toughest challenge ever. I believe many other people have faced similar family conundrums and endured many sad truths about humans in the latter stages of their lives. That is what we consider experience, I imagine!

All these discouraging symptoms of living clearly reflect the poor nature and gullibility of humankind. The whole mayhem is of our own making. We hurt one another and upset ourselves out of habit, usually due to our mindlessness, greed, and arrogance. Unfortunately, we are not intelligent enough to find a means of living together in peace and harmony. That is the biggest human crime and absolute pity! Nevertheless, we must strive to grasp and gracefully accept all these gloomy facts about living and our lousy existence, and to finish somehow the journey we have started with all kinds of hopes and desires.

Sorry for clouding your delicate minds about this journey.

Bon voyage!